Turn up the heat with Julie Ann Walker's Black Knights Inc.

"Julie Ann Walker is one of those authors to be put on a keeper shelf along with Nora Roberts, Suzanne Brockmann, and Allison Brennan."

—Kirkus

"Deft charac̶̶̶̶̶̶̶̶̶̶̶̶̶̶̶ches of humor, and r̶̶̶̶̶̶̶̶̶̶̶̶̶̶̶̶̶̶̶̶hly recommended r̶̶̶̶̶̶̶̶̶̶̶̶̶̶̶̶̶ review

"Filled with highly sensual sex scenes and enough tension to ignite the pages. Fans of Maya Banks's KGI series will also love this."

—Booklist

"Drama, danger, and sexual tension…Romantic suspense at its best."
—Night Owl Reviews, 5/5 Stars, Reviewer Top Pick

"Enthralling, sexy contemporary romantic suspense that will have readers eagerly turning the pages."
—Romance Junkies

"Rollicking, riveting, and romantic."
—Long and Short Reviews

"One heck of a riveting plotline…definitely not to be missed!"

—RT Book Reviews, 4½ Stars

Also by Julie Ann Walker

HELL FOR
LEATHER

BLACK KNIGHTS INC.

JULIE ANN
WALKER

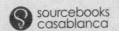

sourcebooks
casablanca

Published by Sourcebooks Casablanca, an imprint of Sourcebooks, Inc.
P.O. Box 4410, Naperville, Illinois 60567-4410
(630) 961-3900
Fax: (630) 961-2168
www.sourcebooks.com

Printed and bound in Canada.
WC 10 9 8 7 6 5 4 3 2 1

To my sister, Pam.

Your wit, whimsy, and overall ability to find the "funny" in most situations taught me early on not to take life, or myself, too seriously. I've had a fuller, happier, far more interesting time as a result of it. Thank you for showing me what a wild, wacky, and wonderful world it really is!

Only those who will risk going too far can possibly find out how far one can go.

—T. S. Eliot

Prologue

Red Delilah's Biker Bar
Chicago, Illinois

MAC WAS DRUNK.

If the sight of the nearly empty bottle of Lagavulin sitting on the bar in front of him wasn't proof positive, then the feel of his eyelids scraping across his eyeballs like thirty-grit sandpaper was.

Shit.

Getting soused hadn't been his intention when he casually tailed Dagan Zoelner into their local watering hole. He'd simply been curious why Zoelner had run like a scalded dog out of the raucous barbeque that had been in full swing back at the shop. And he figured a couple of cold ones might loosen the guy's tongue.

But it wasn't a bottle of Budweiser Zoelner ordered after plunking himself down on a stool at the long mahogany bar, hooking the heels of his biker boots over the brass foot rail. It was scotch. An entire bottle.

And Mac hadn't been able to sit by nursing a beer while Zoelner proceeded to get piss drunk. For one thing, sitting by and watching a friend and trusted teammate get piss drunk, well, it was just...*sad*. And for another thing, he knew when men like them set about getting piss drunk, it was usually because something had triggered past demons to come out and play. Past

demons in the form of dark memories of good men now
dead, of missions or assignments or cases gone horribly
wrong, or of bad calls that drove a guy crazy asking
himself the sonofabitching question of *what if*.

What if I'd done things differently?

What if I'd moved just a little faster?

What if I'd taken a second look at that last bit of Intel?

It was a useless endeavor…asking *what if*. But that
didn't mean all the operators at the privately run covert
government defense firm known as Black Knights Inc.
didn't indulge in it occasionally. Hell, *more* than occasionally. Asking *what if* seemed to come part and parcel
with the job. And tonight it appeared Zoelner was doing
just that…asking *what if* with gusto and single-minded
determination all washed down with a healthy portion of
twenty-year-old scotch—*hiccup*. And Mac, sympathetic
fool that he was, had voluntarily joined in for the ride.

The good Lord knew he'd pay for it tomorrow with a
headache big enough to drop a mule, followed by eight
to ten hours of straight mainlining coffee in an attempt
to combat the effects. But for right now, he felt pretty
good. Except for the gritty eyes, his body was numb
and tingly. His tongue particularly so. Which was why
when he finally turned to Zoelner, breaking the we're-
men-so-we-drink-in-silence thing they had going, and
asked, "So, you gonna tell me why we're sitting here
gettin' drunker than a betsy bug on a Tuesday night?"
the second to the last word came out sounding more
like *Tushday*.

Zoelner, usually known for his smooth movements
and strange bouts of statue-like stillness, turned unsteadily toward him. His slate gray irises were nearly

obscured by the heavy lids hanging over them. The left lid appeared to have suffered the influence of the scotch more than the right because it drooped just a fraction lower.

"First of all," Zoelner said, "has anyone ever told you the big-hat-and-no-cattle Texan comes out in you when you're tipsy?" He grinned lopsidedly. "And secondly," his expression turned serious, "don't go getting mushy on me."

"I'll have you know I grew up with a hat *and* cattle." Mac frowned. "And I'm not gettin' mushy on you. I just thought, you know, you might want to talk about," he made a rolling motion with his hand, "whatever."

Zoelner glanced around the bar, squinting at the red vinyl booths, the burly clientele, and the roaring jukebox like he'd never seen the place before. "Where am I?" He blinked owlishly. "I could've sworn I sat down in a badass biker bar, but at some point I must've been transported into the middle of a chick flick."

When he turned back, Mac made sure his expression was bland.

"Okay." Zoelner rolled his eyes. "So, let's *talk*. Let's delve into the depths of my emotions, of how I'm *feeling*. Then, after we're done doing that," he batted his lashes like he was trying out for a Revlon commercial or something, "we can ask the bartender to exchange our scotch for herbal tea and go find some Indigo Girls on the jukebox."

Mac snorted. His nose filled with the smells of stale beer, crushed peanut shells, and cowhide from the overabundance of leather being sported around the place. Except for the peanut shells, the scents reminded him of home, of The Lazy M ranch where he'd been born and raised.

All hat and no cattle, my ass.

"All right, shitheel," he grumbled. "So maybe you're not too keen on hashing out what's jerked a knot in your tail tonight." Zoelner's wide grin returned, and Mac realized with that last turn of phrase he'd proved the guy's point about the Texan coming out in him after he'd had a few. But he couldn't help it. Nor, come to think of it, would he want to. Because like most Texans, he was good-and-goddamned *proud* to say he hailed from the Lone Star State. *Yeehaw! And pray the creek don't rise!* "But I just gotta know…this doesn't have anything to do with Agent Winterfield, does it?"

Luke Winterfield was a rogue CIA agent who leaked information about the number and location of the U.S. government's black sites to the press. Some called Winterfield a whistleblower. Mac called him a traitor. And just this morning, splashed across the headlines, was news that the bastard had found a country to grant him asylum. It had to be a major blow for every CIA agent out there—even an *ex*–CIA agent like Zoelner.

"Pssshht." Zoelner made a face. "I stopped caring about The Company and its shenanigans years ago. As for Winterfield, I never met the ashhole." Zoelner frowned and rolled in his lips before trying again. "Asshole."

"Then what on God's green earth is tonight all about?" Mac demanded. "Because I gotta be honest. This whole sittin'-here-in-silence-while-we-drink-ourselves-good-lookin' thing has just about run its course with me."

Zoelner tipped his glass of scotch toward the opposite

end of the bar. "I don't want to talk about it," he said. "Actually, I don't want to talk about anything other than that brunette over there, and the fact that she's been eyeing the two of us like we're tall drinks of water and she's been lost in the desert for days."

Mac glanced down the polished length of mahogany and…sure enough. There was a bird in a tight top and buttery-soft biker jacket sitting near the end. She looked like she might've stepped off the cover of a motorcycle magazine—having that whole sexy-without-being-overly-pretty thing going. And when she caught him staring, she licked her ruby-red lips and seductively lowered her thick, sooty lashes.

Can you say invitation, *ladies and gents?* Even in his scotch-addled state, Mac recognized the blatant come-and-get-me-big-boy look in her eyes.

Sorry, darlin'. But you're barkin' up the wrong tree.

"No, thanks," he told Zoelner, sitting back and lifting his glass of scotch to his lips. "She's not my type."

Zoelner hooted with laughter, slamming down his empty tumbler. "Type? Dear God, it's not like you're looking for a blood donor or anything. Type hasn't got a damned thing to do with it. She's hot. She's obviously horny. And one of us should do something about that."

"Be my guest."

Zoelner cocked his head. "You remind me of a giant black hole, sucking all the light and fun out of the evening."

"Me?" Mac turned on the man incredulously. "I'm not the one who decided to spend the night sitting at this…this sausage-factory of a bar, quietly getting stone-cold shit-faced."

"Hmm." Zoelner narrowed his eyes. "Sausage-factory

of a bar, eh? Meaning there are too many swinging dicks and not enough soft and sexies around tonight? Do I detect a hint of melancholy?"

"That's a big word for a drunk man." Mac chuckled.

"I'm not that drunk," Zoelner insisted, and Mac grabbed his stomach, laughing out loud. "Okay, so maybe I *am* that drunk," Zoelner admitted, "but that doesn't mean I'm wrong. My point is, I think you're not interested in the brown-haired Betty over there because you're pining away… Is that how you Texans would put it? Pining? For a certain redhead who's suspiciously absent from the bar tonight."

And *that* strangled Mac's laughter into a cough. He lifted his glass to suck down a drop of scotch. Carefully placing the tumbler back on the bar, he ran his tongue over his teeth and said, "I don't know what you're talkin' about."

"The hell you don't." Zoelner snorted. "Anyone with eyes in their head knows you're hot-to-trot for our usual bartendress. And if all her come-ons are anything to go by, she's hot-to-trot for you, too. Which begs the question…what are you waiting on? Why haven't you hit that, like, a *thousand* times by now?"

"*Hit* that?" Mac pulled a face. "What are we? Fifteen?"

"Dodging the question?" Zoelner countered, and Mac didn't know whether to applaud the man's astuteness or strangle him right where he sat.

Deciding neither scenario would be all that satisfying, he shrugged his shoulders in what he hoped was a gesture of supreme unconcern. "That Woman,"—Mac always thought of Delilah Fairchild, proprietress and namesake of the bar they were currently sitting in, that way, in capital letters—"isn't my type either. And you *know* why."

"Bullshit."

Just the one word. Spoken with complete conviction.

Mac gifted Zoelner with a dirty look and reached for the bottle of Lagavulin. Upending it, he poured the last few drops into his glass, then slowly lifted the tumbler, taking a leisurely sip.

"You know what I think of that whole thing, right?" Zoelner asked. Mac ignored him, wishing like hell he'd never opened his big mouth after that goddamned mission in Somalia. But sitting in a bar in South Africa, basking in the glow of a successful operation—and after having downed a half dozen beers—the whole sorry story had come tumbling out. "Oh, and what? Now you're a mute?" Zoelner inquired after it became apparent Mac wasn't going to rise to his bait.

But what could Mac say? The truth was, he *did* know what Zoelner thought. The guy had flat-out told him he was an idiot to compare one woman to another. *Horseshit* was the word Zoelner used if Mac remembered right. But the guy just didn't understand. He didn't know what—

"Fine," Zoelner spat, shaking his head. "So, we'll pretend Delilah Fairchild isn't your type either."

And, yeah. It *would* be pretending. Because, in all honesty, they both knew That Woman was *every* man's type. Not only was she a perfect ten on the curve-o-meter, but her heart-shaped face, with her clear green eyes and pouty Kewpie-bow lips, belonged on prime-time television. And, as if all that wasn't enough, her pale, creamy skin had to go and be all flawless and shit. Seriously, no matter how closely Mac looked, he couldn't find a single pore to mar her porcelain complexion. To put it quite simply, from the top of her head to the ends of her red-tipped toes, Delilah Fairchild was one hundred percent pure woman. And one hundred percent, no-holds-barred *beautiful*. Beautiful and vivacious and used to commanding the attention of every man in the room. And that last bit made her all too familiar.

Too familiar and too...*dangerous*. And honestly? His life—the one where he masqueraded as a motorcycle mechanic when in fact he was part of a clandestine government defense group that operated as the very tip of Uncle Sam's sword—was dangerous enough already, thank you very much.

And speaking of familiar...

Without warning, the unwelcome image of Jolene flashed behind his gritty eyes. Hair as black as a raven's wing. Eyes the color of Texas bluebonnets. Skin like buttermilk. And a heart as fickle and capricious as a Texas spring...

He shook his head and blinked away the disturbing vision in time to see Zoelner raise a hand and call out to the bald, goateed man behind the bar. "Hey, Brendan! Where's the lovely lady of the house this evening? Not that my rather large, rather slow-talking friend here," Zoelner hooked a thumb in Mac's direction, "is wearing the sulky look of a eunuch in a whorehouse because he's missing her gorgeous face or anything. Because she's absolutely *not* his type."

Right then, Mac made the supremely wise and incredibly mature decision to kick the former CIA agent's booted ankle. Zoelner turned to lift a dubious brow before he hauled off and kicked Mac right back. Which, of course, left Mac with no recourse but to respond with an even *harder* kick and soon they were scuffling like a couple of rowdy college frat boys instead of two highly trained operators. Then again, they were highly *tipsy* as well. So maybe that explained it.

"Delilah's down south," Brendan said, coming to stand in front of them while continuing to wipe wet pint glasses with a dish towel. Short and squatty, Brendan had the physique of a wrestler and the face of a boxer—the bridge of his nose and his cheekbones looked like they'd been flattened more than a time or two by heavy fists. What he lacked in height, he obviously made up for in sheer scrappiness.

"Where?" Zoelner asked, adjusting his leather jacket and shooting Mac a narrowed-eyed glare before turning his attention back to Brendan.

"Southern Illinois," the bartender said, and Mac thought, *Southern Illinois? What the hell is she doin' down there?*

"What the hell is she doing down there?"

He blinked, startled. Had he asked the question aloud? Just how much scotch had he *had*?

But no. It was Zoelner Brendan turned to to answer. Of course, Mac was forced to wonder *again* just how much scotch he'd had when, before any words had a chance to form on Brendan's tongue, the thought *don't let her be down there visiting a lover* whispered through the back of his brain.

Whoa. What? Where the hell had *that* come from? He didn't give two shits what or…or…*who* she was doing down in southern Illinois.

Did he?

He couldn't help but notice his question was answered with resounding, cricket-chirping silence.

Well, hell. That's just the booze talkin'. Because anything else was too disconcerting to contemplate.

"Between you and me," Brendan said, leaning in conspiratorially, "I think she's trying to avoid the bar."

What? Why?

"What? Why?" Zoelner asked.

Mac glared at the mind-reading man. "Who are you?" he demanded. "Carnac the Magnificent or somethin'?"

"Huh?" Zoelner frowned at him in narrow-eyed affront. "Why are you scowling at me like that? Stop it, or that brown-haired Betty over there is going to think you just broke up with me."

As a group, Mac, Zoelner, and Brendan all turned to smile at the woman in question. Zoelner raised his glass and wiggled his eyebrows, which elicited a seductive lowering of the Betty's lashes and a subtle quirk of one corner of her lacquered lips.

"So *why* is Delilah avoiding the bar?" he asked, finding his way back on track more quickly than Mac. Of course, the instant That Woman's name was mentioned, every single thought in Mac's head focused on her like a blue-tick healer pointing out a covey of quail.

Shit, shit, shit.

"After Buzzard's murder," Brendan began, and *oh, great.* Just what Mac *didn't* need to be reminded of right now—the all-out gun battle Delilah had found herself involved in a few months ago, the one where her most loyal patron died. Because that had been the night he almost threw caution to the wind and went against all his better judgment to take her up on one of her offers. She'd been so vulnerable and sad. And he'd wanted to comfort her so badly. "She's been jumping at every chance she gets to hightail it out of here. I think this place holds too many bad memories now."

The three of them fell quiet for one moment. Then two.

"But anyway." Brendan brushed a hand through the air, as if he could wave off the cloud of discomfort hanging over them. "She's on a road trip with her uncle. Something about a visit to an old friend of his, and—"

"Oh, I figured she was down there working her woo-woo magic on the budget of some two-bit municipality," Zoelner said.

Her woo-woo magic…

Zoelner wasn't talking about Delilah's ability to hypnotize a man with her cat-eyed stare or the bewitching way her hips swayed when she walked across the room. He wasn't referring to her talent for whipping up an alcoholic concoction that could taste sweet as candy one minute and knock a man flat on his ass the next or how she could cast a spell over the entire bar simply by tossing her head back and letting loose with that low, throaty laugh of hers. *Huh-uh*. The guy wasn't talking about any of that, though it could all certainly count as woo-woo magic, witchcraft, or, in Mac's not-so-humble opinion, straight-up voodoo sorceress shit. What Zoelner was referring to was the fact that Delilah Fairchild, the sexpot owner of a down-and-dirty biker bar, happened to spend her free time working as a…wait for it…freakin' *forensic accountant*.

Sweet Lord almighty, sometimes Mac still had trouble believing it.

Though, truth be told, he had no trouble whatsoever *imagining* it. He'd spent more than an hour or two daydreaming about her sitting at a desk somewhere, hair twisted up in a bun, reading glasses perched on the tip of her prim nose. In fact, for the last six months—ever since he'd learned what her second gig was—it'd been his favorite go-to fantasy. Something like the tried-and-true naughty librarian dream set on overdrive, because, you know, that whole one-part-proper-lady-and-two-parts-sex-goddess shtick had been a male spanktrovision standard since the beginning of time and—

The front door burst open, slamming against the inside wall. Mac turned to see who was in such an all-fire hurry to get inside the bar. One look had his lungs playing the part of Michael Jordan. They attempted to leap right out of his throat.

Speak of the devil…

Even if he hadn't recognized the long auburn hair cascading from beneath a motorcycle helmet and tumbling around a set of leather-clad shoulders, the shouts of gleeful greeting and the lifted mugs of beer would've told him the woman of the hour had made her way home.

See… Beautiful and vivacious and able to command the attention of every man in the room…

He swiveled back toward the bar, but the hairs on the back of his neck almost instantly alerted him to the fact that That Woman had marched up behind him.

Slowly, with what he hoped wasn't a patently false look of unconcern, he turned around. But before he could open his mouth, she whipped off her helmet and shook out her hair. He was accosted by the spicy-sweet scent of her perfume and the earthier aroma of the open road. Inexplicably, and to his utter horror, Little Mac, the idiot in his pants, defied all convention—not to mention the amount of liquor he'd imbibed—and lifted to half-mast.

Well, for God's sake, he thought with disgust, mentally calling himself *and* Little Mac ten kinds of fool just as Delilah blurted, "Thank goodness you're here."

"Huh?" Okay, and even in his scotch-muddled state, he recognized his response for the gleaming bit of witticism it was *not*.

Delilah frowned. "Are you drunk?" She placed her hands on her hips. Her round, curvy, delicious hips. Her lovely hips that just begged for a man's hands and—

Ah, hell…

"Maybe," he told her, holding his forefinger and thumb an inch apart. "Just a little."

"Goddamnit!" she growled, then immediately yelled for Brendan to bring over two cups of coffee.

"Hey, now. Don't do that," Zoelner objected. "I've been working all evening on this buzz and I—"

"Can it," Delilah cut him off. Mac lifted his eyebrows in surprise. Not that Delilah wasn't a speak-her-mind, in-your-face kind of broad, because she was. But this was something different. The tone she'd taken with Zoelner bordered on rude.

"I need you." She pointed a red-tipped finger at Zoelner's nose, causing the man to go cross-eyed when he attempted to focus on it. *Whoa. What?* She needed… *Zoelner?* Then she turned to include him in that stomach-churning statement. "I need both of you."

Zoelner's face pulled down in a considering frown. "Just to be clear, I'm not usually the kind of man who likes to share his pleasures." Okay, and just the thought had a lurid emotion—*not* jealousy, definitely *not* jealousy—buzzing at the back of Mac's head like a swarm of angry Texas yellow jackets. "But if you've a mind to—"

"Not like that," Delilah hissed, color climbing in her already flushed cheeks.

All right. Something…Mac tilted his head, blinking…*isn't right here*. Unfortunately, the discombobulating combination of scotch and Delilah's nearness ensured he couldn't *quite* put his finger on it. Then she saved him the trouble of trying to figure it out when she blurted, "My uncle is missing. And I need you guys to help me find him."

Well…hello, sobriety.

Chapter One

Outside Theo Fairchild's Brownstone
Thirty minutes later…

DON'T PANIC…

Delilah Fairchild had been repeating those two words to herself for hours. She said them when her uncle wasn't back at the motel when he said he'd be. She breathed them the first—and the *thirtieth*—time she called his cell phone only to be transferred straight to voice mail. She muttered them after a half-dozen inquiries to the area's hospitals turned up exactly nada. She combined them with a rather poetic curse when the local police told her she had to wait twenty-four hours before the missing person's report she filed would get any real attention—her uncle being an adult and all, and possibly just holed-up in a hotel somewhere getting his knob polished. For the record, the policeman hadn't actually *said* that, but his intent had been clear. And she echoed them over and over inside her motorcycle helmet the entire four-and-a-half-hour, hell-bent-for-leather ride back to Chicago.

But the truth was…she was starting to panic.

Big time.

Of course, it didn't help matters that two of the guys she'd been depending on to assist her in finding her uncle happened to be drunk as the proverbial skunks. When she stormed into her bar, intent on running upstairs to the apartment she lived in above the place in order to grab the spare keys to her uncle's new townhouse, she'd been beyond relieved to see two of the Black Knights occupying center barstools.

That relief had lasted all of about ten seconds.

Because the only thing more exasperating than dealing with drunks was dealing with drunks when you *desperately* needed them to be sober.

And speaking of drunks…

A yellow taxi pulled up behind her motorcycle, its headlights bathing her in sharp white light. She raised a hand and squinted against it as she toed out her kickstand and hooked her helmet over the chrome handlebars of her Harley chopper. Bryan "Mac" McMillan and Dagan Zoelner, each wearing faded jeans, summer-weight leather jackets, and T-shirts advertising the custom motorcycles of Black Knights Inc., climbed out of the vehicle. Silhouetted against the light, they both looked big and mean—Mac much more so, with hulking muscles and a perpetual scowl—and, wouldn't you know? They were just what she needed right now.

If only they were sober…

Of course, as her Uncle Theo liked to say, she could wish in one hand and shit in the other and see which one filled up faster. Which in this case meant drunk or sober, she was taking Mac and Zoelner any way she could get them.

"So, what are we looking for here?" Zoelner asked, coming to stand beside her. The guy stumbled slightly when he tipped his head back to take a sip of the coffee she'd made Brendan pour into Styrofoam cups. He swayed again when he glanced up at the three-story brownstone her uncle was in the middle of restoring to its former glory. The dimly glowing streetlamps cast the building's warm rock facade in sharp planes and dark shadows. And for some reason, perhaps it was nerves or maybe it was the adrenaline that had been flooding her system all day, but it struck her as slightly…foreboding. Perhaps even…malevolent?

Okay, and now you're being ridiculous, she scolded herself. "We're looking for an address book, a phone number, *anything* that might tell me where Charlie lives or…or even something that has his last name written on it would be helpful."

"Charlie?" Zoelner inquired.

"The friend my uncle went to see."

"Ah." Zoelner nodded, taking another slightly unsteady sip of coffee as Mac passed loose bills to the cab driver through the open window. She was gratified to discover his path to sobriety seemed considerably farther along than Zoelner's. As the taxi drove away, he strode forward on legs that appeared remarkably steady, his big square face drawn in a set of harsh lines made more severe by the shadowy light of the city street. Between the two men, Zoelner was the more classically handsome, with slate-gray eyes, high cheekbones, and wavy brown hair.

But there was just something about Mac…

Maybe it was the intensity of his piercing blue gaze, or the character in his slightly crooked nose. Perhaps it was the stubborn jut of his substantial jaw or that too-damn-sexy dimple in the center of his chin. Or it could be that he seemed to emanate danger in a sort of testosterone-laden cloud, something felt but not seen. Although, in all honesty, it probably had much more to do with the fact that to meet him was to fear him. Just a little. Or a lot. And she'd always kind of had a thing for bad boys.

Mac was definitely a bad boy. The guy had an alpha male swagger that could be spotted a hundred yards away. And when you combined that with the mystery of him—he was an ex–FBI agent turned *secret* agent who was now working undercover as a motorcycle mechanic—it drove her absolutely nuts. We're talking barely-able-to-keep-her-hands-to-herself, panty-dropping nuts.

Unfortunately, Mac had made it abundantly clear her feelings weren't returned. The big jerk. Of course, the silver lining here—if such a thing could exist in this god-awful situation—was that the sting she usually felt when thinking about his repeated rejections was completely eclipsed by the far more pressing fact that, you know, her uncle seemed to have vanished into thin air. *Poof!* Houdini couldn't have done a better job had he tried.

Damnit, Uncle Theo! Where the hell are you?

She mentally hurled that question into the ether. But like it'd been doing all day, the ether chose to ignore her, refusing to point her in the direction of the man who, after her parents died in a terrible car crash, gave up his bachelor lifestyle in order to settle down and raise a brokenhearted seven-year-old girl. The man who was father, friend, and confidant all rolled into one. The man who was the one person on the entire face of the planet she could call her own…

The tears she'd been holding at bay burned behind

her eyes, but she refused to let them fall. One, because she wasn't a crier, *damnit!* And two, if she let them fall, it would be like she was admitting the possibility that the worst might actually come to pass. That she might never see Theo again and—

"So, fill me in on what you know so far," Mac commanded in his slow-as-molasses drawl, yanking her from her thoughts. It was just as well. Those thoughts had been heading down a gloomy path. One she wasn't willing to tread. Not yet, anyway.

"What I know so far?" she asked with a snort that was far too close to a sob for comfort. "Well, that'd be a big ol' helping of jack with a nice side of squat."

Okay, and *that* sounded slightly more petulant and decidedly more ungrateful than she'd meant it to. She was *glad* they were here with her. She really was. Because waiting the prescribed amount of time for the Marion police to do something wasn't an option. Not when she figured the first twenty-four hours after a person went missing were the most critical. Not when she knew that enlisting the help of the bad-to-the-bone boys over at Black Knights Inc. could give her a leg up. Which meant she should be falling to her knees and thanking them for hopping-to without a second's hesitation instead of answering what was a rational, straightforward question with a mouthful of biting sarcasm.

Damn. She hated feeling vulnerable. It turned her into quite the bitch. *Double, triple, quadruple damn…*

Shaking her head at herself, she made a face. "Sorry," she mumbled, biting the inside of her cheek. "I'm just… I can't…" She stopped, rolling in her lips. Then all she could do in her own defense was shrug.

The look on Zoelner's face was one of sympathy. But Mac?

Well, Mac was tougher to read. The high king of inscrutability. And, man-oh-man, on the list of things that annoyed the ever-loving shit out of her, that usually ranked right up there close to number one. As a dyed-in-the-wool bartender, having seen and served drinks to every kind of man from the fanciest-schmanciest big city politician to the simplest, down-home shift worker, she liked to think she was pretty good at getting a bead on people.

She'd never been able to get a bead on Mac.

Thankfully, his next words provided the reassurance his familiar stony expression did not. "It's okay, Delilah." His low, rumbling voice always reminded her of Sam Elliott's. "You've got nothin' to be sorry for."

She had nothing to be sorry for? Could that be true? She sure as hell didn't feel like it.

"If I'd taken the time to ask Uncle Theo just a few simple questions this morning before he took off…" She stopped, squeezing her eyes closed, and replaying the scene in her head. "If I'd asked him to tell me *exactly* where he was going instead of rolling over to pull the covers over my head, I might've—"

"Coulda, woulda, shoulda," Zoelner interrupted. "There's nothing you can do to change this morning."

"He's right," Mac added. "You can't go beatin' yourself up for things you had no way of knowin'. After all, there's that whole hindsight and 20/20 thing."

Stop beating herself up… It was good advice. And even though this was one of those situations that fell under the heading of Easier Said Than Done, she figured she better do her damnedest to take it. Because agonizing over what she *could* have done, what she *should* have done, was only pushing her closer and closer to the brink of a total mental and emotional breakdown. And *that* wouldn't do anyone any good. Not her. Not these fiercely capable—even if slightly drunk—guys who were trying to help her. And certainly not her uncle.

Squaring her shoulders, she jerked her chin in a sharp nod. "You're right." Then, hoping she was demonstrating far more aplomb than she was feeling, she marched up to the tall, wrought-iron gate surrounding the front of her uncle's newest property. The same gate she'd watched him lock only the evening before.

Holy crap… One day? Really? Had it really been just over twenty-four hours since she agreed to the road trip that landed her here? Now? Her uncle God-knows-where and her entire world turned upside down?

Jesus, she felt like she'd lived a lifetime…

"It all started yesterday afternoon when my uncle got a text from his old Marine buddy, Charlie…something. I don't know the guy's last name, and that's part of the problem. Truth is, I've never met the man even though Uncle Theo usually makes a trip out to see him at least once a year." She was determined to oblige Mac's request to fill him in on what she knew so far, this time *without* the sarcasm. *Sheesh.* "Anyway, Charlie invited Uncle Theo down for a visit. But Uncle Theo told me he didn't really feel like making the ride by himself. I convinced him to go. Told him I'd go and we'd make a road trip out of it. I said it'd be fun."

And it *had* been fun. Up until the point when her uncle didn't show up when he was supposed to. She lifted the key ring only to discover that, despite her best efforts at composure, her hand was shaking as badly as an alcoholic's after twenty-four hours locked away in the drunk tank.

Don't panic. The two words flitted through her head for the millionth time. Only now it appeared her psyche was fed up with the mantra because it quickly answered back with *Yeah right, sister. Not gonna happen.*

Okay, and great. That's just what she *didn't* need, her own subconscious mutinying.

Mac crumpled his empty coffee cup and lobbed it toward a nearby trash can before gently taking the keys from her hand. And with far more dexterity than she would've thought possible given the amount of scotch she suspected he'd consumed—she didn't know if it was him or Zoelner or the two of them combined, but the air around them reeked so strongly of whiskey she feared what would happen if they chanced by an open flame—he neatly inserted the key in the lock, twisted his big wrist, and pushed the gate open. It squeaked on its hinges, and the eerie sound streaked up her spine like the tip of a steel blade, further abrading her already raw nerves. *What the hell is wrong with me?*

And either she winced, or Mac simply used those superpowers of deduction he'd been bequeathed upon his graduation from the FBI Academy, because he frowned fiercely. "Take a breath, Delilah," he instructed sternly. "You look like you're either about to toss your cookies or faint."

And that made sense, since she *felt* like she was either about to toss her cookies or faint. Or maybe she'd toss her cookies, *then* faint.

For crying out loud, get it together!

"I didn't know your uncle was a Marine," Zoelner said, supporting himself against the gate and sipping noisily at his coffee.

"He doesn't like to spread that particular bit of information around," she admitted.

"Why the hell not?" Zoelner asked. "What happened to the *proud* part of *The Few, The Proud, The Marines*?"

"Because of his age." *Just breathe, Delilah. Just… breathe.* "When he tells people he was a Marine, they all assume he did a tour in Vietnam."

"He didn't?" Zoelner lifted a brow.

And, okay, it was that expression right there that made her understand why her uncle preferred to keep his stint in the military on the DL. So many good men had died in that war—or else come home irreparably changed or damaged—that to admit he was a Marine who never saw any action seemed somehow worse than saying he'd never been in the Armed Services at all.

"No. He was an analyst or an engineer or something," she said, grateful when Mac suddenly interrupted their conversation with, "I seriously doubt her uncle's combat status of thirty-some-odd years ago has anything to do with his disappearance today. So, let's get back to the point, shall we?" Yes. The point. Of her uncle missing… *Dear God!* "Delilah, I need you to take me step-by-step through the last day."

And perhaps it was the fact that his electric-blue eyes never wavered from her face, or maybe it was the grounding effect of seeing the soft summer breeze ruffle his thick brown hair over his brow, but the sharp edges of the fear she'd been carrying around all afternoon and evening seemed to smooth out. Just a bit.

"Uncle Theo and I rode down to Marion yesterday evening." Was it her imagination, or was her voice a little steadier than it'd been only seconds ago? "We checked into a motel because Uncle Theo said Charlie's house is a dump not fit for company. I gather Charlie doesn't actually *live* in Marion but outside of it somewhere. And the fact that I have no idea where is *another* part of the problem." She shook her head at herself. Why, *why* hadn't she asked her uncle more questions? "But anyway, this morning Uncle Theo woke up early to drive out to Charlie's. He told me they'd likely do nothing but talk about the old days and I'd be bored to death. So, he left me to sleep in and catch up on some reading. He was supposed to come back for lunch. We were going to go to the diner across the street to grab a burger before hopping on the bikes to make the return trip. It was all going to be easy peasy."

It occurred to her then that it was funny—not funny "*ha-ha*" but funny "*sucky*"—how quickly things could go from easy peasy one minute to freakin' shitty the next.

"He didn't show up for lunch. He's not answering his phone. The local hospitals haven't admitted a man with his description. And the Marion police told me I'd have to wait twenty-four hours before they'd open an investigation. But I *can't* wait twenty-four hours." She reached out to grab Mac's muscular forearm where the sleeve of his motorcycle jacket was shoved up. His coarse male hairs tickled her palm, and his flesh was hot against the pads of her fingers. A *zing* of awareness shot up her arm. She tried to ignore it. It worked. Sort of… "I *know* something's wrong. He wouldn't just disappear like this. Something's happened to him, Mac. S-something *bad*."

And just like that, all her momentary calm disappeared. A sob she fought desperately to control strangled the back of her throat.

Don't panic.

The words of the mantra had lost their meaning and, with that, their power. Truth was, she was beyond panicked. She was straight-up, without-a-doubt terrified. Terrified with a capital T. Terrified right down to her very soul.

A muscle ticked in Mac's five-o'clock-shadowed jaw, and the look on his face was—

"Shh, now. You don't know that for sure," Zoelner whispered, throwing an arm over her shoulders.

"But I *do* know that for sure," she insisted, her eyes imploring Mac to believe her. Despite all rationale, despite their rocky relationship—or more like their rocky *non*-relationship—it was only *his* opinion that mattered.

She thought she saw him nod, just a quick jerk of his dimpled chin. Then again, perhaps the dim light of the street was playing tricks on her, because the words he growled were, "We'll just have to wait and see."

She opened her mouth, but she was stopped from pressing her case further because suddenly and unceremoniously Mac grabbed her wrist and yanked her out from under Zoelner's arm. Then, before she could utter a squeak of protest or, more likely, slug him on the shoulder for manhandling her, he hustled her up the steps until they were standing in front of the brownstone's wide wooden door.

"Geez," she huffed, rubbing her wrist. Although, in

all honesty, she didn't *really* mind his manhandling. Because his manhandling meant that he was touching her. And the feel of his calloused palm was—

Holy shit! Seriously, Delilah? How pathetic can you be? How many times does the guy have to tell you "no" before you'll get the hint? And how screwed up are you to be mooning like some lovesick teenager when Uncle Theo is freakin' MIA?

The answers to those questions were simple. In order, they were: one, very pathetic; two, apparently at least one more time; and three, pretty darned screwed up. Then all thought flew from her head when Mac used the keys to unlock the front door and the smell of sawdust mixed with cigar smoke immediately assaulted her nostrils. Those two scents would always remind her of her uncle. And, just like that, she lost hold of the tenuous thread she'd managed to keep tied around her emotions.

Her chin began to wobble.

Never a good sign…

And her nose began to burn.

An even more petrifying harbinger of things to come…

No, no, no. Don't do it. Don't you cry like a weak-kneed ninny.

But it was too late. The waterworks broke past the levee and now there was no stopping them.

At least that's what she thought.

Then she felt Mac reach down and lace his thick, warm fingers through hers…

———————

Mac was *still* drunk.

It was the only way to explain why he'd unceremoniously

yanked Delilah from Zoelner's embrace in order to satisfy the demands of the green-eyed monster that roared to life inside him the moment the former CIA agent threw an arm around her shoulders. Because there was no doubt whatsoever that he shouldn't care one whit whether or not another man was comforting her...touching her. Not after he'd spent most of his life avoiding women like her. And certainly not after he'd spent the last handful of years avoiding her *in particular*.

The fact that he *did* care *had* to mean that, yessiree, he was still drunker than ol' Cooter Brown. And *that* would also explain why, when he saw her little chin start to wiggle, he went against the grain and all his good sense and grabbed her hand.

Then again, maybe he was giving too much credit to the booze for that last move because, truth was, he'd always been an easy mark for a pretty little gal with tears standing in her eyes.

And Delilah's tears?

Man-oh-man! They were *particularly* gut-wrenching because usually she was the kind of woman who, as his father used to say, wouldn't think twice before charging hell with a bucket of ice water. Although, when he glanced down, it was to find her eyes dry as bones and wide as pie plates.

No doubt her shock was due in large part to the fact that he was actually, factually, *willingly* touching her. Especially since it was no big secret he'd spent a good amount of the time they'd known each other endeavoring to do exactly the opposite.

See, the problem was, he'd always kind of figured touching Delilah was similar to taking a hit of crack cocaine. Once was enough to get a guy good and hooked for life. And when he felt her cool, slim fingers hesitantly close around his, when the softness of her breath tickled his chin because she was gaping up at him, succulent mouth open in a little O of surprise? Well, you can bet your bottom dollar Little Mac took notice. And *Big* Mac? Well, he knew he'd been right all along...

He may have stopped the tears that had threatened to spill down Delilah's cheeks, but he also just took that first hit of crack.

Mistake, asshole. Huge mistake!

Dropping her hand like the thing was a molten-hot cattle prod, he cleared his throat and turned to find Zoelner standing directly behind them. The guy was wearing an infuriatingly sly smirk as he lifted his Styrofoam cup to noisily slurp at the last of what had to be disgustingly lukewarm coffee.

Mac narrowed his eyes and pinned him with a look that clearly stated, *Whatever it is you're thinking of sayin', you better check it at the back of your teeth lest you find those teeth shoved straight down your throat.*

But either Zoelner was still too sloshed to recognize the unspoken threat in his eyes, or, more likely, he just didn't give a rat's ass, because his sly smirk morphed into a devilish grin right before he opened his mouth. Luckily, Mac was saved from feeding Zoelner a five-finger sandwich—obviously men should never be allowed to drink; it caused them to revert to their lowest common denominator: i.e., freshman year of college—when Delilah cleared her throat and said, "Let's do this, shall we?"

Stepping over the threshold, she flipped a switch.

Instantly, the room was washed in bright light from the single bare bulb hanging from a socket in the center of the ceiling, and Mac realized what it was he'd been smelling...

Sawdust.

It covered the large space in a fine powder, dusting the drop cloths lying over the bare wood floors, blanketing the power tools stacked here and there, and standing a centimeter thick on the sawhorses set up in the center of the room.

"So this is Theo's latest project, huh?" Zoelner asked, pushing Mac from behind, forcing him to follow Delilah into the house. "What happened to that old Victorian he was fixing up in Lakeview?"

"He finished it two months ago," Delilah said, walking toward the sawhorses.

"Did he end up selling it for what he was hoping?" Zoelner inquired, strolling over to a big thirty-gallon trash can pushed into one corner and tossing his empty coffee cup inside.

"About fifty grand more than he was hoping for."

"Wow." Zoelner whistled. Delilah turned to gift him with the first smile...well, half-smile, really...she'd worn all night. Mac felt his hands curl into fists.

Whoa. What the hell is that *all about?* Perhaps it was still a remnant of the scotch? Though, if he was being honest with himself, that excuse had just about run its course. "Am I mistaken, or did we come here for a reason?" he demanded, feeling unaccountably...*something*. Something he refused to name.

"Yes." Delilah nodded, her smile disappearing as quickly as it'd arrived. And, *damnit,* now he wanted to

kick his own ass for being the cause of that. "Yes, we
did. I'll run upstairs to the room he's using as his office.
I know, way back in the day, before he plugged everything in to his iPhone, he used to keep an address book
in the top drawer of his desk. Maybe it's still there. And
maybe it has Charlie's information in it."

Aloud Mac said, "Sounds good." But inwardly he instructed himself *not* to watch her climb the steps to the
second floor. Unfortunately, what he *told* himself to do
and what he *did* were two entirely separate things. The
truth was, Delilah was dynamite from any angle. But
with a set of buttery-soft leather chaps hugging her legs
and revealing the jean-clad wonder that was her perfect,
heart-shaped derriere, the view from behind was, in a
word, *staggering*. He hadn't heard Zoelner cross over
to him, so he jerked when the guy clapped a heavy hand
on his shoulder.

"She's the kind of woman you hate to see leave but
you love to watch go. Am I right?" Zoelner winked
at him.

"I don't know what you're talkin' about," he insisted,
his back teeth grinding so hard he wasn't sure if it was
them he heard crackling or the plastic drop cloth beneath
his booted feet.

"*I don't know what you're talkin' about*," Zoelner
mimicked, doing a fairly good impression of a Texas
drawl, before snorting so loudly Mac figured it was a
wonder the guy didn't swallow his tonsils. "You keep
using that phrase in reference to your relationship with
our oh-so-tempting bartendress. Which leads me to believe you're completely full of shit."

"First of all, I don't *have* a relationship with our

oh-so-tempting bartendress. And secondly, I believe you're still piss drunk."

"You might be right," Zoelner admitted with a lopsided grin. "About the piss drunk part, anyway. But tomorrow I'll be sober, and you'll still be full of shit. So, there."

And, *see*, that little tit-for-tat proved Mac's theory about the lowest common denominator. He frowned, which only caused Zoelner's grin to widen. Then the guy shrugged and glanced around the room. "Man," he said. "Ol' Theo sure has his work cut out for him with this place."

And *that* reminded Mac of what had been bugging the holy hell out of him for the last few minutes. "How in the world do you know so much about what's goin' on in the lives of Delilah and her uncle anyway? I mean, a Victorian in Lakeview? Seriously?"

Zoelner slid him a look that questioned the validity of his college degree. "I know so much about what's happening in their lives because I, you know," he made a sarcastic gesture with his hands, "actually *talk* to her and stuff when I go into her bar to have a drink."

"As opposed to?" Mac inquired.

"Grumbling and growling and giving her dirty looks all the time."

"I don't do that."

Zoelner's face flattened. "Dude," he said, "you really have no idea just how bad you've got it, do you?"

Mac refused to respond to that question based solely upon its preposterousness. He knew what it was like to "have it bad." He'd had firsthand experience with "having it bad." And *he* most certainly did *not* have it bad for Delilah. In fact, he'd go so far as to say—

A hard *thump* sounded directly above their heads. And Mac discovered what it was like to have a full-on heart attack. Because that *thump* was immediately followed by the sound of Delilah's bloodcurdling scream…

Chapter Two

DELILAH HAD JUST SWITCHED OFF THE OVERHEAD fixture to her uncle's upstairs office, plunging the space into inky darkness, when the faint light drifting up the stairwell from the lower level illuminated the fact that the door beside her…moved. And not the kind of movement usually seen in an old house full of loose hinges, strange drafts, and suffering from the occasional effects of a settling foundation.

Oh, no. This kind of movement had purpose behind it. It had…a *person* behind it!

Everything that happened next occurred in ultra-slow motion, like an old 45 vinyl record being played at 33 RPMs. And for what seemed an eternity, she watched, dumbfounded, completely transfixed, as a large shadow emerged from behind the door.

On instinct, she stumbled back, her legs moving like the soles of her biker boots were mired in Super Glue, her heart skipping a couple of sorely missed beats. A million half-formed thoughts had time to spin through her brain—not the least of which was *What the hell?*— right before she slammed into the doorjamb, hitting her head.

Crack!

All thought ground to a halt, extinguished by the sharp pain cleaving her skull in two. A bright kaleidoscope of stars burst before her eyes, momentarily stunning her

and distracting her from the set of arms that reached out
to seize her around her waist.

This isn't happening…

This can't *be happening!*

Fortunately, her instincts took over for her bruised
brain because she let loose with a scream to do a Chicago
Bull's cheerleader proud. A sweaty hand clamped over
her mouth.

"Shut up, bitch," an accented voice hissed in her ear
just as the world ubiquitously decided that, *yep*, the need
for the weirdo, slow-mo time warp had passed. Time
once more resumed its usual course, and it was then she
realized her heart and lungs were set on overdrive, each
threatening to come bursting through her ribs. "If you
behave, I will not have to hurt you."

Yeah, well she couldn't promise the same thing.
Because she was going to take the first opportunity she
could find to inflict some serious damage to the guy who
was holding her hostage. And it *was* a guy. The deep voice
and large body told her as much, even if the darkness
precluded her ability to see him. Of course, the fact that
the stars dancing in front of her eyes had suddenly grown
propulsion packs and were zinging across her vision in a
dizzying array of luminous flashes wasn't helping matters.

Don't you dare pass out. You have to fight back!

And yeah. She could do that. With an old trick her
uncle taught her when she turned fourteen and grew a
set of D-cups…

Lifting her leg, relying on her sense of touch and
location alone, she kneed the sonofabitch straight in the
happy-sack. Soft flesh gave way to the hard crunch of
her attacker's pelvic bone.

Bull's-eye!

She mentally shot a fist in the air as her assailant howled in agony. She used his distraction to twist out of his grip. Unfortunately, he was blocking the doorway, so the only direction she could run was back into the pitch-black office.

She didn't hesitate. She stumbled inside and allowed the darkness to swallow her whole.

"Delilah!" Mac's voice boomed up the stairs.

It seemed as if minutes had passed since she'd screamed in terror, but in reality she figured the whole struggle had barely lasted two seconds.

"Delilah! Answer me!" Mac thundered, his tone sharp with fear. But answering wasn't an option. She couldn't allow the intruder to discern her exact location within the room. She didn't know if he had a gun. She didn't know if he—

Her thoughts screeched to a halt when her hip slammed into one corner of her uncle's desk.

Oh, thank heavens, the desk! If I crawl beneath it, maybe he won't be able to find me. Maybe that will give Mac enough time to—No, wait! The letter opener! She'd seen it lying on the corner of the desk when she was searching—turns out quite unsuccessfully—for her uncle's old address book. It was a weapon! *Hallelujah!*

But where was it exactly?

Her hand silently scrabbled across the wooden surface. Searching…searching…

She detected movement by the door. A shadow, dimly outlined by the miniscule amount of light, straightened and took on the vague shape of a man just as her hand landed on a smooth length of cold steel. Then the shadow shifted, sliding into the darkness, and Delilah knew this was it. Not daring to move, barely daring to breathe, she listened…and waited…

She could hear Mac and Zoelner's footsteps pounding down the hallway as her eyes searched the darkness to no avail. Her fingers curled around the hilt of the letter opener so tightly her knuckles ached.

"Delilah!" Mac yelled again, much closer now. Oh, how she wanted to answer him, just shout out his name so he could come and save the day. But it was too risky. She had to rely on herself here. Only herself…

Off to her left, something rattled, and she blindly turned in that direction, holding the letter opener out in front of her. Then, heavy footsteps. Very close by.

It was time.

The moment had come.

Her blood raced through her veins and roared between her ears, making it difficult to hear anything besides the pounding of her heart. Then a large hand landed on her arm and with a banshee yell, she turned and struck.

The blade of the letter opener hit something hard yet yielding and a loud "mmph" was immediately followed by a muttered curse. Delilah pulled her hand back to stab again just as the room blazed into view. Her arm froze in mid-strike, because it was *Mac* who was standing beside her. Zoelner, over by the doorway, still had his hand poised in front of the light switch.

For a few interminable seconds, they all seemed frozen in a motionless tableau, each of them blinking against the sudden glare. Then a rustling sound drew their attention to the far side of the room where jean-clad legs were quickly disappearing out a window that had been covered by a large, black garbage bag.

"Get him!" Mac bellowed and Zoelner sprang into action, racing across the office and lunging for the set of brown Timberland boots slipping over the windowsill, missing his mark by no more than a hairsbreadth.

"There's scaffolding!" Zoelner yelled, yanking the garbage bag from the window casing, revealing the missing panes of glass and the rusted rails of the framework attached to the back of the house. "I'm pursuing! You stay with Delilah!"

"Roger that!" Mac shouted as he grabbed her hand and hustled her toward the door, half-dragging, half-carrying her because her legs seemed to have transformed into wet noodles. The letter opener fell from her nerveless fingers to clatter dully against the floorboards.

She turned back in time to see Zoelner hop over the sill—obviously the adrenaline coursing through his system had negated the effects of the booze—just as Mac gave up on her ability to ambulate by herself. With a quick dip, he hooked an arm under her knees and then…weightlessness…as she was lifted into the air and pressed tight against his broad chest.

"Mac, I—"

"Hush." He cut her off, running toward the stairs, taking them two at a time. Later she would marvel at the sheer strength of him, at the feel of his hard muscles moving against her, but right at that moment, her head was spinning so fast it made it impossible to think.

He jumped from the third step, and they landed on the lower floor with a *thud* that had her back teeth clacking together and the pain in her abused head ratcheting up another degree. Then Mac raced to the center of the front room where he carefully lowered her next to the sawhorses. And it was a good thing he chose that precise spot, because, to her utter chagrin, she found herself relying on the sawhorse's support to remain upright.

Gulping in great mouthfuls of air, she watched helplessly as he yanked a mean-looking black handgun from the small of his back. Quickly and efficiently he pulled back on the slide and the *clicking* sound, indicating a round had been chambered, seemed particularly vicious in the harsh quiet hanging over the room like a death shroud.

"I have to check the rest of the house. There might be others," he told her, his blue eyes blazing with a light she'd never seen before.

It was the light of battle.

And it startled her almost as much as it fascinated her. Because right there and then, she realized that in all the years she'd known Mac, this was the first time she'd ever really *seen* him. The *real* him. Which shouldn't have surprised her, she supposed. Because if it walked like a hero and it talked like a hero, then it was probably—

"I need you to stay here," he told her brusquely as he bent to remove a small pistol from a holster secured around his ankle. Straightening, he handed her the weapon and she was surprised at how light it felt. And how warm. His body heat had seeped into the metal. "This is a Beretta 3032 Tomcat," he said, quickly explaining the gun's basics. "You have six in the clip and one in the throat. That's only seven bullets total. So if you have to fire, you better make sure your shots count."

She nodded jerkily, and he ducked his chin, peering into her face. "Are you okay? Can you handle this?"

And those were fair questions. You know, considering he'd had to *carry* her down the stairs.

Geez, way to instill confidence, Delilah…

But even though her heart was racing about a hundred miles per hour, and even though she was still dizzy, she'd be damned if she continued to play the pathetic damsel in distress card with him. She was Delilah Fairchild, the ass-kicking, Harley-riding, shotgun-toting beer-slinger-from-hell! And, *yes,* she could do this!

"No problem," she said, press checking the chamber to see that, indeed, he hadn't been lying about the one in the throat.

"Good." He nodded, something that looked gratifyingly close to admiration sparking in his eyes. And then he did something even more stupefying than earlier when he grabbed her hand…

He leaned forward and planted a kiss in the center of her forehead. It was quick. Just a fast press of his warm, surprisingly soft lips against her skin, but it was enough to erase her fear and shock and have her toes curling inside her biker boots. Then he leaned back and grinned. And, as if her mind wasn't already blown to freakin' kingdom come, he went one step further and *winked* at her.

Holy hell! Bryan "Mac" McMillan kissed her. Then grinned. And then *winked.*

Okay, maybe that knock to the head had been harder than she thought, because that couldn't be right, could it? She blinked, hoping that might help clear away what had to be a mirage…or else a delusion brought on by a concussion. But no amount of eyelid flapping erased the sight of Mac's big, square teeth flashing whitely against the dark shadow of his beard stubble.

And the cray-cray just kept on coming, because then he reached up and chucked her on the chin. She was gaping at him when he turned to disappear through the doorway leading to the back of the house.

What the hell is happening? She felt like she'd been eating at the buffet of the bizarre all day, but that little display of Mac's definitely put the cherry on top of the weirdo dessert of it all.

In the span of a few minutes, he'd gone from his usual Mr. Cranky-Pants to Sir Kissy Smiles-A-Lot.

"Lower level's clear," he said, reappearing suddenly, causing her to jump and instinctively raise the weapon he loaned her. "Whoa!" He lifted his hands, splaying the last three fingers of his right hand wide while his thumb and forefinger kept hold of his pistol. "Ventilating any mofo that comes at you is the general idea, darlin'. But I was kinda hopin' you wouldn't think to do as much to me."

"S-sorry," she said, lowering the little handgun and gulping in sawdust-tinged air that scratched at her already dry, itchy throat. "I just...I'm not..." She stopped and shrugged.

And that's when he did it *again*. He freakin' went and *winked* at her before turning to jog up the stairs.

Okay, so now it was all crystal clear. Somewhere, at some point, she'd fallen into a parallel universe. Shaking her head at this place heretofore referred to as Bizarro-Land, she winced when the movement caused her bruised brain to jostle against the sides of her skull.

Lifting a hand, she rubbed at the lump forming on the back of her head—*ow*—just as the front door burst open. Spinning, she raised the pistol, supporting the butt with her free hand just as her uncle had taught her, then blew out a harsh breath when she realized it was Zoelner stepping over the threshold.

"He got away," he informed her, panting as he placed his hands on his hips and bent at the waist. "Fucker disappeared into the labyrinth of alleys around here, and I didn't dare follow in case he was packing. Didn't want to find myself stuck in a fatal funnel."

Huh? "What's a—"

That's all she managed to get out before Mac reappeared on the stairway. "Fatal funnels are hallways and alleys," he answered the question she'd been in the middle of asking. "And they're the last place a guy wants to be when the bullets start flyin'."

"Oh." She nodded. "Makes sense." And that was about the only thing in this entire weird-ass day that *did*.

"Who was he?" Zoelner asked, and Delilah's chin jerked back when she realized he was looking directly at her.

"You're asking me?" Unconsciously, she used the pistol as a pointer and aimed it at her own chest. When she looked down and realized what she was doing, she gulped and carefully set the weapon atop one of the sawhorses. "I...I have n-no idea. I didn't get a chance to see his f-face, and I certainly didn't recognize his v-voice."

Oh, good grief. Why in the world were her teeth ch-ch-chattering like she was standing in the bar's walk-in refrigerator? She'd been in worse situations than the one upstairs. For heaven's sake, she'd actually taken part in a bona fide shoot-out!

Okay, and *that* was the dead-last thing she wanted to remember at this particular moment. Because anytime she opened the mental door to that terrible afternoon, the entire sad scene would inexplicably flash before her eyes. And, yup, right on cue, she saw it all again. Buzzard, her wiliest and most loyal patron slumped on a barstool, blood pouring from him in a thick, ghastly river, his eyes glassy and vacant and...*dead*.

Her chest suddenly felt like it was supporting the weight of an elephant. And from out of nowhere came the thought that perhaps her uncle was somewhere in the same condition. Sitting or lying or crumpled in a heap, covered in blood and lifeless...

Oh, God!

"He spoke to you?" Mac queried, dragging her from her wild speculations. *Thank goodness*. She'd just about played the part of a nuclear reactor and had herself a good ol'-fashioned meltdown. "What did he say?"

And the memory of that voice, not to mention the feel of the assailant's hot breath brushing against her ear, caused her to shudder. Crossing her arms, she chafed her biceps, inexplicably cold despite the warmth of the late spring evening. "Well, he called me a bitch for starters," she recalled, trying to play down the fear she'd felt in that moment by rolling her eyes and making a face. "And then he said if I behaved he wouldn't have to hurt me."

"Lord almighty," Mac growled, his wide jaw sawing back and forth as he crossed the room to retrieve the pistol she'd abandoned. Bending with a graceful fluidity that was incongruent when compared to his large physique, he resecured it in his ankle holster. "What the hell was he doin' here? Do you suppose it has somethin' to do with your uncle's disappearance? Or is it possible he was simply taking advantage of your uncle's absence to break in and steal stuff?" He straightened and glanced around the room. "There's got to be thousands of dollars' worth of tools in this place."

"But he wasn't down here loading up the tools," Zoelner said, a hard look of contemplation knitting his brow. "He was upstairs in Theo's office."

"But that's where Uncle Theo keeps his safe," Delilah offered. "Maybe the guy thought there was a bigger payday to be had up there."

She shuddered at the memory of the man's arms around her, his words in her ear. When Mac saw her continuing to chafe her arms, his frown turned so severe she feared his eyebrows might slide right down the middle of his nose. He reached for her wrist and dragged her next to him. Then he threw a heavy arm around her shoulders. *See*, Bizarro-Land. And as she absorbed some of his warmth, she admitted she was beginning to like it here.

"I don't believe in coincidences," Zoelner declared.

"Neither do I," Mac agreed, lifting his free arm to rub a wide palm over the back of his neck.

"Is your Spidey sense acting up?" Zoelner asked.

Delilah frowned. *Spidey sense? What the—*

"Sure as shit," Mac said. "But that could be because we just witnessed some dude in Timberlands take a header out of a two-story window."

"Yeah." Zoelner shrugged. "Or it could be because Mr. Timberlands is somehow mixed up with Theo's disappearance." Just the thought had another chill snaking

down her spine. She shivered, and Mac absently chafed
her arm. "And speaking of," Zoelner turned to her, "I
don't suppose you found your uncle's old address book?"

"No." She shook her head. "No address book. No
files. Nothing that would tell us who Charlie is or where
he lives."

"All the more reason to find out just who the hell Mr.
Timberlands is."

"No argument here," Mac agreed. "We can hack into
the city surveillance cams back at headquarters. Maybe
we got lucky and they caught an image that Ozzie can
run against his facial recognition software. We can do
that while we're simultaneously searching phone records, military records, and anything else we can think
of to find out just who this Charlie guy is and if it's
possible he has any connection to Mr. Timberlands. Is
that all right with you?" Mac dipped his chin again, and
there was that damn, tempting dimple.

For a moment, she was too distracted with having to
curl her hands into fists lest she reach up to press the
pad of her finger against the thing—something she'd
been daydreaming about doing for years, *and, oh, for
heaven's sake, Delilah, now's not the time*—to realize
what he was asking. Then it sank in.

"You mean am I willing to let super-secret agents
with contacts at the top tier of government take the
lead on the investigation to find my uncle?" She made
sure her expression adequately matched her scoffing
tone. And, okay, so she couldn't *completely* dispense
with the sarcasm. "Uh, yeah. I think that'll be all right
with me."

"Good then." Mac nodded. "It's a plan."

A plan. She should feel elated. Unfortunately, she was too terrified for elation. Stepping out from under the comforting weight of his arm, a sticky warmth against her side had her glancing down. Pulling aside the edge of her lightweight riding jacket, she gasped when she saw bright red blood staining the bottom of her neon pink T-shirt.

"What?" She gulped, pressing her hand against the blood. Had her assailant somehow wounded her? Had the adrenaline kept her from feeling it? "What?" she croaked again, staring at the smear of red on her fingertips when she pulled her hand away.

"Don't worry," Mac told her. "It's not yours."

"Not my—?" She blinked at him uncomprehendingly.

"It's mine."

"Y-yours?" Her gaze shot down to his side.

Sure enough. A circle about the size of a Frisbee stained the black cotton of his T-shirt, making it appear shiny. And then she remembered.

The letter opener...

"Jesus Christ, Mac!" she yelped, rushing forward to lift his shirt. A deep gash about three inches long sliced through the perfection of his tan flank and leaked blood sluggishly.

"It's nothing," he told her, dragging down the hem of his shirt. "It's only about half an inch deep. Not something to worry about."

"It's *not* nothing," she insisted, all her anxiety and terror suddenly joined by twin helpings of dismay and guilt. She wasn't usually a wilting lily when it came to the sight of blood, but knowing she'd wounded a man who'd only been trying to help her made her sick to her stomach. Literally. The stupid organ turned upside down and proceeded to disgorge acid up into her throat. "I-I *stabbed* you!"

"Eh." He shrugged his big shoulders. "People get stabbed all the time."

"In what universe?" she demanded incredulously. "Most folks I know get hangnails, not knife wounds!"

"Really?" Zoelner asked, reminding Delilah of his presence. She'd completely forgotten about him. Of course, who could blame her when every fiber of her being was focused on the fact that she'd freakin' *stabbed* Mac. *Holy shit!* "Maybe that means we're in the wrong business, Mac. Because I've seen plenty of stab wounds, but I can't recall ever laying eyes on a hangnail."

"Are you thinkin' a change of career is in order?" Mac asked Zoelner, one corner of his mouth twitching.

Seriously? *Seriously?*

"That bump to my head must've been harder than I thought," she declared. "Because you two can't really be standing here *joking* about the fact that I stabbed Mac." *I mean, Jesus!*

"I told you it's nothin'," Mac assured her. And before she could open her mouth to refute his statement a second time, he wrapped a hand around her bicep and started guiding her toward the front door. "Now, let's get back to the shop so we can get Ozzie going on findin' out who Mr. Timberlands is, and so Zoelner and I can get going on findin' your uncle."

Oh, yeah. Finding her uncle. And there was that. *Sweet Mary and Joseph, will this god-awful day ever end?*

Chapter Three

"THE PRODIGAL SONS HAVE RETURNED! AND THEY'VE brought Delilah back with them!"

A cheer sounded from all those gathered in the dark courtyard located behind BKI's warehouse facilities. And the raised beer bottles, lively music, fire crackling in the pit, not to mention the canoodling couples lounging in mismatched lawn furniture around the pit, were the whole reason Dagan Zoelner had quit the scene four hours earlier in order to hail the first cab to Red Delilah's Biker Bar.

Because the Black Knights, his colleagues…or, okay, so despite the ignominious way in which he'd joined the group, he supposed he could now count them as his *friends*…had decided to throw an impromptu party. And if there was one night a year when the dead-last thing he wanted to do was pull a Will Smith and "get jiggy wit' it," this was it.

Tonight of all nights, he had absolutely nothing to celebrate and a whole hell of a lot to lament. Beginning and ending with the five lives that had been lost six years ago because of his colossal fuckup…

And to tell the truth, though he was sorry as hell for Delilah and the pain and anguish she was going through—then there was his *own* anxiety surrounding the matter; he happened to like Theo Fairchild immensely—he wasn't sorry to have something other than the anniversary of that clusterfuck in Afghanistan to occupy his mind. Because, try as he might—and you can bet your ass he'd been trying with *all* his might—he hadn't been able to wash away with good Scottish whiskey the memories of that hot desert afternoon and the gruesome images that flashed behind his lids anytime he closed his eyes.

And, yes, he fully realized that numbing his pain at the expense of his liver was anything but mature, and he usually made a concerted effort to be out on a mission when this particular date rolled around. But with one of the Knights' wives about to pop out a mini Knight at any moment, Boss, the esteemed leader of their little group of covert operators, had done his best to make sure as many of the guys as possible were on hand to witness the blessed event.

And, wouldn't you know, Dagan's last mission had ended three days ago, and since then, nothing pressing had come over the wires necessitating him to head back out to parts unknown. Which meant that he was stuck. Here. Waiting on the arrival of a bouncing bundle of joy and unexpectedly finding himself in the middle of a party he wanted no part of...

Then again, that wasn't *totally* true. Because he *was* happy for his fellow operator. Honestly, he was. Even now, as he looked at Ghost rubbing the lower back of his *extremely* pregnant wife, Ali, he couldn't deny the tiny spark of satisfaction...*and is that longing?*...that flashed deep inside him.

The Knights' transient lifestyles, while thrilling,

tended to make them a bad bet for solid relationships. Being hell and gone all the time seemed to curtail serious attachments. But somehow this guy, this hard-driving, hard-fighting operator, had managed to make it work. He'd managed to find a measure of peace, a little bit of happiness, despite the oftentimes spectacular pile of shit that was their under-the-table and off-the-books work for Uncle Sam. And standing there, watching him grin at his wife like he'd just won the lottery gave Dagan hope that maybe someday he, too, might discover a love that could repair all the broken things inside him. A love that could bring him some small level of contentment, that would…he didn't know…make it all, all the struggle and pain, all the regret and sacrifice, worth it.

On the other hand, Ghost was a grade-A, stand-up guy who didn't have the blood of five innocent people on his hands, so—

"Three more barley pops for the new arrivals, Steady!" Ozzie, the Knights' on-staff computer whiz, called cheerfully to the ex–Army Ranger medic who now served as BKI's in-house sawbones. "And while you're at it, pass me one, too."

"I thought you said you were headed out to sow your wild oats," Steady retorted as he popped the top on the big cooler positioned beside his bright red Adirondack chair.

"Sow his wild oats?" Becky, BKI's wunderkind motorcycle designer/mechanic, scoffed from her position on Boss's lap. She was simultaneously sucking down suds and lapping at one of her ever-present Dum Dum lollipops. And just imagining that particular taste combination made the scotch in Dagan's stomach threaten a reappearance. "Is that what you call getting more ass than a sorority house toilet seat?" A wet, slightly fishy-smelling breeze blew in from the nearby Chicago River and teased the ends of her long blond ponytail. Then her smile quickly morphed into a frown as she pointed the end of her sucker in Ozzie's direction. "And you can wipe that look off your face right this minute."

"What look?" Ozzie asked innocently.

"The one that says you know what color panties I'm wearing."

"Well, I can't help that." Ozzie grinned, reaching up to adjust an invisible tie around his neck. "Guessing the color of women's drawers is just one of my *many* talents."

"Ozzie…" Boss warned.

"Now back to this sorority house toilet seat comment," Ozzie blazed ahead. "I thank you for the vote of confidence in my manly prowess, but if we're talking manwhores, we need to turn the spotlight off me and shine it on this guy sitting beside me."

"Me?" Steady hooked a thumb at his chest. The firelight flickered across his swarthy, Hispanic features and flashed in his laughing black eyes. "I'm not the one who goes through women like Kleenex, *cabrón*."

"Pfft." Ozzie waved him off. "I may *technically*," he stressed the word, "have a few more notches on my bedpost than you do." Dagan rolled his eyes. Surely they weren't keeping a running tally. *Surely.* "But at least I'm not the high king of one-night stands. At least I'm gentlemanly enough to take them out to dinner a couple of times afterward, make some kind of connection. I think you're known around town as Mr. One-and-Done!"

"Okay, children." Boss clapped his hands together. "That's enough." Frank "Boss" Knight was well versed in riding roughshod over a group of overgrown men who liked slinging bullshit at one another almost as much as they liked dangerous missions, high stakes odds, and bright, shiny new weapons. Usually Dagan enjoyed the good-natured camaraderie, the relentless ribbing. But not tonight. Tonight he either wanted to wallow in his own self-pity or find something to take his mind off the weight of his unremitting guilt. The scotch had been helping him, albeit marginally, to do both… "Let's not forget we're here to celebrate the imminent birth of a little hellion," Boss continued. "So how 'bout those beers, Steady?"

"Coming right up," Steady said, but Mac stopped him before he could fish the bottles of Honkers Ale from the sea of ice. Part of Dagan couldn't help but grieve the lost opportunity for a frosty brew. Because, unfortunately, the last blessedly numbing drops of Lagavulin had worn off right about the time he was chasing Mr. Timberlands down the street.

"We're gonna have to pass on the suds, folks," Mac drawled while simultaneously trying to bat Delilah's administering hands away from his side. From out of nowhere—or maybe from out of one of the saddlebags on her Harley—Delilah had produced a travel pack of tissues, and she'd been doing her best to tend to Mac's stab wound ever since. It'd been Dagan's experience that most women took the Boy Scouts' *always be prepared* motto to heart.

"And while we're on the subject," Mac continued, flashing Delilah a look of utter exasperation when she refused to quit dabbing at his injury all while making tutting noises like an old Jewish grandma, "we need *you* guys to put a lid on this little celebration, too."

Holy fuckballs, do those two have it bad, Dagan thought. And it was his heartfelt belief that should Mac ever wise up and stop wearing his ass as a hat—he knew Mac's history, knew just how sordid it was, but the guy gave new meaning to the phrase *once bitten twice shy*—then Dagan would have the honor of bearing witness to *another* fairy-tale ending.

"What? Why?" Becky asked. Then she noticed Delilah's ministrations. "Whoa." Her chin jerked back. "What the hell happened to you, Mac?"

"Delilah stabbed me," Mac deadpanned.

Delilah sputtered like a backfiring motor as Boss hooted with laughter, gleefully slapping his knee. "And I'm sure you totally deserved it!"

"I most certainly did *not*," Mac harrumphed, crossing his arms over his chest, his brows angled down his slightly crooked nose.

"Of course you did," Ozzie declared. "You have, after all, been taking those penis-enlarging pills recently."

This time it was Mac's turn to sputter. "I most certainly…what the *hell* are you talkin' about?"

"The fact that you've been a bigger dick to Delilah in the last handful of months than ever before," Ozzie asserted, his eyes sparkling with mischief. The whiz kid turned to bump knuckles with Steady as a dull roar of laughter competed with the *snap* and *crackle* of the fire. Dagan couldn't help it, despite this night and the horrendous anniversary it observed, he felt his lips twitch. Ozzie had a biting wit that was equally amusing and annoying, depending in large part on whether or not you happened to be the one on the receiving end of his rapier repartee.

"Shut the fuck up, Ozzie," Mac growled. Dagan wasn't surprised to discover the ex–FBI agent had fallen into the *Ozzie's Sense of Humor is Annoying* group on this particular occasion.

Ozzie quickly replied with, "Seriously, though, Mac. Just give me ten minutes alone, and I might be able to help you remove that giant stick from your a—"

"Ozzie." Mac's eyes were drilling into Ozzie with so much force it was a wonder the guy didn't spring a couple of leaks from the set of through-and-throughs in his head. "Don't push me tonight."

"All right," Ozzie capitulated, sighing dramatically. "We'll just leave it where it is then. All safe and secure."

Mac opened his mouth to respond, then snapped it shut again, shaking his head. "Look, folks. We don't have time to—" He sucked in a hissing breath when Delilah hit a particularly sore spot. "Ow! Damnit, woman! Will you leave off, already?"

"And let you bleed out?" she yelled back, her pretty green eyes overly bright even in the dim light cast by the fire. "I've already stood by and watched one man bleed to death because of something I did! I'll be damned if I stand by and watch it happen again!"

A stunned silence settled over the group as everyone looked on in fascinated horror while one of the toughest women they knew went ahead and lost her shit. It started out slowly, with just a slight wobble of her lower lip. Then her stubborn chin followed suit. Finally, her chest heaved once, and it was game over. The waterworks exploded like a main pipe had busted.

Mac looked stunned for all of a half-second, before his big, Irish face caved in on itself and he yanked the flame-haired bartendress against him, hugging her tight and muffling the sounds of her pitiful sobs into his chest. So, Brendan hadn't been joking about Delilah's trouble in dealing with her friend's recent murder. And that, combined with the overpowering and stone-cold terror she'd been feeling all day, had finally gotten the better of her.

"Shh, darlin'," the big Texan crooned, rubbing a hand down her hair and kissing her tenderly on the forehead. "Shh, now. There's no need to—"

"Zoelner?" Boss snagged Dagan's attention. The man's craggy face was pulled down into a fierce frown, causing the scar cutting up from the corner of his mouth to pucker angrily. "What the *hell* is going on?"

And as jovial as the party atmosphere had been just seconds ago, that's how somber it was now. It was as if someone had flipped a switch. *Flick!* On to off. Go to stop. Green to red.

Hell, even Ozzie appeared pensive.

"Delilah's uncle is missing," he informed the group. The collective gasp was so strong, he thought it was a wonder the fire didn't instantly flame out from lack of oxygen. "And she's depending on us to help her find him…"

———

Cairo, Illinois

"What happened?" Qasim ibn Hasan barked into the phone, turning to watch as two of his most loyal men lifted the body of the dead American from the rotted wood floor. It'd only been a half dozen hours, but the corpse was already starting to smell, fouling the air inside the dank and musty abandoned building, making it nearly impossible to breathe.

Not that he wasn't used to the stench of rotting flesh. He'd been fighting *jihad* for well over a decade. And living with the stink of the dead and dying was just part of that struggle. But, still...*filthy American pigs. Filthy murderous American pigs...*

"I was interrupted during my search for the woman's address," came the reply from Haroun, his second-in-command. And that was another thing that irked Qasim about the Americans. Why did some of them *insist* on using post office boxes instead of physical addresses?

Haroun's hunt for and abduction of Delilah Fairchild would've been so much easier had their extensive Internet search turned up her place of residence. All Haroun would've had to do was break into her house or apartment while she was at work, wait for her to arrive home, and incapacitate her before delivering her straight to Qasim. *As easy as one, two, three,* as the Americans liked to say.

Unfortunately, counting to three had not been their destiny...

"Then you must find a way to take her away from her workplace or en route from her workplace to her home," Qasim instructed. "Those are our only other options."

"But they are not," Haroun said, instantly piquing Qasim's interest.

"No?" he asked, his lip curling with disgust as his men carted the remains of the old Marine by him. When

the light from the low-burning kerosene lanterns revealed a drop of coagulating blood falling from the body
to the dusty floor, barely missing the toe of his shoe, he
frowned at Sami and Jabbar.

"Idiots," he growled, jumping from the cheap plastic
chair they'd managed to scrounge up from the wreckage
of this sad, forsaken town, "mind where you are going
with that lump of filth."

"Yes, sir."

"Sorry, sir."

After Charles Sander died of a heart attack within
hours of beginning his interrogation and torture, Qasim
had wondered if perhaps he'd been sent on a fool's mission. If perhaps Allah himself wasn't laughing down at
him for thinking he could accomplish what so many of
his brethren over the years had not. But then, just as he
was howling over his lost leverage—he'd intended to
use Charles and Theodore against one another, tortur-
ing one to make the other talk—he'd opened Theodore
Fairchild's wallet to discover what would undoubtedly
be the ultimate chink in the man's armor. Photographic
evidence of a girl—a *niece* Qasim had discovered after
a quick Google search—whom Theodore had raised
as a daughter. *She* was just the bargaining chip Qasim
needed to make the old Marine give up the information
stored inside his head. And it was at that moment that he
began to think that *qadar*, or Fate, had once more swung
in his favor...

Praise Allah! This might actually work!

"Shall we just drop the body next door?" Jabbar
asked, straining under the weight of Charles Sander and
looking peculiar in his Western-style clothing.

"Take him far enough away so that his stench does not reach us," Qasim instructed his men. Then he turned back to the phone conversation. "What were you saying?" he asked Haroun, lamenting the fact that Jabbar had inadvertently smashed Theodore's cellular phone during the struggle to apprehend the man. Because how much simpler would this whole situation have been had they been able to send Delilah Fairchild a text message from her uncle's phone instructing her to come to Cairo. After all, that exact plan had worked so well using Sander's phone in order to get Theodore here...

Such is life, he sighed pragmatically. *Allah gives us obstacles to overcome in order to make the victory that much sweeter.* And just as soon as he had his hands on Delilah Fairchild, he *would* be victorious. And it *would* be very, *very* sweet.

"It was the woman herself who interrupted me," Haroun explained. Qasim's heart beat faster as hope bloomed in his chest. *Could it be so easy?* "I would simply have grabbed her there, but she was not alone. Two men were there with her. I was forced to abandon the premises." Qasim resumed his seat, his shoulders slumping in disappointment. *No, of course it could not be.* "I hid until they left the old Marine's house. Then followed them to some sort of motorcycle repair shop. The place has high security, so I will wait to grab her when she exits. I do not know how long that could be."

Qasim glanced over at Theodore. The aging, white-haired man was tied to a chair, and the blood dripping from his broken nose stained the gag they'd secured over his large, bushy mustache and mouth, turning the cream-colored material a dingy, repugnant crimson.

That shade would always remind Qasim of the bloody sheets he wrapped his wife and two sons in after a drone strike leveled his village in Pakistan.

It'd been barely a year after the towers were destroyed on September 11th. And the United States had told the media the attack was necessary due to the presence of a high-level al-Qaeda operative in the town. But Qasim didn't know anything about an al-Qaeda operative, high-level or not. And all he found when he returned home to search through the rubble of his life were the mutilated bodies of his friends and neighbors…the shredded corpses of his wife and children.

Before the drone strike, he'd never been tempted to join the groups of bewhiskered men who occasionally came through his village, ranting and raving about justice and the need to perpetrate revenge on all the infidels. But that all changed the night an unmanned plane, flown by a soldier sitting in front of a computer screen thousands of miles away, dropped an AGM Hellfire air-to-ground missile on everything Qasim held dear.

AGM Hellfire air-to-ground missile… He would always remember the name of the ordnance that obliterated his family.

Hellfire…

The newspapers had printed it without thought to what that word would mean to those who'd survived the massacre.

Hellfire…

It was exactly what he and so many others were going to rain down on American mothers and fathers, wives and children, in the weeks and months to come.

Filthy American pigs, he thought again. Though, as

he let his gaze once more travel over Theodore Fairchild, he had to give the man credit for his strength. Even after the beating Sami and Jabbar had given him, and even after watching his friend die a wheezing, eye-bulging death, Theodore remained upright, his chin held high, his aging blue eyes bright with fury.

But that strength would only last so long. And Qasim knew just how to strike fear into the hardened heart of a man like Theodore.

Smiling to himself, he tilted his head at his hostage. Theodore was listening intently to his phone conversation. Not that Qasim was concerned. It was unlikely Theodore was able to understand the stilted Arabic he was speaking—stilted because Punjabi was his native tongue and he'd only learned to speak Arabic after joining The Cause. Still, not being able to understand the words Qasim spoke did not stop the old soldier from straining to hear any recognizable phrase. Which was why Qasim winked before saying, "Excellent, Haroun. I look forward to meeting *Delilah Fairchild*," he emphasized the name, "very soon."

Theodore jerked against his restraints, yelling behind the gag, and Qasim allowed a grin to tilt his lips. "I'm going to bring your beloved niece here, Mr. Fairchild," he said in English, infusing his voice with the promise of death and retribution. "And then you and I are going to make a deal…"

Chapter Four

DELILAH WAS MORTIFIED.

She could not *believe* she'd done exactly what she'd promised herself she'd never do…which was break down like a lily-livered ninny in front of these people. These fearless guys who put their lives on the line each day, and these brave women who stood by, dry-eyed, and watched them do it.

How pathetic was she by comparison?

Pretty damned pathetic, a little voice whispered at the back of her head, to which she immediately replied, *Oh, fuck off*.

Because, seriously? If a gal couldn't rely on her own subconscious to have her back, then she couldn't rely on anyone. *Hmph*. Her inner twelve-year-old crossed her arms and scowled.

Okay, now anger… Anger is good. Anger could fuel the fire that burned inside her. You know, as opposed to the fear that had left her weak and spent and falling apart in the circle of Mac's strong arms. And, yeah, so she could admit the strong arms thing was the bright spot in an otherwise humiliating little display. But, seriously, even *they* weren't enough to overcome *all* her embarrassment. *Some*, certainly. A girl would have to be dead from the waist down not to be comforted by the feel of Mac's embrace—not to mention the warmth of his firm lips on her brow. But not all of it.

And, hey, since she was on the topic, what was *with* him and the forehead kisses, anyway? He'd broken— more like smashed through—his four-year moratorium on touching her only to grant her the lowliest form of affection? Because, come on, the forehead kiss, while sweet, was sort of like the kiss of death when it came to romance, placing the recipient of said kiss firmly in the friend zone. So was all Mac's touchy, feely, forehead-kissy stuff an indication that he suddenly wanted to be friends? Was it an indication that—

"…warm up?" Ali, Ghost's wife, dragged Delilah away from her spinning thoughts.

She looked up from her seat at the long, rectangular conference table to find the heavily pregnant blonde holding a carafe of coffee. At least Delilah *assumed* the black sludge sloshing around inside the glass container was coffee. Truth was, after having taken a sip of the foul stuff, she couldn't be quite sure. It smelled like burned rubber and tasted about the same.

"What did you say?" she asked. Eighties music filled the cavernous space that was the Black Knights' second floor…uh…what exactly would one call this area? The command center?

"I asked if you wanted a warm up," Ali repeated.

"Uhhhh…" She shook her head, covering the top of her mostly full Styrofoam cup. "No, thanks."

"You sure?" Ali asked, hoisting the carafe higher, looking very cute in a flowered maternity sundress studded with rhinestones around the collar and hem. But no matter how well Ali played the part of Vanna White, there was nothing that could force Delilah to take one more drink of that sludge.

"Yeah." She nodded vehemently, then narrowed her eyes when a little smile tugged at one corner of Ali's lips. "Hey, are you screwing around with me? What *is* this stuff?"

Ali's tawny eyes flashed. But before she could answer, her husband whisked the pot from her hands.

"What d'ya think you're doin'?" Nate "Ghost" Weller demanded in that strange mashed-up way he had of speaking. It was almost like he talked in cursive. "The doctor said you're not s'posed to lift heavy things." Pulling out a chair, he gently, as if Ali were a fragile piece of antique china, maneuvered her into it despite her repeated swatting of his hands.

"Oh, for Pete's sake, Nate," the blonde groused, scowling up at her handsome, black-eyed husband. "I don't think a coffee pot constitutes a *heavy thing*." She made the quote marks with her fingers, fingers Delilah noticed were pudgy with retained fluid. She'd been around enough pregnant women in her day to know Ali Weller was about to burst. Or as Uncle Theo liked to say, *primed to pop*.

Uncle Theo… And just like that, she felt the blood drain from her face.

Oh, for heaven's sake, were those tears burning up the back of her nose?

"A coffee pot doesn't constitute a heavy thing?" Ghost asked, his expression dubious. "Mmmph," he finished, shaking his head until his black hair brushed against the collar of his white, 110th Anniversary Harley-Davidson T-shirt.

"Mmmph?" Ali parroted, lifting her brows before turning to Delilah. "I thought I was making progress with him. You know," she fluttered her hands dramatically, "getting him to speak in actual sentences and stuff. But ever since that double pink line appeared on the pee-stick test, he's reverted back to his former caveman vocabulary."

"Mmmph," Ghost grunted again, plunking down in the seat beside his wife.

"See what I mean?" Ali asked, and Delilah was eternally grateful for the distraction from her own self-pity. She opened her mouth to agree with Ali but closed it again when the sound of Steady's heavy biker boots clomping down the metal stairs from the third floor snagged her attention.

From what she'd been able to gather the other two times she'd been in the old menthol cigarette factory that now housed Black Knights Inc., the third floor was the living quarters for the operators, those who still resided onsite, anyway. She'd heard a few of the married guys had moved out—no doubt in an effort to gain a little privacy from what she'd come to understand was basically just a big frat house stocked with hand grenades, guns, and all manner of other ruthless, deadly things that went *boom*.

The first floor, with its soaring ceiling, brightly painted brick walls, and gleaming line of custom choppers, was the state-of-the-art motorcycle shop where all the bike building occurred—and where the cover for the clandestine nature of BKI was maintained.

And *then* there was this second floor…

As far as she could tell, it was the heart of the operation. The large conference area was open on one side to the motorcycle shop below. Off to her right, a row

of metal doors stood ajar and revealed the interiors of
half a dozen private offices. And lining one wall, top
to bottom, was a set of computers and monitors fancy
enough to drive home the fact that, yes, indeed, she
really *was* sitting smack-dab in the middle of a super-
secret spy shop.

"Let me check your head," Steady said. "Make sure
that pop you received didn't leave you with a concussion.
And Mac," he said as he dropped a camouflage duffel
bag on the end of the conference table. It landed with a
muted *thud*. "Come over here and take your shirt off."

Okay… *Mac? Shirtless?* Talk about *one* way to rip
her mind away from heavy, heartbreaking thoughts of
her uncle. She had to concentrate incredibly hard in order
to answer the rather simple questions Steady peppered
her with as his fingers pressed around on her skull. Not
because of any brain injury, mind you. But because Mac
was two seconds away from becoming shirtless. And
when Mac did as Steady suggested, sauntering over to the
conference table from his previous position by the bank of
computers, snagging the seat beside her before reaching
over his head to grab the collar of his bloody T-shirt and
whip the garment off in one fell swoop, she completely
forgot her own name. Thankfully, Steady had already
finished questioning her and pronounced her sound.

Oh, for the love of tequila…

Tan… Mac's skin had that I-grew-up-in-the-Deep-
South, sun-kissed look about it.

Hard… The thick muscles bulging in his chest
and shoulders appeared solid enough to withstand a
hatchet strike.

Manly… Hair grew in a patch between his impressive

pectoral muscles and arrowed down to disappear beneath the waistband of his faded jeans, screaming *male* as loudly as a shot glass full of straight testosterone.

Mouthwatering… The corrugated muscles of his stomach bunched when he bent to the side to allow Steady to swipe an antiseptic cloth over his slowly weeping wound.

Delicious… Soap lingered on his skin, and the smell of it was a seductive combination of cool mint and warm vanilla. It made her think of hard Christmas candies and sugar cookies fresh from the oven.

Ink… Around his bulky biceps twined triple links of black barbed wire. A lone fist-sized red, white, and blue outline of the state of Texas with a star in the center covered the hard muscle over his heart. And maybe it was because she'd been raised around a bunch of rowdy bikers, but she always got a little weak in the knees when confronted with badass tattoos inked into tough, tan skin.

Put it all together, add a pinch of I-haven't-been-laid-in-*way*-too-long, and what did you come up with? A big ol' dollop of *yeehaw, cowgirl!* with a side of *wanna take a ride?*

And, *yes*. She'd been wanting to do exactly that for a very, *very* long time now. In fact, she'd been—

Really, Delilah, that pesky little voice piped up again, *we're back to that? Back to swooning over an emotionally unavailable man? And have you forgotten about your uncle?*

Well, sonofa—No, no…*of course* she hadn't forgotten about her uncle. In fact, now that the adrenaline had worn off, now that she'd gotten past the part where she was running around—as Mac would say—like a chicken with her head cut off, she was horrified to discover that deep down, down where she didn't want to look, down where things got dark and scary, she had a very *bad* feeling that she was never going to see Uncle Theo again.

And just skirting around the very *edges*, the thinnest, farthest borders, of that possibility made her heart contract so hard it sat in her chest like a black stone of terror. She didn't realize she'd spoken her fear aloud until Mac threw an arm around the back of her chair and dragged her close to his side. It was also then that she realized her blood was running colder than the dry ice she used in the zombie cocktails she mixed up each year around Halloween. Because Mac's big body felt hotter than the surface of the sun where it touched the freezing skin on her arm, and his sudden nearness chased away the chill and instantly started a fire burning low in her belly. Despite the fear strangling her heart, a soft ache pulsed between her legs.

Yup. Way too long since I've been laid…

"That's not true, Delilah. You're gonna see him again," he told her, his blue eyes flashing fiercely, as if the sheer force of his will alone could make her believe his words. And honestly, looking at him stoically sitting there while Steady shoved a two-inch needle filled with some sort of numbing solution into his other side, she had to admit, it kind of, sort of, *maybe* worked. Because if anyone could find her uncle, it was Mac. The former all-star FBI agent with a backbone of iron and a mind like a steel trap.

Then, of course, there were all the rest of the Knights…

Sucking in a deep, bracing breath, she glanced around

the conference room. Ozzie, Becky, and Zoelner were seated at the computer bank, typing furiously, scouring phone records and military archives for any clue that might lead them to her uncle and this Charlie guy. They were also combing through city surveillance footage for a glimpse of Mr. Timberlands. And, *Jesus*, how in the world was she ever going to pay them back for this?

How in the world was she ever going to pay *Mac* back for this?

He'd been the one to set the others on their tasks, and he'd done it all with the calm authority of a man who'd been down this road countless times before, a man who had the situation well in hand.

She wasn't used to having to depend on anyone for anything. But she was glad she could depend on the Knights and, more precisely, Mac, for this. And since she *didn't* know how she was ever going to pay him back, she reached beneath the table to squeeze his knee and gave him the one thing she could...

Leaning forward, she went to place a soft kiss of thanks, a *friendly* kiss of thanks, on his whiskered cheek—holy hormones he smelled good—but at the last second, he turned his head and her lips landed directly atop his.

Sweet sonofa—This was a mistake. Not what she'd planned at all. But even so, she didn't want to pull back. Mostly because she'd been waiting *years* to find an excuse to get her lips on Mac, and now that she had one, she wanted to milk the moment for all it was worth. And also because, right then, his mouth softened. Just a little. Just enough to allow his hot breath to whisper across her lips.

And that fire he'd started low in her belly? It exploded into an inferno. And that ache between her legs? It shot up into her center, making her womb pulse. For a split second, she considered opening her mouth to him. But before she could work through all the ramifications of that action, he gently pulled back. And the look on his face when she opened her eyes? It wasn't…well, to put it quite honestly, it wasn't what she expected.

When it came to her, Mac's expressions usually fell into three categories. One was simple dismissal. His patented *I don't have the desire or inclination to give you the time of day* look. Another was flat-out disapproval. The one that said *why do you have to be so loud, so bossy, so brash?* And his last go-to expression was what she liked to call his Mask of Inscrutability. The facial equivalent of a blank page.

But to her utter astonishment, he wore none of those tried-and-true looks. *Huh-uh.* In fact, if memory served—and that was taking a giant leap, since it'd been four long years since she'd allowed a man to seduce her—that particular gleam in his eye was the guy equivalent of twenty minutes of foreplay. Instantly her nipples furled, her womb contracted for the second time, and her heart raced until her blood we all fizzy, like a lime dropped in tonic water.

But then it was gone. Just like that—*finger-snap*—and she was left to wonder if she'd really seen anything unusual at all. Perhaps the fear and fatigue, not to mention the crack to the cranium she'd received, were causing her to imagine things.

"I just—" Her voice sounded like she'd been

swallowing broken beer bottles. "I just wanted to th-thank you for...everything."

He shook his head, causing a dark lock to fall over his brow, his expression now firmly entrenched in the Mask of Inscrutability category. "Darlin'," he said in that deep, smoky voice of his, "no thanks are needed. Helpin' out in times of trouble is what friends are for."

What friends *are for*...

"A-are we friends, Mac?" she ventured, her mouth so dry she was almost tempted to take another sip of the goop that passed as coffee.

"Of course we're friends, darlin'," he drawled again.

"Lovin'! Touchin'! Squeeezin'!" Ozzie belted out in a surprisingly clear tenor, instantly breaking whatever spell she'd been under, severing the tie that had held their gazes locked together.

"Goddamnit, Ozzie!" Zoelner yelled. "If you don't turn off that Journey shit in two seconds I'm going to lose my mind."

"No way, man," Ozzie retorted, never taking his eyes from his computer screen and never breaking the rhythm of his fingers dancing across the keyboard at lightning speed. "Steve Perry sings from the heart *and* the hair. You'd do well to appreciate that."

"I'll give you something to appreciate," Zoelner shot back. "How about my boot up your ass? I can't think straight with that crap on and you wailing like a goat being groomed with a cheese grater."

"First of all," Ozzie said, "I've been told I have a lovely singing voice."

"You can't believe the compliments your mother gives you," Zoelner countered.

"And secondly," Ozzie continued as if Zoelner hadn't spoken, "you need to think straight to run a simple scan of military archives? Pssht! And they try to make us believe that all you government spooks are the cream of the crop. What a crock of—"

"Okay, boys," Becky interjected, yanking a purple Dum Dum from her mouth. "Put away the rulers and button up your flies, because I'm finding jack shit on the city surveillance cams. We've run into a brick wall with the mystery man in Timberlands. The scoreboard says we're down by one, so we don't have time to sit around while you two figure out whose giggle-stick is the biggest."

Giggle-stick? Delilah felt her lips twitch.

Then, "Sweet lord of the rings!" Ozzie whooped, shooting a fist in the air. "Un-bunch those panties, Becky my dear, because *now* we're cooking with gas!" He shoved a finger at his computer screen.

Becky slid her rolling chair next to his—one loose wheel clattered against the hard concrete floor—and leaned in close to his monitor. Turning, Becky pinned Delilah with an excited stare. "Does the name Charles Sander ring a bell?"

—◦◦◦—

Delilah trembled at Becky's question, and Mac instinctively squeezed her tighter to his side. Then he was reminded that, sure as shit, touching her *was* like taking a hit of crack—and let's not even get into what the feel of her soft, warm lips or her hot, moist breath was like. Because *holy shit fire!* That innocent little kiss? He didn't know it was possible to get so hard so fast. And all of this, all the touching and the friendly kissing was getting out of hand, making him forget himself.

Get it together, asshole.

And, yessir. That was a sage bit of advice if ever there was some. Time to take it. Like, *now*.

He jerked his arm out from around her back so quickly that Steady whacked him upside the head. "Be still, *chorra*. Or else it'll look Dr. Frankenstein himself took a needle and thread to you."

Okay, so that was one seriously unsmooth move, you stupid, horny dillhole, Mac chided himself while simultaneously rubbing his sore head and lifting a warning brow at Steady who, like always, chose to ignore the killing gleam in his eye.

Luckily, when he turned back, it was to find Delilah hadn't noticed his total douche-canoe maneuver. Her gorgeous green eyes were glued to Becky like the blonde was made of cane molasses.

"Charlie Sander. I—I don't remember if that's him or not," she said, her breathy voice unusually hoarse, as if she'd swallowed all the gravel on the old ranch road that led to his boyhood home.

*Christ…*that sound just…well, it just *got* to him. He was tempted once more to place a comforting arm around her shoulders. After all, she was so incredibly soft. So amazingly warm. So…*so* much woman—and, yeah, sick, twisted, shitheel that he was, he was referring to her boobs. Her lush, delicious, overly abundant boobs. And having her in his arms just now, and earlier, out in the courtyard, had felt…*something*. Something a far cry closer to *right* than he in any way, shape, or form wanted to admit.

Are you really stupid enough to let history repeat itself?

The question was either posed by the universe or his own subconscious. Of course, where the query originated didn't amount to a hill of beans, because either way, the answer was the same.

No. No, he was *not* stupid enough to let history repeat itself. Because the truth was, no matter how good or how *right* she felt in his arms, That Woman was nothing but walking trouble and heartache.

He'd learned that the hard way...

Boy, howdy, had he ever. Barely a week went by when he wasn't reminded of the pain Jolene's leaving had caused. Barely a month passed when he wasn't wrenched from his sleep by the nightmare of her betrayal and what it had cost him. And sometimes, when he was all alone, he could still hear the sound of a strangled voice calling her name in the darkness.

"We haven't been able to access your uncle's text messages," Becky said. "But we have been able to access his call log and Sander's number is the only one with a southern Illinois prefix. Plus Charlie is a nickname for Charles, and—"

"Well, that's—" Delilah shook her head a little frantically. Her slim, pale throat—a throat Mac *didn't* want to touch and kiss and lick; *liar, liar, pants all the freakin' way on fire!*—worked over a hard swallow. "That's got to be him, right?"

Her excited tone hit Mac in his soft, gooey center. And, *yes*, he had a soft, gooey center. Because even though he may be determined not to let history repeat itself, not to let himself get caught up in her sticky web of seduction, that didn't mean he wanted to see her enthusiasm ground to dust either. Fortunately—*thank you sweet baby Jesus*—Zoelner saved him from the unenviable task of having to be the one to douse that spark in her eye. "Don't get too excited," the ex-spook said. "This could be the guy we're searching for, or it could just be coincidence. We still need to run his name through military records to see if he was a Marine."

"Yeah." Delilah nodded again. "Okay." Mac could tell she was trying hard, and failing miserably, to temper her enthusiasm.

"Then, if he *was* a Marine, we can start looking for his last known address," Zoelner added.

"Sounds good." Delilah licked her lips. The dart of her pink tongue made Mac's—

"Ow! Goddamnit!" he hissed. "Lord have mercy, Steady," he groused, frowning up at the man. "Are you usin' a seven-gauge needle to stitch me up, or what?"

"Oh, pipe down, you big baby," Steady replied. "I gave you a local. And besides, this is just a little stab wound. People get stab wounds all the time."

Mac turned to Delilah, one corner of his mouth quirked, his expression all about the *I told you so*. But he was thwarted from speaking the words aloud when Zoelner yelled, "Bingo!"

"What've you got?" Boss strolled into the conference area from his office, then immediately ordered, "Good God, Ozzie! Turn that shit off!"

"What?" Ozzie lifted his hands, blinking innocently. "I'm kicking mad flava in your ears. I'd think you would all thank me for it."

"I'll thank you by way of a boot up your ass," Boss growled, throwing an arm around Becky's shoulders when she came to stand beside him, bending to smack a quick kiss beside the lollipop stick protruding from her lips.

"What is *with* everybody wanting to put their boots up my ass?" Ozzie asked the room. "I know it's a particularly cute ass, but—"

"Ozzie!" a chorus of voices, including Mac's, yelled at once.

"Sheesh!" The guy held up his hands and Mac noticed his T-shirt was printed with the Starfleet logo and the words: *Are you out of your Vulcan mind?* "Tough crowd tonight," he grumbled, twisting to switch off the music. Boss shook his head before pinning Zoelner with a no-nonsense stare. "What've you got, Z?"

Leaning forward, studying his computer screen intently and still typing, Zoelner said, "Charles Sander *was* in Delilah's uncle's Marine Corps unit. And I'm using his cell phone number to locate a phone bill, which *should* give us his last known address. Uh…give me a second here." More rattling as the former–CIA agent attacked the keyboard. "Well, shit," he said after a few seconds, sitting back and raking a hand through his hair. "I have no idea how to find his last known address. All I'm getting for him is a post office box."

"He has a house," Delilah insisted. "My uncle always talked about what a shithole it was."

"Yeah." Ozzie shrugged. "But how do you suggest we find it?"

For a couple of intense, breathless moments, no one moved. Mac racked his brain, trying to figure out their next move. *There has to be something. There has to be a way to*—And then Delilah came up with the answer for him.

"The IRS," she said. "I know a back door into their database. We can cross reference Charles's name with his PO box and check to see if he's getting a yearly property tax bill."

"No way." Ozzie shook his head vehemently. "There's absolutely no way I'm hacking into the Internal Revenue Service."

"Why the hell not?" Mac frowned, wincing when Steady hit another particularly sore spot. He was beginning to think there'd been nothing but sugar water in that syringe of so-called numbing agent. "You hack into the NSA's and CIA's databases all the time."

"Uh, *yeah*." Ozzie pulled a face. "But the IRS is *scary*."

Delilah snorted and pushed up from her seat, strolling over to Ozzie and his bank of computers. Mac didn't let his eyes ping down to watch the sway of her ass. Or if he did, it was only for a nanosecond…er…okay, so maybe it was *two* nanoseconds. "I do it all the time for the law firm," she said, claiming the seat Becky had vacated. Raising her arms to twist her hair quickly into some kind of sloppy updo thingy, she began lightly, but efficiently typing on the keyboard.

Yessir. It was his naughty librarian fantasy come to life. Little Mac, the goddamned idiot, sure took notice. Which was good and bad. Good because it distracted Mac until he could no longer feel the tug and pull of Steady's needle. Bad because his jeans had suddenly shrunk six sizes. He reached down to adjust himself, ignoring the knowing smirk on Steady's face when the guy caught his move.

"And here we go," Delilah said, pointing at her screen.

"Good God, that was fast!" Ozzie enthused.

"The IRS. They see all. They know all."

"*See*"—Ozzie shuddered dramatically—"and that's why they're scary."

"Where does he live?" Mac asked.

Ozzie leaned forward to squint at the computer screen in front of Delilah. "Some place called Cairo, Illinois. Let me see if it's…" He tapped a few keys on his own keyboard. "Yeah. It's about forty-five minutes south of Marion."

"Mac?" Delilah turned to him then, a wide smile splitting her face and making her eyes sparkle like a field of green wheat after a big thunderstorm. "This is it! We're going to find him!"

She jumped up from the desk and raced toward him, grabbing his hand and squeezing it tight. "We're really going to find him!"

Every cell inside him thrilled to the touch of her fingers. *Holy shit fire,* was all he could think. *Just like a shot of pure crack cocaine…*

Chapter Five

Georgetown, Washington, DC

Music...

The sweet, dulcet tones of Dolly Parton singing about working nine to five filtered into Intelligence Agent Chelsea Duvall's dreams, making her smile. Until her unconscious mind recognized the sound of her ringtone and thrust her into wakefulness.

"Son of a hoochie mama," she growled, fumbling on the nightstand for her glasses. "Ow!" she squawked when, in her mad scramble to get the suckers on her face, she stabbed herself in the eyeball with an earpiece. Squinting her abused eye closed, she glanced at the glowing red numbers on her alarm clock with her one remaining functional peeper.

Eleven p.m. *This can't be good.*

"Agent Duvall here," she answered, not bothering to read the caller ID. There were only a handful of people who'd be phoning her at this hour, and they all belonged to The Company.

"We've got a red flag," came the immediate reply from Joe Morales, her supervisor.

"Roger that," she sat up, throwing back the thick purple quilt her mother made her after college graduation and prior to her recruitment by the CIA. Purple had been her favorite color since she was six years old and fell head-over-heels in love with Fred from the *Scooby-Doo* gang. Her young mind had picked up on the not-so-unspoken attraction between Fred and Daphne, and she'd used her brilliant kindergarten reasoning and deduction skills to conclude that it was Daphne's snappy purple dress that was the big draw for Fred. In the way of first crushes, Fred had eventually fallen out of favor. Not so the color purple…

Reaching over, she snapped on the bedside lamp. Diffuse yellow light spilled around her room, highlighting the piles of file folders stacked on her dresser, chair, and bench. Next to her, two laptops occupied the space usually reserved for a lover.

Such is my life, she thought fleetingly—maybe she needed to revisit the whole Fred thing. Pulling one of the machines onto her lap and flipping up the lid, she blew out a breath. "All right, I'm ready, sir. Where's the breach coming from?"

"The Black Knights."

For a moment, all she could do was blink in confusion. *Was she still asleep? Was this all a dream?*

Before she had the chance to pinch herself, her supervisor barked, "Agent Duvall, did you copy that?"

"Yes, sir." She shook her head and scrubbed a hand over her face. "I…I *think* I heard you say the breach was originating with the Black Knights."

"Affirmative."

Oh-*kay*. But… "So I don't understand how that's a breach then, sir. The Black Knights are—"

"Are you still friends with Dagan Zoelner?" The abruptness of the question, along with that name, *his* name, caused a hard lump to take shape at the back of her throat.

Dragging in a deep breath, the smell of Tide on her freshly laundered sheets grounded her enough to croak, "I wouldn't say that, sir. No."

She hadn't heard from Dagan in almost two years. Not since the day he called her up, asking her for help, and she went and said something stupid like, *what are you involved in this time?* It was the *this time*—basically a blinking neon sign referring to that terrible tragedy in Afghanistan—that'd done it, that'd hammered in the last nail on the coffin of any affection they might have once felt for each other.

Or…more like it had hammered in the last nail on the coffin of any affection *he* might have once felt for *her*.

Truth was, she'd never stopped thinking about him. Never stopped worrying about him and wondering if he was happy with his new job at Black Knights Inc. Never stopped questioning how things might've been different if only—

"Doesn't matter," Morales said. "You were once friends, so that gives us just the *in* we need."

"Sir?"

"I want you to call them up and ask them why they're running a search on the phone records of Theodore Fairchild."

"Should that name ring a bell?" She glanced around at the myriad files she'd *yet* to go through since that treasonous agent, Luke Winterfield, had leaked classified information to the press—and then run like a scared rabbit to hide out in a Central American country with whom the U.S. had no extradition agreement. Of course, if the location of the CIA and NSA black sites had been *all* he leaked, and if the press had been the *only* people he leaked to, she wouldn't be getting calls about red flags from her supervisor at eleven o'clock at night.

"No. It shouldn't ring any bells. At least not yet," Morales assured her. "It could be nothing more than coincidence, but I want to make sure of that. And you're just the agent for the job."

Usually when her supervisor stroked her ego, the ambitious, upstart career woman in her was tempted to purr like a cat. Not tonight, though. Because tonight he was asking her to phone Dagan Zoelner.

"Thank you for the vote of confidence, sir." She hoped he couldn't hear the slight tremor in her voice. "Do I tell the Knights *why* I'm inquiring about their most recent Internet search?"

"No."

Chelsea waited for more. Nothing came.

Morales could be amazingly eloquent and long-winded, especially when he was ranting about terrorist factions and rogue nations. Or he could be frustratingly succinct. At this moment, unfortunately for her, he'd chosen to be the latter.

"If you'll pardon my confusion here, sir," she finally said, "what *do* I tell them if not the truth?"

"Tell them that in our ongoing effort to assist them in their exemplary work for the president and his Joint Chiefs, we've been monitoring the online activity on one of their computers and we were simply wondering if there was anything we could do to help in regard to their most recent endeavors."

Chelsea lifted her brows. *Okay, and* now *he goes for eloquent*? "And what's the *real* reason we've been monitoring the online activity on one of their computers?"

"It's just a leftover from when we were looking for Rock Babineaux," Morales admitted, referring to the huge blunder involving the framing of one of the Knights by a psychotic former government psychiatrist. And, yes, Chelsea knew just how ironic that sounded. Psychotic psychiatrist. *Jesus.* "And you know that once we get our sharp, little eavesdropping hooks in someone, we don't like to let them go."

Did she ever. "Dagan…uh…" She cleared her constricted throat. *Damned pesky lump.* "What I meant to say is that Agent Zoelner—"

"*Former* Agent Zoelner," Morales stressed, obviously still firmly entrenched in the camp of people who placed the blame for that failed Afghani mission squarely on Dagan's shoulders.

"Yes, sir," she capitulated. "Former Agent Zoelner might ask why *I'm* the one calling. What should I tell him?"

"Tell him, given the friendly relationship you two once shared, that you've been appointed the official liaison between the United States Central Intelligence Agency and the covert group known as Black Knights Incorporated."

"Is the official liaison between yada, yada even a real thing, sir?"

"It is now. Congratulations on the promotion, Agent Duvall," Morales said. And, yeah, as well as its sharp, little eavesdropping hooks, the agency was *also* known to come up with nifty titles for people when it behooved them to do so.

"Thank you, sir. Does this promotion come with a raise?"

"Of course not."

Uh-huh. "I didn't think so, sir."

"Get on it, Agent Duvall. And call me back with whatever information you discover."

"Roger that."

After punching the "end" button on her iPhone, Chelsea simply sat and stared at the blank screen as the old grandfather clock in the living room ticked away the seconds.

Oh, quit being such a wuss, her pride finally admonished. And with a shaky finger—really? Were her hands shaking?—she dialed Dagan's number...

"So, what now?"

All the Knights were seated around the conference table, and Delilah felt buoyed just looking at their capable, determined faces. Now that they'd identified Charlie *Sander* and pinned down his address, the cold fear that had squeezed her in its merciless grip, the one that had fostered all those nebulous, terrifying feelings that she might never see her uncle again, finally released its icy hold.

She *was* going to see Uncle Theo again. She wasn't exactly sure how or when. But she was sure of *where* to start looking. Cairo, Illinois...

"It's called a plan, shit for brains," Steady answered the question Ozzie posed to the group, a grin pulling at his handsome, swarthy face. "You know, as in, we need one?"

"Well, *derrr*." Ozzie rolled his eyes. "Thanks for that brilliant—"

"We head down to Cairo," Mac interjected, cutting short what Delilah had come to suspect would be a lengthy back-and-forth. For a group of highly educated, highly trained men, they sure talked a lot of smack. Of course, her years behind the bar had taught her that an overload of testosterone tended to have that effect on guys when they were grouped together. "We check out Charles Sander's house. And if we don't find Theo there, we go door-to-door, flashin' his photo until we locate someone who's seen him."

Yup. And that sounded about right to Delilah. Then again, *most* things Mac said sounded right to her. It was hard for things *not* to sound right when they were spoken in that low, sexy, Texas twang of his.

Oh, pull your head out of your ass, Delilah.

"Yeah, well, good luck with that." Ozzie harrumphed, and for a moment, she wasn't completely sure she hadn't spoken that last thought aloud. Then she saw Ozzie frowning at the laptop sitting open on the table in front of him. "The place is a ghost town."

"All the better," Mac muttered. He'd donned a fresh shirt, and he was swirling a stir stick in a piping hot cup of sludge…er…coffee. It *had* to be coffee, right? "Small towns are notoriously nosy. If Theo and his big, loud Harley rolled through, you can bet your bottom dollar he was noticed."

"No." Ozzie reached up to scratch at his mop of blond, fly-away hair. "I wasn't being oblique. The place is *literally* a ghost town. Says here," he pointed a finger at his screen, "that following some pretty severe race riots in the sixties, the town was mostly abandoned. Then, in 2011 when the Ohio River burst its banks, the Corps of Engineers evacuated most of the residents who were left. It's possible Theo could have come and gone with no one the wiser."

"Or there could be a handful of people still livin' there who know everything about everything that happens in their town," Mac quickly countered.

"Not to get off track," Ali said, her bare feet up in her husband's lap as BKI's ugly, mangy, *obese* mascot of a tomcat attempted to balance himself on her knees while rubbing his furry face over her bulging belly. The feline was purring so loudly it sounded like a small plane about to take off. "But are you guys just going to forget about the man in Timberlands? The break-in and attack on Delilah seem awfully coincidental so close on the heels of her uncle's disappearance." She absently scratched the cat's notched ears, causing him to ratchet up his purring to a rhythmic roar. "Or are those just my paranoid pregnancy hormones talking?" she asked, wrinkling her nose.

"No, those aren't just your paranoid pregnancy hormones talkin'," Mac assured her. "And I'd just as soon bite a stink bug as quit lookin' for Mr. Timberlands, but findin' Delilah's uncle has to be the top priority right now."

"The top priority," Boss interjected, "but not the *only* priority."

"You have something in mind?" Mac asked, eyes narrowed in interest.

"I'm going to report the break-in to Chief Washington. Maybe his boys in the CPD can find Mr. Timberlands for us. If that's all right with you, Delilah." Boss turned to lift a scarred eyebrow at her.

"Hey," she shrugged, "I'm taking all the help I can get. Obviously." She gestured to the men and women gathered around the table.

"Good." Boss jerked his chin. "That'll let us focus all our efforts on the hunt for your uncle without completely allowing the guy in work boots to get off scot-free."

And for the second time, gratitude surged so strongly inside Delilah that she felt overwhelmed. "I don't know how—" She had to stop and clear her throat. "I don't know how to thank you all for doing this. It's just so—"

"Darlin'," Mac's deep drawl, not to mention that knee-loosening endearment, had the words screeching to a stop on the tip of her tongue as if they'd come equipped with a set of airbrakes. "I told you, that's what friends are for."

Friends…yeah… Except when it came to him, she wanted—she'd *always* wanted—something more. *Ack! And we're back to that, Delilah?*

Okay, it was official. She needed a lobotomy, if only to silence that annoying voice.

"So who's goin' on this little fishin' expedition?" Ghost asked, absently rubbing his hand over his wife's pregnant belly.

"Well," Boss said, "since Ali has been… What did you call it the other day, Mac?"

"Storked," Mac replied helpfully. "Down in Texas, we say she's been storked."

Oh, and *why* did she have to go and find stuff like that so freakin' adorable? What was it about the slow-talking, overgrown, Southern boy sitting next to her that she found so fascinating?

Uh, everything, she admitted woefully. It was absolutely *everything* about him. *Damn it all to hell!*

"Yeah," Boss chuckled, slapping a huge, baseball-mitt-of-a-hand on the table. "You Lone-Star staters do have a way with words. Anyway, since Ali has been storked," he snorted, "it's a foregone conclusion Ghost will stay behind and—" Boss stopped in mid-sentence, scowling at Ali. "What the hell is the matter with that cat?"

The tom was now rubbing his entire length over Ali's belly.

"He's a frickin' traitor, that's what's the matter with him." Becky crunched down on her sucker, chewing angrily. "I'm the one who feeds him. I'm the one who bathes him. I'm the one who buys him catnip toys and cleans out his litter box. But do you see him over here rubbing all over me? No. No, you do not."

"It's not *me* he's rubbing on," Ali insisted, shooting Becky a placating look. "It's the baby."

"People," Mac interrupted, "let's get back to the point, shall we? Who besides me is goin' down to Cairo?"

And either Delilah was exhausted or crazy or both, but the way he said that, like it was a foregone conclusion he'd be going with her, gave her a little thrill. Before that idiotic voice could pipe up with something scathing, she preempted it. *Put a cork it, you aggravating little prick! I've had it with you!*

"Ooh, ooh!" Ozzie raised his hand like an overly exuberant kindergartener. "Me, me! A road trip to southern Illinois sounds like fun." He winced, peeking at Delilah. "Sorry. I didn't mean it was fun that your uncle—"

She waved him off. "No worries. I know what you meant." Because she was a born-and-bred biker, and she knew the thrill of the open road better than anyone. Cruising down the highway on the back of a half-ton of hand-tooled leather and high-polished steel was the closest a person could come to flying without ever leaving the ground.

"Yeah," Ozzie shook his head woefully, "but that doesn't—"

He was stopped when Zoelner's phone suddenly came to life, buzzing angrily and vibrating across the table. The former CIA agent flipped over the device and peered at the screen. A look of confusion and surprise came over his face.

"I'm in for Cairo, too," he said. Then, "Excuse me for a second." Standing, he jogged into one of the darkened offices. A light blazed inside the room before the door slammed shut with a *bang* that echoed around the large space, causing the tomcat to pause in his adoration of Ali's belly.

"Becky and I will stay here to monitor the progress of the guys we've still got out in the field," Boss said. It was then that Delilah did a quick head count and realized seven of the Black Knights were absent from the conference table. *Okay, and way to be completely self-absorbed, Delilah. For heaven's sake.*

"So that leaves Steady," Mac said, tipping his dimpled chin toward the dark-eyed man, "to join those of us headed south. The more boots on the ground we have down there, the more area we can cover."

"Agreed," Boss concurred. "It's all settled then. Pack up your saddlebags, boys. You're going on a road trip."

"Wahoo!" Ozzie shot a fist in the air, then kept his hand raised, looking around for someone to slap him a high-five. When no one took him up on his offer, he realized what he'd done and winced at Delilah again. "Jesus. Sorry. Is it too late to take back that *wahoo*?"

"It's okay, Ozzie," she assured him, eager herself to be back out on the road now that they had a plan. "I know you didn't—"

She was cut-off mid-sentence when Zoelner's office door flew open. The former spy—or current spy? Did the Black Knights qualify as that? In all honesty, she wasn't sure—stood on the threshold, a strange look wallpapering his face.

"What's up?" Boss asked. "Who was on the phone?"

"Uh." Zoelner reached up to scratch his ear. "That was Chelsea Duvall."

"Should I know who that is?"

"She's an old…uh…*acquaintance* in The Company. She said she's been promoted to the position of our official liaison to the CIA."

"Our official *what*?" Boss demanded, his tone that of a man who occasionally munched on a baby for breakfast.

"She also said…" Zoelner stopped, scrunching up his face. "How did she put it? She said that in an effort to assist us in our exemplary work for the president and his Joint Chiefs, they've been monitoring the online activities on one of our computers and—"

"The hell you say!" Ozzie exploded. "Which one? I have anti-spy programs running on all of them!"

"Well, they're obviously getting around that somehow, *hermano*," Steady observed.

Now it looked like *Ozzie* munched on babies for breakfast. He attacked his laptop keyboard as if he had a personal vendetta against the poor thing.

"Go on," Boss growled. "They've been monitoring the online activities on one of our computers and *what*?"

"And they were wondering if there was anything

they could do to assist us in our most recent endeavor regarding Theo Fairchild," Zoelner finished in a rush, still wearing a slightly bewildered expression.

"Yeah, well, that sounds like a prime example of my cow done up and died so I don't need your bull," Mac said. "Why would the CIA give one shit, much less two, about helpin' us? I don't trust those people."

"Yeah," Zoelner snorted. "You don't have to tell me. Remember I used to *be* one of those people."

Mac made a face. "Then what *did* you tell her?" And Delilah was curious about that as well. Was it possible the CIA could do something more than the Knights in locating Uncle Theo? Were there…she didn't know… some sort of secret CIA ways and means?

"I told her we were simply looking for Delilah's missing uncle," Zoelner said. "And I told her that unless they had some sort of LoJack on Theodore Fairchild or his old Marine Corps buddy, Charles Sander, there wasn't much they could do."

Okay. Apparently the CIA *didn't* have any sort of secret ways and means. *Shit.*

"Good." Boss nodded. "Sooo," he drew out the word, "barring any more mysterious telephone calls from the CIA, I think we all have our assignments here. Let's get to it."

"Permission to stay behind and figure out how those goddamned spooks are monitoring our Internet activities?" Ozzie said, typing frantically.

"Permission denied," Boss said, causing Ozzie to glance up from his laptop screen. "You've got more important things to do besides getting into a dick-measuring contest with the CIA's tech boys. You go help find Theo. You can whip it out and prove your superiority to the spooks when you get back."

"But—"

"No buts," Boss announced, pushing up from the table.

Delilah stood along with the rest of the group, itching to mount up on Big Red, her beloved custom BKI motorcycle, and hit the road. But a loud squawk followed by a quickly indrawn breath drew her attention over to Ali.

"Uh…folks?" the blonde said, wrinkling her nose and staring down at the floor. "My water just broke."

Chapter Six

HOLY SHIT, I'M SUCH AN IDIOT.

Chelsea reached up to slide her forefinger and thumb beneath her glasses, pinching the bridge of her nose. What were the odds that her supervisor would ask her to call Dagan on *this* night? And what were the odds that she'd completely forget just what *this* night meant?

"I didn't expect to hear from you," had been Dagan's initial salvo. "Not tonight of all nights." To which, *idiot* that she was, she'd responded with, "Tonight? What's so special about tonight?"

The words had been out of her mouth a half second before she glanced at the date on the lower right-hand corner of her laptop screen, a half second too late for her to call them back.

"Oh…" was Dagan's immediate retort, and there'd been no mistaking the hurt in his voice the moment before all emotion whatsoever disappeared. She could picture him getting completely still in that weird way of his, becoming a living, breathing statue. "So, what do you want then, Agent Duvall?"

Agent Duvall…

He never used to call her that. It'd always been Chelsea, or Chels.

To say it'd all been downhill after that would be the understatement of the century. And, yeah, she'd certainly spend a good deal of time obsessing about how she could have handled it better. But for right now, she had a call to make.

Rubbing her hand down her face, she dialed her supervisor's number.

"What'd you discover?" Morales demanded before the first ring finished sounding.

"Nothing," she told him. *Nothing other than the fact that I'm an insensitive* ass, *and Dagan was smart to cut all ties with me*. "They're simply looking for this Theodore Fairchild guy because he's the uncle of one of their friends. That…uh…that bartender who's in on their secret?" she explained. "You know the one?"

A grunt was Morales's only reply. She took it to be an affirmative. *Back to being succinct, are we?*

"Anyway," she continued, "apparently the bartender's uncle was supposed to be visiting a former Marine pal named Charles something or other and has since stopped answering his cell phone. The bartender is worried about him—allegedly going MIA isn't like the man—and she's enlisted the Knights to help her locate him." And unless her boss read more into the situation than she figured was warranted, she quickly added, "But it's been less than twenty-four hours, so I suspect the two old coots just tied one on for old-time's sake and—"

"Sonofa-fucking-bitch!" Morales thundered, and Chelsea was so taken aback, the phone slipped from her hand to clatter against the keyboard of her laptop.

"Sir?" she asked once she retrieved the device, her heart's tempo having gone from a steady *thump-thump* to a racing *bahdahboom-bahdahboom*!

"Was it Charles Sander?" Morales demanded.

"Uh…yeah." She swallowed. "That rings a b—"

"Does the code name BA Repatriate mean anything to you?" he cut her off.

"BA…" She hastily pushed her laptop aside and lunged from her bed, running over to her dresser where some of the alphabetized, highly redacted copies of the files the CIA suspected the rogue CIA agent might have had access to sat in a neat pile. Quickly finding the one she sought, she flipped open the cover.

And although most of the page was blacked out—couldn't worry that a civilian might stumble into her apartment and see highly classified files—the three words scrawled against the top of the page in big, bold letters said it all.

Her stomach immediately took a header, falling to the floor at her bare feet. "Sir? Do we have any idea who Winterfield might have sold this information to?"

"Unfortunately not," Morales admitted, fury vibrating in every syllable. "But you can be certain, *if* he sold this piece of Intel, it was to an organization that *isn't* on Uncle Sam's Christmas list."

Her mind was racing a million miles a minute. The implication of this could be… But, wait… "This file doesn't list the locations of the missing BAs. It just gives the names of the five men who worked the mission."

"All of whom are dead of natural causes except for Charles and Theodore. And apparently, according to the Knights, both of those men have now gone AWOL."

And the hits just keep on coming! But it was part of Chelsea's job not to get bogged down in the details. She was expected to be the "big picture" girl. She was expected to keep everyone from jumping to conclusions. "It's still possible this is all a misunderstanding," she said. "I mean, we're not *positive* which files that prick Winterfield," she winced at the foul language, "accessed and downloaded. This could *still* be a case of two old Marine Corps buddies getting overly lubricated and—"

"Which is why I'm sending you in alone, Agent Duvall."

Okay, huh? He was…sending her in? As in, out into the field? But she wasn't a *field* agent! She was a desk-jockey analyst with lines of code instead of listening devices and reams of Intel instead of incendiary devices. "Uh, sir? I'm…I'm not sure I copied you correctly on that last bit."

"If this *is* just a red herring," Morales said, "I don't want to alert the Knights to the true scope of the problem Winterfield has caused for us. So I'm sending you in to—"

"If you'll pardon my interrupting, sir. The Knights have proved themselves trustworthy time and again. Heck, they're the personal goon-squad to the president and the JCs. How much more proof do you need of their reliability?"

"Loose lips sink ships, Agent Duvall. You know that as well as I do."

Loose lips sink ships, she silently mimicked, rolling her eyes. "Spare me the World War II propaganda, sir," she harrumphed, disliking where this conversation was leading. Disliking the thought of having to lie straight to Dagan's face. "I know better than most how important it is to keep our cards close to our vest. But the Knights—"

"You'll go in," Morales cut her off, "working under the auspices of your new title and you'll assess the situation." And she recognized a red line when she was poised to jump right over it. Her supervisor had made up his mind. Any more argument from her would be flying precariously close to insubordination. "If you think there's more going on in Illinois than a simple misunderstanding, I'll have a team ready and waiting to swoop in. If not, then BKI, and the world at large, will remain blessedly unaware of just what a clusterfuck Winterfield created for us."

"The Knights aren't the world at large," she muttered, unable to help herself.

"What's that?"

"Nothing, sir," she said, biting her tongue so hard she marveled she didn't taste blood.

"Good then," Morales said, finality in his tone. "I'll arrange transport for you immediately."

The line went dead, and Chelsea pulled the phone away from her ear. Her eyes scanned the file in her hand, and she imagined the warm welcome—*not*—she'd receive when she just *showed up* on the Knights' doorstep.

This is bad, she thought. *This is going to be very, very bad…*

—∿∿—

"Blow," Becky demanded, holding Delilah's shiny silver Breathalyzer—a handy device used for checking blood/alcohol level—up to Mac's mouth.

Delilah had taken to carrying the thing around in her saddlebags because anytime she joined one of the local MCs—motorcycle clubs—on a ride, it was inevitable the group would stop at a bar or roadhouse somewhere. Equally inevitable was the fact that some sorry sucker would have one too many, forcing Delilah and the rest of the gang to wait around while the guy—it was *usu-ally* a guy, though once, it had been a gal—sobered up enough to blow below .08%.

"You heard me. Blow," Becky repeated, wiggling the device.

Mac's dark eyebrows winged down in a fierce V, his five-o'clock…no, more like *ten*-o'clock-shadowed jaw clenching. "I'm not drunk," he ground out, crossing his arms over his chest, causing his leather biker jacket to pull tight across the wide expanse of his back.

They were standing in the lower level of the shop, readying their bikes for the ride south following what had been about five minutes of sheer pandemonium after Ali's water broke. Ghost had immediately scooped his wife up in his arms, ran toward the stairs, then turned and ran back to the conference table to snag Ali's purse. It was then that he nearly slipped in the puddle of clear amniotic fluid. Delilah had never seen a group of men move as fast as the Black Knights when, in unison, they'd leapt forward to steady the couple.

"H-E-double-hockey-sticks, Nate!" Ali'd bellowed, whacking Ghost on the arm. "I can walk! It's not like this kid is going to slide out of me or something! And you're liable to get us both killed this way!"

Ghost had ignored her, refusing to put her down. And after slinging her purse over his big shoulder—now *that* had been a sight, seeing a big, tough-looking guy like Ghost shouldering a pink, sparkly Guess tote bag—he'd bolted down the metal steps two at a time, his booted heels thundering and echoing around the cavernous space. Seconds later, the engine of BKI's monster Hummer roared to life. A moment after that, the big garage door at the end of the shop rolled up, and Ghost left rubber on the concrete floor, fishtailing his way out of the building.

It was at that point that Becky yelled, "Ew! No! Bad kitty!"

As a group they'd all turned to find Peanut down on his fat, furry haunches, lapping at the puddle of fluid while purring contentedly. Ozzie made a retching sound. Boss muttered, "I think I might be sick." Becky raced over to the supply closet and pulled out a mop and a bucket, while Steady grabbed the tomcat, holding the beast out in front of him and grimacing like he was about to lose the coffee he'd been swigging.

Some mopping, one quick, disgruntled cat bath, and a couple of packed saddlebags later, and the group heading south was finally ready to go. Well, almost. If Mac would only stop scowling like he'd been sucking on a lemon and blow into the damn Breathalyzer…

"You're not drunk?" Becky impatiently shoved a green sucker into her mouth. The gesture looked like the physical equivalent of *men…why the hell do they have to make everything so freakin' difficult?*

And even if Delilah had not felt obliged to agree with that sentiment based solely on the unspoken pledge between the sisterhood—you know the one, *we gals stick together*—she'd have agreed because, after all, it was *Mac* they were dealing with here. Mac…*numero uno* on her very short list of things that put a kink in her otherwise fairly straightforward life.

"No, ma'am. I'm not drunk," he insisted. "I've had so much coffee that we'll have to pull over every ten minutes so I can pee like a Russian racehorse."

"I've always wondered about the origins of that phrase," Ozzie observed. He'd already mounted up on his custom chopper. Steady was behind him in the process of doing the same. "I mean what's so special about a ruski equine, I ask you?"

Becky ignored him, still frowning up at Mac. "So if you're not drunk, prove it, Gigantor. Puff, puff."

"Fine," he grumbled before sticking the short, plastic tube between his lips and blowing. "There." He showed Becky the digital number on the device's screen, wiggling it in front of her face victoriously. "I told you. So, go cork your pistol."

Becky rolled her eyes before moving on to Zoelner with the Breathalyzer.

After Zoelner blew and proved that he, too, was fit to make the journey, Mac swung astride his monster bike. Delilah watched as his big thighs pulled the fabric of his faded jeans tight. For a second, just a *split* second, the searing image of what it would be like to have those muscled thighs pushing her legs wide burned through her mind. And in that fleeting moment, she imagined she could feel his crinkly man-hair brushing the tender skin at the apex of her legs as he pumped and strained into her. For that one all-too-brief instant, she fancied she could actually feel him there, so big and rough, so hot and hard, and…okay, *crap*. Her mind suddenly shook itself out of La-La-Land, and she realized she was staring at Mac's jean-clad thighs like she was honing her knife and fork, ready to cut a big bite out of each.

You really are *pathetic*. And as much as she hated to admit it, that annoying voice was proving to be right far more often than it was proving to be wrong.

When she felt the top of her head buzzing like her scalp was threatening to lift away from her skull, she looked up to find Mac's eyes narrowed on her and…was that slight reddening of his tan cheeks an actual blush?

Oh, great. Busted. Had her salacious thoughts been written all over her face?

She hoped not. And in the event that they *hadn't* been, she licked her lips before blurting the first thing to come to mind. "Uh…just admiring your bike."

Mac blinked, his expression turning contemplative before it once more slid into that inscrutable mask.

Delilah mentally slapped herself a high five. That *was* some pretty quick thinking on her part. And a believable excuse to boot. Because Mac's custom Harley *was* one badass bike. Its name, Siren, said it all. With its intricate black-and-gold paint job offsetting and highlighting the glinting chrome of the handlebars, engine, battery box, and wheels—not to mention the mean stretch and the eye-catching blue LED running lights—the motorcycle was, to put it simply, flat-out mesmerizing. Enough to distract and draw in even the most disinterested of passersby just like the fabled Sirens of Greek mythology.

Still congratulating herself on her speedy and, moreover, *believable* explanation for the lust in her eyes and the drool on her lips, she mounted up on Big Red. Pressing her helmet over her head, she waited. Waited for the sound she loved. The sound that was the audio equivalent of a full-on, body-shaking orgasm. The sound of rolling thunder…

It didn't take long.

Steady pushed the ignition on his bike and was

rewarded by an immediate guttural rumble. Ozzie followed suit. Then Zoelner. Then Mac. And only when
the full-throated roar of four well-tuned V-Twin engines
filled the vast expanse of the shop did Delilah thumb
the ignition on Big Red. The motorcycle came to life
beneath her, growling and shaking like a steel beast.

A little thrill streaked up her spine...

That feeling, that excitement of being in control of
something bigger and meaner than herself, never faded.
Pressing her kickstand back with her booted heel, she
twisted her wrist and followed the skid marks left by
Ghost's madcap exit from the shop, the four BKI operators rolling out behind her.

As the soft, summer breeze wafted against her face,
she whispered quietly, a warm glow of hope filling her
chest, "Just hold on, Uncle Theo. Whatever happened to
you, wherever you are, just hold on. Because I'm coming. And I'm bringing the Black Knights with me..."

"She is back on her motorcycle," Haroun relayed. The
quiet hum of the small engine on the compact car they'd
rented over the border in Canada barely competed with
the sound of Qasim's second-in-command's voice.
"And she is not alone. She has four men riding with her.
I have followed them onto the highway. It appears they
are headed south, in your direction."

Qasim narrowed his eyes, staring into the near distance. The glitter of dust danced in the beams of the
low-burning lanterns, reminding him of so many of the
other dark, dusty corners he'd been forced to hide in.
"In *my* direction? Do you suppose she's already missing

her uncle and is coming in search of him?" He hadn't banked on that, on the fact that only a handful of hours after they'd captured Theodore, his disappearance would already be noted.

Praise Allah!

"It could be," Haroun mused. "Perhaps she attempted to call him, and his not answering has spurred her concern."

Hmm. That could very well be the case, especially considering how close Qasim suspected Theodore and his niece were. Flipping through the photos in the old Marine's wallet, Qasim was privy to snapshots of the pair's lives together. The photograph on top was apparently the most recent. Theodore had his arm thrown around a stunning, flame-haired woman. A golden turkey sat on a platter atop a long, dark bar in front of them while the sparkle of alcohol bottles stacked on shelves glinted in the background. Both Theodore and Delilah were grinning foolishly, as if they hadn't a care in the world. A pang of envy sliced through Qasim.

The next picture was slightly older, given the fact that Theodore's stark white hair was peppered with black. The former Marine was smiling broadly at Delilah, who was dressed in a graduation gown and holding up a diploma in one fist, her other hand forming a V for victory. Qasim growled. *So much to celebrate for those two. So much promise for the future…*

Beneath the second photo was a third, older still. This one was of Theodore and Delilah on a beach somewhere, both laughing and tan. Theodore looked young and fit, and Delilah had the fresh appearance of a girl who'd just begun to blossom into a woman. Happy times. Blissful times. The kind of times Qasim hadn't experienced since the deaths of his wife and sons...

And last, but certainly not least, was the final photo. It was of Delilah, aged seven or eight by Qasim's calculations, pigtailed and giggling while riding Theodore's broad shoulders. It was *this* picture that bothered him the most. Because seven years old was the age his youngest boy had been the day that Hellfire missile slammed into his village. The day his life changed from one of simple pleasures to one of vengeance, battle, and...*blood*.

And he'd tried. For years he'd tried to sate his thirst for revenge by killing Westerners and those of his brethren who'd fallen victim to the poison of Western beliefs. He'd taken lives and watched others as they were burned down to ashes. Alas, no matter how much blood he spilled, it just wasn't enough. He'd found no solace, no refuge in the deaths of those many innocents. But perhaps this mission, perhaps destruction on *this* scale, would finally be enough. If he was successful here, perhaps he could finally find peace.

And in a slightly ironic twist, he had a rogue American agent to thank for the opportunity. He never would have believed his salvation would come in that form. Though, come to think of it, perhaps he should have. Winterfield had turned against his own country, turned his back on his motherland, for something as simple as money. A *lot* of money—those who headed The Cause had deep pockets—but it was money all the same.

Good old American capitalism and greed have come home to roost, and—

"Qasim?" Haroun asked, and he realized he'd been silent for too long.

Shaking himself, he pushed everything but the mission from his mind. "Make sure you are not spotted," he commanded. The last thing he needed was for Haroun to find himself matched up against a bunch of big, slow-witted bikers. Qasim had watched enough American television to know that the type of men to wear leather and ride Harleys tended to use their fists or pistols first and ask questions later.

Not that Haroun couldn't defend himself; he'd been trained by the best *mujahedeen* fighters on the planet. But still…it was better not to take any chances. "Follow them. But do not attempt to take Miss Fairchild while those bikers are around. Wait until she is alone."

"Do not lose faith in me, Qasim," Haroun said. "I know what I am doing."

"Of course you do, my friend," he assured his second-in-command. Haroun's pride was easily wounded, like that of so many of the staunchest and most fanatical believers. "I just want to ensure we do not fail in our mission. I want to ensure—"

"I know what you want, *habibi*," Haroun interrupted. He only used the Arabic term of endearment and friendship when they were speaking alone. All other times, he remained stubbornly formal. "But we will not fall short this time. This time victory shall be ours."

"*In sha'Allah.*" *God willing*, he said before thumbing off the phone and spinning once more toward his hostage.

The kerosene lanterns were turned low despite the fact that his men had covered the windows with black cloth, assuring no light escaped the dilapidated building to catch the attention of a passing motorist. Though, in truth, the possibility of catching the attention of a passing motorist seemed slim. In the two days they'd been occupying this part of Main Street, they'd only heard one car rumble past. And it was obvious the driver had been lost. The vehicle had turned around at the end of the street before heading back out to the highway.

So, yes, perhaps Qasim was being paranoid by insisting the lanterns be kept at their lowest setting. But he didn't mind the dark. He embraced it, in fact. It seemed somehow fitting. Dark deeds were usually done in dark places, after all. And even in the dim light, he could see that Theodore's left eye was now swollen almost completely shut. A deep gash near the man's temple stained his white hair and leaked blood down his cheek and neck.

The stale air inside the deserted Main Street shop was redolent with the metallic aroma of lost bodily fluid and the much sharper odors of fear and desperation. But even so, even suffering from all that fear and desperation, even though his aged body had to be racked by the pain of the repeated beatings Sami and Jabbar administered with glee, Theodore Fairchild refused to answer Qasim's questions.

That would soon change…

"I have it on good authority that your niece is traveling this way," Qasim said conversationally, examining his fingernails. "She's riding with a group of bikers." Something flashed in Theodore's good eye and Qasim cocked his head. "Friends of yours?" The old man refused to make so much as a peep behind his gag. "Ah." He nodded, smiling appreciatively. "That is perfect. A few more bargaining chips to add to my pile…"

Chapter Seven

Highway 57, 10 miles outside Cairo, Illinois
Five hours later…

MAC HAD SPENT THE ENTIRE RIDE STARING AT Delilah's ass…

Not that he was overly partial to Delilah or any-thing—he wasn't, by God! Well, at least not any more than *any* sighted, red-blooded, heterosexual male would be—but he *was* overly partial to asses. And Delilah's ass, jiggling slightly against the hand-tooled leather seat of Big Red…not to mention the fact that her T-shirt and biker jacket occasionally rode up to reveal the tramp stamp on her lower back—two colorful doves holding a pink ribbon between their beaks with her deceased parents' names inked onto it—and *holy shit fire*! It was a sight to see, to say the least…

Little Mac had been at full attention for most of the journey, and for anyone who's ever tried to ride a motor-cycle with a massive chubby, saying it was painful was belittling the definition of sheer agony. Of course, his own physical discomfort was eclipsed by a sharp spike of…some emotion—it wasn't jealously, but it was a mean-eyed cousin thereof—when they exited the high-way, stopped at a lonely streetlight, and Ozzie pulled up beside him and murmured loud enough to be heard over their grumbling engines, but not loud enough to reach

Delilah's ears, "Damn! That woman sure has a sweet dumper, doesn't she? I'm going to ask her to marry me!"

Oh, for the love of—

Mac couldn't very well tell Ozzie to shove his sweet dumper comment—*I mean, come on, now. Dumper?*—down his throat without alerting the guy to his…*not*-jealousy…*un*jealousy?…so he did the next best thing. He laughed and shook his helmeted head. "I think you've already asked her a dozen times, and I think she's already turned you down each and every one."

"Yeah." Ozzie shrugged laconically. "But that was before I rode to her uncle's rescue—quite literally. *Now* I'm going to the big, strapping hero. And, as far as I can figure, that's pretty much catnip to the feline-esque female of the species."

As much as Mac wanted to brush off Ozzie's comment as a bunch of bull, he had to admit the sentiment actually held some merit. Not only was Ozzie handsome in the way of most movie stars—even *with* his mad scientist mop of blond hair—but the guy was also smart and charming and…*fun*. Delilah was fun. Ozzie was fun. Mac was…*not*-fun…*un*fun? So, yessir, maybe Ozzie was right. Maybe his riding to her uncle's rescue would be just what Delilah needed to nudge her over the line from *no way in hell, Ozzie* to *sure, Ozzie, let's give it a go*.

Unbidden, the image of Delilah arching beneath BKI's tech wizard flashed in front of his eyes. Immediately, his ears began to burn and red edged into his vision. But he wasn't jealous. *Hell, no*. He was just…*something*. Something that *wasn't* jealous.

And instead of going with his first instinct, which

was to tell Ozzie to just keep on dreaming when it came to Delilah *finally* saying yes to one of his myriad proposals, Mac went with, "Yeah, dude. You might be right. This little huntin' expedition might be just the thing to turn her *no* into a *yes*."

Ozzie flipped up the visor on his helmet, gaping at Mac in the dim red glow cast by the overhead stoplight.

"What's that look for?" Mac demanded.

"I just figured," Ozzie lifted a shoulder, "you know, given all the not-so-subtle sexual tension between you two, that you'd be a little less apt to toss her happily my way."

"Hey," Mac lifted one hand from his handlebars, making a dismissive gesture, "I don't have, nor do I *want* any sort of claim over That Woman. The field is free and clear, my man. I say, go all Pat Benatar on her and hit her with your best shot."

Ozzie's chin jerked back as if Mac'd gifted him with a pop to the jaw instead of a magnanimous piece of advice.

"Okay, not that I don't appreciate the '80s music reference, dude, because, seriously? Pat Benatar? High five for that one. But if you don't mind me saying, I think you're completely full of shit."

Why does everyone keep sayin' that? First Zoelner, now Ozzie?

Mac opened his mouth to refute the guy's claim, but, *thank the sweet Lord*, the light flicked from red to green. Twisting his wrist, Siren's big engine growled appreciatively at the influx of high-octane fuel, and he motored out into the intersection, following behind Delilah and her luscious, world-class ass.

He wondered idly how all his teammates could be so wrong when it came to the relationship...*non*-relationship...*un*relationship?...he had with Delilah. The Black Knights were usually a pretty astute group, constant ribbing and one-upmanship aside. But, he was sad to say, they were dead-eye wrong when it came to this...

Outside Charles Sander's House

Ozzie wasn't kidding when he called this place a ghost town...

Delilah might have expected to find the deserted Main Street, the rusting gas pumps, and the crumbling roads that made up Cairo somewhere out west. Somewhere oil or gold, or oil *and* gold, had dried up, leaving the residents nothing to live or stay for. But here? In southern Illinois? Well, a ghost town of this magnitude—it had sprawling neighborhoods, and vast, empty public spaces—was bizarre, to say the least. Downright spooky, to say the most.

Okay, and yeah, she was saying the most. Because on a scale of scary from one to ten—one being slightly foreboding and ten being shit-your-pants terrifying—this whole town fell somewhere around an eight. Eight or nine...

"Lord almighty," Mac breathed. "Looks like hell with everyone out to lunch."

And that was one way of putting it, Delilah supposed. Another way of putting it was to say that Cairo, Illinois, was a horror movie set sprung to life.

She shivered as a gust of cool wind howled down the deserted street, rattling the shutters on the house next door like the ribs on a skeleton. And she tried, *oh, man*, how she tried not to let the gaping black windows of the dilapidated homes remind her of eyes, *dead* eyes. Of course, the fact that the entire block was pitch dark, illuminated only by the headlights of the bikes they'd parked on the street, didn't help matters any.

And, then, leave it to Ozzie to go and make everything that much worse by loudly whispering, "Ahhh! Make the lambs stop screaming!"

Instantly, an image of Anthony Hopkins playing Hannibal Lecter—complete with spooky half-mask— flashed in her mind's eye, and she instinctively reached for the hand closest to her.

It was Mac's. And its warmth, not to mention its strength, kept her from turning around and jumping back on Big Red, leaving a mile-long trail of rubber in her wake as she hightailed it out of Dodge…er…uh, Cairo.

"Holy crow, Ozzie," Mac grumbled. They were all standing on a disintegrating sidewalk and staring up at Charlie Sander's house. And although it wasn't in *much* better shape than the crumbling dwellings around it, it *did* appear to still have all its windowpanes. And the yard, though not manicured by any stretch of the imagination, *did* look like it'd been recently mowed. "This place is creepy enough without any *Silence of the Lambs* references."

"Sorry," Ozzie said, shuddering dramatically. "I just keep expecting some naked dude to come around the corner with his Johnson and nads tucked up between his legs, singing *it rubs the lotion on its skin, or else it gets the hose again*."

Delilah squeezed Mac's hand tighter, inching closer to his side and fighting the urge to glance over her shoulder.

Was something back there? Watching? Waiting to sneak up and devour her soul in one greedy gulp?

Mac chafed her freezing fingers with his free hand before turning to glare at Ozzie. "What did I *just* say about *Silence of the Lambs* references? I swear by all that's holy, Ozzie, if you don't cut that shit out, I'm gonna be forced to feed you my gun."

BKI's tech guru held his hands in the air. "Sorry. Sorry. I just watched it again last weekend, so it's kinda stuck in my head, you know?"

"Yeah," Zoelner huffed, "and now, thank you very much, it's stuck in *all* our heads."

Another gust of damp, moldy-smelling wind. Another bout of bone-rattling shutter noise. Another shiver danced up Delilah's spine.

This was her Uncle Theo's friend Charlie's house? Why would anyone choose to live like this? Why would anyone choose to *stay* in this godforsaken town? And, yeah, she *totally* got why her uncle decided to leave her back at the hotel in Marion…

Okay, okay. Just take a breath and focus on what's important. Focus on why you came here, like—

"Uncle Theo's bike isn't here," she observed, glancing toward the glaringly empty, grease-stained driveway. "Which means *he's* not here." And for a moment, a heavy wave of disappointment overcame her fear.

"It's possible he's parked in the garage," Mac told her, giving her fingers another reassuring squeeze, a *friendly* squeeze.

"Yeah, *hermano*," Steady said, "but the question is, who's gonna go check?"

"Maybe we should state our intentions," Zoelner suggested. "It is," he checked the big watch on his wrist, "oh-five-hundred in the morning, after all. If Theo isn't here, and this Charles Sander guy *is*, he's not likely to be all that keen on a gang of bikers skulking around his house in the dark."

"Agreed." Mac nodded. He cleared his throat and called, "Theo! Charles! Are you guys in there?" His deep voice echoed down the empty street, bouncing back to them a second later. "Theo! Charles!" he tried again. But when no one answered him save for an echo and the cackle of dead leaves flipping down the road on another gust of wind, he changed tactics. "We've got Delilah here! Charles, as I'm sure you know, Delilah is Theo's niece and she's feelin' mean as a mama wasp that Theo's not answering his phone! We're here lookin' for him! So, don't turn us into buzzard bait, okay? We're gonna approach your front porch!"

*Front porch…front porch…front porch…*his words bounced around hauntingly before finally fading. Then, silence reigned over the derelict street.

"Okay," Mac said, chafing her ice-cold fingers one last time. "Let's do this."

Uh-huh. That sounded simple enough, didn't it? After all, she was with four big, tough men. It should've been easy to walk up to that chipped and peeling front door. It *should* have been. Unfortunately, someone, at some point, had glued her boots to the sidewalk.

"*Jesús Cristo*," Steady harrumphed, the first to start stomping up the sidewalk. "Let's hope the inside of this place is better than the outside."

Mac ushered her forward. And was it just her? Or did

the trip up to the front porch feel sort of like *Dead Man Walking*? As if she was heading toward her own funeral...

Okay, and now you're just being fanciful. Stop imagining things.

"Mr. Sander?" Steady pulled the screen door open—well, *frame* of a screen door, really; there was no actual screen attached. "Mr. Sander!" Steady tried again, holding the metal doorframe open with his foot and banging on the front door. The thing might have been bright red at one point, but now it was a dirty crimson color, and the air on the porch hung heavy with the smell of the honeysuckle bush growing over the south side railing. Beneath that lingered the dank, moldy aroma of rotting wood mixed with a hint of dog piss and...was that marijuana? "Are you in there, Mr. Sander? We're friends of Theo Fairchild!"

Silence. Dark, dense silence.

And, as if the place wasn't atmospheric enough already, a barn owl, perched somewhere nearby, chose that exact moment to let loose with one of its screeching calls. Ozzie jumped, unholstering his weapon. "Seriously?" he shuddered. "I mean...*Jesus!*"

"Knock again. If you don't get an answer, try the knob," Mac instructed Steady, still firmly holding Delilah's hand. And it was a good thing, too. She feared his tough grip might be the only thing keeping her on the porch and not beating feet in the opposite direction.

Steady knocked. Once. Twice. Three times. When nothing stirred inside the house, he turned the knob, pushing the door open.

Something huge and snarling barreled out at them. The next thing Delilah knew, she was airborne...

—*w*—

When the large shadow leaped from inside the house, Mac's instincts kicked in...

First thing: *Protect the girl*. He grabbed Delilah around the waist and lunged off the porch, landing on the hard ground on his back—*Ow! Sonofa*—before rolling Delilah beneath him and covering her with his body. Second thing: *Acquire the target*. He reached into his waistband, grabbed his Glock 22 .40 caliber pistol, pulled back the side, and lifted the weapon to stare down the night sights.

Just as he'd been taught at the Academy, he scanned the yard in front of him. *Acquiring target. Acquiring target. Acqu—There!*

"Don't shoot!" Ozzie yelled. "It's just a dog!"

And, sure as shit, Mac'd already figured that out for himself. He glanced over his shoulder to see Steady sprawled on his back in the middle of the porch, his neck wrenched back, his arms over his head aiming his handgun into the front yard. Ozzie and Zoelner had taken up positions behind the front pillars supporting the porch's roof, their weapons drawn, their fingers on the triggers.

Well, good to see we've all still got it, he mused, turning back in time to witness—*oh, goody*—the big, yellow dog squatting down in order to take a mammoth dump on the lawn.

"Well, *that's* not exactly what I was expecting," he heard Ozzie mutter, amusement in his tone.

"Mac?" A muffled voice sounded from beneath him. *Ah, shit*. He'd jumped on Delilah quicker than a duck on a Junebug, and now the poor woman was probably suffocating under his not unsubstantial weight.

"Sorry, darlin'," he apologized, pushing up on his elbows and staring down into her pretty face. There was a smudge of dirt on her chin, and her cheeks were flushed. But other than that, she appeared unscathed. He should have rolled off her. He *should* have.

He didn't.

Because she was soft and lush, and for a moment, during which time he was quite sure he'd up and lost his cotton-pickin' mind, he allowed himself to revel in the sensation of her beneath him. "It was a…" Holy crow, was that his voice? All low and growly? "…a false alarm."

She nodded jerkily. But it wasn't fear he saw in her eyes. *Hell, no.* Fear would not have had every cell inside him screeching to a stop. Awareness would. And that's exactly what was plastered all over Delilah's face. Her awareness. Of him. As a man…

And just as every cell inside him came to a grinding halt, so, too, did the rest of the world. The eerie sounds of the downtrodden neighborhood vanished. His teammates and the big, goofy dog appeared frozen in place. It was just the two of them. Just Mac and red-hot Delilah— her lush breasts brushing his chest on an indrawn breath, her green irises speckled with tiny flecks of gold. Up close like this, he could see that he'd been right all along. Her skin was completely, damnably flawless. Her lips plump and smooth. And speaking of… She opened her mouth on an exhale that tickled his chin and allowed her sweet breath to tunnel up his nostrils.

The stupid things flared of their own accord, and when she saw his reaction, she shifted. Just a little. Just enough so that her leg slipped to the outside of his. Just enough for her fun parts to directly align with his. Little Mac, never one to miss this kind of opportunity, swelled and strained against his zipper. His balls instantly tightened and began throbbing in time with his heartbeat. He was lost. Lost in the sight of her. In the feel of her. In the wondrous—

Slurp! A warm, wet tongue curled under his chin, then journeyed the length of his face to tangle in his hair. *Slurp!* The action was repeated, and he looked up into the bright brown eyes of the Labrador.

Hello, reality. Where the hell have you *been the last twenty seconds?*

"Cut it out, you big goofball." He pushed the dog's massive head away as the world around him once more skipped into action. The Labrador sat back, thick tail thumping the grass, a doggy grin splitting its face. Then the beast let loose with a gleeful, "*Yorp!*"

The bark sounded like something that would come from the throat of a pubescent boy, cracking up an octave somewhere in the middle.

"Well, that's a pathetically wimpy excuse for a bark if ever I heard one," Steady muttered, turning over to rub his tailbone—the thing no doubt bruised from the ass-plant he'd done onto the boards of the porch.

"*Yorp!*"

"Yeah, yeah." Mac pushed at that big, yellow head again when it started nosing in his direction, long, pink tongue poised to strike. "We heard you the first time." He squinted at the flashing, silver pendant attached to the dog's blue collar, and thought, *really*? "Fido, huh? I guess ol' Charles isn't real creative when it comes to pet naming."

"His name is Fido?" Ozzie called from the porch, having holstered his weapon.

Mac was about to turn and nod over his shoulder when he felt movement beneath him. A soft, seductive sort of wiggle.

For the love of Christ! He was *still* sprawled atop Delilah!

Now, he really wished he could say he nonchalantly, just oh-so-casually rolled off her. That would've been the acceptable way to handle the situation. But considering he remembered, at that precise moment, that he'd gone and sprung the world's hardest boner—the thing could've been used to cut glass—it should've come as no surprise that the jackknife maneuver he used to propel himself upward was one for the record books. The World's Most Ludicrous and Uncoordinated Dismounts record books…

"Well, yeehaw, cowboy! Did that pretty filly buck you off?" Ozzie called. "And you call yourself a bona fide Texan? *Pssht.*"

Mac chose to ignore Ozzie because, really, how the hell was he expected to think of a comeback at a time like this? Instead, he reached down, offering Delilah a hand, and hoping beyond hope that she hadn't noticed the spruce tree he'd been packing inside his pants while lying atop her.

No such luck. When he hauled her to her feet, the surprised, slightly speculative look in her eye—not to mention the deep flush staining her cheeks and that deliciously overripe chest of hers—told him she hadn't missed a damn thing.

Well…hell…

Chapter Eight

"HOLY HEMP BALLS, BATMAN! LOOK AT THE SIZE OF this thing! It's Goliath's bong!"

Delilah was sitting at Charlie's kitchen table and frowning at the personal income tax returns and financial records she'd found in the filing cabinet acting as an end table in the nearby living room. A needle in a haystack...that's what she was looking for. Something nefarious in Charlie's dealings that might tell her why *he* was missing along with her uncle. And Charlie *was* missing. Gone for at least two days, by her guess. You know, given the state of the dry, crusty food on the dishes stacked in the sink and the general mayhem the dog had created when he began to worry his owner wouldn't return.

The cushions on the brown, threadbare sofa in the living room were shredded, cotton sticking out everywhere and littering the space in great, white wads that glimmered in the light of the two lamps flanking the front window. Toilet paper was strewn around the downstairs bathroom and glued to the wet linoleum floor—glued because Fido had been using the toilet as his water bowl and he hadn't been very fastidious about it, dropping big, sticky blobs of drool and potty water everywhere. And then there was the bottom of the front door... It looked like it'd gone ten rounds with a wood chipper and lost. The wood chipper being

Fido's teeth and claws in his frantic bid for freedom from the house.

Poor Fido…

She reached down to scratch the Lab's soft, floppy ears and was rewarded with an adoring whine and the promise of eternal love shining in his soulful brown eyes. "Who's a good boy? Who's just the best boy in the whole world? Are you best boy in the whole world?"

"He's probably the most mellow boy in the world if he lives with the guy who smokes this thing," Ozzie said.

She glanced up from the dog to find Ozzie waving around a three-foot-long water bong in eye-bleeding orange. And, oh, how she wished the reason her uncle hadn't been in touch with her was because he'd gotten himself good and baked.

If he'd pulled the ol' Cheech and Chong, she'd be pissed at him for scaring her shitless and doing something that by Illinois law could get him thrown in the nearest eight-by-ten. But at least she'd know what to do… Namely, feed him copious amounts of White Castle and Cheetos and wait for the THC to wear off before hauling his stoner ass back home. As it stood, she was no closer to finding her uncle than she'd been *before* she left Chicago. And, to make matters worse, now she was dealing with *another* old Marine who'd mysteriously gone AWOL.

She glanced back down at the tax filings. There was something here. Something she couldn't quite put her finger on. Besides his Social Security and military retirement benefits, Charlie Sanders didn't have any income. But there were expenditures listed in his—

The air around her heated as Mac brushed by her. She

glanced up, only to find him not paying her the slightest bit of attention—*so what else is new?* Instead, he was in the process of making his third slow circle around the kitchen table. Squatting, he studied the orange and green linoleum floor as if in search of some miniscule piece of evidence. When he stood, she managed to catch his eye, but his expression was back to being dismissive.

So, we're playing it that way, are we? She lifted a brow, hoping the look she wore clearly relayed her thoughts. *We're just pretending nothing happened out there in the front yard? We're just acting like you didn't pitch a stick of wood big enough and stiff enough to hang my bath towel on?*

Mimicking her, Mac lifted a dark brow, his expression sliding from dismissive to inscrutable.

Okay. So I guess the answers to those questions are yes, yes, and yes.

Then and there she decided that, just as she'd long suspected, Bryan "Mac" McMillan was a big, irritating, confusing, A-hole. A big, irritating, confusing, *holy-hell-hot-as-homemade-sin* A-hole. And to make matters worse—as if she *needed* matters to be worse at this point; *thanks, Universe, you giant dickwad!*— ever since he'd sprawled atop her, so warm, so heavy, so very much a *man*, blood had been rushing into parts of her that had been too long ignored. Well…too long ignored if you didn't count the pulse setting on her handheld showerhead—which she most certainly did *not*. Because, if memory served, there was a vast difference between a man's touch and that of her trusty stainless steel bathtub accessory. So, yes. Blood. Rushing. Parts too long ignored. And the sensation was driving her crazy. Crazy enough to throw caution, and all his repeated rejections, to the wind and jump on the man like he was a bouncy house.

"*Yorp!*" Fido sang demandingly, upset that her attention had turned from him.

"So sorry," she soothed, resuming her petting, watching the dog's entire back end swing to and fro with the force of his tail wagging.

"There's nobody on the second floor, and the garage is empty save for a pretty cherry El Camino," Zoelner announced as he descended the stairs and marched into the living room. "I called back to headquarters and had Becky run the plates. The car belongs to Sander. No real surprise there. Oh, and FYI, Becky told me to inform you guys that Ali delivered a daughter. Nine pounds, six ounces."

"Mazel tov!" Ozzie crowed, then, "And, damn! That's a big baby!"

Zoelner nodded. "Anyway, mom and baby are doing well. Though, supposedly, Ghost is a wreck."

"And speaking of big," Ozzie grinned, wiggling his eyebrows, "check out the size of this thing." He brandished the bong in Zoelner's face. "It's Goliath's bong!"

"Yeah, yeah," Zoelner rolled his eyes, yanking the contraption from Ozzie's hand and tossing it on the ruined sofa. "I heard you the first time. Very witty. Now shut up."

"Any sign of a struggle upstairs or in the garage?" Mac asked. He posed the question to Zoelner, but he was staring at a kitchen chair that was tipped on its back. Eyes narrowed, he glanced over to the old-fashioned tin coffee cup turned upside down on the floor before turning to study the newspaper lying beside the table leg.

Obviously, Fido, hungry and looking for any small form of sustenance, had gone after the coffee mug Charlie had left on the table and, in the process, created this little tableau of mayhem. Which reminded Delilah...

She scooted her chair back and walked over to what she suspected was a pantry door. Turning the knob, she nearly lost her balance when Fido rushed ahead of her, barking ecstatically and turning in tight circles within the small space that was, indeed, the pantry. His thick tail whacked against her shins hard enough to leave bruises.

"Okay, okay," she soothed. Then, spotting a thirty-pound bag of Hills Science Diet pushed into the back corner, she nudged Fido aside and used the large bowl she found inside the bag to scoop out a healthy portion of dog food.

"*Yorp! Yorp!*"

"Who's a hungry boy?" she asked in that weird sing-songy voice women tended to don around infants and canines. "Who's just about starving to death?"

"*Yorpyorpyorpyorp!*"

"I gotcha, big boy. Just a second." She exited the pantry and set the bowl of kibble in front of the stove. "Here you go. Eat up."

Fido attacked the food with gusto, his hind end swinging back and forth so forcefully he caused himself to stumble.

"Poor dog," Zoelner observed before turning back to Mac. "And to answer your question, that's a negative on any signs of a struggle upstairs or in the garage. All appears as it should."

"Maybe they were abducted by aliens," Ozzie posited unhelpfully.

"You've been watching too much of the Syfy channel," Zoelner said, crossing his arms and tilting his head at Mac, who was back to staring at that silly, knocked-over chair.

"Yeah, right," Ozzie scoffed. "There's no such thing."

"No such thing as aliens, or no such thing as watching too much of the Syfy channel?"

"Well, the second, naturally." The look on Ozzie's face was dubious. "Because *of course* there's such things as *aliens*."

"Of course?" Zoelner's lips quirked.

"Yeah. I mean, the universe is a pretty big place, right? And if it's just us, that's an awful waste of space."

"You stole that from Carl Sagan," Zoelner accused.

"No, I didn't. I stole it from the movie *Contact*. Maybe *they* stole it from Carl Sagan."

"Whatever." Zoelner waved him off. "The point is, Charles and Theo were *not* abducted by aliens, and—"

"So, I get why ol' Sander decided to stay tucked away in the middle of nowhere, holed-up in this hellhole of a crumbling house," Steady interrupted, emerging from the door leading to the basement stairs. "The guy's got a state-of-the-art grow room set up down there. It's enough to make Jay and Silent Bob weep with envy."

Ah, the marijuana. Delilah *knew* she recognized that smell when she was standing out on the porch. And it hadn't been the dried-out, skunky aroma like the kind emanating from the bong—the odor of *used* Mary Jane. It'd been the earthier, almost sweet smell of freshly growing weed. Not that Delilah was an expert or anything. But her roommate in college, Sarah Moore, had been a philosophy major and had kept a couple of pot plants flourishing under a UV light in her closet for… wait for it…strictly "medicinal/experimental purposes." Feel free to insert eye-roll here.

Of course, the presence of the jolly green downstairs could also account for the discrepancies she'd seen in Charlie's financial records. So then the question became, was it possible his disappearance, as well as her uncle's, was some sort of drug deal gone terribly wrong? As her stomach took a nosedive into her biker boots, she posed her theory aloud.

"Are all the plants still there?" Mac asked Steady, continuing to stare at that stupid chair until Delilah was forced to glance down at the thing. *What in the world is so mesmerizing about it?* But no matter how hard she looked, she couldn't discern anything exceptional about the standard wooden ladder-back.

"*Sí, hermano,*" Steady replied, his Puerto Rican accent lilting in the stale air of the house. "Everything appears to be in order. Nothing missing that I can tell. Nothing moved."

"It doesn't make any sense." Mac shook his head, blue gaze narrowed, the too-sexy dimple twitching in his chin as his substantial jaw sawed back and forth.

"What doesn't?" she asked.

"If Sander was attacked and taken because of some sort of dust-up between pot growers," Mac explained, "if it was a turf war gone bad or something, then whoever eighty-sixed him would've grabbed his plants. They're too valuable to leave here to rot."

Attacked and taken. Eighty-sixed… None of those words were ones Delilah wanted to hear.

"What makes you so sure he was attacked and taken?" Zoelner asked, still eyeing Mac curiously. And when Mac reached up and rubbed a wide palm over the back of his neck, Zoelner lifted a brow. "Is that Spidey sense of yours acting up again?"

Okay, and that was the *second* time Zoelner had used that term. "What in the world are you guys talking about?" she demanded. "What *is* Spidey sense?"

"Spidey sense is Spider-Man's sixth sense about danger," Ozzie supplied. "Except Mac's superpower comes more in the form of an uncanny ability to piece together subtle clues."

"Uh-huh." She nodded, not one to believe in the black arts of extrasensory perception. "You're kidding, right?"

First aliens, now this? Maybe she'd been wrong to enlist the help of the Black Knights for this particular undertaking. Because, apparently, they were all batshit crazy. *Who knew?*

"It's not a sixth sense *or* a superpower," Mac assured her, and she breathed a sigh of relief. "It's just good, ol'-fashioned FBI training."

"Okay, good." She nodded. "So then to reiterate and rephrase Zoelner's question, why does your good ol'-fashioned FBI training tell you that Charlie was attacked and taken?"

"For the record," Ozzie interjected before Mac could speak, "I'm *still* leaning toward alien abduction."

Oh, for heaven's sake…

Delilah, along with the rest of the group, watched as Mac walked over to the coffee cup. Using the steel-toe of his biker boot, he flipped the mug over. Beneath it was a small brown puddle of dried coffee.

"At first I thought Fido here," the dog's tail went from a side-to-side wag to a full-on circle at the mention of his name, "knocked the chair over in an attempt to get at the mug on the table," Mac explained. And, yup. That gelled with Delilah's take on events. "But then I saw there was a ring of coffee surrounding the lip of the cup. No way the Lab would've left that if he was after its contents. He'd have pushed the mug around until he lapped up every last drop. So, then if Fido wasn't after the coffee, I asked myself, *why is the cup on the floor?*"

Delilah lifted a brow, glancing from the coffee mug to Mac.

"No one?" Mac's eyes sparkled in the lamplight as his gaze swung around the group. "Okay, then. Let me demonstrate."

He bent to pick up the tin mug and the newspaper. Then, he righted the kitchen chair before settling himself in it. Holding the paper in his left hand, the coffee cup in his right, he called to Zoelner. "Come up behind me. Grab me and drag me backward like you're tryin' to wrestle me out of the house."

Dumbfounded, Delilah watched Zoelner crouch down and sneak slowly forward. Then the former CIA agent reached out and struck, quicker than—as she'd once heard Mac put it—greased lightning. One of Zoelner's arms wrapped around Mac's throat. His other arm clamped tight around Mac's broad shoulders. A second later, Mac was yanked out of the chair.

The cup went flying. The newspaper fluttered to the ground. The chair tipped, and only after Zoelner dragged

Mac halfway across the living room floor, Mac's boots scrabbling for purchase, did Mac reach up and tap the guy's forearm, saying, "Okay, that'll do."

He stood to his impressive height, adjusted his biker jacket, winced and touched his side like his stitches hurt—yeah, she *still* felt guilty about that—and gestured toward the kitchen. As a group, Delilah and the rest of the Knights turned to look. And, sure as shit, the chair was lying on its back. The paper had settled beside the table leg. And the coffee mug, though not *quite* where it'd been before, was still pretty darn close.

"Jesus," Ozzie muttered, his face void of its usual grin.

Okay, and now Delilah was a convert, a wholehearted believer in Mac's Spidey sense. We're talking ready to prostrate herself in front of the altar of his Spidey sense because...*damn*...

A fresh wave of cold fear crashed over her, chilling her to the bone. Charlie Sander had been attacked and abducted from his own house. And her uncle, who'd come here to meet him, was missing now, too. It was one thing to *suspect* foul play, but another thing entirely to *know* something dark and treacherous had happened here.

She rolled in her lips as all manner of violent scenarios flicked through her head, as every ax-murderer horror movie she'd ever seen scrolled through her mind's eye on fast-forward. And she must've made a noise, or else what she was feeling was radiating around the room, because Fido—finished with his kibble—bumped her limp, dangling hand with his head and stared up at her, whining in doggy concern.

Grateful for his presence—for one, he was warm and wiggly and alive, which was comforting, and two, he gave her an excuse to bend down and bury her face in the scruff of his neck, thereby hiding the tears that threatened at the back of her eyeballs—she hugged him and kissed him and told him he was a *good boy* before getting control of herself enough to lift her gaze to Mac.

"What's going on here?" she asked, not surprised her voice came out sounding like she'd been choking down broken martini glasses. "I mean, seriously, *what's going on here?*"

Mac leveled a look on her. And not a dismissive look, or a disapproving look, or his standard inscrutable look. No. This one was a look of one hundred percent pure confidence. "I don't know, darlin'. But I sure as hell aim to find out."

―∿∿―

"They have stopped at Sander's house," Haroun whispered through the phone, and Qasim sat back in the rickety plastic chair, marveling at how easily things appeared to be falling into place. First Theodore's speedy arrival in Cairo, and now Delilah's. Perhaps *qadar,* along with Allah, really *was* on their side…

"Your plan?" he asked after impatiently signaling for Sami to get off the big, shining motorcycle parked in the center of the dusty room. Ever since riding Theodore's Harley-Davidson into the dilapidated Main Street building—they hadn't dared leave it parked in Sander's driveway for fear it would draw the attention of some random passerby—the silly man had been mesmerized by the thing.

Qasim, for his part, didn't understand the allure. The motorcycle was loud and flashy and obnoxious… *Just like the Americans*, he supposed, curling his lip. It was certainly *not* the kind of vehicle he'd ever choose for himself, preferring the nearly inaudible hum of the two electric cars they'd rented in Canada. Not only were the little rentals stealthy, but they also weren't vehicles likely to draw attention. Just the kind of attributes a man like him both revered and required.

"I am in the backyard, hiding behind a doghouse," Haroun breathed, his voice so low Qasim strained to hear, "watching them as we speak. My plan is to take the woman as soon as she is alone."

"And if she leaves with the men before you have the opportunity?"

"I will follow," Haroun assured him. "I taped the extra cellular phone beneath the seat of her motorcycle. No matter where she goes, I will find her."

Qasim hadn't thought they would have a need for the third phone and hadn't wanted to spend the cash on it *or* the "find my phone" application Haroun had downloaded onto it. But in his firm but respectful way, Haroun had insisted. And that was *exactly* why he'd risen through the ranks to be Qasim's second-in-command. The man was a consummate professional, always prepared for every eventuality.

Qasim rose from the chair to walk toward one of the large cracked windows at the front of the building. Carefully pulling back the thick, black cloth, he peeked outside. The main thoroughfare was as deserted as it'd been since they first arrived, the golden rays of the sun slipping over the eastern horizon dimly illuminating the decaying facades of the buildings, the trash littering the street, and the broken glass globes sitting atop streetlamps that hadn't functioned in years.

"It will be daylight soon," he murmured, as much to himself as to Haroun.

"Which will be perfect," Haroun said. "People drop their guard during the day. And I know how to stick to the shadows."

Qasim knew that to be true. Haroun was like those small, electric cars. Silent, unassuming, and incredibly efficient. Still, even if his second-in-command happened to apprehend the woman... "If you take her, the men with her will tear this town apart searching for her."

"They will," Haroun agreed. "But it will take them time to do so. And, by then, we will have the information, the Marine and the woman will both be dead, and we will be long gone."

Haroun obviously had more confidence in the timeliness of this particular plan than Qasim did. Not that Qasim doubted Theodore would—how did the Americans put it?—*spill his guts* as soon as Delilah's life hung in the balance. But he *did* doubt how long it would take the motorcycle fanatics to find them once they began looking. Thirty minutes, he wondered? Forty? An hour at the most? The town was fairly large and sprawling, but it wasn't a metropolis by any means. Did Haroun's plan *really* give them enough time to secure the information they were after and silently make their escape?

Qasim ran though the logistics in his head, scowling at the number of ways it could all go horribly wrong. On the other hand, it could also go really, *really* right. And Fate *did* seem to be favoring them...

"Yes," he finally decided. "Grab the woman when you can. Be quick and quiet about it."

"Am I ever any other way?" Haroun asked, a hint of pride entering his tone.

Qasim closed his eyes, letting the black cloth drop back into place. "No, dear friend," he assured Haroun. "You are the very epitome of stealth. And I eagerly await your arrival with Miss Fairchild."

Clicking off the phone, he turned and sauntered over to Theodore. The man's head hung limply on the column of his neck, his chin touching his chest. Qasim grabbed a handful of snowy white hair and wrenched the old Marine's head back, gratified by the grunt of pain he elicited and unfazed by the fury sparking in those aging blue eyes.

"My second-in-command has your pretty niece in his sights," he said in English, smiling when Theodore's look of hot fury was replaced by one of cold fear. "She is here. In Cairo. So, now we can... How is it you say? Do this the easy way or the hard way?" He chuckled in delight that he'd found himself in a position to use that particularly charming little colloquialism. "You can either tell me what I want to know, and I will call my man and instruct him to leave Delilah alone. Or you can remain stubbornly mute, forcing me to bring your niece here where I will kill her if you do not give me the answers I seek."

He leaned down until he was nose-to-nose with Theodore, until the smell of the man's spilled blood filled his nostrils. "I suggest you go with the first option," he whispered, loving the way Theodore's chest heaved with emotion.

Struggling against his restraints, the old Marine mouthed something around his bloodied gag.

"What is that?" Qasim lifted a brow, reaching around to untie the cloth.

The minute the gag slid free, Theodore spit in his face, yelling, "Fuck you!"

Sami and Jabbar raced forward, but Qasim waved them back, straightening. He used the hem of his Western-style T-shirt to wipe the saliva from his cheek, the anger he usually kept in check—it didn't do to lose one's head to fury—boiling just beneath the surface.

"Go fuck yourself! You goddamned terrorist sonofa—" That was all Theodore managed, because Qasim slammed his balled-up fist into the man's jaw, effectively knocking him out cold. Haroun wasn't the only one who'd learned a thing or two from the *mujahedeen*.

Flexing his hand, reveling in the pain radiating up his arm, Qasim threw the bloody gag to Jabbar, absently noting the black eye Jabbar had sustained in the initial struggle to bring Theodore down. He was getting very tired of the old Marine's antics. "Put this back on him and then revive him," he said, walking back toward the plastic chair, sinking into it wearily. Anytime he gave into the violence roiling inside him, he felt both elated and, at the same time, strangely drained. "I want him awake when Haroun arrives with his niece."

Chapter Nine

"THIS LITTLE DOOR-TO-DOOR OPERATION WE'RE scheduled to begin in…" Mac watched Ozzie check the big, black Luminox watch on his wrist, "an hour or so would be a whole hell of a lot easier if we knew which residences were actually occupied."

Mac had convinced the group that it would be best to wait until oh-eight-hundred before going around and pounding on Cairo's front doors in order to flash Theo's and Charles's DMV photos. In his experience, people didn't take too kindly to strangers demanding answers from them before they'd had their first cup of morning joe. And given the…uh…self-styled hermits liable to still be inhabiting this defunct town? Well, he figured *they'd* appreciate that kind of intrusion even less.

Can you say answering the door shotgun first, ladies and gents?

And Mac, already a little cranky because he was experiencing the tiniest vestiges of the hangover-that-never-was—a bit of a headache and a craving for greasy cheeseburgers—not to mention the fact that the stitches in his side burned like holy hellfire, didn't fancy the idea of adding buckshot to his current list of ailments.

Delilah had put up a fight, anxious to charge ahead in the search for her uncle. But she'd finally admitted the logic of his decision to give it a couple of hours. And since she'd still been wearing the shirt stained with his boiling just beneath the former agent's surface, "she offered to help. I think this is one instance where we should take her up on it. I mean, geez, it's just a quick infrared scan."

Mac watched the muscle on the left side of Zoelner's jaw twitch, and part of him—the part that could *totally* understand not wanting to get another woman involved here, especially not one who seemed to have the same effect on Zoelner that Delilah had on him—almost told Ozzie, *to hell with it, just hijack the goddamned satellite*. But the *other* part of him, the part he prided himself on, the *professional* part, knew the kid had a point. If the CIA was going to know they were using the satellite system anyway, and if they could do the deed more quickly and more efficiently, why not just let them do it? As an added bonus, it could work as a test, of sorts, to see just how well the spooks were willing to play in the whole "joint assistance" arena.

"Is it *that* much of a problem for you?" he asked Zoelner.

"*No*." Zoelner frowned hard enough to strain a facial muscle. "It's not a *problem*. I'd just rather not have to deal with Ch—" He stopped, forcing himself to take a deep breath before continuing. "With those folks."

Mac hadn't missed Zoelner's truncated slip-of-the-tongue. There was definitely some sort of history between Zoelner and this agent named Chelsea. "Look, man," he placated, "this might be our opportunity to—"

"Fuck it," Zoelner spat viciously. "I'll do it."

Mac opened his mouth, but before he could say anything, a *thump* sounded overhead followed by a strange moaning sound. And a handful of hours after he had his first heart attack, he experienced a second one…

Beyond disappointed, and exhausted to the point of delusion apparently, Delilah spiked her phone into the orange shag carpeting and groaned her misery. Because the thought had occurred to her while she'd been in the shower that maybe her uncle had called. That maybe his disappearance had, indeed, been some kind of huge mistake. That maybe he and his old Marine buddy, Charlie, *had* gone somewhere to pull a Cheech and Chong, or else get their knobs polished—*erp*, she sooo didn't want to picture that—and he'd awoken this morning to leave her a message explaining everything. The idea had taken such a hold on her while she'd been shampooing the highway from her hair, that she'd almost, *almost* convinced herself it was real.

But after hastily pulling on a clean pair of jeans and her favorite T-shirt—the hot pink cotton read *Asphalt Angel* and had been washed so often it was soft as satin—she grabbed her iPhone only to find its screen glaringly blank. And even though Fido snored softly over in the corner of the small, dimly lit bedroom, sprawled on his back, legs bent and twitching as he chased rabbits in his dreams, the stark silence of her phone's empty voice mail messages seemed to scream.

Tossing the damp towel she'd been using to dry her hair to the floor, she collapsed onto the edge of the bed and cursed the tears that pricked behind her eyes.

Don't do it, she fiercely scolded herself. *Don't you give in, yet. Don't you give* up, *yet.*

But to her utter humiliation, she couldn't dispel the sense of helplessness, the sense of...*hopelessness* weighing her down like a lead anchor attached to her soul. And, then, as if things weren't bad enough already, a vision of Buzzard in his last moments invaded her consciousness.

So much blood…

There'd been so much *blood*. Everywhere. All over the bar. All over the floor. And even though she'd had a team come in to scrub it away, even though everybody told her there weren't any stains, every time she walked into the place she would swear she could still see it there, dripping from Buzzard's usual stool, falling into a growing pool of red on the floor.

To put it simply, what happened that afternoon… Buzzard's *death*…it haunted her. And even though she'd moved his favorite song into permanent shuffle on the jukebox, even though she'd started serving shots of his customary whiskey at half price, even though she'd had a plaque with his name imbedded into the bar, even though she'd done *everything* she could think of to memorialize him, she was still…*haunted*. Her heart damn near threatening to burst anytime she was caught off guard, like now, with the memory of him.

Would she soon be attending *another* funeral for someone she loved? Someone who'd still be here if not for her? Because no matter how hard she tried to convince herself otherwise, she couldn't shake the idea that none of this would have happened if she'd been tough enough to get her shit together and get back behind the bar where she belonged, instead of using every excuse she could think of to avoid the place…i.e., encouraging her uncle to go on an impromptu road trip. *Jesus*, if not for her cajoling, Uncle Theo wouldn't have taken

Charlie up on his invitation for a visit, and he wouldn't have gotten embroiled in whatever trouble Charlie Sander was obviously involved in.

Throwing herself back on the blue and orange comforter, causing the bed's rusty springs to squawk in complaint, she tossed an arm over her tear-hot eyes. And that's when a strange thundering sound, almost like that of an earthquake, rumbled in her ears. It was immediately followed by the bedroom door flying open with such force the knob stuck solid in the sheetrock. She sprang upright—Fido doing the same, popping from his corner with a sleepy-eyed *yorp*—in time to see Mac lowering his biker boot from where he'd kicked the door open. He charged into the room in a fighter's stance, his big, black Glock up and at the ready. The rest of the Knights piled in behind him, weapon's drawn, faces like death masks in the dim light of the bedside lamp.

"What the hell?" she gasped, a hand clutching her throat.

"You okay?" Mac asked, quartering the room like a…well, like a pro, she supposed.

"Of *course* I'm okay." Although, in all honesty, that was pretty far from the truth.

"We heard a thump," Ozzie explained, holstering his weapon and bending to shake Fido's paw. The dog, never having met a stranger and too silly to recognize the danger of four locked-and-loaded men, had wagged himself over to the group, thinking this was all some sort of hugely fun game. He was sitting and offering his front leg in greeting.

"I…" Delilah had to swallow and try again. "I had this crazy idea when I was showering that Uncle Theo called and left a message." She pointed a finger she was dismayed to note was shaking at the iPhone lying in the middle of the shag carpeting. "When I realized it was all in my head, I got a little…" Hopeless? Infuriated? Dismayed? Frustrated? All of the above? "…disappointed, and I spiked it into the ground."

"What about that groaning sound that followed?" Mac demanded, having shoved his gun into the small of his back and risen from his fighting stance. He crossed his arms over his chest, the gray of his T-shirt hugging his bulging biceps and pulling up just enough to show the bottom links of the barbed wire tattoos inked there. Now normally, she preferred a man when he was all decked out in a biker jacket. There was just something about the way the leather hung on a guy's shoulders. But Mac? Well, suffice it to say, she liked *him* just as he was right now. Dressed in nothing but faded jeans and a too-tight T-shirt that accentuated the width of his chest, the slimness of his waist, and the flat expanse of his washboard belly. Yeah, there was just something about the sheer height and breadth of him that…well…it just *did* it for her. Did it for her *every which way*.

Which just proved how delusional and exhausted she really was. Because the dead last thing she should be concerning herself with right now was the sorry state of her nonexistent sex life.

Still…they had—she bent to retrieve her phone, pushing the power button and checking the time—about an hour before they were scheduled to start knocking on doors. And there *had* been that look on his face back at BKI headquarters when she'd accidently kissed him smack on the mouth, not to mention the honking big

hard-on he'd popped out in the front yard. So maybe…
yeah…maybe she *should* be concerning herself with her
nonexistent sex life. Maybe that's just what she needed
to keep the helplessness and hopelessness from driving
her shithouse crazy for the next hour.

A plan began to take shape…

"Delilah?" Mac asked worriedly. She was wearing a
strange look. Something he couldn't quite put his finger on.

"Huh?" she blinked up at him, her face even more
beautiful scrubbed free of makeup, the deep red high-
lights in her damp auburn hair catching the glow from
the lamp and burning like living fire. And then, *Lord
almighty*, there was that T-shirt. He'd swear it was thin
enough to blow off in a stiff breeze, and it hugged her
curves so lovingly that had she been braless he'd have
been tempted to eat his own ammo.

Of course, the swift kick to his libido was about as
welcome as a porcupine at a nudist colony, because
not only was he *not* changing his mind about getting
involved with That Woman—he *wasn't*—but he also
felt like a complete cad for lusting after her when it was
obvious she was bone-weary. As his dear ol' dad had
liked to say, *she looked like she'd been chewed up, spit
out, and stepped on*.

Poor little gal… Which reminded him…

"We heard groaning," he repeated.

"Oh." She shook her head, as if she needed the physical inducement to rearrange her thoughts. "That…uh…
that was me, too. Just feeling a little beaten down by
the…weight of it all, I guess."

And, yessir, *that* was enough to punch through his tough exterior straight to his soft, gooey center. Taking a deep breath, he gave her the only piece of advice he'd ever found to be one hundred percent true one hundred percent of the time. "Hard times don't last, darlin'. But hard people do. You gotta hang tough."

Her throat made a clicking sound when she swallowed. And, *damn it all*, he hadn't meant to make tears spring to her eyes, but that's just what he'd done.

"I'm…um…I'm going to go make that call to the CIA," Zoelner said, fleeing the scene. The coward.

"I'm going to…uh…feed the dog again," Ozzie said, grabbing Fido's collar and hauling the panting, wagging canine into the hall, proving that he, too, was yellow as mustard.

Mac turned to lift a brow at Steady, wondering what *his* excuse might be. To his utter exasperation, the man didn't even *attempt* to come up with a justification for his departure. He simply made an *oh, shit* face when he saw Delilah's over-bright eyes and turned on his heel, escaping into the hall, slick as a whistle, pulling the door out of the sheetrock and closing it behind him.

All of 'em are worthless as teats on a bull when it comes to a woman's tears, Mac inwardly groused. But when he turned back to Delilah, it was to discover the wetness had miraculously vanished from her eyes. And not only that, but she was stalking—yes, *stalking*; it was the only way to describe that slow, rolling gait of hers— toward him.

He instantly went from feeling sorry for her to feeling like a fly about to get stuck in a glue pot…

Chapter Ten

"WHAT ARE YOU DOIN'?" MAC DEMANDED, ATTEMPTING to don that inscrutable mask of his, but failing to manage it. For one thing, Delilah could read the wary suspicion in the flash of his narrowed eyes, and she could see the muscles in his jaw jerking, causing that adorable dimple in his chin to twitch.

The sight worked on her like a Tom Hardy nude scene, warming her blood, tickling her womb, and making her realize that one: Mac fully clothed was much hotter than Tom Hardy in his birthday suit—imagine *that,* if you will. And two: She was *right* to do this. Because they'd been circling each other like a couple of heavyweight boxers for way too long, and it was way past time for one of them to throw the first punch and see where the match-up would take them.

Besides, what did she have to lose? The one man in the whole world who loved her just as she was had mysteriously flown the coop. And if he didn't come back to her alive then she didn't know—

No. Don't think about that now.

And, okay, so that was sound advice. Because what would happen later, good or bad, would happen later. There was absolutely *nothing* she could do about that. But she could do something about *this.*

So make like Nike, and "just do it." Mmm, hmm. Alrighty then…

"What am I doing?" She cocked a brow, hoping it looked as sexy as it felt. It'd been a hell of a long time since she tried to work her feminine wiles, which meant she was rustier than the springs on Charlie Sander's bed. "I'm finding a way to take my mind off my uncle for the next hour or so," she told him, lowering her chin so she could stare out at him from under her eyebrows. Was it coming off like she wanted it to? Like a look of pure seduction? Or was it more of the creepy/stalkery type of expression?

In all honesty, it was hard to tell. Especially since the big idiot just stood there. Blinking at her. But then, just when she was about to try another tactic...*bingo*! She'd managed to pull off pure seduction after all, because Mac gulped. Like, she seriously heard an audible *gulp* and saw his Adam's apple bob in the long, tan column of his throat. If she'd been a cartoon villain, this is the part where she'd rub her hands together and laugh maniacally.

"H-how were you plannin' to do that?" he managed, uncrossing his arms and glancing behind him like he was considering making a run for it.

She pointed a finger at her face, stopping a mere foot from him. "You know what I'm planning to do. It's written all over my face."

"Sex." Mac said the word like one might say *mucus*— with a bit of a lip-curl. For a brief moment, just one split second, she was taken aback. But then she recognized his act for what it was...

"Yes, *sex*. Or something close to it," she taunted. "And you can drop the uninterested shtick right now, Mr. McMillan." That sounded a little like Marilyn

Monroe saying *Mr. President*, didn't it? Yes, it did. And, *booyah!* "I know you want to."

She lifted a hand, walking her fingers up the breadth of his chest until she could lay her palm over his heart. To her intense satisfaction, the organ was racing at breakneck speed, belying anything he might try to say to contradict her last statement.

Yeah, that's right. I still got it! If it wouldn't have ruined the mood, she'd have pumped a fist.

"Wh-why would you think that?" he asked, blinking rapidly, *breathing* rapidly.

"Because I felt how hard you got when you were lying on top of me."

"That was just…uh…just the adrenaline."

"Bullshit."

He gulped again. "Okay. But you can't expect me to…just…fall into your trap."

"What trap is that?" She loved this feeling of power. Loved that, for the first time in nearly eighteen hours, she could push the panic and fear aside and concentrate on something she might *actually* be able to accomplish. Namely, the bedding of one Bryan "Mac" McMillan…

"Cut the crap," he growled, glancing pointedly at her boobs. "You *know* what trap it is."

She smiled, making sure the expression was a little sly, like a cat watching a canary. "You see something you like, cowboy?" she murmured, moving toward him, putting him to the shark-bump test. You know the one Great Whites use to see if their prey is weak enough to go without a fight?

It worked just as she'd hoped. The instant her hip touched his, he sucked in a breath, his nostrils flaring.

As they stood there, toe-to-toe, heat poured from his big body. It made her realize the air in the room around them was close and cool, but it was his nearness that caused goose bumps to erupt over every inch of her skin. She curled her bare toes into the thick carpet as her nipples furled into tight, deliciously painful buds.

Mac noticed her body's reaction. Even in the dimly lit room, she saw his pupils dilate. And when he licked his lips, those deceivingly soft lips? Well, it took everything she had not to shimmy up his body like an electric worker shimmies up a pole.

"You think men are led around by their dicks, don't you?" he asked. "You think all we want is sex."

"No." She shrugged, watching him narrowly as she inched just a *tiny* bit closer. "I think men want beer and whiskey, too. Pretzels. Football on Monday nights and—"

"Yeah, I get it." He nodded jerkily, rubbing a finger down the length of his wonderfully crooked nose. "We're just a bunch of shallow, two-dimensional creatures, slaves to our most basic desires, and—"

She pressed a finger over his lips. A *zing* of sensation tripped up her spine when his hot breath tickled her skin. "Why are you trying to change the subject?" she asked him. "And why are you fighting this?"

"I'm not fightin' anything," he scoffed, but there was a spark of…was that fear in his eyes?

But, why?

And then it occurred to her that she might be going about this all wrong. That maybe the best way to blow through Mac's thick, prickly barriers wasn't to come at him sledgehammers out and swinging. He was the standoffish sort and this blatant, in-his-face attack might be doing the opposite of what she intended…frightening him into running screaming in the opposite direction. But, what then? How was she supposed to accomplish her task of turning him into putty in her hands?

And then, as if a blast of divine inspiration was breathed into her, she knew. "You're not fighting anything?" She lifted a brow, tapping her finger ever so gently above the heavy beat of his heart, nudging his hip subtly. "So, prove it, cowboy. Because, see, here's the deal. I've got this…this *thing* where I can't stop thinking about you. Thinking about kissing you again on that spectacular mouth of yours."

"You think my mouth is spectacular?" His chin jerked back.

And how cute was that? The man was unaware of just how absolutely delicious he was in every way, shape, and form.

"I do." She nodded. "And if you must know, it's been screwing with my head for about four years now. So, if you're not up for sex or something close to sex, despite that giant length of wood you slung out there in the front yard," now his fabulous lips pulled down at the corners, "then at least do me the favor of kissing me. I mean *really* kissing me, full-on tongueage. That way I can get you out of my system."

There. Deal made. And now the proverbial ball was in Mac's court…

She worried that maybe she'd read him wrong *again* when he swallowed thickly and took a step back, but then something changed in his eyes. His expression became less…*hunted*—okay, so *that* wasn't very flattering— and turned a bit more contemplative. Speculative, even.

She held her breath. One second. Two.

"Just the one kiss?" He slid her a sidelong glance. "Then you'll stop harassin' me? Stop *propositionin'* me?"

She took offense to the "harassment" part of that, but whatever. Now was not the time to quibble over semantics. "Yes," she said and hoped she wasn't struck down by a bolt of lightning on the spot for lying straight through her teeth. "One kiss. That's all."

The seconds stretched out again. One. Two. Three…

"Okay," he finally said.

"Okay?" She slowly puffed the oxygen from her lungs, trying not to smile from ear-to-ear.

"Yes." He nodded. A swath of dark hair fell across his brow. "Go ahead." His voice was so wonderfully low and gravelly. "Kiss me."

"Uh…" She thought the plan had been for *him* to kiss *her*. But again, no time to quibble. "Okay." She nodded, wondering just how best to do this for maximum effect. And then, apparently, she was still filled with that breath of divine inspiration because she *knew*. She'd *tell* him each step before doing it. Build the tension. So when she *did* finally do it, he'd be so worked up that he'd forget the deal was for one kiss only. *Double booyah!*

"So, first I'm…I'm just going to step into you," she whispered. "Just press myself up against you."

"Sounds like," again with the Adam's apple bob, "a decent start."

"And then I'm going to slowly *sssslide*," she said, drawing out the word, "my arms around your neck."

"Okay, then." He nodded jerkily.

"And then I'm going to reach up on my tiptoes and—"

Before she could finish, he grabbed her waist,

pulled her to him with such force that her breath caught, and slammed his mouth over the top of hers.

Oh...heavens...

There were those lips, so unexpectedly soft. Though, the pressure he applied was all man. All about the plundering and conquering. All about proving that *he* was now the one in control. Which, truthfully, was fine by her. Because, really, who was she to argue with him about running the show? Especially when he was doing it so well?

She opened her mouth to the slick press of his tongue, moaning at the taste of him. At some point he'd chewed on a stick of spearmint gum and his breath was fresh and delicious. *Talk about toes curling into the carpet.* Then, when his tongue delved and retreated, delved and retreated in languid exploration of her mouth, she forgot all about her toes or the carpet or anything else for that matter, because her muscles turned to liquid. They just dissolved into mush at the onslaught of lust roaring through her veins. She fancied it was only the fortitude of her bones that kept her from sliding horizontal.

Mmm, horizontal...

That sounded pretty good. *Damn* good, as a matter of fact and she got distracted from thoughts of wrestling him back toward the bed because, right then, he did something magical. He softly caught her tongue between his teeth, simultaneously sucking and flicking the tip with his own before once more plunging into her mouth.

Holy hell, the man can kiss. Not that she was all that surpri—

Whoa. What?

Just as quickly as the kiss began, it ended. One

minute his tongue was rubbing languorously against hers, his big, warm hands spanning her waist, his hard chest cushioning her aching breasts. The next minute he was just…gone. G.O.N.E. Having broken the seal of their lips and taken a step back.

"How was that?" he asked, panting slightly.

"Uhhh." She coughed, pressing a hand to her spinning head. "Good," she managed to croak. "It was good."

"All out of your system?"

She lifted her eyes to his face, gratified to find it flushed with desire. Not even *attempting* to be sly, she let her gaze slide down to his fly. And, sure enough, there it was. Mr. Woody. And, really, who was he trying to kid?

"Out of my system?" she asked incredulously. "Are you insane?"

Without a second thought, she slammed into him, pushing him back until he stumbled over his biker boots. The instant his back hit the wall, she was up on her tiptoes, ravaging his delectable mouth with every-thing she had.

Now who's doing the plundering and conquering, huh?

Damned if Mac wasn't kissing Delilah right back…

He couldn't believe it. And there was a large part of his brain that was screaming, *What the fuck, dude? It was supposed to be one kiss! Just* one *kiss!*

Yessir, a large part of his brain was screaming exactly that. Over and over. But the rest of him? Well the *rest* of him was yelling something else entirely. Something that started with "oh" and ended with "yeah" and had a "hell" thrown in somewhere in the middle.

Which could mean only one thing. He was dumber than dirt. Dumber than a barrel of hair. If brains were leather, his wouldn't be able to saddle a flea...

Shit. And he *knew* there was a reason this was all so *very* dangerous. He *knew* there was something he should be remembering right now. Something important. But the way she was moving against him made it impossible to latch onto a single thought. She was so sinuous, so...*goddamned sexy*. Like a cat. Like a cat with *boobs*. Great, glorious, gorgeous boobs—excuse the alliteration. But *damn*. He could wax poetic about those things for hours on end, compose sonnets to their majesty, write plays exalting their grandeur and—

"Mac," she breathed against his lips, pressing her hips into him softly, suggestively. And when she felt the steely length of his erection pounding against the metal teeth of his zipper, like a honeymooning couple in Texas, she took things over-the-border, thrusting her pelvis forward to rub against him in the most mind-numbing way.

Mind-numbing. Yessir. That was the only way to describe it. Because in that instant, even the fleeting, insubstantial thoughts in his head clenched right along with his nuts. He was no longer in control. He was a beast bent on rutting. Bent on ravaging this woman who'd been driving him crazy for four long years.

He was so hard he hurt. He wanted to pull those tight-ass jeans from her long, silky legs, yank aside the crotch of her panties, and thrust himself into her wet heat in order to satisfy the ache.

Someone growled. Was it him? He couldn't be certain. What he *could* be certain of was that it *was* him who grabbed her waist and spun her around, pressing her back into the wall and shoving his thigh up high and tight between her legs.

Oh, Lord have mercy, sultry...

He could feel her heat even through the double layer of denim. She was so steamy she damn near set him on fire. His dick pounded in appreciation and in a simultaneous bid for freedom from the close confines of his jeans.

"Delilah," he whispered her name, unable to help himself. Unable to stop the hand that skimmed up the edge of that ball-swelling T-shirt as her deliciously agile tongue darted into the depths of his mouth.

The woman was a witch. She'd cast some sort of spell over him with her killer curves and cat-eyed stare, with her soft mouth and mewling little sounds of encouragement. Not that he needed any encouragement, really. Because he was already skating his hand up the smooth skin of her side, reveling in the goose bumps that met his touch, coming to a sudden stop when his thumb brushed the underside of one gorgeous breast.

Delilah tore her mouth away. Mac watched her, watched those beautiful eyes of hers roll back in her head when he cupped her, weighed her. He growled— yeah, that had probably been him earlier, too—in masculine approval as he rubbed his thumb over the crest of her.

Her nipple was tightly furled. He could feel it through the satin of her unadorned pink bra. It pressed against him in wanton abandon. And when he pinched it ever so lightly between his thumb and forefinger, her breath hitched and her eyes flew open. Her irises had darkened a shade in passion, going from fern green to forest green, and the sight was enough to spur him on.

Pulling the cup of her bra down, he lowered his chin and just…looked.

"My God," he whispered, realizing he sounded a bit like a penitent but unable to help himself. He wasn't a religious man. The only deity he'd ever really known was a .45 caliber bullet in a smooth working piece. But one look at her and he became a believer. Because only God could craft something so beautiful. So completely, unequivocally perfect.

She was lush and round, her skin milky white except where her veins showed through, faint and light blue. Her half-dollar-sized nipples with their little pencil-eraser-shaped tips were almost the exact same color as her hair. Dark with a deep blush of fiery red.

"Kiss me, Mac," she breathed, watching him drink in the sight of her. Her hands coming up to tangle in his hair.

Kiss her. She wasn't asking him to kiss her on the mouth. And as much as he *loved* kissing her on the mouth—ycah, *loved*, and he'd have to worry about that later—right then he wanted nothing more than to duck down and suckle her silly. Suckle her until she writhed against him. Suckle her until she begged him to take her.

Again, it occurred to him that there was some reason he shouldn't be doing this. Some reason… But he couldn't catch the fleeting thought. Especially not when saliva pooled hot on his tongue at the same time blood pooled deep in his testicles. His entire body throbbed with every thudding heartbeat, but most of the ache was centered in his cock. He couldn't help himself. He rubbed his burning length against her, against the sultriness of her, trying without success to combat the pain.

"Mac," she pleaded again, wrapping her ankle behind his knee, grinding into him even as he pressed into her. "*Kiss* me. *Please*."

And that was all it took. That breathy *please* falling from the lips of a woman who was usually too proud to beg.

Cursing beneath his breath, he used his forearm to scrape away the stacks of hunting and fishing magazines littering the top of the oak dresser pushed against the wall beside them. He grabbed her hips, hoisting her onto the piece of furniture—her legs immediately wrapped around his waist, just as he'd hoped they would—and dipped his chin to suck the hard bud of her nipple into his mouth.

Sweeter than stolen honey…

That's how she tasted. Her skin was baby soft against his lips, the tip of her breast hot and firm against his tongue. He laved it, flicked it, groaning when she tossed her head back, the ends of her damp hair tickling the bare skin of his arm. She pressed him closer, digging her fingers into his scalp at the same time she dug her heels beneath his butt. The stitches on his side pulled tight. But the pinch of pain was barely registered, because…

Fragrant as a pie supper…

That's how she smelled. That spicy-sweetness filling his nose was unique to her. He didn't know if it was perfume or lotion. But whatever it was, it reminded him of apple cider and vanilla ice cream. Of everything wonderfully all American and deliciously bad for you.

Skimming the backs of his fingers down her stomach,

he noted the quivering of the supple muscles there. They were shaking with desire, trembling with anticipation. The button at the top of her jeans gave way with very little coaxing, and the zipper seemed to slide down of its own accord. His searching fingertips instantly met the lace edge of her panties. The fabric was warm and soft, he noted, just like her skin. But he knew it wasn't nearly as warm and soft as the intimate flesh it was covering.

Lord almighty, how he wanted to touch her there, *needed* to touch her there. Something inside him, something intrinsic and instinctive, made the urge to feel her heat and wetness an unbearable necessity. He was compelled by some invisible force, some millennia-old urgency to sink his fingers into her, to feel the slickness of her bathe his hand and know that it was all for him. That her body's response was the feminine answer to his male hardness.

Dipping his middle finger beneath the edge of lace, a tiny triangle of silky smooth hair welcomed his touch. Then...farther...his fingertip touched the topmost edge of her channel, and just as he'd suspected, her skin was so feverish it nearly burned him, so delicate he could think of nothing more than unbuttoning his own fly and pressing the length of himself into her in order to feel all that satiny, wet flesh close around him.

"Don't stop," she breathed, arching into him, *melting* into him like the snow used to melt in the rain during Texas winters. "Oh, Mac, don't stop."

He had no intention of stopping. He didn't think he *could* stop. It would take a—

"Hey, guys!" The door flew open a split second before, "Oh, hell! Jesus...uh...sorry."

Delilah's decadent nipple popped free of Mac's hungry lips and he yanked his hand from her panties. Jumping in front of her, he shielded her from the view of their most unwelcome arrival. Her elbows bumped into his back as she frantically rearranged her bra and shirt, quickly zipping and buttoning her jeans.

"What the fuck, Ozzie!" he thundered, reaching up to pat his hair. He could feel it sticking up every which way, courtesy of Delilah's exuberant fingers. "Ever heard of knockin'?"

"Sorry…I…" The guy actually appeared flustered—not at all usual for Ozzie. Then, that shit-eating grin split the kid's face. He leaned against the doorjamb, wiggling his eyebrows. "So that whole Pat Benatar, hit-her-with-your-best-shot advice you were spouting out there on the highway was all a bunch of bullshit, eh? I thought so." He nodded sagely.

"What are you talking about?" Delilah asked. "What Pat Benatar advice?"

"It's nothing," Mac said, then hastily added, "What do you want, Ozzie?" He asked the question while glancing over his shoulder at Delilah.

Mistake.

Her lips were moist and swollen from his kisses. Her chin and cheeks slightly pink from the abrasion of his beard stubble. And all he could picture right then was how the rest of her would have looked, so flushed and rosy, if he'd been allowed to finish what he started.

Or had *she* been the one to start it?

Honest to God, he couldn't remember. His recollection surrounding how his lips initially met hers was a little fuzzy. In fact, his thoughts seemed to be flitting around his head like the honeybees used to skim around the meadow flowers on the east pasture back at the Lazy M. But one thing he *was* sure of was that an unpleasant sense of…he supposed he'd label it *doom* had settled in the center of his chest.

He felt as much as saw Delilah hop down from the dresser. And when she skirted around him, his eyes darted down to her jean-clad ass and that little roll of delectable flesh at the tops of her thighs just below the curve of her butt. The sight nearly had him going cross-eyed. Not to mention the fact that the exercise did *nothing* to dissuade Little Mac who was still beating persistently against his zipper.

But then, like a lightning strike from the clear blue, Mac remembered why he should *never* have let things get so far out of hand. Why he should *never* have allowed himself to kiss her. And why he should be falling at Ozzie's feet and thanking the guy for barging in when he did.

Jolene! Jolene, come back!

And, god*damn*it! Where was that recollection ten minutes ago when he needed it? The night when that broken voice yelled out in the dark, and the long string of days that had followed it when he'd mourned so much he thought he'd die? The one time, the *one time,* he could've really used the memory as a good ol'-fashioned kick-in-the-pants, it'd abandoned him.

"I, uh." Ozzie tugged at his ear, still grinning and glancing back and forth between Mac and Delilah. "I wanted to tell you to come downstairs. Because I think Zoelner's about to kill the adorable little CIA agent who just arrived on our doorstep."

Huh? CIA agent? Well *that* was just what the doctor ordered, the perfect prescription to jerk Mac from his troubling thoughts.

The CIA? What the hell *do they want?*

Chapter Eleven

LIFE IS A SERIOUS SHIT SANDWICH SOMETIMES...

That was the thought that flitted through Dagan Zoelner's brain when Chelsea Duvall cocked her head and, with one small finger, pushed her glasses up the length of her nose. Because imagine his surprise when, after escaping downstairs, he dialed her number only to hear the sweet sound of a Dolly Parton ringtone—Chelsea's favorite and don't get him started on *that*—emanating from just beyond the front door. Without a second thought, he'd wrenched open the ruined slab of oak, only to immediately start arguing with her as if it'd been mere moments since they'd last seen each other instead of a handful of years.

And, to top it all off—add the olive to the shit sandwich, if you will—how was it possible to be unaccountably *pissed* and unfathomably *delighted* all at the same time? The state should be a biological impossibility. Unfortunately for him, it wasn't. Because, despite everything, she looked *good*. And it was *good* to see her. Even if her inauspicious arrival set his internal gyroscope twitching.

Taking in the black sedan parked out by the curb, an obvious government issue job, he narrowed his eyes and demanded, "How the hell did you find us?"

She rolled her eyes. "Seriously? You do remember who I work for, right?"

Yes. He remembered. Which made it worse. She

accurately read his expression, because the next words out of her mouth were, "Come on, Z." That low, rusty voice of hers was so familiar it almost felt like a part of him. "I'm just here to help."

Uh-huh. Sure. "You'll excuse me if I call bullshit," he said, crossing his arms, staring down at her as she continued to stand on the threshold of Sander's house.

The early morning light filtered into the decrepit old neighborhood and glinted off her pixie-cut black hair and the warmth of her café au lait–colored skin until it glowed around her like a halo. He wouldn't have been surprised if the heavens opened up with a chorus of angels singing *awwwwww*. Of course, in reality her sudden appearance should've been accompanied by the *dum, dum, dummmm* sound effect of a thickening plot. Because, baby, her being here meant the plot had *definitely* thickened.

"Why is it," she asked, narrowing her copper-colored eyes and mirroring his stance, crossing her arms over her plain white, button-down shirt, the strap of a big, black carryall bag tightening against her shoulder, "that special operations and federal agencies tend to attract a certain kind of man?"

Annnnddddd, here we go. Let me put on my boxing gloves. Because no matter what *else* had changed between them in the years since he'd left The Company, it appeared their tendency toward, not to mention love of, verbal sparring hadn't diminished.

"I'll play," he said, vaguely aware that Ozzie, Mac, and Delilah were tromping down the stairs behind him. "What kind of man is that?"

"A dog. A stubborn, unruly dog that tries to bite the hand reaching out to feed him."

"Nice." He nodded, marking up one point in her favor on his mental scoreboard. "So then what kind of *women* do those fields attract, Miss *CIA Agent*?"

She grinned. The dimples in her cheeks winking at him. "Why, bitches, of course." She uncrossed her arms to give him a shove. When he stumbled back into the house, she followed him inside, allowing the front door to slam behind her. "It's all in the tail-wagging family."

And point number two for the lovely Agent Duvall…

"Uh-huh." He refused to let his eyes dart down to the curve of her ass, hugged so tightly in a pair of black slacks. Chelsea tried to hide her figure behind severe clothes, but with a rack like hers, not to mention that bodacious booty, it was an impossible endeavor. She might be short, probably no more than a couple inches over five feet in Zoelner's estimation, but she had the curves of an Amazon woman. There was a lot of *boom* and *pow* packed onto that tiny frame, and, if you can believe it, he'd once heard her lament being fat.

Fat? Oh, hell no. Well…according to the ridiculousness of today's fashions—skinny jeans and whatnot—perhaps she was a bit…*plump*. But in his humble opinion, that little bit extra she was carrying around meant that she was straight-up, lip-smacking delectation on two legs. The kind of woman men dreamed of sinking into. Soft, warm…

Good to know that *hasn't changed either. Fuckballs…*

"So now tell me why you're *really* here," he demanded, watching her nod to the people who'd gathered around her. His teammates wore various looks of intrigue, consternation, and…um…okay, so Delilah and Mac looked more like cats caught in the cream. And was that pinkness around Delilah's mouth a beard stubble rash? Momentarily distracted, he mentally slapped Mac a high five, silently congratulating the guy on *finally* pulling his head out of his ass. Then Chelsea snagged his attention when she said, "Like I already told you, *I'm here to help*."

"And like *I* already told *you*, that's…survey says? Complete bullshit."

"Wow." She nodded. "With sweet talk like that, it's almost hard to believe you're not married by now, Z."

"Many have tried, babe." He smirked at her. "Many, *many* have tried."

She rolled her eyes and lifted a hand toward Delilah. "Hi," she said, flashing that friendly smile that had been the first thing he noticed about her during a sit-rep— situation report—down in some windowless room at Langley. Well, that, and her amazing rack. "I'm Agent Chelsea Duvall, and you must be the intrepid Delilah Fairchild. It's nice to meet you. I'm so sorry to hear you're short one uncle for the time being, but I'm hoping I can help with that."

"H-hi," Delilah said, making no effort to hide her curiosity as she took Chelsea's hand. And on the introductions went—*What is this? A goddamned tea party?*—until finally Chelsea came to Ozzie. BKI's techno guru grabbed her hand, lifted it to his mouth, and kissed the back of it while wiggling his blond eyebrows at her enticingly.

"Ethan Sykes at your service, ma'am," he murmured like one might say *meet me in bed in two minutes*. "But everyone calls me Ozzie." And, then, apropos of nothing, "You have beautiful eyes. Has anyone ever told you that?"

"Well…" Chelsea raised her free hand to her throat, batting—*yes*, actually *batting*, for God's sakes—her lashes.

Dagan had had enough. "Cut it out, Ozzie," he groused. "And stop slobbering over her hand like it's a medium-rare steak."

"Tsk, tsk," Ozzie said, sliding him a measured glance. "Doth my eyes deceive me? Or is that a little green monster sitting atop your right shoulder, Zoelner?"

And now *Dagan* was the one to find himself in the position of labeling Ozzie's rapier repartee annoying. It was *not* a little green monster. He told the guy as much while avoiding Chelsea's searching glance. "It's a little *red-eyed* monster sitting there. And he's pissed because he doesn't appreciate the giant plate of horse crap Agent Duvall is trying to feed him."

"I beg your pardon," she harrumphed, fisting her hands on her hips, looking for all the world like a bespectacled, pint-sized version of Wonder Woman.

"Beg all you want, Chels," he pointed a finger at her adorable button nose, "but the fact remains when it comes to you CIA types, it's better to find out what the strings are before they're even attached. So, spill. Why are you *really* here?"

"Are you *deaf*?" she huffed. "I've been appointed the CIA's liaison to Black Knights Incorporated. And my supervisor sent me here on a goodwill mission in an effort to assist you in your exemplary work for the president—"

"The president and his Joint Chiefs, yada, yada, yada," Dagan finished the sentence for her. "Yeah. You already played me that tune over the phone. Which is another thing. Where exactly *were* you when you made that call?"

"Huh?" Her smooth black brows crinkled. "What do you mean?"

"I mean, were you in Chicago, New York, DC?"

"I...I was in my apartment in Georgetown," she said, thrusting out her stubborn little chin. The woman could do mulish like nobody's business. Most days, he admired that aspect of her character. Right now, it made him want to put his fist through a wall. Because there was *something* she wasn't telling him. And—*yes, goddamnit*—it *hurt* that she didn't trust him enough to give him the truth.

Will I never *get out from under that catastrofuck in Afghanistan?* His guilt, usually relegated to the recycle bin of his subconscious—except for on the anniversary of that disastrous date—suddenly popped back up to be reused. *Oh, great. As if my day wasn't* already *circling the drain.* But he'd be damned if he'd stand there playing the poor-me card when he could do something more productive. Like, say, raking the ever-exasperating Agent Duvall over the coals.

"And your supervisor flew you here in the middle of the night—a CIA agent who has *no* jurisdiction on U.S. soil—just to find one missing old man?"

"*Two* missing old men," Chelsea corrected. "Because unless I'm mistaken and you've got him tied up down in the basement, Charles Sander is also *persona in absentia*."

"Oooh." Ozzie placed his hand over his heart, stumbling back like he'd just been hit by one of Cupid's arrows. "A woman who speaks Latin. Marry me, Agent Duvall. Marry me right this minute."

"Shut *up*, Ozzie," Dagan thundered when Chelsea

turned to gift Ozzie with another beatific smile. "And before you go getting too flattered, Chels, you should know that he asks everything with breasts and ovaries to marry him."

"Can I butt in here?" Delilah asked, and Zoelner blinked, having momentarily forgotten about the other people standing in the dingy little living room. "*Why* doesn't the CIA have jurisdiction on U.S. soil?"

Dagan opened his mouth to answer, but Mac beat him to the punch. "The Central Intelligence Agency is chartered to work internationally." The former Fed's slow Texas drawl made that last word sound about a hundred miles long. "The FBI is the federal agency that deals with domestic issues."

"Oh." Delilah frowned. "So, then why *is* she here?"

"Exactly!" Dagan threw his hands in the air.

"Look, people," Steady cut in. "I hate to be the one to mention it, but does it really *matter* why she's here?"

"Considering the CIA just *loves* to stovepipe the rest of us?" Dagan replied. "Yeah, I'd say it matters."

"I'm not stovepiping," Chelsea insisted.

"Zoelner's right. It matters if she's stovepiping," Ozzie said in an aside to Steady.

"Even if she *is* stovepiping, her arrival here might be—" Steady began, only to be interrupted by Chelsea yelling, "I'm *not* stovepiping!"

"What the heck is stovepiping?" Delilah asked, and all heads turned toward her. The room was so filled with tension at that point that Dagan felt like he was defusing a bomb. Defusing a bomb while being chased by a psycho killer and running through a minefield filled with hungry lions...

Yeah, that about covered it.

Mac, still managing composure despite the volatile atmosphere, supplied helpfully, "It's when one agency doesn't help the other because they're stingy when it comes to their Intel."

"I'm *not* stovepiping," Chelsea repeated sullenly.

"I don't believe you." Dagan scowled down at her, narrowing his eyes when the slightest wash of pink tinged her cheeks. "Aha!" He pointed at her, but before he could say anything more, Steady stepped in again.

"Whether you believe her or not is inconsequential, *hermano*, because, the fact remains we were going to call for her help anyway, so—"

"You were?" Chelsea grinned at Dagan, one victorious brow raised.

"Just for access to the infrared on Eyes in the Sky," he admitted irritably.

"Well, *why* didn't you say so?" She slung the black carryall around in front of her to dig out an iPad. Punching the button on the Bluetooth device hooked around her ear, she simultaneously sat on the arm of the couch and started issuing commands to whomever was on the other end of the line. "So, what do you need?" she asked as she powered up the iPad.

"We need heat scans of the entire town," Ozzie told her. "We're hoping to go door-to-door to ask if anyone has seen Charles or Theo, and that exercise would go much more quickly if we actually knew which houses were occupied."

Had *everyone* lost their friggin' minds? They were just going to ignore the ten-ton elephant—aptly named Chelsea's Bizarre Appearance—that was tap dancing over there in the corner? Because why in the world would—

"Dagan?" When she used his given name, he realized two things. First, it made his skin prickle. And next, it was the second time she'd tried to get his attention.

"What?" he demanded, feeling as if his head should be spinning around atop his shoulders à la Linda Blair in *The Exorcist*. *See*…Ozzie wasn't the only one quick with the horror movie references…

"I asked if there was a specific grid you'd like me to start with," she said, frowning up at him. "My technician," she pointed to her earpiece, "is telling me it'll take about two minutes to reroute the satellite and begin uploading the scans."

"Tell him to start with downtown and make his way back toward our current location," he said, irked that she'd somehow managed to take over the situation without first coming clean about her mysterious arrival. Diversion and avoidance. Yeah, he'd learned that pretty little trick in spy school, too.

Chelsea relayed the information, simultaneously tapping on her iPad. Then she grinned up at him. "Has anyone ever told you when you get pissed, your voice gets all raspy? I can't imagine how you handled that out in the field. It's a tell that—"

"And has anyone ever told you that your observations are about as welcome as an itchy asshole," he cut her off.

"Yeesh." She suppressed a grin. "You'd be the first."

"And don't think just because I'm agreeing to your help right now that it means I'm swallowing that load of hogwash you're dishing."

"First it was horse crap and now it's hogwash?" She

wrinkled her nose. He did *not* make note of how cute it was. "None of that is very appetizing, is it?"

"I mean it. The minute we find Delilah's uncle," he pointed a finger at her, "I'm going to be all over your ass like a bad rash until you come clean with whatever it is you're hiding from me."

"A bad rash, huh? I've heard calamine lotion works wonders for that."

"I'm dead serious," he warned.

"Ooh." She shivered dramatically. "I love it when you bring out the sound and fury."

"Oh, shut up."

"Spoken like a true scholar."

He scowled down at her. She grinned up at him. And the Black Knights appeared to have been stunned into silence. The air around them vibrated like a yawning black hole of complete conversational failure. Then Chelsea's iPad dinged and a set of real-time infrared scans appeared on her screen.

The Knights gathered around her as the first image took shape and Mac leaned in close, whispering, "Well, I tell you one thing, she's got some snap in her garters."

Yeah, Dagan thought uncharitably, that's *one* way of putting it. *Another* way of putting it would be to say she was a serious pain in the ass.

———

The Knights were eyeing the CIA agent with differing levels of curiosity and suspicion, and Delilah had to admit that Chelsea Duvall was not what she imagined in a government spook. Short, slightly plump, and adorably cute with her mixed heritage and smattering of freckles, Chelsea looked more like she should be teaching kindergarteners their ABCs and 123s and less like she should be chasing bad guys around the globe.

Then again, perhaps that was the whole point. A spy wasn't supposed to *look* like a spy, right?

Mac's knuckles brushed the back of her hand when he stepped up to get a closer look at the screen on Chelsea's iPad, and Delilah would swear she felt the touch somewhere much more intimate. A slight shiver convulsed her muscles, and she just barely held back a gasp as she glanced into his big, square, unfairly attractive face.

Oh, goody-goody-gumdrops. So the Mask of Inscrutability has returned!

And how he could manage to look completely unfazed when mere minutes ago he'd been sucking her nipple and grinding the hard, hot length of his erection against her she'd never know. For her part, she couldn't seem to come down from the high. Her body was still piano-wire tight, the blood rushing through her veins as sharp and warm as the hot toddies she liked to serve when a nor'easter blew through Chicago.

She now knew what it meant when those historical romance novels she liked to read claimed the heroes "ravaged" the heroines. Because, really, considering the way Mac had held her, stroked her, kissed her, tongued her, there was no other way to describe it. And if she was going to call it a ravaging, then she also had to call Mac completely, deliciously beastly. He'd been growling and groaning and—*for the love of tequila*—to say it'd been hot would be like calling lukewarm bathwater hot. Because enigmatic, self-disciplined, Bryan "Mac" McMillan losing control of those reins he usually kept such a tight hold on had been way *beyond* hot. It'd been volcano-hot, surface-of-Mercury-hot, exploding-star-hot. So hot she was still feeling singed, and he was...

Well, he was ignoring her and watching the CIA agent's screen with concerted interest.

Ugh. She didn't know if she should be depressed or *im*pressed.

"*Yorp!*" Fido sang from his position by the back door, wagging his tail enthusiastically. Obviously, he had no interest in what Agent Duvall was showing them, and Delilah sort of envied the big yellow dog. How nice would it be to have no worries except for when your next meal or game of fetch would be?

Then again, that wasn't necessarily true. Because poor, sweet Fido had lost his master as surely as she'd lost her uncle. And, okay, so that was *one* way to take the edge off the lust still zinging through her system. Thoughts of Uncle Theo...

"Check that out," Ozzie said, pointing a finger at the screen. "Why are there four people in that building downtown?"

Delilah couldn't help herself, she moved in closer so she, too, could see what Ozzie was motioning toward. To her utter consternation, she couldn't understand the information on the agent's iPad. It just looked like vague gray outlines in a series of geometric shapes with four green dots moving around inside one of them.

"Squatters?" Mac supplied. "Or kids in there havin' a toke?" When her arm brushed against his, he took a small step back. She glanced up at his face and was rewarded for her effort with an expression that was no longer the Mask of Inscrutability. That was the good news. The bad news? Well, now he'd reverted back to his second most favorite look. Disapproval.

Oh, you've got *be kidding me!* Her feelings must've been evident on her face because disapproval quickly morphed into dismissal.

Wahoo! We're three for three, folks! And, oooh, where was a rock when she needed one? Something small and hard that she could zing toward his stubborn head? Just *whack!* Knock some sense into him with one blow. She was stopped from glancing around the room in search of a serviceable item when Ozzie replied, "Mmm. Yeah, you're probably right. Ask for the next scan, Agent Duvall."

Chelsea repeated the request into her Bluetooth device, and the screen dissolved to black a second before another image appeared.

"*Yorp! Yorp!*" Fido caught sight of his own wagging tail and decided to chase it.

"That dog is a wonder of stupidity," Mac observed.

"*Yorp! Yorp!*"

"Oh, for Christ's sake." Irritation was evident in his tone. "Delilah, will you let the damned dog out so he'll stop makin' that racket?"

A part of her—a larger part than she'd like to admit—wanted to tell him to take his orders and shove them somewhere extremely uncomfortable. She deserved to stay here and look at these scans just as much as *they* did. It was *her* uncle they were looking for, after all. At least that's what the petulant, ego-sore, just-got-summarily-rejected-by-way-of-a-glance woman in her wanted to shout. But then logic, that little *bastard*, intervened and reminded her that for one thing, she didn't know what the heck she was looking at. And for another thing, they *were* here helping her, so a little patience and forbearance, not to mention cooperation, on her part wasn't too much to ask.

"Fine," she hissed before spinning on her heel. She marched through the kitchen toward the back door, and all along the way, beneath her breath, she called Mac unsavory—if somewhat creative—names. Her favorite was *booby-licking, jerk-faced bastard*. But *shit-talking, lug-headed butt-monkey* came in a close second.

"*Yorp! Yorp! Yorpyorpyorp!*" Fido sang happily, spinning in delight upon her arrival.

"Okay, okay," she soothed as her shins took a beating from his tail. She bent to grab hold of the thick, whip-like monstrosity lest she need a set of crutches, and Fido took this to be a wonderful new game. He nipped at her fingers playfully, stepping on her bare toes.

"Geez, you're a menace," she laughed when he panted up at her happily.

"*Yorp!*"

"Yes, you are," she crooned, unable to stop herself from using that sing-songy voice. "You're just a big ol' pain in the patoot, you know that?"

"*Yorp!*"

"Delilah! Goddamnit!" Mac thundered from the living room. "We can't hear ourselves think!"

Turning, she placed her hands on her hips and made the supremely wise decision to stick her tongue out at him. His adorably dimpled chin jerked back. Then he blinked and shook his head in exasperation.

Yeah, okay. So, that wasn't necessarily my smooth-est move. But, goddamnit! He irritated and confused the hell out of her, all while making her so hot under the collar she couldn't think straight.

Sighing dejectedly, she pushed the back door open and watched Fido shoot out of the house like a rocket. The yellow dog launched himself from the top of the steps, barking excitedly all the while.

Daring one final glance over her shoulder, she was amazed to discover Mac's eyes *not* on the iPad screen as she'd expected, but instead glued to her butt. When his gaze jumped to her face, she curled her lips in a grin that was the facial equivalent of *caught ya!* Feeling instantly better, she followed Fido into the yard…

Chapter Twelve

"WHO'S A GOOD BOY?" DELILAH CALLED TO FIDO, skipping down the three steps leading from the back porch to the fenced-in yard. The hungry look on Mac's face when she busted him ogling her booty was clear in her mind's eye. And, considering everything she was dealing with right now, it made her unaccountably happy.

She did a little victory dance complete with a hip shake and finger snaps while watching Fido thunder down the long expanse of lawn—Delilah would bet it was thirty yards if it was an inch. He latched on to something behind the whitewashed doghouse near the back fence. She could see his furry butt protruding from the little structure, his hind legs bent forward as he growled and tried to wrestle out whatever he'd found.

"Ow!" she cursed as she stepped onto the lawn, lamenting the fact that she hadn't taken the time to put on her biker boots when the sharp blades of dry grass poked into the soles of her bare feet. Hopping over to a patch of dirt, she called out, "What is it, boy? What've you got?"

Oh, and brilliant. What did she expect? The dog to stand up and start talking? *Sheesh*. She glanced around, glad for once that the neighborhood was empty as the proverbial drum. "*Grrrr! Yorp!*" Fido intensified his struggle, his back legs scrabbling against the dry lawn, kicking up little puffs of brown dust.

Please don't let it be a squirrel or a rabbit, she

thought as she once again hopped from her relatively
safe patch of dirt onto the needle-like lawn. She may
be the ass-kicking, Harley-riding, shotgun-toting beer-
slinger-from-hell, but she was also a big softie when it
came to fuzzy things. She didn't know what she'd do if
Fido was mauling something—

Uh, was that a shoe clamped between Fido's jaws?
She broke into a run, uncaring now about the blades
of grass stabbing into her feet. She drew closer. Ten
yards. Twenty.

Yes, yes, that's definitely a shoe.

For a moment, she thought perhaps she'd found the
infamous pot-growing Charlie Sander. Maybe Mac had
been wrong. Maybe the guy hadn't been attacked and
dragged from his kitchen but instead had a heart attack
out here in the backyard. But, then...no. Because she
thought she recognized that shoe, or boot, actually. It
was a brown Timberland and—

"*Arp!*" She saw the blade on the big hunting knife
flash in the rays of the rising sun and could do nothing
but watch helplessly as it imbedded itself into Fido's furry
chest. She stumbled back when the dog's yelp of pain and
confusion echoed in her ears, a scream of gut-wrenching
anguish building like a tidal wave at the back her throat.
She opened her mouth to let it loose, but in that instant the
dark-skinned man launched himself at her, hands curled
into claws, an ugly snarl plastered on his face.

Oomph! All the air exploded from her lungs when
his weight slammed her to the ground. *Bam!* Her head
bounced against the dirt and grass, stunning her, making
her ears buzz and her vision narrow until it appeared as
if she was stuck inside a dark tunnel.

It was a strange thing, but during that moment when she lay still, unable to move, unable to draw breath, unable to think, she noticed the sky above her was pink and purple and orange. The rays of the early morning sun glinted off the clouds in a brilliant display at the end of the dark shaft that was her vision. Then, seemingly from a place very far away, a hand came up to cover her mouth, just as it had the first time.

The first time…

In an instant, the ol' cerebral cortex jump-started its synapses and her muscles immediately came to life. She wriggled and writhed, bucked and heaved, trying to scramble out from under the unbearable weight pressing her into the yard. But nothing she did seemed to dislodge her attacker.

She couldn't believe it. She couldn't believe her would-be abductor had followed her here. To this place. And he was going to try to take her. *Again!*

Oh, hell no!

Even as her mind raced with questions—*Who is he? Why is he here? Is he just after me, or is he mixed up in Uncle Theo's disappearance? What does he want?*—she fought with everything she had, opening her mouth to try to bite at the hand. But it was to no avail. And, inexplicably, no matter how hard she punched and kicked and tossed about, she couldn't unseat her assailant. And then he placed an arm against her throat. Instantly, her brain became starved for oxygen. Her movements began to feel sluggish, weighted, as if her limbs were no longer her own…

She tried to shake her head, to jolt loose the hand over her mouth, but all she managed to do was to turn her chin.

It was overtaking her now. The darkness. The empti-
ness. She struggled to drag in a breath as her bleary gaze
alighted on Fido, lying on his side. The dog's wonderful
brown eyes were bright with misery and bewilderment,
his tongue hanging out as he panted in what had to be
his death throes.

I'm so sorry, she thought, watching Fido's bright
red blood leak from around the blade of the knife still
imbedded in his chest, matting his fur and staining the
grass beneath him. *This is all my fault. I brought this
man here. And I'm so, so sorry.*

Even terribly injured, the brave dog sensed her desperation and attempted to drag himself closer. But it was
too much. Every move resulted in a loud, soul-tearing
yelp that rang sharply in her ears and felt like a hatchet
strike to her heart. Hot tears burned up the back of her
throat, pouring from her darkening eyes to slide across
her cheek and nose and drip into the earth beneath her.

Shhh, shhh, she wanted to tell Fido. *Don't fight it.
You're a good boy. Be still. Be quiet…*

But death wasn't something a body—be it man's
or beast's—did gracefully. It struggled and strained
against the inevitable end with everything it had. She
should know. This wasn't the first time she'd seen the
specter of the Great Beyond hovering close. The blood.
The fear. The all-out battle to draw one last, shuddering
breath of life. It'd happened before…

*Just like with Buzzard. Just like…had it been this way
for Uncle Theo? Will it be this way with me?*

The thoughts whispered through her sluggish mind
as white stars danced before her eyes. Her under-
oxygenated brain begged her to draw a breath. Her chest

burned like she'd swallowed a box of fireworks. But she blinked off the encroaching darkness, holding on a second longer. If she could just hold on a second longer…

Locking gazes with poor Fido, she wanted nothing more than to take the dog's agony and anguish and confusion into herself. To reach out to him and offer him comfort in these last miserable moments. And maybe she could. Maybe if she could just reach—

Letting go of her assailant, she strained toward the whimpering, suffering animal with one arm, her fingers outstretched, her diaphragm quaking with her muffled sobs and her body's intense desire to suck in a huge, glorious lungful of oxygen.

Please, God! Let me help him! Let me touch him!

But her prayer went unanswered. The big yellow dog was too far away. Too far away, and she was fading now. Her vision dimmed to nothing more than faint, barely intelligible shadows. And, then, to her astonishment, the dying canine dragged himself forward another inch, enough to allow her fingertips to reach the soft pad of his nose. As her eyes rolled back in her head, she gently rubbed that warm, dry nose, giving what small measure of peace she could until the darkness consumed her…

———

"Okay. Bring up the next one," Ozzie said as they all watched the screen on the CIA agent's iPad fade to black while the satellite changed the angle of its lens. Mac was more than happy to let the boy wonder take the lead in this particular endeavor. Ozzie *was* the most qualified among them, after all. And *someone* needed to keep an eye on Agent Duvall's keystrokes. You know, make sure she wasn't feeding them a big bunch of hooey for…whatever reason.

Because talk about something…er…some*one* to make Mac's Spidey sense jump up and down while waving semaphore flags. Zoelner was right. Chelsea Duvall wasn't here out of the goodness of the CIA's black heart. Something more was going on. Something she was refusing to tell them. But whether it had anything to do with the disappearance of Charles and Theo, or if it was just The Company's way of keeping tabs on the Knights themselves, Mac didn't know.

"Jesus. This place is even more deserted than I thought," Ozzie murmured, implying with a rolling finger that Agent Duvall should ask for the next scan.

And Ozzie wasn't kidding. Besides the four heat signatures in the building on Main Street, only two other houses in the entire town appeared to be occupied. And both were clear on the other side of the municipality. Meaning it was a pretty sure bet that even if Theo *had* made it here to visit Charles, those folks wouldn't have been close enough to hear the big engine on his Harley and make note of it.

Shit. This was turning into a classic case of not having a pot to piss in or a window to throw it out of. And it certainly wasn't the news he'd hoped to offer Delilah.

Delilah…

The look she'd given him a minute ago when he skedaddled away from her touch would've made a hornet look cuddly. Seriously, if looks could kill he'd be checking into the Wooden Waldorf, planted in the fossil farm, and pushing up daisies. But could he blame the gal?

For the love of Christ, no. Because even though the thought of him being a tease sat about as well as a raw catfish dinner, he had to admit that that's exactly what he was. A tease with a capital *T*. A tease in the classic sense of the word. Hot one minute, cold the next. Beckoning her closer with one hand while pushing her away with the other.

It had to be confusing as hell…

And the good Lord knew she didn't deserve it. After all, she couldn't see the future laid out before them the way *he* could. She didn't know about the history he refused to see repeated… Of course, what she deserved and didn't deserve would have to play second fiddle to him figuring out how in the world he was ever going to go back to the man he'd been before that little scene upstairs. The man who could resist her come-on-cowboy looks and blatant propositions.

She said she'd lay off if you gave her one kiss, he reminded himself. But that was all a big, smelly pile of cow manure—and he should know; he'd dealt with his fair share. Because she'd gone back on that deal almost as soon as she'd made it.

Boy howdy, did she ever. He could still feel the strength of her fingers digging into his hair. Still taste the sweetness of her tongue as she kissed him to within an inch of his life. Yep, she'd reneged on the deal faster than a bee-stung stallion out of the gate. And now here he was…sporting half a hard-on and having to curl his hands into fists lest he use them to reach out and strangle someone.

He'd prefer it was *her* neck he wrapped his fingers around. Unfortunately, not only was she absent from the room, but throttling her meant he'd also be *touching* her again. And he knew what sort of tomfuckery *that* led to. For shit's sake, this situation right here was the whole reason the term *FUBAR* came into being.

"And there *we* are," Steady said, diverting Mac's attention from his unsavory thoughts. The image had finally rendered, displaying Charles Sander's house, as well as the houses around it in a one-block radius. The five of them, huddled together so tightly, showed up as one giant green blob. Two more fluorescent dots of heat appeared in the backyard, Delilah's signature about twice the size of Fido's. Other than that, the block was empty of life.

So what else is new, Mac thought ill-temperedly. And, okay, the truth was, despite his pseudo ire at Delilah's blatant lie when it came to that whole one-kiss-only business, he desperately wanted to help her locate her uncle. Because, *damnit*, not only did he like Theo, but he also liked *her*. Liked her spunk and grit. Liked her sultry laugh and easy smile. And despite the fact that he couldn't give her what she was asking for in terms of them sharing some sort of relationship, the idea of being a hero for her was more than a mildly satisfying concept.

There. He admitted it.

Of course, admitting he liked her and craved playing the part of her knight in shining armor—or Black Knight in shining armor; yeah, he could be corny occasionally—didn't change anything. So, then where did that leave—

"Okay," Ozzie sighed, disappointment evident in his tone. Obviously, he was coming to the same conclusion that Mac had already reached. Simply put, going

door-to-door in Cairo would be a useless endeavor.
"Let's keep moving. Bring up the next scan."

But just as the image on the iPad screen began to
fade, something strange happened. The dot that was
Delilah separated into two distinct blotches. And it was
like the Grim Reaper himself scraped a broken nail up
the length of Mac's spine.

"What the hell?" Zoelner said, but Mac was already
in motion, hurtling the coffee table and knocking over a
kitchen chair in his mad dash toward the back door. Had
he thought it possible, he'd have left a Mac-shaped hole
through the sucker—just Supermanned his way right
through it—but instead he skidded to a stop, yanking
the slab of warped oak open.

The scene that met his eyes was enough to stop his
thundering heart. A dark-haired man was busy heaving
a limp Delilah into his arms. And Fido, the poor beast,
was bleeding from a wound to his chest while valiantly
trying to drag himself closer to the man's boots.

Boots…

Timberlands…

Delilah's mystery man? *What the hell?*

Mac's Glock was in his hand before he made the
conscious decision to reach for it. "Halt!" he yelled,
pointing his weapon at Mr. Timberlands' back. "Or
I'll shoot!"

Had he had a *clean* shot, he'd have gone ahead with it
without giving Mr. Timberlands a warning. But Delilah's
slack form pressed all along the man's front prohibited
him from squeezing the trigger. He couldn't chance his
bullet slicing through the guy and entering her.

Timberlands swung around, his eyes bugging out of

his head like a horny toad trying to shit a chicken bone when he saw Mac drawing down on him. Delilah hung limply in his arms, her head dangling until her fiery hair obscured her face, the red-painted tips of her toes barely touching the grass. Mr. Timberlands held the length of a bloody knife to her throat.

Blood...

Delilah's blood?

Mac's pulse roared between his ears, his scalp on fire and feeling as if it was trying to crawl off his skull. But, no. Save for the few crimson drops that had fallen from the knife to stain her pink T-shirt, she appeared unscathed. *Unconscious*—which was bad enough—but otherwise unscathed.

He drew in a shaky breath and whispered a quick prayer of thanks as he tracked the guy's every move down the length of his Glock's sights. His finger was on the trigger, ready to pump out lead the very moment he got the opportunity.

"Holy crap on a cracker," Ozzie murmured, dropping down to one knee beside Mac, his handgun up and aimed. Steady and Zoelner quickly took up positions on his other side, weapons out and at the ready.

"I need satellite surveillance on my location *now*," Agent Duvall barked into her Bluetooth. She was standing behind Mac, turkey-peeking around his back at Timberlands. "A suspect is in sight and attempting to abduct Delilah Fairchild. I need facial recognition, ASAP. Who is he?"

Mac didn't give a flying fuck who the guy was. All he cared about was introducing him to the full measure of BKI meanness. Just as soon as he had a clean shot, the dude was dead. Dead as in dead. Dead as in six feet under, dirt-nap dead.

"You shoot me," Mr. Timberlands called, his accent thick, "and you might hit the woman!" The man was slowly scooting the last few feet toward the open gate at the rear of the yard.

"Anybody have a clean shot?" Mac asked from the corner of his mouth.

"No."

"Negative."

"Wish I did," were the responses he received. *Shit, shit,* shit.

Okay. And like any good card player, Mac knew when it was time to bluff. "I'm a better shot than you think," he yelled. And in all honesty, he *was* good. All the Black Knights were. But regardless of what people saw on TV and the movies, trying to hit a moving target from thirty yards away wasn't as easy as it looked. In that split-second from the time he squeezed the trigger until the bullet found its mark, Mr. Timberlands could jerk or move just an inch or two and Delilah could end up hit. Of course, it was always possible Timberlands didn't know that. "Now either I can put a hole clean through the center of your forehead, or we can skip the bloodstains and you can drop the woman! Dealer's choice!"

"If you thought you could do it," the guy called, nearly to the gate, "you would have done it already."

And, *goddamnit*. So they weren't dealing with a man a few bricks shy of a full load here. *Talk about dumb luck*. What were the odds this criminal, whoever he was, would have some brains in him?

Mac flicked his gaze to the right, to the left, wondering how in the world this standoff would end. Maybe if he started closing the distance, he could distract the man while the Knights moved in to flank him. Maybe if he—

But then something amazing happened. Fido lunged forward with a mighty heave and sunk his teeth into Mr. Timberlands' ankle. It was enough to distract the guy into losing his hold on Delilah. She slid down his front, just a bit, but it gave Mac the advantage he needed.

In the blink of an eye, his heart slowed, his vision sharpened, his muscles relaxed, and on a silent exhale he applied three pounds of pressure to the Glock's trigger. The *boom* was deafening in the close confines of the back porch, but he barely noticed it, too busy jumping from the top step to the yard below.

His bullet nicked Mr. Timberlands' upper shoulder, and Mac landed on the lawn in time to witness the force of the round's impact spin the guy like a top. He dropped Delilah in the process, and she crumpled to the ground like a rag doll, arms and legs akimbo. The moment she was free and clear, Mac let loose with all his fear and fury.

"Halt, you motherfucker!" he roared, welcoming the burn of his thighs as his long strides ate up the distance. But, Mr. Timberlands didn't heed his warning. The man managed to regain his balance, and, turning on his heel, fled.

Chapter Thirteen

BOOM! MAC SQUEEZED HIS TRIGGER AGAIN. THIS TIME his shot flew wide, slamming into the fence, shattering one brittle length of wood into a hundred splinters. A flurry of gunfire rang out behind him, the BKI boys joining the party. And though the fence line was instantly blown to smithereens, reduced to matchsticks in some parts, Mr. Timberlands serpentined his way the last few steps and managed to miraculously slip through the gate.

"Get him!" Mac yelled as his legs churned over those last few yards. He might be slow with his words, but, by God, he was fast on his feet. Then, in a move any MLB player would envy, he slid across the final distance, ending up on his side before throwing his body over Delilah's inert form. If there was more gunplay, he needed to make sure she wasn't hit by a stray bullet or flying fence debris. But to his utter dismay, not one additional shot echoed out over the abandoned neighborhood. Which meant the Knights didn't have a clear bead on Delilah's assailant. *Sonofa—*

He could hear them charging toward him, but he didn't dare raise his head until he felt them draw near. Zoelner flew past him first, boots pounding, arms pumping. Ozzie was right on his heels, pistol locked and loaded, up and ready to fire. When Steady pulled even, Mac reached out and snagged his foot.

"*La madre que te parió!*" Steady bellowed in Spanish as he tripped, arms flailing, legs pinwheeling before his quick, operator reflexes kicked in and he righted himself.

"The dog." Mac pointed to the animal, lying on its side no more than two feet away, its panting breaths fanning the dirt of the yard. "He may've just saved her life. Now you have to try to save his."

Steady gulped as he looked down at the dog, his expression pitying. Then he nodded and knelt beside the animal.

Carefully, Mac pushed into a seated position, tucking his Glock into his waistband as he gathered Delilah in his lap. She was so still. So pale.

"Delilah." He gently tapped a finger against her satiny cheek, taking comfort in its warmth. "Darlin'…you need to wake up, now."

Nothing. Not one move. Not one whimper. His heart hammered hollowly against his ribs.

Letting his gaze slip down to her throat, he noted with intense satisfaction that her pulse was hammering there, and when his eyes slid farther down, to her chest, he wanted to crow with victory when he saw it rise on a shallow breath. *Come on, darlin'. You can do it. Wake up.*

"*Hijo de puta,*" Steady cursed, whipping off his shirt to press it to the wound in Fido's chest. "I don't know dick about canine physiology, Mac."

"Just do your best," he said, softly rocking the woman in his arms, murmuring to her as he continued to caress her dirty cheek.

And you know that soft, gooey center of his? Well, it was melting like a Hershey's bar left out in the summer

sun. Because not only was he witnessing what were probably the last moments of one very valiant dog—was that a
goddamn tear in his eye?—but seeing Delilah like this…
so limp, so quiet…was like watching a raging inferno
sputter and die. All that fiery energy was just…gone.

He ran his hand over her head, trying to feel for
bumps or for the warm wetness of blood. Had Mr.
Timberlands hit her with something? With the hilt of
his knife, perhaps? Was her brain even now swelling
inside the confines of her skull, causing her to slip into a
coma? But his searching fingers found nothing, nothing
to account for the fact that she was still out cold. *Dear
God, I promise you that if you let her—*

His prayer was cut off when her pale lids fluttered
open, her green eyes dazed and disoriented. "M-Mac?"
she whispered in confusion.

And, sweet Lord almighty, had he ever heard anything more wonderful than his name on her lips? If so,
he couldn't remember. "Yeah, darlin'. I'm here."

When her gaze finally focused on his face, she slowly
reached up to touch the dimple in his chin, the pad of
her finger cool against his skin. She smiled bemusedly
before her lips curved down in a frown. "Th-the man
from Uncle Theo's house…he's here. H-he s-strangled
me, and—" Strangled? The sonofabitch had probably
cut off the blood supply in her carotid artery. It was a
dangerous maneuver. Done incorrectly, it could end in
death. The hairs on Mac's arm lifted at the thought. "I
think he—"

"Shh," he soothed, brushing a lock of auburn hair
from her forehead—noting how soft and silky it was.
"I know."

She swallowed, blinking in consternation. Then her expression changed, becoming alarmed. "Wh—" was all he managed before she sat up so fast the top of her head clocked him under the chin. His jaws slammed together and it was a wonder his back molars didn't crack. "Ow! Sonofa—"

"Fido!" she screamed, scrambling from his lap in such an all-fired hurry that her hip smashed his nuts into the ground.

"Oomph!" He cupped himself and barely managed to keep from crumpling sideways. The pain shot up from his testicles to radiate out to all parts of his body. He broke out in an instant sweat, his stomach doing flips like it was auditioning for a trapeze act in the circus that used to roll through town when he was a boy. And he really feared he was two seconds away from hurling chunks…

Of course, he felt like a complete wuss when Delilah—barely having regained consciousness—scrambled over to Steady and Fido, holding a hand to her obviously spinning head, and asking, "Wh-what do I do? How do I help?"

Damn, she sure is something, he thought, only slightly distracted by the agony in his balls when his chest swelled with…what was that exactly? Pride, maybe? And, yessir, since he was in the admitting mood today, he'd go ahead and admit that he was good and goddamned proud to know her. This strong, independent woman. This paragon of wonderful, exasperating, disturbing bullheadedness. And sometimes, like now, he wished things could be different. He wished he didn't know what he knew because, *damn*, he was sure tempted to take her for a ride. To let their relationship just play out until its inevitable, disastrous end. But, unfortunately, he *did* know how things would turn out. And that meant he also knew that the short-term pleasure wasn't worth the long-term pain.

"Hold this!" Steady instructed, and Mac watched him press her hand to the T-shirt wadded against Fido's chest. "I have to run and get my medical bag."

Mac managed to cowboy-up and drag himself over to Delilah and the dog a second or two after Steady beat feet toward the house. Letting go of his throbbing nads, he helped her apply pressure to the wound and used his other hand to softly stroke Fido's big, block head.

"You're a good boy," Delilah whispered over and over again, uncaring of the tears trickling down her cheeks, leaving dirty trails in the dust covering her face. Fido whined pitifully, but the tip of his tail wagged despite the terrible pain he was in. And, sure as shit, that *was* a tear in Mac's eye. *Damnit!*

The Lab reminded him of his father's old ranch dog. Dutch had been his name. And he'd studiously kept the coyotes away from Lazy M cattle for fifteen long years. He'd been a big, rangy canine just like Fido here. But where Fido was happy-go-lucky, Dutch had been about as friendly as a bramble bush. Still, there was nothing quite so satisfying as owning a good dog. And nothing quite so heartbreaking as watching a good dog die.

"Wh-what happened?" Delilah asked, her eyes wide when she glanced up at him. "Where'd he go?"

And Mac knew she was asking about Mr. Timberlands.

"Don't you worry about it," he told her. "Zoelner and

Ozzie have gone after him." Though, the longer the minutes stretched out with no sound to break the stillness of the neighborhood, the more concerned he became. The only reason the BKI boys would be in stealth mode was if they'd lost the guy and were now quietly hunting him.

"Give me your keys!" he heard Steady demand and looked up in time to see him standing in the middle of the yard, holding a hand toward Agent Duvall. Mac had forgotten all about her. "If I can get the dog's bleeding stopped," Steady lifted the medical bag gripped tight in his other fist, "he might just make it to the closest vet. But I'm gonna need your car."

Chelsea nodded and dug into the hip pocket of her slacks, all the while barking instructions into her earpiece and never taking her eyes off the screen of her iPad. After retrieving a key ring and tossing it to Steady, she jogged with him toward Mac and Delilah and the injured dog.

"Okay," Steady said, dropping down beside them. He reached into his camo duffel bag and came out with a pack of QuikClot. "Now when I say *go*, I want you guys to remove my shirt and hold the dog down. When I shake this shit into his wound, it's gonna burn like hell."

Mac saw Delilah nod hastily, tears standing a quarter-inch thick on her lower lids. But she was holding steady, by God. Again, the thought *she sure is something* whispered through his head. But he didn't have time to dwell on it, because Steady ripped the foil case of biological sealant open with his teeth, spit out the fragment of packaging, and said, "Go!"

They tossed the T-shirt aside—*Holy crow, there's a lot of blood*—and threw themselves over the dog.

Delilah held Fido's rear end in place; Mac kept the pooch's front legs and head under control.

Steady was quick on the draw, pouring the powder into Fido's wound. But besides a low whimper, the dog did nothing to fight them. In fact, he went so far as to lick Mac's hand. And damned if that tear in Mac's eye didn't up and decide to spill over.

Thankfully, more were stopped from joining the fun when he heard Agent Duvall bark, "Patch me over to Agent Zoelner's number! Now!"

"What's up?" he asked, looking away from Fido's wound only after he noted with gratification that the QuikClot was working. The bleeding had instantly slowed. Fido certainly wasn't out of the woods. But now, at least, they'd given the fearless animal a fighting chance.

"We've got thermal imagery of the guy," the CIA agent relayed, keeping one hand on her earpiece, listening intently to whatever was happening on the other end. "And I need to let Z know which house he's hiding in."

Mac nodded, turning his attention back to the dog.

"Help me lift him," Steady said, bending to get both hands under the animal. "Careful, now. *Mierda!* We don't want to jostle that wound."

Mac and Delilah helped Steady stand, the canine cradled gently in his arms. Fido whined weakly but still managed to bathe Steady's face with his long, pink tongue. And unless Mac was mistaken, the medic's eyes were unusually bright.

Yep, the Knights may deal with and deal *out* death on a daily basis, a bunch of hard-nosed, hard-hearted operators, but hand them one dumb-as-dirt, critically injured dog, and they all turned into big bags of mush…

"Okay," Steady grunted once he'd taken all of Fido's weight, clearing his throat. "I've got him. I'll get him to the nearest vet." He turned to Mac. "You keep me informed of what's going on here, *hermano*."

"I'm going with Steady," Delilah declared, rubbing the back of her hand over her cheek, smudging her tears and the dust on her face in a long line as she bent down to grab Steady's medical bag.

"No." Mac snagged her wrist when she turned to follow Steady's careful steps, noting the soothing warmth of her skin against his callused fingers. Crack cocaine. Pure and simple…

"What?" She turned to him, brow puckered. "Why?"

"Because until we have Mr. Timberlands in custody, and until I know what the hell is goin' on around here, I'm not lettin' you outta my sight."

When she jerked out of his grip to catch up with the medic, Mac thought he might have a fight on his hands. But then she swung back to him, shouting, "I'm just going to help him to the car!" She lifted the camo duffel bag. *God love her*. Another wave of relief crashed over Mac, and he figured it was a wonder he wasn't drowning in the stuff.

Of course, when Agent Duvall whispered into her earpiece, "Z, he's in the garage of the house directly across from you," any respite he'd enjoyed lit out of him quick as a hiccup. The fact that Mr. Timberlands was holed up inside a house meant Ozzie and Zoelner were going to have to kick in a door. And *that* was a tricky business, especially seeing as how a guy never knew what he was going to find behind that door. It could be Christmas morning or World War III…

———

"You must get out of there," Haroun hissed the moment Qasim answered the phone.

"Why?" Qasim asked, jerking forward, the plastic chair squeaking in objection.

"I was not able to secure Miss Fairchild, and now I am forced to evade," Haroun relayed, and Qasim glanced around the darkened, dust-heavy room. *Forced to evade…* Never a situation one wanted to find oneself in but a situation Qasim and all the others were used to since joining The Cause. They'd effectively been *forced to evade* nearly every Western government for years.

"Forced to evade the motorcycle fanatics?" he asked, motioning and barking at Sami and Jabbar to begin gathering their belongings. He didn't question Haroun's orders when it came to something like this. If his second-in-command said it was time to go, then it was time to *go*.

"The heavily *armed* motorcycle fanatics," Haroun clarified, and Qasim's blood ran cold. He'd figured as much, but to hear it confirmed was another thing entirely. "They saw me attempting to drag the woman from Sander's backyard and opened fire. I am wounded."

Qasim sucked in a ragged breath.

"It is nothing," Haroun assured him. "A flesh wound only. But plans have changed. This place is no longer safe. If they have not called the police to report my assault already, then they will soon. This town will be swarming with men in badges. You must retreat to our second location." Their second location… *Praise Allah, we have one*. "I will come to you once I have secured Miss Fairchild."

"No." Qasim shook his head even though Haroun couldn't see him. "Forget about her for now. Just get yourself to safety. We will try different torture methods on Theodore. It has only been a day. We may still get him to talk by—"

"Ah, *habibi*," Haroun chuckled softly. "I always say you worry like a *sitto*." And, yes, Haroun was known to compare Qasim's continual fretting to that of an old grandmother. He was the only man in Qasim's circle who would dare. Years ago, Qasim had killed men for such insubordination, and his reputation still preceded him. But, Haroun...well, Haroun had been by his side since almost the beginning, and as such was allowed certain latitude. "By all means continue to try make that old Marine talk, but in the meantime, allow me to carry on with my mission. I will use the signal on the phone attached to her motorcycle to follow her like her own shadow. And when the time is right, I will grab her."

"You have already attempted to grab her twice before," Qasim reminded his second-in-command, wondering if they'd gotten so close to reaching their goal only to be thwarted at the last minute. Allah might be on their side, but unfortunately, *qadar* was now living up to her reputation as a fickle mistress.

"Yes." There was a note of indulgence in Haroun's voice. "But what is that American phrase you like to use about the third time someone attempts something?"

Despite himself, despite the left turn their mission had suddenly taken, Qasim felt the corners of his mouth twitch. Haroun was one of the few people who knew of his secret fascination with the English language. "They say the third time is a charm."

"Yes. It is indeed. Now, go. I will call you again when I once more have the woman in my sights."

Qasim could only hope it would be that easy, "God be with you, brother," he said.

"And with you, *habibi*."

Qasim punched the "end" button on the phone and turned to find his men had already packed up their meager supplies. They were standing at attention, awaiting his next order.

"Put the old Marine in the car," he told them. "We are retreating to our secondary location."

"And Haroun?" Jabbar asked, his black eye now swollen almost completely shut.

"Will meet us there with the woman." At least Qasim *hoped* that would be true. A troubling sense of foreboding had invaded his spirit since disconnecting the call. But he thought perhaps it was just because he worried like a *sitto*…

———

"Be careful, Z," Chelsea whispered, standing with Mac and Delilah on Sander's back porch. She didn't care that the CIA technician listening in on the line could hear the distress in her voice. *Screw it. Let him hear. This is a distressing situation, after all.* Made more so because it was *Dagan* out there in harm's way. Dagan, the only field agent who'd ever looked at her as something more than a bespectacled computer lab rat. Dagan, the only man who'd ever made her feel like, maybe, just maybe, there was something…*sexy*…about short, plump, mixed-race *smart* girls. "From what we can tell, he's sitting in a car. He could run you down if you approach him from the front. I suggest engaging from a side or back entrance, if that's possible."

"Chels?"

Chels… Her heart tripped at the familiar nickname. "Yeah, Z?" She licked her lips.

"Shut up, will you? I know what I'm doing, but having you yakking in my ear isn't helping me concentrate."

Okay. And any warm fuzzies she might have been feeling were instantly doused in gasoline and set ablaze. She fancied she could see them racing around inside her head, arms flailing, flames licking out behind them.

"I'm just trying to help, you ginormous ass," she hissed, even as she continued to watch like a hawk the three green dots on her iPad screen that were Ozzie, Dagan, and the suspect. From the corner of her eye, she saw that Mac was standing by one porch post, swatting at Delilah's hands as the woman lifted the hem of his T-shirt to reveal a bandage soaked with blood. She made note of the fact that the big former Fed had a fresh wound that was obviously bleeding anew since his Ty Cobb-worthy slide across the yard, but she gave it only a fleeting thought. With Dagan seconds away from kicking in a door with who knew what behind it— they couldn't be sure whether or not Delilah's assailant had been packing more than a hunting knife—the extent to which she didn't give a shit about Mac and Delilah's scuffling could not be measured. Because, not to be a broken record or anything, but it was… *Dagan* out there…

"What did I just say about your yakking?" he replied.

She opened her mouth to take issue with him but she got distracted when the technician cut in with, "Excuse me, Agent Duvall. We have the suspect's identity."

"Who is it?" she asked, holding her breath, hoping beyond hope that, despite the man's appearance and thick accent, he was nobody, some convict who'd simply been hanging out in this dilapidated old neighborhood to escape the notice of the five-oh. Hoping beyond hope that Charles Sander and Theo Fairchild would turn up with a very good explanation as to their disappearance. Hoping beyond hope that this wasn't the kind of clusterfuck Morales feared it might be.

"His name is Haroun al-Hallaj," the technician relayed, and her heart sank even before he continued with, "He's a noted member of an off-shoot al-Qaeda organization that operates mostly in the Arabian Peninsula."

"Goddamnit, Chelsea!" Dagan hissed, having listened to the whole thing through his joint connection. "What the hell have you gotten us involved in?"

She didn't have time to correct him by telling him that *they,* the Black Knights, had been involved long before *she* arrived on the scene, because she was too busy screaming, "Patch in Director Morales! Now!" to the technician.

While the secure connection was being made, she could hear Dagan breathing heavily. "Do we proceed, Agent Duvall?" he whispered.

Agent Duvall. So they were back to that, were they? Well, she shouldn't be too surprised. After all, with these most recent revelations, it was clear that her sudden appearance on their doorstep wasn't as innocent as she'd tried to make them believe. Which meant that

Dagan now knew, without a doubt, that she'd been lying to him.

"Negative, Z," she said, waiting for her supervisor to pick up the damned phone. "Hold your position until—"

"Agent Duvall," Morales barked. "I've been following your situation and have two teams en route. ETA is approximately thirty seconds. Tell your boys to hang tight."

"We're not *her* boys," Dagan growled through the joint connection. "Or yours, for that matter, Morales. So you can go f—"

Whatever he was about to say—and Chelsea figured she had a pretty good idea—was cut off by the low muttering of two stealth Comanche helicopters as they zoomed overhead. Flying in at a low insertion profile so they wouldn't trigger the FAA's radar—couldn't have the civilians knowing there was a super-secret op going down right under their noses, could they?— and so both teams in the helos could fast-rope in at the drop of a hat, the smell of aviation fuel drifted down to burn Chelsea's nose. She watched the choppers disappear down the block, then turned to find both Mac and Delilah gaping first in the direction of the helicopters and then at her. She winced and shrugged, hoping her expression accurately conveyed her remorse at having been forced to deceive them. *I swear I didn't want to. I swear I didn't.* But then Dagan's voice shouted through her earpiece. "He's fleeing! He's fleeing! The suspect is fleeing!"

Chelsea heard the squealing of tires coming from down the block and saw the tops of the trees swaying before the two helicopters mushed up from their position atop the canopy and raced forward to keep up with the escaping vehicle.

Morales barked instructions in her ear. The technician kept up a running monologue of al-Hallaj's movements as he watched the activity via satellite feed. And Dagan cursed her six ways from Sunday and beat feet back here, if the sound of his labored breathing was anything to go by. But it was Mac who grabbed her arm, ducking his chin until his tan face was an inch from hers.

It occurred to her then, as he bent to bring them nose-to-nose, that the ex–FBI agent was about a foot taller than any normal human male should be.

"I don't cotton to being lied to," he growled, his deep voice rumbling through her chest like fireworks on the Fourth of July. And like those fireworks, she knew Mac, if not handled properly, could blow up in her face quicker than she could say *I'm so sorry it had to be this way*.

"And I like it even less," he continued, still manacling her bicep, "when those lies might've gotten a good dog killed," *God, I hope not*, "and a good woman," he hooked a thumb toward the redheaded bartender, "*nearly* killed. So, you're gonna tell me what the hell is goin' on here, Agent Duvall. And you're gonna do it right now."

He motioned toward the pistol he'd moved to the front of his jeans. It was a big gun. What most operators like to call *a huge persuader*. She gulped.

"Or else," he added, "I might be tempted to empty a clip in you and any other government asshole who comes my way based on principle alone."

She nodded in acquiescence—screw Morales and his orders to keep her mouth shut—just as Dagan and Ozzie barged through the back gate. Dagan was still holding his cell phone to his ear, listening in on every word being spoken.

"Mac!" he yelled furiously, his voice echoing out over the yard and neighborhood. "If there's anything left once I've finished with her, you can be my guest!"

Chapter Fourteen

IF DELILAH DIDN'T KNOW THE MEN OF BLACK KNIGHTS Inc. as well as she did, she might have feared for the life of the little CIA agent. All three operators surrounded Chelsea Duvall, who was perched on the edge of Sander's ruined sofa.

At first, Delilah expected them to fire up the engines on their motorcycles and take off to join the chase for Mr. Timberlands. And even though her head was still spinning slightly from being choked out, she'd been ready—more than ready—to accompany them. *No one attempts to kidnap me twice and gets away with it. Wonder Twins, unite!*

But when she'd said as much to Mac, he'd quickly informed her, "We're better off lettin' the spooks risk life and limb tryin' to catch him. Choppers are better equipped to tail him anyway. Besides, we need to stay here and protect you."

And to say she'd been peeved by the *need* for protection was an understatement. But what with that whole *two attempted abductions* thing she had going for her, she didn't really see a way to naysay him. Which meant that she now found herself standing in the middle of Sander's living room, watching three grown men bully one small woman. And they *were* bullying Agent Duvall, insomuch as they were towering over her.

"You all stop looking at me like I killed your canary," Chelsea said, lifting her chin in defiance.

You go, girl, Delilah thought as a proud, card-carrying member of the sisterhood. On the other hand, the CIA agent *was* here under what Delilah was now certain were nefarious circumstances, so her support of the woman didn't go much further than that.

"Not our canary," Ozzie said, crossing his arms and shaking his shaggy head. "But you may've been instrumental in the death of a dog." *Fido…* Tears pricked behind Delilah's eyes. "I mean, did you guys *see* that? It was straight out of *Turner and Hooch*!"

"What was?" she asked, running a hand under her nose. She couldn't help but notice her fingers smelled like dirt and dog, and *gah!* That just made everything so much worse. *God, Fido. Don't die.* "What was straight out of *Turner and Hooch*?"

"Fido chomped onto Mr. Timberlands' boot like the thing was made of jerky," Mac said without taking his eyes off the CIA agent, without uncrossing his powerful arms.

"Haroun al-Hallaj," Agent Duvall corrected, her voice only slightly tremulous. "His name is Haroun al-Hallaj."

Mac made a face that clearly stated he didn't give one shit, much less two shits, *what* the guy's name was. It was cold, that expression of his. Ice cold. Delilah shivered in response. This Mac, this frigid mountain of a man, was hard to equate with the hot, growling lover who'd given her such intense pleasure upstairs just… She glanced at the old Felix the Cat clock ticking away on the kitchen wall and realized in astonishment that it'd been less than thirty minutes since she'd been burning up beneath his ravishing kisses.

It felt more like a week had passed.

"Fido's bite caused the man to drop you," Mac continued, "which is the only reason you're here with us now instead of…wherever the hell he'd been planning to take you."

The tears behind her eyes pricked more forcefully. Mac must've recognized her trouble because, with a back-and-forth grind of his jaw and a twitch of that delectable chin dimple, he held out his hand, beckoning her under his arm.

She went gladly. Sidling up to his warmth, his strength. Hating herself for needing either. Loving the fact that he offered both.

For Heaven's sake. You're one sad sack.

What did I tell you about fucking off, huh? she demanded of that infinitely bothersome voice. Though, secretly, she was glad for its presence. It always pissed her off. And she heartily preferred being angry to being on the verge of another humiliating breakdown.

Of course, her flying thoughts crash-landed back into the conversation when Zoelner cocked his head and demanded, "Okay, Agent Duvall. You want to try this again, and tell us why you're *really* here?"

"I—" Chelsea began, but Zoelner cut her off.

"And before you think to feed us anymore of your bullshit—"

"It wasn't bullshit," Ozzie interrupted, his usually jocular expression now as somber as death. Delilah wasn't sure she'd ever seen the guy look quite so…*threatening*.

"No?" Zoelner asked.

"No." Ozzie shook his head. "Her coming here and *stovepiping*," he emphasized the word, "us while insisting oh-so-innocently that she wasn't, was some serious, fucked-up shit, which is an entirely different bouquet."

"Indeed," Zoelner agreed, still frowning down at Chelsea. "I believe you're right, Ozzie. So, Agent Duvall, before you think to try to feed us anymore of your serious, fucked-up, I'm-just-here-as-your-liaison, *stovepiping* shit, please understand that although we're used to backdoor dealings, double crossings, and back-stabbings from the likes of your kind, we—"

"You used to *be* one of my kind, Z," Chelsea interrupted.

"Exactly." Zoelner nodded. "Which is why I, along with my colleagues here, won't hesitate to take everything we know and the huge amount we obviously *don't* know straight to POTUS. See what *he* thinks about The Company's shenanigans here."

Delilah had to think about that one for a bit. The Knights were always using weird acronyms. But then it hit her…POTUS. President of the United States.

"I was following the orders of my s-supervisor," Agent Duvall said, shifting uncomfortably.

"And throwin' us under the bus in the meantime," Mac added. Delilah could feel the tension radiating through him as if she was holding on to a live wire.

"I wasn't throwing you under the bus," Chelsea insisted with a huff, crossing her arms to mirror the men's stances. "I was following *orders*. Surely you guys remember what those are. Surely you haven't been calling your own shots for so long that you've forgotten—"

"Agent Duvall," Mac rumbled, "Zoelner's already explained this to you, but let me put it another way. We're not farmers, so stop tryin' to sell us a load of fertilizer and just tell us what the hell is goin' on here."

Okay. And, yeah. Despite being a card-carrying member of the sisterhood, Delilah had to agree with Mac's insistence. After all, she herself was more than a bit curious as to what the hell was going on here.

Chelsea frowned up at them, hesitated a second more, then finally shrugged. "Have you guys been keeping up with the headlines chronicling the misadventures of an ex–CIA agent named Luke Winterfield?"

"Of course," Ozzie said. "He just fled to Nicaragua, right?"

"I thought it was Honduras," Zoelner said. Delilah had been under the impression it was Guatemala.

"It doesn't matter *where* he is." Chelsea waved an impatient hand through the air. "What matters is that along with copies of the files pertaining to the locations of our government's black sites, we also suspect he took copies of…other files."

A curious sense of dread bloomed in the pit of Delilah's stomach.

"What other files?" Mac demanded.

"A *lot* of other files," Chelsea admitted. "But the one we're most concerned about right now, in this situation, is labeled BA Repatriate."

"BA…" Zoelner's chin dropped down as if someone had unhinged his jaw. For a moment, Delilah thought he resembled a handsome Pez dispenser. "You don't mean broken arrows."

Chelsea nodded. "That's exactly what I mean."

The room grew so still, so quiet, Delilah could hear the hum of electricity in the lamps beside the sofa. Mac was literally vibrating beside her. And that bloom of dread in her stomach? Well, it grew to the size of redwood. "I don't think I really want to know, but..." she licked her lips, "what are broken arrows?"

"I take it you're not a big John Travolta fan," Ozzie said.

Huh? "What in the world are you talking about?"

"You know that '90s movie with the train and the—"

"Broken arrows are missin' nuclear warheads," Mac cut in succinctly.

Delilah shook her head, digging a finger in her ear. "I'm sorry," she said, "I thought you said missing *nuclear warheads*."

In answer, Mac gave her a squeeze. It was meant to be comforting, she was sure, but the gesture missed the mark. *Holy hell, did it ever!* Because that simple little squeeze was an affirmative that, *yes,* in fact she *had* heard him correctly.

"We have missing nuclear warheads?" she screeched, jerking out from under his arm so quickly she thought perhaps her head spun in a circle. She had to lower herself to the arm of the sofa lest she wilt to the dirty shag carpeting.

"If by *we* you mean the U.S. of A. then, yes," Ozzie concurred. "Eight at last count."

"No." Chelsea shook her head. "It's five now. The two lost in the Mediterranean in '56 were recovered nearly forty years ago. And the one that rolled off the deck of the USS *Ticonderoga* and fell into the Pacific Ocean was finally recovered in '76."

"Huh." Ozzie raised his brows. "Well, what do you know? That's good news."

Good news? *Good news?* The U.S. was still missing *five* freakin' *nuclear warheads*, and Ozzie considered this *good news*?

That's it. She'd suspected it before, but now she knew for sure. The Black Knights were crazy. Without a doubt, do not pass go, do not collect $200, batshit crazy. But right now the more pressing question was, "What in the world do five missing nuclear warheads have to do with my uncle?"

Chelsea turned to her, reaching up to adjust her glasses. *Again* Delilah couldn't help but think the woman would be better suited to a kindergarten classroom. "You know your uncle did a stint in the Marines during Vietnam, right?"

"Yes." She nodded emphatically. *Yes, yes,* yes. She was well aware of that fact. It'd been brought up enough in the last twenty-four hours.

"Do you know *what* he did?" Agent Duvall eyed her curiously.

"He was an engineer or a technician or something."

Chelsea laughed. "Yeah. Or something." Blowing out a breath that barely ruffled the short, dark bangs hanging over her forehead, she said, "Now, it goes without saying that what I'm about to tell you guys is highly classified."

Highly classified. People really used that phrase?

"We have clearance," Zoelner growled. "We've had clearance from the get-go. Probably higher clearance than you have, come to think of it."

"Yeah, yeah." Chelsea waved him off. "You've already bent me over. There's no reason to break it off up in there, too."

"I just don't enjoy getting pissed on from a great height."

Chelsea rolled her eyes. "And cue sad, slide whistle sound."

Delilah saw Zoelner's hands clench and heard him whisper something under his breath. She couldn't quite make it out, but Ozzie obviously could. "Whoa," Ozzie said, stepping back, his gaze darting between the CIA agent and the *ex*–CIA agent. "Shots fired. Shots fired."

"Uh-huh." Chelsea nodded, so much heat in her eyes Delilah was surprised Zoelner's eyebrows didn't burst into flames. Obviously, *she'd* heard what Zoelner said, too. "Well, you might want to pack a coat for your stay at the Moral Highground, Z. I've heard it's quite chilly up there."

"Cut the shit, Chelsea." Zoelner leaned in until his nose was barely an inch from hers.

"You better back the hell off," Chelsea growled, "or I'm liable to do something to you that'll make walking impossible."

"Come sip from the cup of destruction. I dare you."

Delilah watched as Chelsea changed tactics. Instead of making good on her threat, she batted her lashes, smiling like a debutante. "Oh, Z," she said breathlessly, "you had me at destruction."

Ozzie choked. Mac groaned. And Delilah couldn't tear her eyes away from Chelsea and Zoelner. She figured she was about ten seconds away from witnessing the two throwing punches or ripping each other's clothes off.

But just when the strained atmosphere reached a pressure point—Delilah actually scooted back on the arm of the couch in preparation for the explosion—Mac cut through the tension with, "Sweet Lord, I need an aspirin. It's either that, or I'm gonna to have to pull my weapon and start shootin' some of you. Or *all* of you."

He ran a big hand through his hair and instantly Delilah was reminded of how soft and warm those thick locks had been between her fingers. How wonderfully rough the calluses on his palm felt when he gently molded her breast. How—

Okay. Enough of that. She had to cross her legs in an attempt to squeeze away the sudden sensation throbbing between them. And, lamentably, it was true. She really was a sad sack.

"Zoelner," Mac continued, "why don't you stop antagonizin' Agent Duvall, huh?" Zoelner grumbled but straightened away from Chelsea all the same.

"And Agent Duvall," Mac scowled down at her, "I hate to be the one to tell you this, but when it comes to a showdown between you and Zoelner, you don't have any more chance than a Junebug in a chicken coop. So quit rufflin' his feathers, will you? And get on with the damn explanation. I'm growin' old here waitin'."

Ooooh, Delilah just loved it when he got authoritative and down-home countrified all in one breath. Was there anything sexier?

Um, not that I can recall.

Sad sack, whispered the voice.

Shut it!

Chelsea cast Zoelner one last fulminating glance before sighing resignedly and loosening her shoulders. "During the Vietnam conflict," she said, "it was decided that having eight nuclear ordinances from a bygone era spread willy-nilly around the globe wasn't really in our country's best interest."

Delilah barely contained a snort. "You think?"

Chelsea made a face and shrugged. "Well, it's not as bad as one might suppose. Most of the lost weapons were at the bottom of the ocean or submerged in swamps so deep they were impossible to recover. But others…"

Delilah shivered at the thought of the "others."

"Well," the CIA agent continued, "by that time technology had progressed enough to make their recovery somewhat feasible. Problem was, in many instances, we didn't know the exact locations of the warheads. Enter a five-man team of Marine Corps Advanced Sonar Specialists."

"Including Theo Fairchild and Charles Sander," Ozzie said, uncrossing one arm to rub a finger under his chin, his expression contemplative.

"Affirmative." Chelsea nodded. "And low and behold, those go-getter guys not only pinpointed the exact locations of those few ordinances that were salvageable at the time, but they pinpointed the whole damn lot."

Delilah couldn't believe it. Her uncle had been part of some super-secret, nuclear missile detection team back in the day, and he'd never once breathed a word to her about it.

Is no one what they appear to be? First, she had to go and learn the Black Knights weren't really a rowdy motorcycle club but were instead Uncle Sam's most terrifying, tip, tip, tippity-top of the spear. And now this? *Seriously?* She tossed the question out into the ether. Surprisingly, this time the ether answered back. *You mean like you're not really a bartender, but one of Chicago's most sought-after forensic accountants?*

And touché. Delilah gave credit where credit was due.

"So this file, BA Repatriate," Zoelner said, "I suppose it gives the global coordinates of the remaining five weapons?"

Five freakin' *missing nuclear weapons!*

"No." Agent Duvall shook her head, adjusting her glasses again. "That's just the thing. The file containing the actual *locations* of the weapons was above Winterfield's security clearance. He couldn't access it. The only thing he could access was the file detailing the original mission and the names and ranks of the men who worked on it."

"Of whom two are now MIA," Mac murmured.

"The only two who are still alive," the CIA agent confirmed.

"Christ," Mac swung away, cursing a blue streak under his breath.

"And you didn't think to raise a red flag and put a protective detail around Theo and Charles when the *first* three men turned up dead?" Zoelner demanded.

"Considering one of them died in '78 of an overdose and the next two died in the nineties, one from a heart attack and the other in a bizarre fishing accident," Chelsea declared, "*no!* No, we did *not* consider a protective detail!"

Ozzie plopped down on the coffee table, repeatedly running a hand back through his hair. And if Zoelner had looked like he wanted to kill Chelsea Duvall before, now he looked like he wanted to beat her senseless and *then* kill her.

"Do you really believe it's possible, that after forty-some-odd years, these two men still remember the exact coordinates of the missin' warheads?" Mac interrupted, his back still turned.

Chelsea hesitated a beat. "Obviously the *terrorists* believe it." She shrugged and added, "And, honestly? Yeah. If it was *me* tasked with pinpointing a handful of nukes, you bet your ass I'd remember. Wouldn't you?"

"Goddamnit, Chelsea!" Zoelner roared. "And you didn't think that type of information warranted you going against your orders!"

"We weren't *certain* there was any need for alarm!" Chelsea yelled right back, jumping up to slam her hands into her hips. "We didn't know *for sure* which files Winterfield snagged. We just knew which files he had access to. And until ten minutes ago, we thought it was entirely possible Fairchild and Sander were just holed up somewhere tying one on!"

Delilah's mind raced to reach the same conclusions the Knights evidently already had. "Excuse me," she said after a beat, raising her hand like she was still back in school. "Can someone please explain to me what in the world all of that means? I mean, I get that you guys are under the impression that this al-Whoever guy—"

"Al-Hallaj," Chelsea added helpfully.

"Yeah, okay." Delilah nodded. "So, I get that you think Winterfield sold the files to al-Hallaj. And I get that al-Hallaj took Sander and my uncle in order to try to…uh…get the locations of the warheads from them." She couldn't bring herself to voice the word *torture*. "Am I correct in believing that once again technology has advanced to a point where some or all of the remaining five might be salvageable?"

The CIA agent nodded, and Delilah's heart sank. If she wasn't mistaken, the thing was hanging out somewhere in the vicinity of her kneecaps.

"So, let's not get into the discussion of why *we*, the United States of America, haven't gone to secure the warheads, and jump instead to the question of why *I've* been targeted twice. It doesn't make any sense."

"Unfortunately, it does," Mac murmured, the muscles in his mile-wide shoulders twitching fitfully.

"It does?" she asked. "But, why?"

Mac turned his face slightly, his distinctive profile in view. And if she'd ever seen a jaw looking harder than his, she couldn't remember the occasion. That redwood of dread in her stomach hit a growth spurt, sending branches up to strangle her throat.

"It means they've been unable to get the information from the men by traditional means." *Traditional means*. She knew he meant torture. "So, they're *attemptin'* to use *you* as leverage."

Uh-huh. Okay. Right. So…terrorists—freakin' frackin' *terrorists*—wanted to use her as leverage. Against her uncle. In order to find nuclear weapons…

She bent at the waist, trying to decide if she was going to puke or pass out. Fortunately, she was saved from doing either when the soft muttering of helicopter blades sounded overhead a mere second before the front door exploded open. What was left of the ruined slab of oak disintegrated on impact with the wall.

She bolted upright just as three men in full-on SWAT gear poured into the house, their huge, black machine guns up and at the ready. The Black Knights answered in kind, handguns whipped from waistbands and holsters in the blink of an eye. Each group aimed for the other. Each group yelled for the other to drop their weapons. It was a rootin', tootin', gun-totin' Yosemite Sam melee.

And Delilah was caught smack-dab in the middle of it. *Yippee!*

Chapter Fifteen

"GET BEHIND ME," MAC BELLOWED TO DELILAH, barely sparing her a glance as he kept his weapon trained on the intruders. But that quick peek was enough to tell him her face had completely drained of blood. It was as white as the chalk he and his father had used to paint the cattle with during culling season.

"Don't move!" yelled one of the three men decked out in expensive tactical gear.

Mac knew a CIA wet unit when he saw one. Not that he was all that impressed. After all, whatever training these spooky boys had gotten back at Langley, he knew it couldn't possibly compare to the rigorous, months-long physical hell Frank "Boss" Knight had put him through before allowing him to join the ranks of Black Knights Inc. *You might not officially be a Navy SEAL*, Boss had thundered more than a time or two while watching him struggle to keep from drowning in the frigid waters of Lake Michigan or having him fire so many rounds that his fingers went numb, *but, fuckin'-A, I'll make sure you should have been*.

Mac had survived that ordeal. And many, *many* more in the years since. Which meant that although he had a small amount of respect for the skills of the black-suited men in front of him—*small* being the operative word—he'd still bet a dollar to a doughnut that he and the two Knights lined up beside him could drop the fancy boys faster than a buckin' bronco could blaze out of a chute.

"I said, *don't move*," the man—obviously, he was the team leader—yelled again when Delilah started to head for Mac. And then the idiot made his second mistake. His first had been daring to come at the BKI boys with guns hot, of course. But now the dumbass had the unmitigated gall to train his weapon on Delilah.

"Uh-uh," Mac tsked, his finger tightening on his trigger, every muscle in his body tensing to absorb the coming recoil should he have to fill Dumbass SWAT Guy full of hot lead. "You best keep pointin' that iron at me, friend. Because if you don't, I'll drop you so fast you'll be kissin' St. Peter hello within a second."

The guy must've known Mac wasn't whistling Dixie. He hesitated barely a heartbeat before once again aiming the black eye of his quick-firing Colt in Mac's direction.

"That's better." Mac jerked his chin in a nod, his anger going from a rapid boil to a slow simmer. "Now, we're all just gonna hold our fire and our breath while Delilah makes her way over to me, *capisce*?"

"I'm on orders to take Miss Fairchild into protective custody," the guy said, one small drop of sweat glistening on the bridge of his nose. Besides his eyes and the tops of his cheeks, that was the only part of his face not covered by the black, tactical balaclava he wore.

"You'll take her over my dead body," Mac growled.

Delilah quickly flitted across the room. When she ducked behind him and shoved her fingers into the top of his waistband, he heaved a secret sigh of relief.

"Your dead body can certainly be arranged," Mr. Asshat SWAT-man retorted, the smug, self-satisfied

gleam in his eye all but screaming that he was the win-
ner in the big dick lottery, the hot girlfriend competition,
and the sharp-shooting championship. And although
Mac was well versed in dealing with the immeasurable
arrogance of Company Men—even as a Fed he'd had
to suffer their occasional association—he discovered he
had an intense desire to wipe that look off of Asshat's
face with a well-placed strike from his handy-dandy Ka-
Bar. Or a well-aimed bullet. Either one would do nicely.

"Oh, for the love of—" Agent Duvall jumped into
the fray. "Are you guys kidding me with this? I mean,
I'm just spitballing here, but aren't we all on the same
friggin' team?"

"Morales informed me the Black Knights might
not be willing to hand over the woman," Mr. Asshat
explained. "In which case, I'm instructed to take her
by force."

Mac's finger twitched on his trigger as the fire under
his anger flamed with new life.

"Jesus Christ," the little CIA agent huffed before
screaming into her earpiece at whatever now-deaf technician was on the other end. "Get Morales back on the
goddamned line!"

As she waited for the call to go through, she let her
gaze ping-pong back and forth between the two oppos-
ing groups. "This place could seriously use a Xanax salt
lick," she muttered, shaking her head in exasperation.

Ozzie chuckled despite the charged atmosphere.
"You're funny, Agent Duvall. Has anyone ever told
you that?"

"Not since I gave up stand-up comedy for a regular
ol' nine-to-five," she said, tapping her foot impatiently.

This time Ozzie barked with laughter. "There are two things I know for certain," he said, and Mac would have rolled his eyes had he not been inclined to keep his blinkers trained on Asshat SWAT-guy. Because he was fully aware of what was coming.

"Oh, yeah?" Agent Duvall asked, falling hook, line, and sinker. Mac was pretty sure that grumbling noise he heard was coming from Zoelner. "And what two things are those?"

"Number one," Ozzie began, "Warrant is one of the most underrated hair bands of the eighties."

"Oh-*kay*. And number two?" the little CIA agent prodded when Ozzie hesitated.

"You're going to marry me someday."

Mac felt Agent Duvall's look of disbelief more than he saw it. "Are you serious?" she demanded. "Are you really doing this right now? Flirting with me?"

"Yeah." Ozzie shrugged. "I figured I'd just go for it."

When Agent Duvall opened her mouth to say, "You know what? You're not as good-looking as you think," with a hint of laughter in her voice, Mac peeked over at Zoelner, not surprised to find the guy had settled into that weird state of statue-like stillness.

"Not as good-looking as I think?" Ozzie retorted. "I find that hard to believe. I *do* own a mirror."

This time Agent Duvall laughed outright, and Zoelner hissed, "Why don't you stop being such a goddamned hemorrhoid, Ozzie."

With that, Mac's suspicions about Zoelner's feelings toward Chelsea Duvall were confirmed. Because, unless he was mistaken—and he very much doubted he was— the ex-spook was absolutely green with jealousy.

And, okay, given the fact they were in the middle
of a good ol'-fashioned standoff, Mac fully recognized
how ridiculous the entire last three minutes—aka the
circus that was Ozzie, Zoelner, SWAT Guys, and Agent
Duvall—had been. In fact, he reckoned the only thing
they were missing here was a clown car. But it was the
sheer absurdity of the entire thing that made his anger
dissipate enough for him to realize Delilah had pressed
herself against him, turkey peeking around his shoulder
at the scene being played out like some sort of poorly
written slapstick comedy.

And even though he had one very large machine gun
pointed at his chest, the only thought to run through his
mind in that instant was...*boobs*...

Great, glorious, good-God-almighty boobs...

Then he was distracted—*thank you, sweet Jesus*—
when Agent Duvall lifted a hand to the Bluetooth device
in her ear and said, "Sir! Excuse my French, but what
the *hell* is going on here? I've got three guys in full tactical pointing weapons at me and saying they're working
on your orders to take Delilah Fairchild into custody."

"What do you mean I'm not safe with the Black
Knights?" Delilah demanded in response to the decla-
ration Chelsea made after *finally* signing off with her
supervisor. The call had lasted five eternal, god-awful,
soul-sucking minutes. And Delilah figured if she heard
one more, "Yes, sir. I understand, sir," she was going to
grab Mac's gun and shoot the CIA agent in the ass. After
all, it was *her* they were talking about here. The fact that
they wanted to take *her* into custody.

"I mean just that," Chelsea said. "You're not safe with the Black Knights."

Delilah was no longer hiding behind Mac's back because the mysterious Morales had apparently issued an order for the three Men in Black to stand down, and the tension in the room had leveled out in response. Oh, it was still a pretty hairy environment, what with six heavily armed, testosterone-laden males scowling and posturing toward each other, but at least now Delilah felt safe enough to stand in the middle of them, hands on hips, scowl pasted firmly in place.

Not safe with the Black Knights? Preposterous! If she wasn't safe with *them*, then she wasn't safe with *anyone*. She flicked a quick glance toward Mac. Unfortunately, she could read nothing behind the Mask of Inscrutability. Her heart skipped a beat. *Give me a sign, Mac. Let me know Chelsea is chock-a-block full of crap...*

And maybe he was a mind reader, or maybe his Spidey sense worked for more than just piecing together clues, because his electric blue eyes alighted on her face for a brief second, one heartbeat...then two. But it was enough. Because the flicker of dead-eye certainty she saw in his gaze took the tiniest edge off her screaming nerves.

"We lost al-Hallaj," Chelsea said. "And since the Black Knights have not been unable to assure your safety from him on two separate occasions, my supervisor would feel more comfortable keeping you under the CIA's protection until such a time as we have al-Hallaj in custody." She gestured toward the Men in Black. "And these men are here to—"

"We *might* have," Zoelner interrupted, his voice so

low and raspy Delilah wondered who'd been shoving tacks down his throat, "been able to keep Delilah safe had *someone*," he lifted a meaningful brow at Chelsea, "told us there was a fucking *terrorist* on the loose!"

"As I already *explained* to you," Chelsea shouted, two red flags painting her cheeks, "we weren't *certain* of that fact at the time!"

"Oh, so you're saying it's perfectly fine for *you* guys to fuck up. But when *we* do it, you think you have the authority to—"

"Can we get back to the real issue?" Ozzie interrupted. "Which is that your idiotic CIA compatriots went and *lost* al-Hallaj? I mean, honestly, how the hell did you manage that? He was driving a wimpy little hybrid and you had choppers and…uh…" he snapped his fingers, "oh, yeah, *satellites*!"

Chelsea turned to Ozzie, frowning and pushing her glasses up the bridge of her nose with a brusque finger. "He drove under an overpass in a heavily wooded area and the helos lost sight of him," she explained. "Then he abandoned the car on the other side of the overpass and ducked into a large drainage pipe that ran for more than a mile. In the couple of minutes it took the pursuing team to fast-rope into a nearby clearing, hump it back to the overpass and realize that's how he'd made his escape, he was already gone. They gave chase and we trained the satellites on the truncating location of the drainage pipe, but it was too late. We've got men scouring—"

Ozzie rolled his eyes and held up a hand in the classic traffic cop "stop" signal. "Whoa, there, Long Windy. Is it possible to get the tweeted version of this saga?"

The look Chelsea sent him very clearly stated that

whatever headway his earlier flirtations had made with her had instantly been lost.

"In short," Zoelner grumbled beneath his breath, "you lost the guy, and now we've got a big, steaming pile of jack shit."

"Which really sucks out loud," Ozzie added.

And Delilah had to agree. The whole situation sucked. Silently. Out loud. Every which way. She turned when she saw the lead SWAT guy lift a hand to his ear, pressing his earpiece closer to his head. He nodded tersely before informing the group, "My supervisor just told me we've got five minutes to secure Miss Fairchild. Then we're moving out."

Mac took a threatening step forward and Ozzie muttered something about the SWAT guy's cornhole and what should be stuffed in it.

In response, SWAT Guy made a move toward his weapon. Ozzie's handgun was up and aimed before Delilah could blink. And suddenly World War III was about to break out all over again as every man in the room armed himself anew.

"Agent Duvall," Zoelner hissed. "Now would be an excellent time to call and tell Morales that the only way Delilah Fairchild is walking out of this house is over our corpses."

"I've already said that can be arranged," SWAT Guy growled.

Delilah barely resisted rolling her eyes. *God, save me from this sea of testosterone.* She fancied if she squinted just right, she'd be able to see the stuff sloshing around the room in great, heaving waves.

"And make that call fast," Ozzie added. "Because,

according to shit-for-brains here, we've only got five minutes before the bullets start flying."

"Are you all kidding me right now?" Chelsea demanded.

"About the flying bullets," Ozzie said, "or about the fact that this guy does, indeed, have shit for brains?"

"Go fuck yourself," SWAT Guy growled at Ozzie.

"Better than fucking you, Middle-Aged Mutant Ninja Turtle," Ozzie retorted.

And that one got her. Despite everything, despite the fact that she was horrified about the terrorist, scared shitless for her uncle, and damn near dead on her feet from thirty-some-odd hours of no sleep, Delilah felt her lips twitch. Because, what with the all-black suit, the balaclava, and the pack attached to his back, SWAT Guy *did* kind of look like he could pass for the fifth member of the TMNT gang.

"Oh, shut up, all of you!" Chelsea barked, holding her Bluetooth device in place with one finger. She turned her back on the group and proceeded to throw out accusations like buckets of hydrochloric acid to whoever was talking in her ear. Then Chelsea was quiet for a long moment, during which time every eye in the room was focused on her back. Well, except for Zoelner's. When Delilah glanced at the guy, she couldn't help but note *his* eyes were focused like laser pointers on Chelsea's butt.

Men. She shook her head. *Such wonderfully simple creatures.*

Chelsea suddenly ended the conversation with, "I'll convince them this is the right move, sir." Delilah's heart sank. "Yes. Yes, you can depend on me."

Holding her breath, she watched as Chelsea turned to face the room. "Morales says you guys can play the part of Delilah's PSD," Chelsea said, "as long as you agree to remain in the area in case the CIA needs to question her and as long as you allow Agents Fitzsimmons and Wallace here," she nodded toward two of the guys in SWAT gear, "to remain with you."

Remain in the area? Okay, check. Delilah wanted to do that anyway since this was the place where her uncle had disappeared, and being here allowed her to feel close to him. Let a couple of CIA agents hang around as bodyguards? Check, check. The more guns the merrier, she figured. After all, a freakin' *terrorist* was out to get her. And have the boys of BKI play the part of her PSD? Uh…triple check? Because, even though she had absolutely no idea what in the world a PSD could be, she got the distinct impression that whatever it was, it meant she was going to be able to stay with them.

She allowed her gaze to flit around the room, measuring each expression. The SWAT guys were hard to read since their eyes were the only things visible on their entire bodies. Chelsea looked apprehensive as she gnawed on her bottom lip and darted looks back and forth between the Men in Black and the Knights. Zoelner had gone back to being a Greek statue. Ozzie's head was cocked contemplatively, his eyes narrowed. And Mac? Well, you guessed it. He was wearing the Mask of Inscrutability.

To break the tension, Delilah asked, "Will someone please tell me what the hell a PSD is?"

"Personal security detail," seven voices rang out simultaneously. The unexpectedly loud, in-stereo response startled her into stumbling back. Mac's hand darted out quicker than a snake strike, cupping her elbow to steady her before releasing her just as swiftly. The stupid skin on her arm tingled in response to his touch.

"Sure." She nodded, rubbing at her elbow. "And as much as I hate to admit it, I think I could *use* a personal security detail right about now. So, then, um…if we're all in agreement here, why are we still standing around and staring at one another like someone's about to pull the pin on a hand grenade?"

Of their own accord, her eyes darted to the three SWAT guys. And, sure as shit. Those were definitely hand grenades attached to the straps of their suits. *Gulp*.

"I'm just waiting for Fitzsimmons and Wallace to kiss," Ozzie said. "I love it when chicks make out."

"Get bent," Fitzsimmons…er…Wallace?…barked angrily.

"Go eat a bowl of dicks," Ozzie shot back.

And just when Delilah sensed fingers going back on triggers, Chelsea stepped in.

"I just went out on a limb for you guys," she said, addressing the Knights. "And believe me when I say my boss knows how to handle a chainsaw. So, cut the shit. All of you. But especially *you*, Ozzie." She skewered BKI's computer guru with a look sharp enough to run him clean through.

"As for you guys," Chelsea turned to the Men in Black, "I'm in charge. Fitzsimmons and Wallace," two of the men stepped forward, "you're with me. Jacobs, you're to report back to your team. They're converging downtown."

When MIB III, er…Jacobs, slung his gnarly looking machine gun over his shoulder, nodded to his two compatriots, and slipped out the front door, Chelsea made

no effort to disguise her sigh of relief. "Morales is rent-
ing rooms for us at a motel outside the town of Olive
Branch." She snorted. "And, yes, I fully appreciate
the irony in that name given our current situation. It's
only a few miles away. It's clean. It's secure. It'll work
quite nicely as a base of operations while we continue
to search for al-Hallaj, Fairchild, and Sander. And it
means we'll each have a bed to sleep in when we aren't
taking a shift guarding Delilah. If I'm not mistaken,
every single one of you could use a nap."

"Yeah," Lead SWAT Guy spoke up. "You all look
like hammered shit."

Ozzie answered back with a colorful rejoinder about
the guy's lack of paternity.

"Oh, yay," Delilah said, rolling her eyes and shaking
her head. "I can tell this is going to be tons of fun."

Chapter Sixteen

Noel Motel, Outside Olive Branch, Illinois
Thirty minutes later…

"Well, hi there," the scrawny, greasy-haired guy manning the front desk said to Delilah's boobs after Mac watched her tiredly prop a hip against the wobbly piece of furniture. If the dickhead noticed the little drops of blood on her T-shirt or the dirt still smudging her cheeks, he sure didn't show it. "Need something for the day? Or just for an hour or so?" Greasy wiggled his wiry eyebrows, smiling licentiously. His crooked teeth were stained a disgusting shade of baby-shit brown.

Probably from years of chewin' Copenhagen and drinkin' cheap whiskey, Mac thought. Because even now, even from four feet away, and even though it was barely oh-nine-hundred in the morning, he could smell the dude's breath. As his father used to say, *it's so strong you could hang the washin' on it.*

Behind Greasy, sprawled in a green faux-leather recliner, was a woman. Greasy's sister? Girlfriend? Wife? Whoever she was, she sported a stringy mop of platinum-blond hair with two-inch black roots. Dressed in a faded muumuu, she was watching reruns of the Maury Povich show on an old tube television and smoking Parliaments. *Chain*-smoking Parliaments, if the overflowing ashtray beside her was anything to go by.

Taken as a pair, the two were incongruous. What with Mac estimating Greasy didn't weigh in at over a buck and a quarter soaking wet while Mrs. Greasy had to be pushing the scales at close to four hundred pounds.

This is the clean, secure place Morales reserved for us? he thought, glancing around the wood-paneled office with its row of dusty tchotchkes in the window and the lone gumball machine by the front door. The ceiling fan whirled drunkenly overhead, off balance and doing little to cut through the smoke floating near the ceiling.

The flickering neon sign outside proclaimed the place was the Noel Motel, but from the looks of Mr. and Mrs. Greasy—not to mention the hourly rates, the rickety row of doors leading to no-doubt questionably cleaned rooms, and the off-street parking located in the back of the place—Mac figured it might as well have been named the No Tell Motel. And if Delilah hadn't looked as though she was about to collapse in her tracks, like her giddy-up-and-go done got up and went, he might have insisted they go somewhere else.

"My boss called and reserved some rooms for us," Agent Duvall announced as she shouldered through the front door, Zoelner, Ozzie, and the SWAT guys—now dressed in civilian garb—ambling in behind her. Quick as a cricket, the CIA had replaced the agent's car while simultaneously supplying Fitzsimmons and Wallace with new duds. Mac had to give it to the spooks. They were grade-A number ones when it came to pulling rabbits out of hats.

"You're the Land Management folks who're in town to check on our water quality?" Greasy asked, dragging his eyes away from Delilah's breasts in order to assess the newly arrived group. He grinned again when he got a load of Agent Duvall's rack.

Talk about ten pounds of shit in a five-pound bag, Mac thought uncharitably, moving slightly in order to draw Greasy's attention away from the women. It worked. When Greasy saw his unfriendly expression, the guy's smile faltered.

"That'd be us," Chelsea concurred, pushing her way up to the desk.

"You come to find out why the water outta the tap smells like swamp ass some days?" Mrs. Greasy inquired, never taking her eyes off the television screen. Smoke curled from her nostrils as she used the butt of one cigarette to light the tip of another.

"Sure did." Chelsea reached into her carryall to whip out a credit card stamped with a picture of a pine forest and the words *Land Management*.

See… Rabbit out of hat. Mac shook his head, then narrowed his eyes and stepped over to Delilah when she swayed slightly. She lifted a hand to her temple and squeezed her eyelids closed.

Okay, and just call him Mr. Stuck Between a Rock and a Hard Place. Because the Southern boy in him, the *gentleman* in him, couldn't stand there watching her wilt right before his eyes, not when it would be so easy to lend her his support. Then again, there was the whole crack cocaine thing. And, truth be known, his little addiction had only gotten worse since that scene up in Sander's bedroom.

Christ. How did I let it go so far? How could I have forgotten about the past? About Jolene? About not falling into that same ol' trap that—

The decision of whether he should or shouldn't lend Delilah a strong shoulder to lean on was made for him when she opened her eyes and lifted her gaze to his face. Her expression was sad enough to bring a tear to a glass eye. And—*ah, hell*—that was it. He couldn't stand it a second longer. He threw an arm around her shoulders.

"Okay," Agent Duvall said to Greasy after having run her credit card. "We're good here. Thanks for the hospitality."

"Any time," Greasy answered the CIA agent's chest. Zoelner looked like he was ten seconds away from ripping the guy's head off. And, yessiree, Mac certainly knew the feeling.

Luckily, he and Zoelner were saved from being forced to hone their decapitation skills when Agent Duvall turned, motioning for the group to follow her. And like a troop of well-trained goslings, they tailed Mother Goose out into the motel's patchy front lawn.

"Morales booked it so you men are bunking two to a room," she said, sorting through a handful of old-fashioned keys. The bits of dull metal were attached to key rings that were themselves attached to plastic circles sporting numbers. Apparently, Mr. and Mrs. Greasy hadn't upgraded the Noel Motel's locks to that of twenty-first century standards.

Again, Mac couldn't help but think *clean and secure? This place?*

It was almost like Agent Duvall's supervisor was pulling a giant joke on them. And, come to think of it, he wouldn't necessarily put it past the guy. After all, BKI's relationship with The Company had been on shaky ground ever since the CIA erroneously listed Rock, the

Knights' resident interrogator extraordinaire, as a rogue operator. And then there was the fact that the Black Knights had happily taken on Dagan Zoelner after the spooks booted him out. So, yeah, giant joke. Had to be.

Then again, Agent Duvall didn't *look* like there was a hidden candid camera behind one of her shirt buttons. In fact, she looked serious as death while untangling the mess of keys. "All the rooms have two full-sized beds in them," she said. "So it shouldn't be a problem for you boys to double up."

"Don't tell me the CIA is too cheap to spring for individual rooms," Ozzie harrumphed, crossing his arms. "Or maybe you guys spent all your money on those two-hundred-dollar ashtrays and four-thousand-dollar toilet seats?"

"Z," Agent Duvall said, completely ignoring Ozzie, "you and Mac are in room three." She handed Zoelner the key. "Delilah gets her own room, number four."

Mac watched Delilah reach forward to take the key and noted her hand trembled ever so slightly. He instinctively pulled her closer to his side. She tucked her thumb through one of his belt loops, and why that one small move—her subtle message of trust—should simultaneously thrill him and scare him shitless he didn't know.

"Fitzsimmons and Wallace," Agent Duvall handed a key to the now jean-clad, T-shirt-wearing Fitzsimmons, "you guys are in room five. I figure with Delilah between both groups, no one will feel left out." And *that* was a bit political for a spook. Generally, they weren't known to be all that accommodating. "I'll be in room six. Which leaves Ozzie and Steady, once he returns, to take up residence in room seven."

As if speaking the man's name aloud somehow con-jured him up, Mac's phone vibrated in his hip pocket. Pulling out the device, he saw the medic's encrypted number on his screen.

"Go," he barked, listening intently. Then, "Steady, man, I know details aren't your strong suit," BKI's medic was notorious for being overly—and most times confusingly—concise, "but I'm gonna need more than a simple report of *situation stable, medical intervention commencing*." Steady blew out a blustery breath on the other end of the connection before deigning to oblige him. Ending the call, Mac quickly relayed Steady's news. "Fido's bleedin' has stopped. He's bein' wheeled into surgery. The vet says chances are good the big jughead will make it."

Delilah lifted her free hand to her mouth, her big green eyes brightening with tears. When her chin started to wobble, Mac knew the fear, fatigue, and overwhelm-ing doses of adrenaline she'd been running on for more than a day had finally taken their toll. She needed a hot shower and soft bed. In that order. And fast.

"He's really going to make it?" she asked, trying to blink away her tears. One lone drop defied her efforts and slid down her dusty cheek.

"He said chances are good," Mac assured her, tak-ing the key from her hand and nodding for the rest of the group to carry on as he escorted her to her room. Inserting the key into the lock, he had to wiggle it a bit, but the knob finally turned. Pushing the door open, he hit the light switch on the wall and discovered, much to his surprise, that the Noel Motel's room number four was decently clean.

Oh, the bedspreads on the two beds were faded, and the carpet sported a faint stain under the window air-conditioning unit. But the walls appeared to be freshly painted. The furniture seemed to have been made sometime within the past decade. And the air smelled of cleaning supplies, furniture polish, and freshly laundered linens. Apparently, Mr. and Mrs. Greasy were smart enough to employ a decent maid staff.

Who woulda thunk it?

Maneuvering Delilah over the threshold, he allowed the door to swing shut behind them. Well, *almost* shut. It caught on the doorframe at the top and remained open a tiny crack. *Yeah, super secure spot Morales picked out for us. Pfft.* Not bothering to wrestle the aperture into place, he turned back to find Delilah watching him. And it was then he realized he was alone. With her. In a motel room. With *two* beds.

His stomach began a freefall like the time he'd been on a BKI mission that required him to execute a HALO—high altitude/low open—jump out of a Boeing C-17 over the spiky mountains of the Hindu Kush. That particularly hairy assignment had almost killed him. He wasn't completely certain this situation right here wasn't just as dangerous.

"If you're okay here, I'm gonna head next door," Mac said after he switched on the window air-conditioning unit. It hummed to life, filling the room with the sharp, dry aroma of chemical coolant.

Delilah turned to find him backing toward the door, the look on his face wary and slightly…alarmed?

Wha—She blinked, narrowing her eyes as her weary brain tried to make sense of his expression. Then it hit her when his gaze darted to one of the beds and lingered there a moment.

Really? He's scared I'm going to jump his bones?

She resisted the urge to roll her eyes. And then, blame it on exhaustion or frustration or mental whiplash from riding an emotional roller coaster for the last thirty-six hours, but she found, in that moment, she very much wanted to prove him right. She *did* want to jump his bones. If for no other reason than to wipe that ridiculous look off his face.

Crossing her arms, she tilted her head. "What's with you, anyway?"

He blinked. "Huh?"

"I mean, all this time, I thought you didn't particularly like me. Thought maybe you didn't like red hair." She lifted a lock off her shoulder. "Or thick thighs." She motioned toward her legs. "But then there was that whole deal up in Sander's bedroom and—"

"You don't have thick thighs," Mac muttered, not quite meeting her gaze. "I don't know why women always think they have thick thighs…"

"*That's* what you took away from what I just said?"

He *did* meet her gaze then. And what do you suppose the big, irritating, lug did? He shrugged. Shrugged! *Ooh!*

"Okay," she huffed. "Let me put it another way. How can you have spent the last four years sneering at me like I'm something stuck to the bottom of your shoe, and then suddenly claim last night that you're my friend? How can you claim to be my friend last night, only to kiss me cross-eyed up in Sander's bedroom this morning?" She enumerated her points on her fingers as she made them. "And how can you kiss me cross-eyed this morning, only to turn around and sneer at me down in Sander's living room five minutes later? It's like you can't decide whether you like me or loathe me."

He hooked his thumbs in his front belt loops and rocked back on his heels. He may've been trying to pretend supreme indolence, but the air around him, the air between them, crackled with electricity. And his expression might've suddenly gone all lazy, Southern boy, devil-may-care, his stare heavy lidded, but his eyes were absolutely full of guarded calculation.

"Like you said," he mumbled, "given the evidence in Sander's bedroom, it's quite obvious my feelings toward you fall *firmly* in the 'like' category."

"I'm not talking *physically*," she stressed. "I get now that your boy parts like my girl parts, thick thighs and all, but—"

"You *do not* have thick thighs!"

"Why the hell are we still talking about my thighs?"

"Because you keep bringin' them up!" He'd dropped the easy-going act. Now his wide jaw was sawing back and forth, and he crossed his arms over his chest. Yep. There were those barbed wire tattoos. And *there* were those bulging biceps.

"Answer the *goddamned* question, Mac!"

"It's not that I don't like you!" he roared, then caught himself and blew out a breath. For a second, he did nothing but give his jaw muscles a workout as he scowled down at the floor. Then, slowly he said, "But the thing is, I don't want to get involved with you…with a woman *like* you."

Whoa. Huh? Her hackles twitched to life.

"You might want to clarify that last statement," she warned, fisting her hands on her hips as she stalked toward him. He retreated a hasty step in response. "What do you mean a *woman like me?*"

He swallowed, his Adam's apple jerking up the tan column of his throat.

"I just meant…uh…a woman who's beautiful and vivacious and used to being adored and…um…stuff."

"Because…" She made a rolling motion with her finger, his pseudo-compliment having fallen on deaf ears because the way he said *beautiful* and *vivacious*, they might as well have been dirty words.

"Because I've seen what happens." He swallowed again when she took another step forward, then another, until the steel toes of her biker boots were barely an inch from his.

He was trapped between her and the motel room door. And not that he couldn't pick her up and toss her aside as easily as he could a cocktail napkin, but for now she had him right where she wanted him.

"And what exactly happens?" Her heartbeat was slow and steady, efficiently fueling the fire building in her blood.

"Delilah." When he said her name like that, all low and Sam Elliott throaty, she had to suppress a shiver. "I think very highly of you. I do. But…"

The word hung in the air for what seemed like forever. In reality it was probably only a second or two, but it was a second or two longer than Delilah had the patience for.

"But *what*, Mac?" she demanded.

He stared at her for a second more, his eyes narrowed like he was trying to see into her soul. She let him look. She had nothing to hide. Then he shrugged. "It's just that women like you aren't cut out for—" He stopped and shook his head. "You're nothing but trouble," he finally finished.

"Nothing but trouble?" If her jaw hadn't been attached to her head, it would've dropped to the floor. "Jesus Christ, Mac. You're a goddamned misogynist! I never would've believed that."

His chin jutted out stubbornly, making him look even more...*stubborn*. She didn't want to press a finger to that fascinating dimple now. She wanted to slam a fist into it. *Pow!* One hit in the name of all womanhood!

"I'm *not* a misogynist," he growled. "I love women. Everything about them. But I have firsthand knowledge of certain types of women, and I know my tendencies and limitations as well as theirs."

"You almost had me convinced," she sneered. "Up until that last bit, which was spoken like a true misogynist."

For a moment they just stood there, glowering at each other. Delilah fancied the flashing in her peripheral vision was actual sparks crackling through the air. The fine hairs on her arms and the back of her neck stood up as if in warning of a potential lightning strike. And then it happened. But the thunderbolt wasn't a burst of electricity from the sky, it was Mac's next words...

"Would a misogynist have resisted you all this time because he knew he couldn't offer you anything more than a hard fuck?" And not that she wasn't used to him cursing. He could sling a blue streak as well as anyone. But what she *wasn't* used to was him being so crude about it. "Would a misogynist have suffered innumerable hard-ons just to save you the ignominy of a one-night stand?"

Of their own accord, her eyes darted down to the fly of his Levis. Sure enough, there it was. Mr. Woody.

"I was *protectin'* you, goddamnit!" he nearly shouted, causing her eyes to fly to his face. "I know you're lookin' for more than a scratch for your itch. And since I can't *give* you more, I was savin' you the hurt and humiliation!"

"But…" She knew she was about to open herself up for more rejection. "*Why*? I don't understand!"

He threw his hands in the air before pushing her aside so he could pace in front of the double beds. "We've already gone through this." His booted steps thudded angrily against the carpet.

"Humor me," she said, folding her arms over her chest, chafing her biceps. Cold. She suddenly felt very cold. Because of the air-conditioner? Or because she somehow sensed just how chilling Mac's next words would be?

"I knew a woman once," he said. "A woman who reminds me of you in some ways. She ruined…everything. And I'm not *willin'* to stand by and watch history repeat itself."

She felt she'd just taken one punch to the chin and another to the stomach. "B-but that's not fair," she whispered. "You can't hold me accountable for something—"

"Fair?" His expression turned ugly. "Let me be the first to tell you, darlin', life ain't fair. In fact, it's a goddamned—"

A hard knock sounded on the partially closed door. Ozzie immediately popped his head in. "Damn," he said.

"I was hoping to catch you kids going at it again." He wiggled his eyebrows. Then his grin faltered when he sensed the strained atmosphere. "Is…uh…is everything okay in here?"

Okay? No. Everything was *not* okay.

"We're fine," Mac grumbled, sparing her a quick glance. She wanted to gouge his pretty blue eyes out. "What's up?"

Ozzie hesitated a second, frowning at Delilah.

Damnit! Tears burned behind her eyes. But this time they weren't sad tears or frightened tears. They were pissed-off tears! *I'm-going-to-punch-Mac-in-the-balls* tears!

"I feel like I'm missing something here," Ozzie ventured.

"Yeah," Delilah told him. "You're missing the fact that your pal," she motioned to Mac, "is an enormous asshole."

One corner of Ozzie's mouth twitched. "Nah. I've known that for years, and I—"

"Ozzie." Mac cut him off, that wonderful drawl of his grating against Delilah's nerves like sharp teeth sawing on bone. "What was it you came in here for?"

"Oh, uh, yeah. So, Chelsea has a few updates to share with us. She wants us to gather in Zoelner's room."

And that, effectively, was a verbal blanket thrown over the fire of Delilah's fury. Updates. *Uncle Theo…*

Her lungs squeezed down inside her chest, causing her next exhalation to wheeze out of her like a tire that had just rolled over a nail.

Screw Mac and his cowardly, warped sense of reality. She had more important things to deal with…

Chapter Seventeen

"You come through with that," Chelsea said into her Bluetooth device as she sat on the bed closest to the window, quickly swiping images on her iPad. It was Dagan's bed. The one he'd chosen for himself. But he wasn't going to ponder that. "And I'll kiss you on all four cheeks."

His back molars set. Flirting. Chelsea Duvall was flirting with whatever douchebag technician was yapping in her ear, and it made him want to spit nails.

"Come through with what?" he demanded, flicking a glance at the two CIA agents standing on either side of her, their eyes glued to her device's screen. From here on out, he was going to refer to Fitzsimmons and Wallace as Tweedle Dee and Tweedle Dum, the Bobbsey Twins of synchronized scowls and whispered exchanges. And, *yes*, he was fully aware he was mixing up his fictional characters, but right now he didn't give a rat's ass.

Because it was obvious he was the extra wheel here, The Company folks having teamed up in an Evil Agency Trifecta. Or maybe he was just still fuming over the fact that Chelsea had lied to him. *Lied straight through her pretty white teeth.* And there was a large part of him that couldn't help but wonder if she would have done the same six years ago, or if her lack of faith in him *now* stemmed entirely from that colossal fuckup in Afghanistan.

Something told him it was the latter.

Pushing the familiar pain aside, he demanded again. "Chelsea, what's going on, damnit? Come through with *what*?"

She frowned and he braced himself for the impact of her molten eyes. He'd once heard Mac characterize a woman as whiskey in a tea cup—pretty on the outside, kickass on the inside—and he couldn't help but think the description suited Chelsea to a T. And just as he expected, when she lifted her gaze to his, it was like a potshot to the gut.

"Hang on just one minute, you impatient *ass*," she hissed at him.

"I prefer *Mr*. Impatient Ass, thank you very much." Yes, he liked to push her buttons. So sue him. Currently, it was the only advantage he had and—The door burst open, admitting Ozzie closely followed by Mac and Delilah.

Whoa, he immediately thought. *Who ate your bowls of sunshine, thunderclouds?*

Because one look at the last two arrivals told him that whatever understanding the pair had reached earlier, the one that had resulted in Delilah sporting a fresh, pink beard stubble rash, had since been blown to smithereens. Delilah's color was so high he worried for her blood pressure. And Mac? Well, Mac managed to look simultaneously pissed and pensive.

Jesus, you big, dumb Texan. Back to wearing your ass as a hat, are you?

And then Mac proved him correct when the guy leaned down to whisper to Delilah, "I don't know why you've got your panties in such a twist over this." Dagan raised a brow. Because telling a woman her panties were in a twist always worked in a guy's favor. *Not.* "And I don't know why *I'm* the bad guy here. In fact, if you'll just settle down and think about it, you'll see I probably deserve a goddamned medal for Herculean self-control."

Delilah's invitation for Mac to shove his opinions *and* his hypothetical medal where the sun didn't shine was issued and immediately ignored.

"Darlin'," Mac began.

"Don't you darlin' me, you overgrown ape!" Delilah snapped. "I've had quite enough of your *darlings*. In fact, if I hear one more *darlin'* fall out of your mouth, I swear to God I'm going to haul off and punch you in the balls."

Mac's chin jerked back, his eyes narrowing. *Uh-oh.* Dagan knew when a man was about to dig himself into a hole that might be impossible to climb out of. He opened his mouth to try to save Mac, but the idiot beat him to the punch.

"Oh, yeah?" He taunted Delilah. "Well, you're welcome to try it, sugar pants. See where it gets you."

Sugar pants? Dagan winced.

"You did *not* just call me sugar pants," Delilah snarled.

If Dagan had to give a title to the expression Mac suddenly donned, it would be Extreme Disinterest. And *that*, along with accusations of twisted panties, was *another* thing universally known not to sit too well with a woman, especially not one a guy was in the middle of having an argument with. Dagan imagined he could actually *see* Mac heaving a shovelful of dirt over his shoulder.

"You just said you didn't want me callin' you darlin'."

The former Fed shrugged. "And of the *other* two names that came to mind, sugar pants seemed the nicest."

Dagan watched Delilah's eyes narrow to slits, her lips flattening into a thin line. He began to worry for Mac's balls when her hands curled into fists. "Mac," she hissed, "I swear to God, I'm going to—"

"Hey," Chelsea cut in, having signed off with that douchebag of a technician, "can we roll the credits on this little feel-good movie and get down to brass tacks?"

"By all means. Let's do that," Mac said, shooting Delilah a look that had morphed from disinterest to disapproval. And, yep. There went shovelful number two.

Dagan's gaze flicked to Delilah. With a tinge of admiration, he watched as she physically pulled herself together. Taking a deep breath, she briefly closed her eyes before squaring her shoulders and saying to Chelsea, "Yes, Agent Duvall. Please fill us in on what you know."

When he was sure Delilah's attention was diverted, Dagan reached over and socked Mac on the shoulder, scowling, his expression yelling, *what the hell, dude?*

The look Mac offered him in response couldn't be mistaken. Quite simply, it was the facial equivalent of *mind your own fucking business*.

Shovelful number three? Four?

Dagan just shook his head. Who was he to try to save a guy who didn't seem to want saving?

"The good news is," Chelsea said, "we've found your uncle's motorcycle."

"You did?" Delilah breathed, reaching up to place a hand over her mouth.

"Yes." Chelsea nodded. "It was parked inside one of the buildings on Main Street back in Cairo." She turned to Dagan then, and he could still read her well enough to know what was coming next. *Christ*. They'd been so close. "The same building we saw the four green dots in on the thermal imagery earlier this morning. The same building that is, as I'm sure you've already guessed, now empty."

"H-he was there," Delilah whispered, her eyes wide. "My uncle was there in that building, only a few blocks away, while we were in Sander's house."

"Yes." Chelsea nodded. "We're certain he was."

Dagan picked up on her inflection. "Certain? What do you mean by *certain*?"

Chelsea lifted her hand to push her glasses up the length of her nose. He knew it for the stalling tactic it was. Whatever was coming next, it wasn't good news.

"There was blood at the scene," she admitted, her eyes trained on Delilah. "And though our labs are going to need a DNA cheek swab from you to verify it's source, initial indications are that it *is* your uncle's. We have his blood type on file from his time in the military. The sample at the scene is a match."

And speaking of blood…every ounce drained from Delilah's face. Her cheeks had been red as cherry bombs when she entered the room a minute ago. Now they were whiter than the snow that blanketed the Windy City in January.

"But we view this discovery in a positive light," Chelsea continued, attempting to provide Delilah with hope. "Because even though there's blood, the fact that he was taken means he's still alive. And that's what you need to focus on."

Delilah blew out a blustery breath, and Dagan watched Mac curl his hands into fists in an obvious attempt to keep from reaching out to comfort the woman. *Jesus, dude. Just do it. Just show her how much you care.*

"Which is more than I can say for Charles Sander," Chelsea admitted, and Dagan's chin snapped around, his eyes landing on her face. "We found his body in another abandoned building. Our MEs are saying he's been dead about twenty-four hours. Initial indications are that he had a heart attack or a stroke while under-going…uh…"—she hesitated, seeming to search for words—"rigorous questioning."

"You can say torture," Delilah whispered. "I can handle it."

Chelsea's expression was sympathetic. "Your uncle is now the *only* person who can give the terrorists the information they seek. Which means they're going to do everything they can to keep him alive until they get it."

And then Delilah proved just what a bright bulb she really was. "But that also means they're going to do ev-erything they can to make him talk, right?"

Chelsea swallowed uncomfortably, nodding.

"Jesus." Delilah turned her back on the group, and Ozzie threw an arm around her shoulders, bending to whisper something in her ear. Mac's jaw ground with such force, Dagan was surprised little bits of tooth enamel didn't come flying out of his ears.

"There's more," Chelsea said. "An investigation into the car that al-Hallaj left behind revealed he rented it, along with a similar vehicle, over the border in Canada."

"Canada?" Dagan shook his head. "So, *that's* how he made it into the country?"

"Yes. From what we've been able to determine, he snuck into Canada on a cargo barge that docked in the

Port of Quebec. Then, using false documents, he made his way inland. Highway photos taken from Canadian Border Services reveal that after he rented the two vehicles, he crossed into the U.S. with three compatriots. One of whom is Qasim ibn Hasan."

The minute the name was spoken, a cold chill snaked up Dagan's spine.

"Oh, crap," Ozzie muttered at the same time Mac said something under his breath that wasn't worth repeating.

Delilah glanced around at the faces of the men, her brows pulled down in confusion. "And who is Qasim ibn Hasan?" she asked.

Dagan wasn't too surprised by her question. Most Americans didn't pay all that much attention to terrorist attacks on foreign soil, even when the news of the attacks was splashed all over their television screens and headlining their newspapers.

"You remember hearing or reading about the bombing of the Grand Hyatt hotel in Istanbul?" Chelsea asked. Delilah rolled in her lips, nodding. "How about the series of bus bombings in Dublin and the murder of schoolgirls in Iraq?" Again Delilah jerked her chin up and down. "Well, Qasim ibn Hasan is responsible for all three, and likely a whole lot more that we're not certain of."

"And he has my uncle?" Delilah rasped.

"Indeed he does. But we're doing everything we can to find him."

Qasim ibn Hasan...Jesus, Dagan thought. And if he wasn't mistaken, that sound he was hearing was the sweet, dulcet tones of the shit hitting the fan.

"Why?" Delilah asked, and he cocked his head, staring at her in confusion.

"What do you mean?" Chelsea asked.

"Why would he bomb hotels or blow up city busses or kill schoolgirls? Why does he hate everyone so much?"

Ah, the search for reason in the unreasonable. Dagan knew the exercise well.

"Not *everyone*," Chelsea corrected. "Just us. Because even though his previous targets were all on foreign soil, each of those countries is one of our allies. And all of his victims were either Westerners, like those in the hotel and on the buses, or they were proponents of Western ideals, like the Iraqi girls who had the unqualified gall to try to get an education."

"Then why does he hate *us* so much," Delilah asked, shaking her head. "I mean, what did we ever do to him?"

"Killed his family," Tweedle Dee spoke up for the first time.

"What?" Dagan snapped.

"It's true." Chelsea nodded. "His wife and two boys were victims of a drone strike about a dozen years ago. Before that, Qasim was a simple merchant. Now, he's one of America's Most Wanted."

"For fuck's sake," Mac grumbled, running a hand over the back of his neck. "Sometimes I don't know if we *make* more enemies with predator drone strikes than we kill."

Dagan snorted. "Fire from above does tend to radicalize men who would have otherwise remained neutral." After much consideration on the subject, years in fact, the only sense he could make of it all was that drones were an imperfect solution to an incredibly complicated issue.

"So it's revenge he's after?" Delilah asked.

"Yes," Chelsea admitted. "But it's warped revenge. What you have to remember is that his family was killed by accident. As terrible as it is to say, they were unfortunate collateral damage in a war. The war on terror. It happens. But *he* is deliberately taking his remorse and vengeance out on innocent targets. I mean, schoolgirls? Grannies and single moms riding the bus? There's no reciprocity there, no equality of grievance. If he targeted military bases or embassies? Sure, I could see that. Give credence to his actions, even. A war is a war, after all.

"But he's *not* going after soldiers or diplomats." She shook her head. "He's deliberately going after women and children. And that makes him a monster in my book. Whatever kind of man he might have been *before* that bomb landed in his village doesn't matter. Now he's evil. An evil man doing evil deeds."

It was an impassioned speech given by a passionate woman. Chelsea was a true patriot. And she *believed* in the U.S. government. Even through all its missteps and mistakes, through all its self-serving appointments and support of totalitarian dictators, through all its posturing and bullying, she believed *America* was still a beacon of hope the world over. They'd had many discussions on the subject long ago, and it seemed her stance hadn't become jaded in all the years since.

But she wasn't finished. "We all, each and every one of us standing in this room," she slid a glance toward him, "have lost people we love in this war. But you don't see us killing indiscriminately. You don't see us searching for nuclear weapons to unleash on an innocent civilian population."

"Yeah." Delilah nodded wearily, lifting a hand to her temple. "I…I understand. I really do. I just can't help but wish my uncle wasn't caught up in the middle of it."

"You and me both." Chelsea's smile was compassionate. "But we're doing everything we can, using satellite imagery and scouring traffic camera footage to try to locate that second rental vehicle. We're going through phone records, recent online chatter of known domestic terrorist groups, and much, *much* more. I assure you, the minute I hear something, you'll be the first to know. In the meantime, why don't you head next door and get some sleep."

Delilah shook her head. "I don't think I can."

"Then just lie down and rest for a while. We don't know how long this thing will last. But regardless of whether its hours or days, you're going to need your strength."

"Yeah," Delilah conceded on a heavy sigh, looking a little lost and a lot beaten down. "Yeah, you're right."

"And you don't have to worry about al-Hallaj making another attempt to snatch you. These guys," Chelsea motioned to the Knights as well as Dee and Dum, "will be taking shifts guarding both your door and your bathroom window around back."

"Thank you," Delilah said wearily, allowing her gaze to alight on every face in the room in turn. "Thank you all for everything."

"No thanks are necessary," Dagan assured her.

She gifted him with a sad, tired smile before turning for the door.

"I'll take first shift out front," Mac declared, stepping up behind her.

"Hey." Dagan stopped him with a hand on his shoulder. "Why don't you let me do that?" He lowered his voice so only Mac you hear him. "Then you can go make right with her whatever it is you just made wrong with her."

"I didn't make *anything* wrong with her," Mac insisted. "And I'm *takin'* the first shift."

Dagan released the big Texan, shrugging and thinking, *well, like my mother used to say, there's no use trying to make chicken salad out of chicken shit...*

Chapter Eighteen

Three hours later…

SITTING IN THE PLASTIC CHAIR HE'D POSITIONED BESIDE the door of the Noel Motel's room number four, Mac closed his eyes and counted to ten. Twice. Then three times. And when that didn't work, he went in for a fourth.

None of it helped. He was still hornier than a bull separated from the heifers in the herd. And why should that be, do you suppose? Well, because five minutes ago, when he knocked on Delilah's door to hand her the turkey sandwich and bag of chips Ozzie procured from the local Subway, she answered his summons in her T-shirt.

In her T-shirt, and nothing else…

Oh, sure. She'd been wearing panties. Pink panties, to be exact. Pink panties with a little red bow on the front—not that he was obsessing about them or anything. Okay, so maybe he was obsessing a *little*. But, the pink panties alone wouldn't have put him in this particular predicament—hot and hard and fidgety as a woodshed waiter—had they not also been paired with a clean white T-shirt that she'd donned after taking yet another shower. And let's not even get him *started* on the earlier agony of what it had been like to sit *out*side her door, listening to water running *in*side, all the while picturing her naked and wet, because *that* was another issue altogether.

No. When he said she answered the door in her T-shirt and nothing else, what he really meant was that she'd been without a bra. And he'd been able to make out the shape of her nipples. Her decadent, rosy-red nipples. Those nipples he'd licked and laved and sucked just a few hours back. Those nipples that, despite everything he told himself to the contrary, despite everything he told *her* to the contrary, he wanted quite desperately to lick and lave and suck again.

Christ almighty. He was in a bad way. And it didn't help matters that, for the last three hours, he'd been soundly chastising himself for the way he handled things after she flat-out asked him why he didn't like her.

Didn't like her? Was she crazy? *Of course* he liked her. What wasn't to like?

But, in true *guy* form, when he tried to convey that it wasn't *her*, that it was *him*, it'd somehow come out sounding all wrong. Accusatory, almost. And offensive, certainly.

"Holy shit fire, man," he muttered to himself. "You gotta get it together."

And while he was at it, he'd also do well to yank his head out of his ass. Because too much more of *that* kind of thinking, of obsessing about Delilah, about what he should or should not have said, about how gorgeous and sexy and flat-out provocative she was, and he might be tempted to say *fuck it* to all his hard-earned life lessons, *fuck it* to everything, and just give in. Give in to the needs of his body. Give in to her desire to see where things between them might lead…

But while he was damn sure he could pull off the first of those two things, he was also just as certain the second would be asking too much. He may like Delilah immensely, respect her grit and her spunk, but…God's honest truth, he didn't…well, he didn't *trust* her. Or, more accurately, he didn't trust himself *around* her.

Think of Jolene, he told himself. *Think of that god-awful morning when the bank came to take the ranch…*

And, yessir. That helped to instantly cool his ardor. Because, not counting the day his father died, the day he lost the Lazy M was the worst of his entire, sorry life.

It'd been gone. Just like that. The land his ancestors had worked for three generations. The big, rambling house that had seen the births and deaths of his father, grandfather, and great-grandfather. The cattle herd he'd helped breed, brand, and build. All of it was taken from him in the blink of an eye. And all because the blessedly few extra pennies that had been in the ranch's coffers had gone to finding Jolene…

Lawyers, private eyes…hell, even a former police detective had milked the estate dry. And then the inheritance taxes had come due, followed by a balloon mortgage payment, and that was that. Game over.

Aimless, set adrift when his entire world, his entire *future*, was snatched from him, he'd enrolled in the criminal justice program at Texas A&M. Four years later, he was accepted into the FBI Training Academy. And a handful of years after that—*thank you, U.S. government, for your zealous record keeping*—he was the one to finally locate Jolene.

Living in California with some big shot movie executive, she was as lovely as he remembered. And even *knowing* what kind of woman she was—the kind to run out on her husband, her home, and…*everything* with only a simple Dear John letter reading *I'm unhappy. I'm leaving*—he'd still been amazed at how uncaring she'd been to learn he lost the ranch after his father's death.

"Good riddance," she'd told him. "That place was like a prison. I never hid how much I hated it."

And that was true. If she'd expressed her loathing for the Lazy M once, she'd done it a thousand times.

"It was *awful* there. Endless days of housework, of staring out at boring ol' fields and fat, smelly cattle," she went on, tossing her long black hair over her shoulder. "I was the Belle of Lee County before the marriage. Did you know that?" Of course he knew that. It's all she'd ever talked about. "I was respected and admired and invited to all the best parties." Her blue eyes took on a dreamy, faraway expression before suddenly sharpening. "And then I moved out to the Lazy M." Her top lip curled. "Where there *were* no parties. No people to respect or admire me. No excitement. No fun." She shuddered dramatically, then turned her beautiful, vivacious smile on him. "So I did what was best for everyone and left."

And although he found it impossible to believe, he could see she actually thought that was true.

"And just *look* at me here." She motioned around the massive house. "I'm the belle again! Oh, Bry-Bear," she cooed, reaching forward to smooth a hand over his cheek. The old nickname, once so cherished, sounded like an obscenity, and her touch repulsed him. "Now you're free of the ranch, too. Everything worked out! Isn't it wonderful?"

Wonderful? No. Nothing about what she'd done was wonderful. He'd never *wanted* to be free of the ranch. Being free of the ranch felt second only to death.

He left rubber on the movie executive's immaculate driveway on his way out. And sitting on Redondo Beach later that day, staring out over the seemingly infinite expanse of the Pacific Ocean, he promised himself two things. The first was that he would never allow history to repeat itself. And the second was that, someday, he was going to make enough money to buy back the Lazy M.

In the years since he made that vow, he'd managed to accumulate about half the funds necessary to put in an offer on the ranch—his work for the Black Knights and the sizeable government paychecks that came with that work having helped substantially. As for history repeating itself?

Enter Delilah…

With her bold nature and fiery beauty, she was *just* the kind of woman he found most desirable. The kind to light up the room. The kind of woman guaran-damn-teed to—

Bzzzz. Bzzzz. The buzzing of his cell phone pulled him from his troubling thoughts. Reaching into his hip pocket, he yanked out the device to find Steady's encrypted number blinking on the screen.

"Talk to me," he barked. And for once, Steady did, throwing out a litany of medical terms. From the corner of Mac's eye, he watched Ozzie approach, sub sandwich in hand. "All right, Steady," he said when BKI's medic wound down. "We'll see you here in a bit." Then he stood and motioned Ozzie over. "I need you to take over for me here while I go in and give Delilah the news on Fido."

And considering he was seconds away from having to knock on her door and see her in those goddamned pink panties and that goddamned might-as-well-be-see-through T-shirt, it was no wonder dread was circling around in the pit of his stomach.

"Sure thing, Mac my man." Ozzie plopped into the plastic chair. A warm, dry wind blew against the motel, tunneling fingers through Mac's hair and wafting the smell of the mustard and salami on Ozzie's sandwich up his nose. His stomach growled. He realized he hadn't touched his own sandwich, too caught up in hot thoughts of Delilah and the cold grip of old memories.

"While you're in there," Ozzie said, pulling out a pickle and munching contentedly, his standard grin firmly in place, "don't do anything I wouldn't do."

"Well, hell," Mac told him, pulling a face as he rapped his knuckles against the baby-blue door. "That doesn't leave much, now does it?"

—◦◦◦—

"It's open," Delilah called. She was curled beneath the linens of the bed farthest from the door. The TV atop the dresser was tuned to *The Price Is Right*, the volume up in an attempt to distract her from constantly obsessing over her uncle. Or Mac. She seemed to go back and forth between the two men when she wasn't muttering to the contestants on the game show that their bids were too high.

I mean seriously, Janelle from Wisconsin, do you really think a seven-piece dining set costs thirty thousand

dollars? What do you suppose that table is made of?
Antique ivory? The tears of archangels?

And not that she had anything against Drew Carey,
but she really missed Bob Barker.

"Delilah," Mac said, tipping his chin by way of
acknowledging her presence in the room. And it was
amazing, but she'd never found the sound of her own
name more irritating. Add to that, he was wearing her
second favorite expression.

"Wow, Mac," she grumbled. "You could really
start a business with that look of disapproval. You're
Mud, LLC."

A muscle ticked in his jaw. And how was it possible
that even standing clear across the room he could still
make her skin tingle and her heart race?

Her shirt suddenly felt two sizes too small, squeezing
her breasts, brushing her nipples. *Sonofa—*

"I wanted to tell you…I…wanted to say," he began
hesitantly. Then, "Screw it. Look, I'm sorry for the way
I handled things earlier, okay? I didn't make myself very
clear, and I—"

"Oh, you made yourself perfectly clear."

"No." He forced out the word. "I should have just
said, it's not you, it's me."

"Jesus, Mac." She rolled her eyes. "It's like you're a
walking cliché."

"Maybe so," he admitted on a sigh. Then his eyes
flicked to the paper-covered sub sandwich lying beside
the lamp on the bedside table. "You haven't eaten."

"I'm not hungry," she assured him. And although it
was true, she hated that the three words came off sounding petulant.

"Stress burns calories," he said, crossing his arms, revealing his tattooed biceps. *For the love of tequila! Why do I have to find that so sexy?* "And unless, by the time we find your uncle, you want there to be nothin' left of you between your horns and your hooves but your hide, I suggest you force yourself to eat."

"Did you come in here just to badger me and throw out absurd cowboy-isms?" she demanded, refusing to look at him—he was just too tempting. Instead, she kept her eyes glued to the television screen.

"No. I came in here to give you something."

"Is it a shot of whiskey, a clean pair of jeans, or the promise of world peace?" she asked.

"No."

Sighing dramatically, she made sure her expression was bored when she finally turned to him, pointing a finger at her face. "Then this is me, interest having waned."

He frowned before sauntering in that loose-hipped way of his over to the dresser. Flicking off the TV, he said, "I came to give you an update. I just got a call from Steady."

"Fido?" she asked, dropping all pretense. Throwing back the bed sheet, she swung her legs over the edge of the mattress. "Is he…"

She couldn't bring herself to voice the next word. Alive? Dead? The first adjective might elicit an answer of *no,* and the second adjective might elicit an answer of *yes.*

"He made it through surgery." She released her pent-up breath. "Steady says, barring anything unexpected, he's gonna be humpin' legs and pissin' on hydrants in a couple of weeks."

"Thank God," she whispered, placing her elbows on her knees and bending forward. Her hair fell around her face in a curtain. She didn't attempt to brush it back. Tears of gratitude had sprung to her eyes, and she didn't want Mac to see them, see her being weak yet again.

The truth was, she hadn't known how desperately she needed some good news until she heard it. And the fact that Fido made it out of this horrendous, soul-sucking situation alive stoked the flame of hope burning inside her that perhaps her uncle, too, might just be blessed with the same fate.

And then, a thought occurred…

"I want him," she said, lifting her head, surprised to find Mac had taken a seat on the bed across from her. She hadn't heard him move, either because he'd employed his super stealthy covert operator skills or because she'd been too focused on keeping a firm hold on the reins of her emotions to pay attention to anything but her own breathing. Whichever, now he was facing her, his elbows resting on his muscular thighs, his big, tan hands laced together between his knees. Knees that were nearly touching hers, but she did *not* notice the delicious heat pouring from him. No, she most certainly did *not*.

"What do you mean you want him?" he asked, his brow furrowed.

"Charlie Sander is…uh…dead, right?" He nodded. "So, I want Fido."

After all, the dog had saved her life. The very least she could do now was provide the big goofball with a warm and loving home for the rest of *his*. Besides, every good biker bar needed a resident canine, right? Right.

"Uh." Mac reached up to run a hand over the back of his neck. "I suppose we'll have to make sure Sander didn't have any relatives who want him. But, yeah. Okay. If no one steps up, I reckon he's all yours."

"Good." She nodded, feeling like, for the first time in a long time, she was taking control of the situation. Making decisions instead of just allowing events to blow her around like the wind blew around the discarded peanut shells on the floor of her bar whenever someone entered or exited the place during a winter storm.

And since it felt so darned good to make that first decision, she resolved then and there to make another one. "And you know that one-night stand you were talking about earlier?" she asked, watching his eyes round slightly.

"Yeah?"

"I agree."

"Uh…" There went the hand again, rubbing over the back of his neck. She'd never noticed before, but he seemed to do that when he was deep in thought, troubled by something, or else uncomfortable. She figured in this case, it was the latter.

Good. She was glad she made him uncomfortable considering the effect his nearness had on *her*.

"What do you mean you agree?" he finally asked. "You agree that I was right to—"

"I agree to a one-night stand," she told him.

And too bad her iPhone was way over on the dresser. Because the litany of expressions that flashed across Mac's face was absolutely priceless, worthy of being preserved for posterity via a set of digital photos. First there was shock, then disbelief, quickly followed by denial, and finally a penetrating sort of...*interest*.

And maybe she was nuts, completely off her rocker—or else delirious from lack of sleep, which was entirely possible—but she couldn't help but think *what the hell*... After all, she'd been waiting *years* for him to take her up on one of her offers. And even though he was right when he said she wanted more from him than a scratch for her itch, something was better than nothing, right?

And, besides, there *was* that whole human tendency to want what you couldn't have. So, maybe, just maybe, once she *had* him, she'd stop wanting him.

The little voice in her head attempted to speak up, but she immediately shushed it.

"Y-you're not serious," he said.

"As a heart attack," she assured him, pushing to a stand.

He jumped up like the bed bit him on the ass, and was that...? Holy hell, Mac actually looked a bit scared. She fought a grin as she took a step toward him. He immediately began to skirt the bed like a jumper inching along the lip of a ledge.

"Whoa there." He held up a hand. "Slow your roll, darlin'. We need to talk about this."

"I'm all talked out today," she told him, stalking him across the room. "And, besides, this will kill two birds with one stone."

He lifted a brow.

"It'll scratch that itch you were talking about earlier. And it'll help me take my mind off my uncle."

"But—"

She grabbed his forearm and yanked him forward. "Shh." She placed a finger over his lips, shivering when his hot breath moistened her skin. "I'm handing you the golden ticket, Mac. Giving you the keys to the kingdom with no strings attached. Are you really going to stand here arguing with me?"

His big chest rose on a shaky breath. "No strings?" he asked around her finger.

"None."

"No hurt feelings afterward?"

"None," she promised, ignoring the little voice when it gleefully sing-songed *liar, liar, liiiiar…*

Chapter Nineteen

MAC KNEW DELILAH WAS STILL TALKING. HE COULD see her lips moving. But, for the life of him, he couldn't make out her words. All he could hear was his own heartbeat, fast and fierce and...unimaginably *hungry*.

The golden ticket. That's what she called it. But it was more than that. It was the golden ticket, a get-out-of-jail-free card, and a royal flush all rolled into one. Everything he'd never dared to hope for but simultaneously fantasized about. Delilah. His for the taking. With no strings attached. With no chance of heartbreak for... either of them.

He wished he could say he hesitated a moment, really thought about it, weighed all the pros and cons. But he didn't. In fact, the only thing he thought was *git along little doggies*. Or, in his case, git it *on* little doggie. *Yeehaw!*

He grabbed her around the waist and pushed her across the carpet. Lifting her atop the dresser, he slammed his mouth over hers. And that was it. They went from neutral to overdrive in two seconds flat.

The instant their lips met, their tongues clashed and fought for supremacy, his stroking hers, hers tangling with his. Her hands were everywhere, running over his shoulders, knotting in his hair, grabbing his ass. It was like being caught up in storm. He could feel the crack of electricity that was in the air, highlighting the raw, untamed power of it all. The pleasure was searing, seething, all-consuming.

In the back of his mind, he wondered if he should apply the brakes. At this rate, it was going to be over in minutes. Hot, hard, *fast* sex atop the Noel Motel's dresser. Fuckin'-A. But, really, who was he trying to kid? Stopping wasn't an option. Not when he'd already grabbed the hem of her T-shirt, whipped it over her head and tossed it over his shoulder. Not when he was already cupping her plump, beautiful breast and lifting it, running his thumb over the beaded nipple before ducking his chin to suck it into his mouth.

"God, you taste good," he moaned, dragging the smell of her in deep, reveling in the delicateness of her skin against his lips. Her nipple was a hard button pressing against his tongue. He stabbed at it and was rewarded with her groan of pleasure.

"Oh, *yes*, Mac," she sighed, tossing her head back, hooking her heels beneath his butt in order to rub herself over his raging length. He could feel her through the silk of her panties. Feel how hot she was. How wet. His cock pulsed behind his zipper, begging to be set free, pleading to sink into her soft, sultry depths.

A hundred emotions slammed through him. Joy. Passion. Fear…

Because being here, locked in her embrace reminded him of something. Of what it was like to be… *home*. But at the same time, he was lost. Lost in the feel of her hands. In the heated wetness of her mouth when she grabbed his face and dragged him up for a ravishing kiss.

She opened her lips wide to the bold press of his

tongue. But no matter how hard he pulled her against him or how strongly she grasped him to her, it wasn't enough. Wasn't *close* enough. He wanted to dissolve into her softness and warmth. Wanted to lose himself in her completely. And, *holy crow*, he couldn't recall anything ever being this hot. This fast. This…*crazy*.

He knew the bargain she'd struck with him was doomed. Once wasn't going to be enough. Not nearly enough. But he'd have to think about that, deal with that, later. For now? There was Delilah. Delilah with her warm, lush breasts. Delilah with her fast, feverish kisses. Delilah with her tempestuous, demanding hands…

She pulled his T-shirt over his head and flung it aside, her breath catching at the back of her throat as her eyes drank him in. And that look right there was enough to make a man think he could leap tall buildings in a single bound.

"Holy crap," she whispered almost reverently as she ran her hands over his chest, gently tracing the Texas tattoo over his heart. Then her fingers slid down his belly, causing his muscles to quiver and clench beneath her fingers. Delilah didn't have smooth, delicate hands. No. They were firm, slightly rough. The hands of a woman who'd spent her life twisting off bottle tops and washing pint glasses behind a bar. But the rest of her… Dear Lord, the rest of her was ungodly soft. "You're beautiful, Mac."

His lips quirked as he hooked his thumbs into the waistband of her pink, satin panties, the fabric silky against his fingers. He pulled back just enough to slide them down her long, lovely legs, past her delicate, red-tipped toes.

"Isn't that supposed to be my line?" he asked.

Her eyes were impossibly green when she met and held his gaze. Then she grinned, catching her bottom lip between her teeth, and he was totally dunzo.

Because she was temptation personified. Everything female and wonderful all packaged up and presented in one darling woman. From the gentle slope of her shoulders to the plump thrust of her breasts, from her small waist to the dramatic flare of her hips, she *was* femininity. Even her goddamned bellybutton looked girlish. Small and oval and begging for the dip of a man's tongue. *His* tongue.

"Does this hurt?" she whispered, pressing a soft finger to the fresh bandage over his stitches.

"Darlin'," he said, rubbing a hand over her hip, moving it around so he could palm her ass and pull her against him. And now, oh, she was *really* hot. Her wet channel riding the distended ridge of his fly. "Right now, I don't feel anything but you."

"Mmm," she said, bending forward to flick her wicked tongue over his Texas tattoo, then lower, to his nipple. "That's a really good answer."

Little Mac jumped with every dart of her tongue, every tug of her lips, and he couldn't stand it a second longer. Bending to open the middle drawer on the dresser, just a bit, just enough to create a tiny ledge, he placed her heels atop it. Putting his hand on the insides of her knees, he moved back slightly so he could see her, watch her as he spread her thighs wide.

And talk about femininity. There was the heart of her. Right there. Right in front of his face. She was flushed and pink. Ripe and swollen. Her small patch of pubic hair was auburn, shaved into a tiny triangle just above the entrance to the wet, warm wonder of her center. He couldn't see her clitoris, but he knew when he brushed his thumb up her silky channel, he'd find it distended, throbbing.

He dragged in a shuddering breath, and the smell of her, the smell of desire and sex and *woman* filled his nose, causing saliva to pool in his mouth, hot and heavy, causing his balls to pull tight against his body.

He glanced at her then, gauging her mood. Was she embarrassed by his blatant study? Some women didn't understand or appreciate the beauty of their bodies, their sex in particular.

But he shouldn't have worried. After all, it was Delilah. Bold, brazen, fearless Delilah. There was not one ounce of bashfulness in her expression, not one drop of chagrin. Just the opposite in fact, one elegant brow was arched, the light in her eyes nothing less than breathtakingly carnal.

"Jesus," he breathed in awe, trailing his hand up from her ankle to her calf, standing when he reached the soft, white expanse of her thigh. She *didn't* have thick thighs, no matter what she said. Like the rest of her, her thighs were soft and satiny and wonderfully, exotically feminine. "You're absolutely perfect," he told her, delighted by her low, husky chuckle.

"Hardly," she said. And then he couldn't pay attention to her next words, because she reached for his zipper...

⌁

Delilah was on fire.

From head to toe, she burned, ached, throbbed. And

she needed Mac. Needed him to take her, fill her…fuck her. She wanted to revel in the sensations. In the feel of his callused hand rubbing a slow trail up her inner thigh. In the smell of him, so hot and male and uniquely Mac. In the taste of him when he leaned forward to claim her lips…

Fumbling with his zipper, she cursed against his lips when it snagged. His big hands came up to help her, his fingers long and tan and deft. The *scrrritch* of the metal teeth sounded far away when he slowly unzipped his jeans, hard to hear over the rushing of blood between her ears.

Pulling his Glock from his waistband, he checked the safety before setting it aside. Then, with one deft move, he shoved his Levis and boxer shorts down his thighs. And there he was… Thick as her wrist, violently red, and heavily veined. The head of him was plump, weeping, twitching beneath her ravenous, startled gaze.

And he called *her* perfection.

She could hardly breathe, hardly think for the sheer, masculine beauty of him. And she wanted him. All of him. Inside her. Pumping, straining, coming. But…he was…big. And it'd been four years, and—

She stopped thinking altogether when he reached forward with one hand, gently spreading her labia, finding her clitoris in an instant and pressing it with his thumb. Sensation exploded through her, the ache skyrocketed to an intolerable level.

"Oh, God," she breathed, taking him in her hand, wondering at the sheer heat of him, the sheer breadth of him that strained the capacity of her grip.

"So soft," he murmured, stepping forward to seal

their lips. His tongue slid into her mouth at the same time one thick finger slid into her body. She moaned. He answered in kind.

"Stroke me," he growled, and she hastened to accommodate him. Rubbing her fist up his shaft and back down again. She rejoiced in the throb of his veins against her palm, in the silky wetness that seeped from his tip, in the satiny skin that moved over a core of hot, living steel.

A second finger teased at her opening, playing, petting.

"Open yourself to me," he demanded, and she usually didn't like anyone telling her what to do. But when it came to Mac and sex, she appreciated the caveman that came out in him. It only added to the pleasure, the excitement.

Repositioning her heels on the lip of the dresser drawer, she spread her thighs wider. He rewarded her obedience by slowly, so unbelievably *slowly*, working his second finger inside her. It was a struggle to accommodate him, but she loved the stretch, the burn. It both soothed the ache and simultaneously ratcheted it up another notch.

"So tight," he said against her lips, nipping, laving, sucking. "So damned tight."

And, God, it felt good. Felt good to be filled, to be brimming with warm, male flesh. But it wasn't enough. The nerves inside her cried out for more stimulation.

"Mac," she begged, "please. I need—"

"I know exactly what you need, darlin'," he said, and he wasn't lying. Because he began to pump his fingers in and out of her, slowly at first, and then more quickly, all while rubbing the rough pad of his thumb back and forth over the distended nub of her clit.

And that was it. Her climax slammed through her

violently, arching her back, straining the tendons in her neck as she held back a scream of unimaginable pleasure. When her thighs tightened around his hand, she didn't know if she was groaning, or if it was him, or the both of them together.

―〜〜―

Delilah didn't climax. She detonated. Squeezing his fingers so hard his knuckles rubbed together, screaming and melting and coming and coming and *coming*.

In the back of Mac's mind, he did some quick calculations. Seven feet. Seven seconds. That's how far it was to the nearest bed, and that's how long it would take him to pick her up and cart her there.

They weren't going to make it...

Not when she was so soft and wet. Not when she was throbbing around his fingers. Not when her hand was stroking him toward insanity, stroking him until he was so hard and hot he hurt. *Sweet Jesus*, he couldn't seem to draw breath for what she was doing to him.

No. They were definitely *not* going to make it to the bed.

He needed to be inside her. Needed to feel her sultry walls closing around him. Now. Thirty seconds ago when she first exploded. He slowly withdrew his fingers from her body, glancing down to find her labia quivering, pulsing slightly with the aftershocks of her monumental orgasm.

She was sucking in great gulps of air, whispering his name over and over again. He couldn't help himself. He lifted his fingers to his lips, licking away the evidence of her passion, savoring the earthy smell of her, the salty-sweet flavor of her, until he couldn't take it a second more.

"Wrap your legs around me, darlin'," he growled.

She did as he instructed, angling the head of him toward her entrance. He watched, mesmerized, muscles tensed, breath bated as she placed his swollen tip against her most tender flesh. Watched as she rubbed the length of him up her silken channel, pressing the head of him against the throbbing bundles of nerves at the top of her sex, moaning. And then she changed the angle of her hips and he was suddenly pressing into her.

And there, *there* were the brakes he couldn't apply earlier. Because in that instant, as he watched his hard length disappear into her, as her watched her body give, watched himself take, everything slowed. Way. Down.

The sensations… Good God, they were incredible, so intensely…something. Sweet, maybe? Decadent, certainly.

"Christ." He gritted his teeth. "You're tight."

"F-four years," she rasped, then squeaked and bit her lip when he slid an inch further.

Four years? What did that mean? And then it hit him. "You haven't been with a man in four years?" he asked, his entire body going bowstring tight. His breath caught in his lungs.

She shook her head. "There was the b-bar." He slid in a bit more. "And then getting my side job as an FA started. Ahhhh." There was another inch. "And, th-then I met you. Oh, God! Mac!"

Something wonderful and terrifying burst inside him, in the region usually relegated to his heart. She'd waited…for him? He couldn't fathom it. Didn't want to acknowledge it, but the truth was shining in her emerald eyes. And then she wiggled, just a little, just enough to elicit a gasp from both of them.

"Am I hurting you?" he managed to ask.

She shook her head, her silky hair brushing against her shoulders, rasping over the red, ripe tips of her up-thrust breasts. "God, no," she whispered, grabbing him and pulling him to her so she could plant a kiss on his chin. He felt the tip of her tongue dart out to tickle the dimple there. His balls tightened in response. "You feel amazing," she whispered in his ear, nipping the lobe. "Please don't stop."

And just like back in Sander's bedroom, stopping was the absolute last thing on his mind.

He trailed kisses along her neck, sucking lavishly on her pulse point, rewarded for the effort by her silky walls convulsing around him, squeezing him, milking him. Everything about her, about this, about what they were doing together, was amazing. The sound of her sighs, the feel of her heels hooked together above his ass, the swollen delectation that was her hot, hungry mouth…

When he grabbed her hips to push forward the last two inches, seating himself to the hilt with one final, forceful jab, and his tip pressed tight against the hard entrance to her womb, she speared her fingers into his hair. Sealing their lips, her satiny tongue darted deep. And he was completely awash in the smells and sounds and sensations of sex.

It'd never been this good. Never, never. And that's when it occurred to him.

"Condom," he croaked.

"Mary and Joseph," Delilah groaned, resting her forehead against his.

When her inner walls squeezed around him again, he gasped, "Stop that."

"Can't help it," she husked, biting her lip, each of them holding still. Holding perfectly still. Because one small move, one slick slide, might be all it took to send both of them careening over the edge.

"I-I don't have—" he began, lamenting the fact that he didn't carry a spare condom or two in his wallet like the rest of the Knights. What was the point? He wasn't a horndog like Ozzie or Steady. He didn't bed everything on two legs. When he had a woman—and he *did* have a woman on fairly regular occasions despite what some of the boys at BKI might say to the contrary—it was always planned ahead of time. A nice dinner. A movie. And the inevitable fall into bed. *Then* he came packing. A true-blue Boy Scout to the core. But now? Nada. Zippo. Zilch. How the hell could he have let it go this far? Where was his head?

Oh, right, offline right now because Little Mac was doing all his thinking for him.

Delilah drew back. "I'm on the pill. If you want—"

That's all she managed because, in the next instant, he pulled himself from the decadent warmth of her body only to slam back home on a stroke that rocked her against the top of the dresser. The pill? That's all he needed to know. Because the monthly physicals and blood work he was required to undergo working for BKI told him he was clean and free of disease. And four years for her? Yeah. No worries. She squeaked at the force of his thrust. But one look at her face told him everything he needed to know. It wasn't a squeak of pain; it was a squeak of pleasure. So he repeated the move, over and over. Slipping, sliding, impaling. She met him stroke for stroke. Her hands on his ass, her nails digging into his flesh.

"Yes, Mac!" she moaned against his lips, her breath hot and sweet. "Yes!"

He felt it then. That fist sharp edge of release building in his balls, racing along his shaft. He wanted to stop it. Wanted to keep on taking her forever. It was so good. Too good. But he couldn't stop it. He didn't have the strength or willpower. Not this time. Maybe later. But this first time his hips pistoned wildly. This first time, his mouth greedily devoured her lips and tongue, her cries of pleasure.

And then she did it. She threw her head back and screamed his name right before she detonated. Her back arched. Her breasts thrust up at him, the hard, wet tips a temptation for his eyes. The walls of her vagina squeezed him like a hot fist. *Lord have mercy!* His orgasm answered in kind, bursting through him. And it was the most explosive, heartrending, gut-twisting, delicious, melting, decadent sensation he'd ever experienced.

He had no idea how long his body spasmed as he held himself deep, as he poured himself inside her. It seemed like forever. And all that time she clasped him to her, kissed him, her mouth so unbelievably sexy, so unmistakably greedy.

"Delilah," he finally groaned, pushing himself deep inside her one last time, reveling in the little tremors of residual pleasure that shot up his shaft.

She squeaked again when he wound an arm under her butt, lifting her from the dresser. Making it to the bed took some doing, what with his jeans bunched down around his ankles, but he managed it. When he separated himself from her body to toss her atop the bed, the sudden feeling of loss shocked him with its strength. But he quickly pushed the sensation aside, reaching down to drag off his boots, his ankle holster, his jeans.

She lay on the bed like the incarnation of provocation. Eyes heavy lidded and sparkling. Lips red and swollen. She drove him crazy when she lazily ran a finger back and forth over the tip of one violently puckered breast. Her right knee propped up, allowing him a small peek at the plump, wet flesh between her legs.

"I thought this was a one-shot deal," she said when he crawled up to her, over her, her eyes darting down to his dick. Little Mac, the boy wonder, had already begun to harden with new life.

"That first one had to be done to take the edge off," he told her. "Now we're ready to start the real show."

And if *that* wasn't the sexiest, naughtiest, most delicious thing a man ever said to a woman, she didn't know what was.

"Mac. Oh, God, that feels good." She speared her fingers into his hair as he slowly kissed his way down her body, stopping to swirl his hot tongue into the hollow of her bellybutton. And she'd never noticed it, never seen it on any of her biology class diagrams, but there was obviously a nerve that ran from the navel straight to the clitoris. Her toes curled into the sheets, her hips lifted from the mattress.

She *wanted* his mouth on her, his tongue *in* her. She wanted to feel his beard stubble rasp against her most private parts. In the simplest terms, she wanted sex. All of it. Every which way. Until she couldn't think. Until she couldn't lament that this time, this one time, would be all she had…

"I love the way you smell," he told her, kneeling between her legs, his broad shoulders forcing her thighs wide. "I love the way you look." His eyes were on her. Drinking her in. "And," he said, palming the globes of her ass in his warm, rough hands, lifting her hips, pressing one all-too-brief kiss to her heated core, "I love the way you taste."

"Mac…" His name was sigh, a prayer, a curse… But then all thought escaped her. Because his tongue lapped up the length of her, tapping against the distended bud of nerves at the top of her sex, and her center pulsed, becoming a throbbing void of yearning. Of hunger. And then…

Oh…he wrapped his lips around her clitoris and started flicking his tongue in a rhythm that drove her straight to the edge. Two fingers filled her, pumping, rubbing. His growls of triumph and pleasure echoed in her ears.

She strained. Strained toward release and away from it at the same time. She wanted an end to the glorious misery. And yet she wanted it to go on for eternity. Stretching out to infinity.

Her head thrashed on the pillow. She plucked at her own nipples. Mac bit her, ever so gently, catching the nerve-bundle between his teeth. And that was it. She exploded. Her orgasm hitting her with the force of a runaway train.

She screamed…something. She didn't know. She didn't care.

Divinity. She'd heard the word. Knew what it meant. But never had she experienced it until this moment. The sensations Mac pressed on her as he continued to coax more and more from her were divine. Mystical. Spiritual.

This was making love. *This* was what it was supposed to be like. She never knew. Oh, God, she never knew…

"Again," Mac told her when the last pulse of orgasm ran through her. He pressed up on his knees, grabbing his shaft by its thick base and angling his plump head toward her entrance. "Do it again just like that. With me inside you."

⁓

Mac had lost his mind. His body was in control now. And it wanted to devour Delilah, claim her, mate her, leave its mark on her until she'd never be able to look at herself in the mirror without thinking of him. Of them.

Of this time together when their two bodies became one in what had to be one of the most phenomenal, cosmic couplings since the beginning of time.

He was so hard he could barely bend himself enough to press into her tight channel. With a growl, he adjusted his position, letting go of his shaft in order to plant his palms beside her head. He used his knees to spread her thighs wider. Ducking his chin, he thrust forward, watching the raging head of his cock separate her silky folds. Watching himself grow shiny with the evidence of her passion. But just when he gathered himself, tensed his hip muscles in readiness to flex forward, she tilted her hips, changing the angle.

He moaned. In frustration. In unspeakable, horny delight when she grabbed him, rubbing herself against him before pressing the head of him tight against her throbbing little clit. He was nearly cross-eyed, but he could still see her mouth fall open on a gasp of pleasure when he pulsed against her.

"You like that, don't you?" he asked, rocking back slightly, supporting himself with one arm so he could grab his shaft and tap his tip forcefully against the hard bundle of nerves guaranteed to send her to the moon. She sighed blissfully, her knees falling to the sides. He kept up the motion until he thought he'd come, until he thought *she'd* come. Then, in one smooth stroke, he plunged home.

Delilah climaxed instantly, writhing against him, scratching his back, neck arched in a lovely bow. With gritted teeth, he held on until she finally quieted. Then he began to move. Slowly, steadily, the tension in his balls, the pleasure along his shaft building with each glorious glide.

"I want you to come again," he told her, pressing kisses into the damp hair along her brow, breathing in the scent of her. "And this time," he reached down between them so he could rub her tiny nub with the pad of his thumb, "I want you to take me with you."

"Yes," she breathed, fisting her hands in his hair, claiming his mouth as she drew her thighs higher along his sweating flanks. "Yes, Mac. Oh, *oh*, yes."

He rode her then. Drove into her over and over again. Staked his claim. Marked her. And when she began to shatter, he went with her, holding himself deep, flooding her with his passion.

When it was over, he lay atop her, body spasming, breath sawing from him and ruffling the ends of her fiery hair fanned out beneath his face on the pillow. Finally, he gathered enough strength to pull back, and he choked out a laugh.

Delilah…was asleep. Eyes closed. Lids fluttering every so often. A soft little snore grumbling from between her lovely, kiss-swollen lips.

Holy smokes, he'd screwed her unconscious. And if he wasn't such an evolved guy, he might just slap himself a high five.

Then it hit him. Just how exhausted she must be. How scared. How…vulnerable.

Shit. Had he taken advantage? Had he made a mistake?

Slowly, with infinite care, he rolled off her. She murmured her dislike of his sudden absence, the desertion of his heat, shivering slightly when the air from the window AC unit raised goose bumps all over her body. Her nipples tightened and, in response, his spent cock jerked with interest.

With a frown, he admonished Little Mac for being a wit-less wonder. Then he pulled her close, brushing strands of fragrant hair away from her temple so he could press a kiss there. Brave Delilah. Strong Delilah. Wonderful Delilah…

He didn't want her to regret this. Didn't want her to hurt because of him.

Daring Delilah. Charming Delilah. Beautiful Delilah…

She was the kind of woman to make a good dog break his leash. And she made *Mac* wish everything was dif-ferent. She made him wish *he* was different. A man with fewer emotional scars, a man who didn't know better than to lay it all on the line and give it a go. Sweet Lord almighty, she just made him…*wish*.

And wishing was a dangerous business. After wish-ing came hoping. And after hoping came *what the hell; let's try*. And after *what the hell; let's try* came—

Jolene! That broken cry from that ravaged voice echoed in his head. He could still feel the unfathomable ache in his chest.

As he looked down at Delilah, so pretty, so…every-thing a woman should be, he knew he could fall, if he let himself. Perhaps he *had* fallen…just a little. And that right there was enough to scare some cotton-pickin' sense into him.

This is a one-night stand, asshole. Nothing more. You'd do well to remember that.

Good advice. *Great* advice. And since it *was* just a one-night stand, he'd be damned if he wasted one single, solitary moment of it.

"Darlin'," he murmured, rubbing his burgeoning cock against her silky hip, thumbing one of her delicious nipples to rigid life. "Wake up. I want you again."

Her pale lids fluttered open. Her eyes impossibly green in the lamplight spilling across the bed.

He wasn't sure she was fully awake, but she turned in his arms, eagerly offering her lips. He took them like the heartless, ravenous bastard he was…

—◆◆◆—

Delilah would say this for the man, he was certainly thorough.

She'd fallen asleep on him twice, and twice he awakened her to wild positions and mind-blowing sex that shattered her psyche and decimated her body. He'd bent her over the bed, forcefully thrusting into her from behind while his fingers did things to her clitoris that made her scream. He'd had her on her knees, murmuring titillating commands to her on just how she should suck him, stroke him, cup him. He'd even taken her up against the wall, heaving into her over and over and *over* again until she shattered into a million tiny pieces and couldn't remember her own name, much less his.

What wonderful delights would he show her next?

Without opening her eyes, she reached for him, her outstretched fingers searching the rumpled sheets next to her. The linens were cool, and…empty…

She bolted upright, pushing her hair from her eyes. A quick glance told her two things. One, she'd been asleep for a while because the sun was sliding toward the western horizon, sending tendrils of golden light through the slats of the aluminum blinds, highlighting the dust motes dancing in the air. And two, Mac wasn't in the room.

"Mac?" she called quietly, her heart giving her rib cage a quick kick. She ignored it. He was just in the bathroom.

Mmm. Sex in the shower. That was one they hadn't tried yet. Water, slippery soap, their bodies slapping together. Yes. She could go for some of that.

Sliding from the bed, she smiled at the little twinges and aches that were proof her body had been well-used, well-loved. Bending to grab her panties and T-shirt from where they'd fallen to the floor—fallen? More like been *hurled*— the memory of his fervor caused a shiver to race up her spine. She hoped he'd be just as anxious to undress her again. With a little giggle, she shimmied into the garments.

"Mac?" she called again, padding to the bathroom, knocking hesitantly on the partially closed door. It squeaked open under the pressure of her knuckles, revealing…nothing. Just the standard motel shower, sink, and toilet. But no Mac.

No Mac…

It was then she realized. True to his word, he'd given her one gloriously decadent afternoon. And that was it. Done. Finished. *Over.*

She slumped against the doorjamb, biting her lip as tears instantly filled her eyes. Thoughts spun through her head like tornados, threatening to destroy everything in their path. That ball of broken glass was back, tearing at her lungs, scraping against her heart, shredding her until the sob she held at the back of her throat broke through.

The sound was pathetic, even to her own ears. Desperate. Devastated.

You made the bargain, the voice whispered.

But that was before I realized I loved him! she argued

in her own defense, then covered her mouth with a shaky hand because she knew that wasn't true.

She'd known she loved him. Hell, if she was honest with herself, she'd known she loved him for years...

In fact, she'd fallen in love with his chin dimple and crooked nose the very first time she laid eyes on him. A few months later, when Ozzie told some raunchy joke and he tossed back his head, belly laughing, she'd fallen in love with the crinkles at the corner of his eyes. Then there was the day he valiantly came to the rescue of a woman whose husband was pushing her around out in the alley behind the bar, and she'd fallen in love with his courage. Fast forward to just a few months ago, when he held her close after she lost Buzzard, and she'd fallen head-over-heels in love with his compassion.

Yes. From the beginning, she'd loved him.

And now I have to live with it being...over.

She glanced wearily at her reflection in the mirror. Her eyes were red and shiny, her hair a rat's nest of tangles. The skin around her mouth was pink from Mac's whiskers and...what was that? She pushed away from the doorjamb, leaning against the sink as she turned her head to the side, examining the skin on her neck. A love bite. Just a small one. But it was a reminder of how well, how *thoroughly* he'd taken her. Made her his in every which way.

A reminder... A memory...

It was all she had now. And it would have to do.

She was Delilah Fairchild, after all. The ass-kicking, Harley-riding, shotgun-toting beer-slinger-from-hell. What was a little heartbreak to a woman like her?

"Everything," she admitted to her reflection, wiping

at the tears slipping down her cheeks and dropping from her chin. "It's everything. But you can't let him know."

Because she'd promised there would be no strings, no hurt feelings. And if she couldn't keep her word, the least she could do was never show him how much she suffered.

So toughen up, buttercup, she scolded herself, sniffling and pressing a hand to the ache in the center of her chest. Shaking out her hair, she forced herself to take a deep, cleansing breath, and turned on the faucet. In the middle of splashing cold water on her face, she jumped when the CIA agent tasked with guarding the rear of the motel tapped on the large frosted window positioned behind the toilet.

"May I have a glass of water?" he called, his voice hoarse and slightly muffled.

Poor guy. He'd been out there in the sun all afternoon. He was probably about to shrivel up and die.

Out there all afternoon…

Her cheeks flamed when it occurred to her that he might have heard *everything* that been happening inside the motel room, that whoever was positioned at the front had probably heard it, too. She wasn't known for being a quiet lover, after all. And Mac had been nearly as vocal. Growling, groaning, yelling in triumph during orgasm like he'd just won an Olympic race or something.

"Well that's just *great*," she muttered to herself, embarrassed, wondering how she'd ever look any of these people in the eye again. I mean, really. What must they think of her? Her uncle was missing. Nuclear warheads were about to fall into the hands of terrorists. And what was she doing? Yep. You guessed it. She was getting her groove on. Getting her groove on and getting her heart broken all at the same time.

Pathetic. Deplorable. Unfor—

Tap. Tap. She could just make out the shadow of a hand knocking against the glass. "Just a second!" she called, bending to grab one of the plastic drinking cups from the shelf beneath the sink. Unwrapping it from its hygienic covering, she filled it with cold water before reaching to unlatch the window. It was a bit tough. The windowpane having been painted a few times. But it finally gave way and she threw up the sash.

"Here you g—"

That's all she managed before a hand grabbed her wrist, yanking her forward. Her forehead slammed into the window sash, causing stars to dance in her field of vision. She was half hanging out the window, her knees atop the toilet tank, the cup having fallen from her hand to bounce on the ground below. In confusion, she watched it land atop Agent Wallace…

He was lying in the dirt beneath the window, his lifeless gaze staring vacantly into the sky above—a look that chilled her to the bone as it instantly re-minded her of Buzzard—blood pooling beneath his head from the giant gash flaying his throat open in a gruesome, macabre smile. His foot was twitching. She didn't know why she should notice such a thing in the split second it took her to open her mouth to scream, but she did. She saw it. That awful, twitching foot. She heard it. That terrible scuffling sound it made against the ground.

Then…pain. White-hot agony. It exploded at the base of her skull. From the corner of her eye, she glimpsed a familiar set of brown Timberlands, felt the brutal bite of terror as it sank its sharp fangs into her galloping heart. The second blow to her head cut off the cry lodged at the back of her throat. And then…lights out…

Chapter Twenty-one

Mac was a coward.

That's all there was to it. Because he'd wanted to stay with her while she slept. Hold her in his arms. Pet her. Kiss her. Watch her dream…

But he couldn't. He *had* fallen…just a little. And he didn't dare risk it. He was too *afraid* to risk it.

On the other hand, it'd been nearly three hours since he slunk from her room like the lily-livered cur that he was, and that probably meant she'd be waking up soon. He couldn't stand the thought of that, of her rolling over to discover his dastardly desertion.

Yes, he was determined to stick to his guns, to let their dalliance end here, today. But that didn't mean she deserved to be treated like some nameless, faceless hook-up. Like some woman he'd taken home from the bar only to ghost out on her in the middle of the night. Because she *wasn't* that. She was so much more. She *deserved* so much more, so much *better* from him.

Christ almighty, what the hell was I thinking?

"Ozzie!" he barked. The guy was down at the end of the building, filling a bucket with ice from the machine. "Come take my place, will you? I need to talk to Delilah."

"Talk?" Ozzie snorted, sauntering toward him. "Yeah. By my count, this will be the, uh, *fifth* time you guys have…*talked*."

"I'm serious," Mac growled. "And remember what I told you I'd do to you if you tell her you heard us?"

"Oh, I remember," Ozzie said, eyeing him askance. "The imagery of your description is sure to give me nightmares for years."

"Excellent." Mac winked, lifting his hand to the knob of the Noel Motel's room number four. He was stopped from turning it when Agent Duvall burst from her room, running to rap hard knuckles against Steady's door. She turned and pounded on the door of the room Fitzsimmons and Wallace shared before marching over to Mac. Instantly, his operator senses were on high alert.

"What have you got?" he asked.

"Let's wait until…ah," she said when Fitzsimmons poked his head out of his room followed quickly by Steady down the way. "Good. Come join us, gentlemen."

"What's going on?" Zoelner said, wrenching open the door beside them, wiping sleep from his eyes.

"We've got a lead," Agent Duvall announced, her gaze bright with excitement. Mac felt all the cells in his body slow down and come to attention. A lead… Those two beautiful words still spoke to his Federal Agent heart. "We found footage of Hasan and al-Hallaj buying cell phones from a store up near Thunder Bay, Ontario. We got the model and product numbers from the receipt. Now we're talking with the phone company to try to determine which wireless numbers are assigned to those particular phones."

"And once you know the numbers, you can monitor when that device pings local cell towers, thereby allowing you to triangulate their locations," Ozzie said.

"Exactly." The agent nodded.

"And now?" Mac asked, his eyes darting to Delilah's door.

"And now we wait for the numbers."

Wait. He was usually a patient man, but when it came to an op, he hated the word *wait*. Huffing out a sigh, he immediately thought, *oh, sweet Jesus*. Because he could still smell her on his breath, still taste her on his tongue. Swallowing, he glanced around, wondering if anyone else noticed that he was absolutely covered, head-to-toe, in Delilah Fairchild. Delicious, delightful, delectable Delilah Fairchild...

"You want to be the one to tell her?" Chelsea asked, nodding toward the baby-blue door. "While you're doing that, I'll run around back and alert Wallace to the progress."

Dipping his chin in acknowledgment of Chelsea's plan, he stepped up to Delilah's door, waiting to push it open until the group dispersed. He'd left her naked, sated, and sprawled atop the mattress, her plump ass — and that wonderfully kissable tattoo inked above it — there for all the world to see. And, call him crazy, or territorial, or...yeah, just crazy, but he wanted what they shared, the glory of her nudity, to be his and his alone.

Can you say *dangerous thinking*, boys and girls?

Shaking his head at himself, he stepped into the room, blinking against the gloom in sharp contrast to the bright glow of the setting sun outside. The instant his eyes adjusted, he noted her absence from the bed. The sheets were rumpled and messy, proof of her presence, of *their* presence — *Lord almighty, what an afternoon*. But *she* was gone.

Shit. She *had* woken up to find him missing. He *had*

subjected her to that particular humiliation. Someone should definitely kick his ass. And, no joke, he volunteered to be first in line.

"Delilah," he called, marching toward the bathroom. "We've got some good news. Agent Duvall—"

A loud gasp sounded from the bathroom, followed by a whimpering kind of squeak. He threw open the door, only to find the space…empty.

Huh? Then where had the sounds—

The window. It was open.

He was across the bathroom in two steps, placing his palms on the windowsill in order to lean out. The first thing he saw was the pint-sized CIA agent. She was holding one hand to her mouth, her eyes trained on the ground in front of her.

Mac glanced down. "Son of a goddamned *bitch!*" he roared, instinctively reaching into his waistband for his sidearm, his heart growing teeth and trying to gnaw its way through his breastbone. Wallace's inert, bloody form lay in the dirt, staring unseeingly at the sky above. And Delilah was…*gone.*

―――

Qasim stood at the entrance to the cave, his eyes searching the twilight gloom of dense woods beyond. "Where are you, Haroun?" he said into his cell phone. "I do not see you."

"I am coming, *habibi*," Haroun grunted. "Almost there. The woman is heavier than she looks."

Qasim's heart beat with wild anticipation. When Haroun called earlier to tell him he'd captured the woman, Qasim tempered his excitement. Much could happen on the hour-long drive from Delilah Fairchild's motel to the spot they'd chosen as their secondary location. And he'd learned over the years not to get his hopes up.

But now Haroun was calling to say he'd made it, and Qasim allowed himself to breathe a sigh of relief, to experience this crystalline moment of joy. Because, finally, *finally*, after all these years, it was beginning to look like he would have his revenge. It was beginning to look like he would, indeed, discover the location of the nuclear weapons. And then, he would sit back and watch American cities burn...

The anticipation sent a thrill skittering along his nerves, heightened his senses, intensified his breathing. People liked to believe love was the strongest of human emotions. But Qasim knew better. It was hate. *Hate* was the strongest. It was *hate* that had fueled him for more than a decade. He felt its powerful pull much more than he ever felt the pull of love for his wife and children. And someday, hopefully someday soon, he'd sit by his television and watch as all his hatred was made real by the countless deaths of the wives and children and brothers and sisters and husbands of capitalist pigs. He'd sit and—

There. Through the trees...

Qasim blew out his pent-up breath when Haroun stepped into the small clearing in front of the secluded cave. Even in the waning light, he could see that the man looked terrible. Blood stained Haroun's Western-style T-shirt. His hair was a mess. His face filthy with dust and sweat. But there was a smile curving his lips when he slapped a hand against the panty-clad bottom of the unconscious woman draped over his left shoulder.

"Did I not tell you this was our chance?" Haroun said. Qasim could hear his voice through the cellular connection but also across the short distance. He thumbed off the device and shoved it into his pants pocket. "Did I not say trust in Allah and all would be well?"

"You did indeed, brother." He squeezed Haroun's shoulder when his second-in-command pulled even. He glanced down at the limp, scantily dressed woman and spotted the small patch of blood matting the back of her head. He raised a brow. "You hit her?" he asked as they carefully made their way inside the cave, moving toward the lamplight dancing at the back.

"I had to act fast. But, rest assured, she isn't too badly hurt. We can revive her with the smelling salts." Smelling salts...a standard component of any torture arsenal. After all, pain didn't work nearly as well when the one being tortured was unconscious.

Haroun grunted when his ankle turned on a loose stone. Qasim reached out to steady his second-in-command. In doing so, his hand brushed against Delilah Fairchild's soft hip. Curiosity...and lust...stirred at the contact. His lips curved into an anticipatory smile as it occurred to him that perhaps his initial plan of holding a gun to Miss Fairchild's head in order to get Theo to talk wasn't necessarily the most expedient course of action. After all, forcing someone to watch the rape of a loved one was not only a tried and true method of information gathering, but also there were times when it was *more* powerful and motivating than the promise of death...

They made their way into the small circle of light cast by the kerosene lanterns and Qasim found everything just as he'd left it. Theodore was on the ground,

his back propped against a wet boulder, his broken
leg stretched out in front of him. With his hands tied
behind his back and his head bent forward—he'd been
losing consciousness often from shock and loss of
blood—the old Marine couldn't see their approach.
But soon…soon he'd understand Qasim was a man of
his word.

Sami and Jabbar stood on either side of Theodore.
Jabbar munched on an apple, his blackened eye having
turned an angry purple, and Sami sucked down a can of
Coca-Cola through a striped straw. Both smiled widely
when they laid eyes on the nearly naked woman. It was
obvious that they, too, had ideas about how the interrogation should proceed from this point on.

Haroun bent to carefully lay the redhead on the
ground and Qasim sucked in a startled breath. Because
she was even more beautiful from the front. Ripe, round
breasts. Even, lovely features. His cock swelled inside
his trousers.

Yes, he rubbed his hands together, *this could be
quite fun*.

Jabbar tossed away his apple, stepping forward to
hand Haroun a handkerchief to be used as a gag and
a plastic zip tie to be used on the woman's wrists.
Haroun applied both, then glanced up at Qasim. "Shall
we begin?"

Oh, yes. Qasim was very, *very* ready to begin. With
his blood running hot, he smiled at his men and nodded.
"Let us enjoy this first step, my friends, on the journey
that will see our names immortalized…"

Delilah jolted from the darkness to discover her heart pounding, her brain buzzing, her lungs heaving, and her head…

Ow!

With her eyes squeezed tightly shut, she reached up to touch the tender spot—

No. No, she did *not* reach up, because something was tied around her wrists. Something was tied around her wrists, and something was tied around her mouth, and—

Timberlands! The terrorist! It all came back to her in a flash.

Her eyes flew open, but she could make no sense of her surroundings. Darkness? Dancing light? Craggy shapes?

She blinked. Trying to focus beyond the splitting ache of her head. Eventually the world snapped into view, and she could see a low rock ceiling hanging above her. Flickering yellow light created macabre little shadows in its crevices and glinted on the droplets of water occasionally falling from it. Beneath her was cold, wet stone, but she could hardly feel the chill for the hot terror burning through her blood. The smell of wet earth and bat guano filled her nose just as the dark faces of four men filled her vision.

She recognized one of them. Al-Hallaj… He'd taken her. Against all odds, against four Black Knights and three CIA agents, he'd managed to take her. It seemed impossible. And she might have thought she was in the middle of a nightmare had not the excruciating pain in her head been so unmistakably real.

Crying out when two of the men reached down to grab her shoulders, she absently noticed how the noise was muffled against the salty-tasting gag pulling the corners of her mouth tight. *Crunch!* The sound of her kneecaps slamming into the rock floor echoed in her ears a split second before her central nervous system registered the agony.

Somebody screamed. Was that her?

Her face felt hot. Were those tears?

She knew she was on her knees. Knew there were hands supporting her. Knew the air inside the cavern was cold. But she could feel none of these things. Not when her body was inundated with pain signals from every direction. Her head pounded. Her knees throbbed. Her shoulders ached from having her hands wrenched behind her back.

But all of that was nothing compared to the agony in her heart when her eyes fell on her uncle. This time she *knew* the scream that echoed around the cavern was hers. It was her uncle's name, garbled by the gag.

Oh God, Uncle Theo... Her mind tried to make sense of it all, to claw through the thick, sticky cobwebs the pain and disorientation had stitched through her mind. *Uncle Theo...*

She couldn't tell if he was dead or alive. There was so much blood. It matted his white hair and stained his shirt, dripping onto the stone floor from a cut near his temple. She couldn't see his face. His chin was touching his chest. But the blood. So much blood. Just like that awful afternoon with Buzzard...

She screamed again, struggling against her captors, her heart like a flame, her lungs on fire. And now she knew the wetness on her face *was* tears, rivers of them. They poured from her burning eyes as she screamed over and over again, despite the sledgehammers bashing away at the back of her skull. Trying to wake Theo. Praying she *could* wake him.

"Aren't you a vocal one?" observed one of the men as he skirted around in front her. He was dark like the others, with a hawkish nose and a cruel mouth. Was this Qasim? The man Agent Duvall spoke of? The mass murderer of innocents? He didn't look all that impressive, below average in height and underfed. But he *did* look like he could be the leader of the group. It was the way he held his chin high, his spine straight.

"Fuck you!" she yelled around her gag, crying out when one of the men holding her in a kneeling position slapped her across the face. Her head whipped to the side. Her lip split open. Pain seared. Blood trickled and dripped from her chin. She could smell it, the iron richness of it. But she didn't cry out. She *wouldn't* cry out. Not again. She wouldn't give them the satisfaction. *The bastards!*

Slowly turning back to face the leader, she didn't attempt to hide her hatred. It was there in the hot glow of her eyes, in the wide flare of her nostrils.

The leader tut-tutted when he saw her bloodied lip, frowning at the man who hit her. He said something in a language she couldn't understand before smiling down at her. The expression reminded her of a snake. Vicious. Venomous. *Savage*. She gulped. She couldn't help herself.

"Would you like me to tell you what I just told Sami?" he asked conversationally, as if this was a social occasion and not an abduction and precursor to what she knew would be a torture session.

Torture session…

Would she be able to withstand it? She prided herself on her strength, but she never bargained to be put to the test this way. *Mac! Where are you? Are you coming for me? Do you even know I'm gone?*

"Miss Fairchild," the leader spat, his smile fading. "I asked you a question. I expect an answer. This will go easier for you if you cooperate."

"Fuck you," she snarled again, but the volume was gone from her voice. All that screaming had shredded her vocal cords. When she swallowed, her tears ran down the back of her nose and burned her damaged throat.

"Indeed," the man said. "That *is* the plan. Which is why I told Sami he would have to wait to bloody you. Because the rest of us like our women to look pretty while we fuck them."

Her limbs began to shake uncontrollably as the fire in her blood turned to glacier ice, as the flames that had mere moments ago been her lungs and heart banked, leaving the organs frozen solid.

Evil…

The word whispered through her head. And, yes. As she stared into the soulless pools of Qasim's dark—he had to be Qasim, right?—eyes, she knew she was seeing pure evil. There was no humanity there. No compassion. Just ugly malevolence and…*death*.

And that's when it hit her. She was going to die here. But first…she was going to experience horror.

Jesus, help me! Mac…!

———— ᴡ ————

"If you think we're stayin' here," Mac thundered at Agent Fitzsimmons as they stood in the small clearing around an abandoned ranger's station in Shawnee National Forest, "you're crazier than a shithouse rat!"

"You have no jurisdiction," Fitzsimmons snarled impatiently, slipping an extra clip into his pocket. The guy was back in SWAT gear, flash-bang stun grenades attached to his vest, headset radio clamped around his ear, and a Spyderco knife velcro-ed up near his shoulder. Even in the twilight filtering through the softly swaying trees, Mac could see that his face was like a hurricane. Not that he blamed the guy. Less than an hour ago, Fitzsimmons had watched his buddy's body being covertly loaded into the back of a black SUV, the pool of Wallace's blood cleaned away as if it'd never existed.

Which was *exactly* why Mac was insisting he and the Knights join the CIA wet team going in after Delilah and Theo. Well, that and the fact that he trusted his skills and those of his teammates over anyone else's, but right now that was beside the point. Because, given Wallace's brutal murder, he wouldn't put it past these spooky boys to go in weapons hot. Exacting a little revenge for their downed comrade, and damn the two innocents caught in the crossfire.

No lie, Mac would sooner slit his own throat and the throats of every single CIA bastard gearing up around him than allow that to happen.

Delilah… For the love of Christ, he could hardly *breathe* for the fear squeezing his chest. Barely *think* for the terrible images ripping through his brain like mortar rounds.

Ten minutes after they discovered Wallace's body—the

longest ten minutes of Mac's life—Agent Duvall finally received word on the numbers assigned to the three cellular phones Hasan and al-Hallaj purchased in Canada. It took two minutes more to pinpoint the locations of the devices. Well...*two* of the devices, anyway. The first had been taped beneath the seat of Delilah's motorcycle—which was obviously how al-Hallaj had been able to track her to the Noel Motel. The second phone trace put the caller smack-dab in the center of the Shawnee National Forest. But the CIA had some trouble tracking the third device. Something about spotty cell tower coverage, an issue with triangulation, marginal signal strength, yada, yada, what the fuck ever. All Mac had cared about was getting to the Shawnee National Forest...

The drive from Olive Branch, Illinois, to the park should have taken seventy minutes. Mac and the BKI boys mounted up and made it in thirty-five, even beating the CIA wet team that arrived via chopper a few seconds later.

Which brought them here, to this moment. One very pissed-off CIA agent squaring off against one unspeakably terrified BKI operator. Of course, Mac couldn't let anyone *see* how terrified he was. How his heart was pounding out of control. How his kneecaps felt like they'd been replaced by globs of Jell-O. How his hands shook before he curled them into fists.

And, really? At a time like this, the guy had the audacity to bring up jurisdiction? Mac considered giving Fitzsimmons a little sermon about the dangers of, as Mac's father used to say, hanging his washing out on someone else's line. But Mac had neither the patience, nor the inclination to lecture the man. Instead he went with, "You're one to talk about jurisdiction, Mr. *CIA*"—he made sure to emphasize the word—"Agent. *We*," he motioned to Steady and Ozzie who were lined up beside him, "have more jurisdiction than *you* any day of the week and twice on Sunday."

"Shut up, shut up." Agent Duvall, who was looking over a map of the park, waved him to silence. She cupped her hand over her ear, listening intently to whatever information was being relayed to her, and Mac waited with bated breath. "Are we absolutely positive?" the little CIA agent asked after a beat. More listening. More waiting. Mac thought he was about to go insane, then, "Affirmative. We'll move out in ninety seconds."

"What is it?" he demanded, barely resisting the urge to reach out and strangle the woman when she took the time to drag in a deep breath. The evening air hung around them, heavy with the earthy smells of moist undergrowth and spring leaves.

"We were finally able to pinpoint that third phone," she said. "It's now joined the second one in the middle of the park." She folded a section of the map over her arm. Popping a penlight in her mouth to add some light, she pointed with her finger at a dot on the map labeled Devil's Den. Beside the name was a number with a red hash mark through it.

"What does that mean?" Mac flicked a finger at the symbol.

Agent Duvall unfolded the map until she found the legend. Removing the penlight, she said, "Says here, it's a cavern. One that's been closed to the public for over a decade due to a cave-in near the back."

A cave. That made sense. Dark. Quiet. Secluded. Just what a group of terrorists would need.

Mac welcomed the hard kick of adrenaline that made his pulse jump, his muscles clench. "Let's go," he said, reaching around to pull his Glock from his waistband.

"I *said* you're not invited," Fitzsimmons growled.

Mac wanted to punch the guy but couldn't afford to waste the time or the effort. Not with Delilah in the hands of terrorists. He felt every ticking second like it was a physical blow. "And I thought I made myself clear I wasn't waitin' on an invitation," he spat. Hopefully his immovability on the issue was as evident in his sneer as it was in the quick movements he used to slide out his clip, find it full and rip-roarin'-rarin' to go, and slam it back home with the edge of his palm.

Fitzsimmons took a menacing step forward before Agent Duvall stopped him with a hand to the chest. "Hold on a second, Agent," she said, pushing her Bluetooth closer to her head, her color rising as one second stretched into two. Then she lowered her hand and gritted, "We've just had orders that the Knights are to lead this mission."

Mac's chin jerked back. Not only go on the mission but *lead* it? *What in the world?* Then, from the corner of his eye, he saw Zoelner standing off to the side, quietly talking into his cell phone. "Thanks, Boss," the ex–CIA agent said, nodding. "And be sure to thank the president for stepping in like this."

Mac saw Fitzsimmons' jaw nearly fall off his face a split second before the guy snapped it shut.

"Sorry, Chels," Zoelner said as he jogged over to

them. But it was obvious from his expression that the *last* thing he was feeling was sorry. "But I thought you guys had been in charge for just about long enough. And besides, I work for the president now. My loyalty belongs solely to him. To be quite honest, it was making me antsy that you were keeping him in the dark."

And not for the first time, Mac realized how nifty working directly for POTUS could be. *El Jefe* himself had put the Black Knights in charge, and that was music to Mac's ears. Had he thought he could grab Zoelner and kiss him smack on the mouth without receiving a knee to the groin for his effort, he would have done it. Instead, he simply showed his appreciation with a terse dip of his chin. Zoelner smiled, returning the gesture.

"Get them geared up, Fitzsimmons," Agent Duvall said, her jaw working back and forth. "We move out in sixty."

"Excuse me, Agent," Zoelner said, "but I believe that's our call. Mac?"

"We'll take Kevlar, extra clips, and radio headsets," Mac informed Fitzsimmons. "And we'll gear up on the go. Because we're moving out," he waved two fingers in the direction of the dark forest and the cave known as Devil's Den, "right now."

Sometime later, he would appreciate the look of utter disgust on the spook's face who was forced to hand him his gear as he jogged toward the tree line. But right at that moment there was only one thought, one name, one person on his mind. *Delilah… Hold on. I'm coming…*

Chapter Twenty-two

DON'T TELL THEM, DELILAH BEGGED HER UNCLE WITH her eyes, biting into the gag, holding back a sob as Qasim reached forward to dip a hand into her shirt and painfully squeeze her left nipple. The skin on his palm was hot and damp, evidence of his excitement.

And as terrifying as it'd been when her uncle was unconscious, it was nothing compared to the horrible moment they roused him with a vial of something held under his nose. Nothing compared to the moment his pain-filled eyes met hers, and she saw his expression morph from shock to anguish to heartrending sorrow. And it was nothing compared to the absolute misery sketched across his features now, when he was given the choice of telling the men the coordinates of the missing nukes or watching as they defiled her one-by-one.

"What will it be, Theodore?" Qasim asked. One of the men kept Delilah from turning her chin with a hard fist curled in her hair. But from the corner of her eye she could see Qasim use his free hand to rub the length of his erection. She fought the urge to retch as her bare toes curled away from the cold stone beneath them, the tops of her feet beating inconsequentially against the ungiving ground. "Will you give us the information we seek now? In which case, I can make this quick and painless for both of you." He moved his hand from his erection to the butt of the pistol protruding from his waistband. "Or you can remain as stubborn as you've been all along. In which case, I will see that you both suffer unimaginably."

Don't tell them… she mentally cried again. Because she knew, regardless of whether or not her uncle gave them the information they wanted, Qasim and his men were going to rape her. She knew it because she recognized lust when she saw it. She knew it because she recognized the look of a man who'd made up his mind.

Which meant now all she could hope to do was to drag out the ordeal long enough to give Mac the time he needed to find her. *Mac? Are you coming? Please, please be coming!* Or, barring salvation, simply withstand as well as she could whatever they forced on her, accept her death, and keep the world safe from the likes of these disgusting, soulless animals. Because, if it came down to her life or the lives of thousands, there was no choice.

She wasn't being selfless. She was simply being realistic. If the terrorists found and used nuclear bombs on American soil, World War III would soon follow. The U.S. government would unleash hell on one faction after another, one rogue nation after another, allies would come to the aid of allies until the whole world was in flames. And it all, *everything*, hinged on this one moment. On two people being able to stay strong. Stay… silent. Endure.

"I am waiting, Theodore," Qasim sing-songed, removing his hand from her shirt. She huffed out a soft breath of relief, but the feeling was short-lived. Because Qasim drew back his hand and punched her left breast. The blow was enough to knock her from her kneeling

position, her ass landing on her ankles and driving her
shin bones into the cool, wet rock.

Again, she had to bite into the gag to keep from crying out. Pain buffeted her from all directions. It was
searing, relentless, savage. And she knew it was about
to get worse.

Her uncle's furious yell rang in her ears like a death
knell. The sound of his boots scrabbling against the
stone and echoing around the cavern was macabre as
he fought to free himself from the man holding him.
But he was far too weak to manage anything more than
ineffectual struggles. And when she pressed herself back
up to her knees, lifting her chin—they could beat her
bloody, but she promised herself she would not yield;
she would *never* yield—she saw the tears streaming
down her uncle's battered face. Her thundering heart
ached for him, bled for him. Then the organ slowed and
stopped altogether when his look of anguish slid into
one of desperate indecision.

Oh, God. No! She tried to shake her head, but the
hand in her hair precluded the moment. "Don't tell," she
garbled around the gag. "Uncle Theo, don't tell."

Her head was wrenched back and a traitorous squeak
of misery slipped from her ravaged throat. She squeezed
her eyes closed, felt hot tears seep from the corners.

"Sorry," she heard her uncle choke, and her eyes shot
wide, her breath shuddering from her lungs. *No. Surely
he wouldn't…*

The man with his fist in her hair allowed her to lift
her chin, and she did so with trepidation. She didn't
want to see defeat in her uncle's eyes. She didn't think
she could stand watching him surrender. But one quick

glance at his beloved face, one swift look into those blue eyes she'd always adored, and she knew…

Her uncle wasn't apologizing for giving in to the terrorists. He was apologizing because he *wasn't* giving in to them. He was apologizing because he knew they were both going to die here today. And he was apologizing for the pain they were both going to suffer beforehand.

She'd never been prouder of the man than she was in that moment. It took everything she had to hold back the sob burning like a bonfire in her throat. And she *couldn't* hold back the tears continuing to stream down her face, soaking into the salty gag and stinging her split lip. But she raked in a deep breath and managed around the gag, "Love you."

His chest quaking, his face crumpling as he sobbed uncontrollably, her uncle nodded. And then, three precious words… "Love you, too."

Qasim threw back his head and bellowed his fury to the ceiling. He'd been watching the exchange. He knew what'd just passed between them. He understood the pact they'd made. Delilah's entire being, body, spirit, and mind, trembled at the terrible sound of rage as it echoed around the cavern. She'd never heard anything like it. It was awful. Obscene. She closed her eyes against it. Wished she could close her ears against it.

And then, as quickly as it began, it ended. Like a switch had been flipped.

She swallowed, glancing up to find Qasim staring at her.

Evil… Again, the word whispered through her head. Then Qasim snarled something to the men holding her. She didn't understand it, but then he translated,

"I told them to throw you to the ground so I can fuck you bloody."

Her uncle howled and struggled against his captor. She kicked and bucked as two sets of hard, bruising hands pushed her to the floor. The bones in her tied arms cried out as the appendages were smashed between her back and the rock. A knee landed on her chest, digging into her breastbone, making it impossible to breathe. Cruel fingers bit into the skin of her thighs, wrenching them wide. The tart smell of unwashed male bodies tunneled up her nose, causing her to gag.

She crushed the cloth between her teeth with such force her jaws popped. But she didn't make a peep. She refused to—

BOOOOOMMMM!

The explosion was tremendous. Thunderous. It shook the earth.

A split second later, the knee was gone, the hands were gone. Bodies fell around her, slamming into the cavern floor with disgusting-sounding *thumps* and *crunches*. Confused, disoriented, she dragged in a shuddering breath, staring up at the ceiling, at the golden light playing with the shadows.

Wha—

And then she could hear the hollow thud of boots against stone, the steady beat of running feet. The sound was distant, empty, competing with the ringing in her ears. She turned her chin, blinking, trying to make sense of the scene laid out before her. The four terrorists were sprawled around, dead to a man, blood pooling beneath their heads.

And then she knew. It hadn't been *one* massive

explosion; it'd been four *simultaneous* ones. Four shots from four guns that had instantly taken out the threat. And, *sweet Jesus!* Was it over? Could it really be over?

The sobs shuddering in her chest broke free as she finally allowed the shock and the terror and the pain to pour from her.

"Delilah!" She heard her name. Heard *his* voice.

"Mac!" she tried to yell, but the only sound to issue from her throat was a pitiful, hiccupping wail.

"Delilah!" And he was there, beside her, gathering her up in his arms, peppering her face with kisses, reaching around to undo the gag. He crushed her to him, burying his nose in her neck—God, he smelled good. Like Mac—and that's when she saw it.

Movement…

The terrorist closest to them, the one who'd had his fist in hair. He was reaching for the pistol tucked in his waistband, the deep bloody furrow along his temple proof he'd only been grazed.

"Mac!" she screamed, bucking in his embrace, her hands still tied behind her back.

Later she would marvel at Mac's speed, at the battle-honed reflexes that allowed him to raise his gun, aim, and fire all in a split second. But right then she was too busy wincing at the deafening roar of his Glock, at the bright flash as the bullet left the muzzle, at the hot spray of blood that landed on her arm and leg when the terrorist's skull exploded like an over-ripe melon.

No one moved for a beat. The shock of it all overwhelming. Then Mac recovered and yelled over his shoulder, "Somebody bring in a stretcher!" before gathering her shaking form close once again, murmuring, "Shh, now, darlin'. I gotcha. It's all over..."

-------∿∿-------

Northwestern Memorial Hospital
Chicago, Illinois

Delilah turned from her uncle's bedside and gifted Mac with an ear-to-ear smile. He felt the jaws of a trap—one that was both deadly and strangely alluring—closing around him.

In the forty-eight hours since the spooks choppered them to a farmer's field just outside the city, then loaded them into an SUV for a quick ride to the hospital, Mac had had to tell the story of the "backwoods car wreck" that caused Theo and Delilah's injuries a total of one time...to the attending ER physician when they first arrived. That's it. Just the once. Explanation...swallowed whole. It was almost as if he heard an audible *gulp*.

And even though he was a bona fide covert operator, living all that cloak and dagger stuff day-in and day-out, there were times, like this one, that even *he* felt the need to shake his head at the...uh...surreal-ness? Was that even a word?...of it all. Because, no one, not the nurses or the doctors or, hell, even the night janitor had the first clue that the real reason Delilah had a concussion, bruising, and scrapes, and Theo had a broken leg, lacerations, and contusions, was because a group of *terrorists* bent on securing *nuclear warheads* had *kidnapped* and *interrogated* the pair inside of a...wait for it...freakin' *cave*.

But, seriously, why *would* they suspect it? Even for

Mac it was damn near unbelievable. The stuff of poorly written, overly dramatic spy novels, and—

"Mac?" Delilah jerked him from his thoughts. "Are you okay?"

Okay? No. *Hell, no,* he was not okay. Not even close to being okay. Because in the last forty-eight hours, as he watched her stoically suffer pokes and prods from the medical staff, as he watched her answer a gazillion questions from the civilian-clad CIA agent sent in to debrief her, as he watched her refuse to leave her uncle's bedside, he'd come to the awful conclusion that he'd not only fallen a little bit…but *a lot* in love with her. As in, all the way. Ass-over-tea-kettle.

Delilah Fairchild, with her smile and charm, with her bravery and grit, had stolen his goddamned heart. Like a thief in the night. Or maybe it was more like a thief in the *day.* Because she'd made no bones about her pursuit of him. Not even at the very beginning. So, yessir, the fact that he'd reneged on his pledge to himself was nobody's fault but his own.

Which pissed him off. And…scared him to death.

Goddamn history…*why* did it have to go and repeat itself?

"Mac?" Delilah said again. "You're starting to scare me. What is it? Is Fido—"

"No, no," he assured her, shaking himself out of his own head. "Fido's fine. In fact, Steady said the vet will release him tomorrow mornin'. We can make sure someone transports him up here. If you'd like, he can be at the bar waitin' when you bring Theo home." He motioned with his chin toward the softly snoring old man.

And there it was again. That goddamn smile. The one that said he hung the moon and had the ability to jump over it. It was a problem, that smile. It made him want to throw caution to the wind.

"I'd like that very much," she said, pushing to a stand.

He gulped as she strolled toward him. She was wearing her standard daily get-up of painted-on jeans and a soft, body-hugging T-shirt. And that sensual, hip-swaying gait of hers? Well, there should be some kind of law against it. It was just too mesmerizing, reminding him of all they'd done together not so very long ago, taunting him with the things he'd never allow himself to do again. And it was no surprise when Little Mac, the prick—ha!—took notice of her approach. He had to adjust his stance.

"Were you able to get the bikes transported up?" she asked, stopping barely a foot from him. Close enough so that he could smell the spicy sweetness of her. Close enough so that he could see the golden flecks in the centers of her pretty green eyes. He loved those little bits of yellow, like the first autumn leaves turning on a tree.

Oh, for the love of... And now what am I? A freakin' poet?

He nodded. It was all he could manage with his tongue threatening to hang out like a dog's. She was so beautiful. *Too* beautiful.

"Good." She nodded. "Thank you for that."

"No problem," he somehow managed to say while keeping his tongue clamped firmly between his teeth.

"Mac?" She tilted her head, her sleek auburn brows angling down. He loved it when they did that. The smooth arches curling at the innermost edges, a delightful little wrinkle forming between them. *Good God, and now you're going on about her eyebrows?* He really was in sad, *sad* shape. And that…well…he wasn't too proud to say, made him feel the need to vamoose himself, like, yesterday. The soles of his feet were actually itching to send him running far and fast and… *farther* away from her. "Are you sure you're okay?"

No, goddamnit! He was *not* okay! Because somehow he'd allowed himself to fall, despite everything, despite *knowing* better. And he was a damned fool. A glutton for punishment. Doomed to follow the path of—

He shook the half-formed thought from his head. "Did you, uh, think any more about that offer to work on the Winterfield case?" And, yeah, that was good. Work. He should be focusing on work.

Now that the "powers that be" had proof Luke Winterfield had, indeed, sold state secrets to the highest bidder, he was officially listed as a traitor to the United States of America, *persona non grata extraordinaire*. And POTUS himself had tasked The Company with finding the guy in his South American hideout. Considering Delilah's unparalleled expertise in following the convoluted path of money trails and given her close ties with and personal stake in the case—much to Mac's surprise—the CIA had actually had the good sense and foresight to try to bring her on board as an asset. *Will wonders never cease?*

"I did." She nodded. He couldn't help but notice the way it caused a lock of auburn hair to drift over her shoulder. It reminded him of how she'd looked atop the dresser in the Noel Motel, head back, breasts lifted, her long hair playing hide-and-seek with her rosy, delicious

nipples. *Jesus Christ!* And now Little Mac, good soldier that he was, was standing at full attention. "The…
um…" She glanced around to make sure no one was
listening in, before leaning in close. Her sweet-smelling
breath tickled his chin. "The Company is installing a
secure server back at my place as we speak. As soon as
I get Uncle Theo settled, I'm going to start digging." She
cocked her head. "I…I think it'll be…sort of…*cathar-
tic*, I guess would be the word."

"Yeah." Mac swallowed.

"Mac?" Her soft palm landed on his arm, reminding him of how it'd felt when it was wrapped firmly
around his erection, tugging, stroking, bringing so
much pleasure.

He couldn't take it anymore. "I gotto go," he blurted,
causing her wonderfully piquant chin to jerk back.
Piquant? Okay, and could a chin even *be* piquant? Or
was that just his silly, fanciful, ridiculous obsession with
her—and every single, itty-bitty part of her—coming out?

"O-okay?" She blinked. And, yeah. He could go on
about her lashes for a while, too. About how long they
were. About how he loved that the tips glinted blond
in the light when she wasn't wearing any mascara, like
now. *Fuck…*

"There are…" He had to stop and clear his throat.
Someone, at some point, had shoved a big ol' wad of
cotton down there. "Uh…things back at the shop that—"

"It's okay, Mac." And there it was *again*. That goddamned smile. He barely resisted lifting a hand to his
chest in an effort to stymie the ache of his heart. "I
understand. You've been playing nursemaid and right-
hand man to the both of us," she hooked a thumb toward

her uncle, "for long enough. We're good now. Really. Go take care of what you need to take care of."

What he needed to take care of? He needed to take care of the idiotic, ill-timed, ill-*fated* love he'd developed for her. That's what he needed to take care of.

"Delilah, I—" He stopped. Unsure of how to go on. Uncertain, even, if he should. How did he tell her all the things he felt, all the things she meant to him now and *couldn't* mean to him in the future? How did he tell her about—

"What is it, Mac?"

He swallowed. *Damn,* were those *tears* burning the back of his nose? "I'll…uh…I'll see you later, darlin'."

And with that, he turned tail and ran like the yellow-bellied coward he was.

Chapter Twenty-three

Red Delilah's Biker Bar
Three weeks later...

I'LL SEE YOU LATER, DARLIN'...

Whenever it was quiet and empty in the bar, like now, Mac's last words echoed through Delilah's head, taunting her.

For the first week, those five words had filled her with hope. Hope that he would walk through her door at any moment. Hope that he would take her in his arms and tell her he'd been crazy not to give her, give *them*, a chance. Hope that he would see that what they had was too precious and rare to let slip away before it was ever given an opportunity to really start.

But one week slid into two, and he'd done none of those things. Her hope had been replaced with disbelief. Disbelief and *hurt*. She couldn't understand why he was avoiding her. That had never been part of their bargain. And if it *had* been, she wouldn't have signed herself up for it. Because she'd never, *never* been prepared to give up everything. To give up his friendship. To give up the chance of seeing his dazzling smile or his adorably crooked nose. To give up ever hearing his slow, Texas drawl.

And then it'd occurred to her that perhaps he wasn't avoiding her at all. That perhaps he was simply out on a mission somewhere, deep in a jungle or sweating in some desert. He *was* a super-secret spy-guy, right?

But she'd quickly been relieved of that little misconception when, one night after a handful of the Knights came in to enjoy some peanuts and brews, she'd oh-so-casually let slip a question to Ozzie about Mac's "secret" whereabouts. Ozzie had frowned and informed her that there was nothing *secretive* about it. Mac was back at the shop, cleaning out the fuel lines on Siren.

Uh-huh. And there'd gone *that* little glimmer of optimism, crushed beneath Ozzie's words as surely as Roscoe Porter—one of her most loyal patrons—crushed beer cans against his big, wrinkled forehead.

Which brought her to today. Three weeks into what she'd come to call The Great Disappearing Act. And even though the words *I'll see you later, darlin'* still accosted her from time to time, they no longer brought with them hope or disappointment or hurt. Nope. Now they just pissed her off.

What the hell is wrong with him? The man doesn't even have the decency to—

"You're going to slice off a finger the way you're handling that knife," her Uncle Theo observed. She was behind the bar, cutting up lemons and limes to be used in cocktails. When she glanced at him—he was sitting on a stool across from her, the *Chicago Sun-Times* in one hand and a cup of coffee in the other—she couldn't stop the little sigh of relief that whispered from between her lips. He was healthy. And *alive*. And save for a little scar near his temple and the crutches he still had to use, no one looking at him would know what a harrowing ordeal he'd been through.

But *she* would never forget. Never forget the fear in

his eyes. The tears streaming down his face. The blood. *God,* there'd been a lot of blood…

No, she'd never forget. Not if she lived to be a hundred years old. She wiped her hands on her apron and reached across the bar, squeezing his hand.

He made a clucking noise, his bushy, white mustache drooping at the corners. "How long until you stop needing to touch me every thirty seconds to assure yourself I'm really here?"

She swallowed the lump in her throat. "I don't know. It might be a while yet."

He opened his mouth to respond, but a sharp knock on the front door sent Fido scrambling out from under her feet and racing around the end of the bar. His doggy nails scraped against the hardwood floor, alerting her to the fact that it was probably time to take out the clippers. Dog ownership had its own learning curve, one she was enjoying immensely. And besides seeing her uncle healthy and happy—well, as happy as he could be considering he'd watched one of his oldest acquaintances die at the hands of terrorists. She knew he was still struggling with that—nothing gave her more pleasure than to know Fido had completely recovered. The dog had nothing to show for his close brush with death except for a six-inch scar furrowing through the yellow hair on his chest.

"*Yorp! Yorp! Yorpyorpyorp!*" he sang happily as both Delilah and her uncle yelled toward the door, "We're closed!"

"It's Zoelner!" came the reply from outside, and Delilah's hand jumped to her throat when her heart tried to escape from her body via that route.

Mac…. Something had happened to Mac and—

She hopped over the bar, not bothering to use the hinged ledge at the end. Hurdling a barstool, she was across the room in two seconds, twisting the locks and throwing open the door. Zoelner stood on the threshold in jeans and a leather jacket, his expression unreadable.

"Mac," she said, or at least *tried* to say. Her throat was so restricted by the presence of her heart that it came out sounding more like a wheezing *Mahhh*. She swallowed and tried again. "Is he okay? Is he hurt? Do you—"

"Relax," Zoelner said, grabbing her elbow and steering her back into the bar. "Mac's fine." A whooshing sigh of relief gushed from her, and it was then she realized her knees were shaking like the overhead fixtures tended to do on Wednesday nights when a troop of local line-dancers took over the place. When Zoelner spotted her uncle sitting at the bar, he dipped his chin. "Theo. You're looking well. I can't tell you how glad I am to see that."

"Thanks to you and the boys of BKI," her uncle said.

Zoelner waved off his comment. "No need for thanks. Just doing our jobs."

And Delilah still couldn't quite believe how blasé her uncle had been when she explained to him in the hospital—after getting the go-ahead from Frank "Boss" Knight, of course—what exactly the Black Knights were and why exactly they'd been there assisting in his rescue.

Yeah, that makes sense, was all he'd said in answer to her revelation. Then he'd gone back to eating pudding while watching the Cardinals trounce the Cubs on the television hanging from the hospital ceiling.

Makes sense? *Makes sense?* she'd thought at the time. *In what world?* But then she figured it made sense in the covert government mission world her uncle had been a part of back in the day. And, go figure, they'd not mentioned a word of it since.

Men, she thought with an eye roll. Then she decided to narrow that down to *super-secret former and/or current government men*… They were seriously exasperating.

"When does the cast come off?" Zoelner asked her uncle, bending to scratch Fido behind the ears. The dog was sitting in front of him, holding a paw up for a shake.

"Next week, thank goodness," her uncle said. "I've had an itch I haven't been able to get to for six days now."

"Sounds awful." Zoelner grinned, rubbing Fido's belly when it was presented to him. The big goofy canine was on his back, thick tail swooshing across the floorboards, head thrown back so his upper jowls sagged and made him look like he was smiling maniacally. Delilah could only shake her head and grin, wondering how she'd ever lived without the dog's daily antics to make her laugh. Then Zoelner glanced up at her. "You got a couple of minutes? There's something I'd like to talk to you about."

"Sure," she said, brow puckering. "You want some coffee?" She glanced at her watch. It was only ten o'clock in the morning, but the look on Zoelner's face told her he could maybe use something a little stronger. "Or a beer, perhaps?"

"Coffee's fine," Zoelner said, standing and walking with her over to the bar. He grabbed a stool while she skirted the long mahogany length. This time she took the time to lift the hinged section at the end before slipping in behind.

While she poured him a cup of joe, her uncle folded his newspaper, grabbed his crutches, and said, "I'm gonna head outside to smoke a cigar." He shot her a meaningful look. "And I don't want to hear a word about it."

"The doctors say you should stop smoking those things." She placed her hands on her hips, completely ignoring his second sentence.

He rolled his eyes. "The doctors *also* say I've got the cholesterol levels of a twenty-year-old." He began hobbling toward the door at the back of the bar, the one leading to the alley. "So I figure I'm ahead of the curve. Besides, a man my age has to enjoy what pleasures he can."

"And speaking of pleasures," she called to him, "stop sharing your stogies with the agents in the surveillance cars. You're a bad influence!"

He simply lifted a hand to wave her off.

"He's a tough old coot," Zoelner observed.

"And stubborn," she agreed, smiling after her uncle. "He insists there's no reason for the CIA to keep an eye on him even though the head honchos in that al-Qaeda group know he's now the only living person with the exact coordinates of five missing nuclear warheads."

"Three," Zoelner said.

"Huh?"

"It's only three now," he told her. "Given this most recent development, the DOD decided it behooved them to allocate a portion of their healthy budget to the retrieval of the nukes. Two have already been raised from the sea floor. The salvage of the remaining three is underway."

"About damn time, if you ask me," she said, wondering, not for the first time, at the idiocy of a government that would *not* put the recovery of nuclear weapons at the very top of its to-do list.

Zoelner shrugged, and there was that look again. The one that made her wonder if she should renew her offer of a beer. She tilted her head. "You're not here at the bequest of Agent Duvall, are you? Was I wrong? Did the Intel I gave them on the ghost accounts Winterfield set up in Argentina not pan out? Does she want me to—"

"I don't want to talk about Chelsea Duvall," Dagan spat the name like one usually spits out rancid meat. "She was a pain in the ass while I worked for The Company, and now, thanks to her spiffy new title, she's a pain in my ass again."

Uh-huh. Pain in the ass. Did Zoelner realize when he said that, it sounded like a euphemism for *my wildest fantasy come true*? Usually she would have called him on his bullshit, but there was that look again. It was really beginning to trouble her. "So, then, um…what *did* you want to talk about?"

"Do you love Mac?"

"Say what?" She must have misheard him.

"Do you love Mac?" he repeated, and yeah, okay, so she *hadn't* misheard him. He'd asked it. That question. *The* question. Her scalp began to tingle.

"I don't know how that's any of your—"

"Because he loves you."

Thunk. The sentence landed with the weight of a tractor trailer. Was the room spinning, or was that just her head? Then, reality—and the words *I'll see you later, darlin'*—slammed into her. She shook herself.

"Yeah, right!" she scoffed, grabbing the coffee pot to top off his nearly full cup. She needed something to distract herself, to keep him from seeing just how much his words affected her. "The man has been avoiding me like I'm a plague carrier. If that's how he treats someone he loves, I'd hate to see how he treats someone he hates."

Zoelner reached into his jacket pocket and pulled out a photo, slapping it down on the bar. She leaned forward, examining the picture. A woman. Black hair. Blue eyes. Nice face. Curvaceous figure.

"She's pretty," she said, trying to stymie the wild race of her heart. *Because he loves you.* Zoelner couldn't know just how much she wished that were true. "Who is she?"

"She's the reason Mac refuses to take a chance with you," Zoelner said. Delilah picked up the photo, examining it closer. This was the woman who'd ruined Mac? The woman he said reminded him of her? She *was* pretty. And there was something—

"She's his mother," Zoelner said, and Delilah felt her jaw fall open. It was a wonder the thing didn't land at her feet.

"H-his *mother?*"

"Yep. And I want to tell you a story. But before I do that, I have to know if you love him."

His *mother* was the mystery woman? Delilah stared at the photograph. She could see it. Mac had those same eyes. That same smile… His *mother?* But why did he—

"Hey." Zoelner snapped his fingers in front of her face. "Earth to Delilah. Come in, Delilah."

"Sorry," she said, blinking, her brain spinning in

circles the way Fido did when he got bored and caught sight of his tail.

"I have to know," he repeated. "Do. You. Love him?"

She swallowed, a little afraid to admit it aloud for the first time. But then she took her own advice and toughened up, buttercup. Harley-riding, beer-slinging, yada, yada, yada, right? Dragging in a deep breath, she looked Zoelner square in the eye. "Yes. I love him." *God, it feels good to say it*.

"Good." He nodded. "Because, like I said, he loves you, too. And the fact that he does scares him to death."

Could it be true? Did she dare hope? "Scares him? But why?"

"Because of Jolene." He tapped his finger on the photo. *Jolene?* Mac's mother's name was Jolene? "Because she was a faithless cow who ran out on Mac and his father when Mac was only twelve, leaving behind nothing but a selfish, insipid farewell note that didn't contain a single regret or apology."

She winced. Twelve? Such an impressionable age. An age when a boy *needed* his mother for guidance on how to start behaving like a man. "That's awful." She frowned her confusion. "It really is. But I don't understand what the hell it has to do with me."

"Hang on a second," Zoelner said exasperatedly. "I'm getting there."

She made a face. "Then, by all means," rolling her hand, "carry on."

Zoelner lifted his mug of coffee, taking a hasty sip. "Apparently Mac's father was devastated by Jolene's desertion. See, the man was deeply, tragically, and, if you ask me, a little *madly* in love with her. Like,

seriously, I think Mac's father went a little coo-coo."
Zoelner whirled his finger in a circle next to his temple.
"He spent the next seven years of his life and his very
last dime—money that *should* have gone to running the
ranch that'd been in Mac's family for generations—
trying to locate her. No luck. And, according to Mac,
even on his deathbed, having finally succumbed to a
broken heart and pancreatic cancer, his father was still
obsessed, crying out her name."

"Jesus," Delilah breathed, shaking her head, chills
rippling up her arms.

"Yeah." Zoelner nodded. "But it gets worse. See,
Mac adored and idolized his father. And after the banks
foreclosed on the ranch, he busted his ass to get into the
FBI Academy so he could finish what his father started,
using every resource The Bureau afforded him in order
to continue the search for Jolene."

She lifted a hand to her throat, her thumb resting atop
her thundering pulse point. "Did he…" She had to lick
her suddenly dry lips. "Did he ever find her?"

"It took a couple of years, but he finally located her
out in California. She was happy as a pig in slop to be
living all the glitz and glamour and excitement of the
LA scene. And when Mac confronted her about aban-
doning him, it was only to discover she was completely
unrepentant. She even had the gall to tell him it was
for the best. Because she'd been so *unhappy* living on
the ranch."

Delilah shook her head, her eyes wide. It was like
something off daytime television. All the treachery and
drama but with none of the happy endings.

"Of course," Zoelner took another hasty sip, "when

the FBI found out Mac was using Bureau resources for personal pursuits, they fired his ass."

"Holy shit," she breathed. "It just keeps getting worse and worse."

"Eh." Zoelner shrugged. "It all worked out in the end. After all, Boss took him under his wing and made him a Black Knight. And it's a pretty sweet gig, if you want to know the truth of it."

Delilah's brain was spinning. She had to shake her head like Fido shaking off water after a bath in order to organize her thoughts. "O-okay, but I *still* don't understand what any of that has to do with *me*."

"Mac's going to buy back the ranch. It's his second goal in life."

Huh? "Uh...pull out the non sequiturs much, Zoelner?" she asked. Then what he'd said sank in. "Wait. His *second* goal in life? So, what's his first?"

Zoelner smiled sadly. "His first goal is to make sure he doesn't follow in his father's footsteps. To make sure he doesn't fall in love with a gorgeous, thrilling woman who's so used to being the center of attention that she could never be happy living way out in BFE Texas. Hell, he even named his motorcycle Siren to remind himself of the kind of woman he should avoid at all costs."

It was all making sense now. That stuff he was rambling on about in the motel. She shook her head, her heart a pounding fist inside her chest.

"And then *you* walked into his life," Zoelner said, lifting a brow along with his coffee mug. "Delilah Fairchild... The epitome of beauty and vitality and," he motioned toward her position behind the bar with his mug, "the *literal* center of attention of everyone who comes in this bar."

———

Black Knights Inc. Headquarters
Twenty minutes later…

"President Thompson trusts the Secret Service." Mac watched as Boss glanced curiously at the files in his hand before continuing. "But these are his daughters we're talking about. And since the NSA thinks the on-line chatter concerning the supposed abduction of one or both of his children is credible, he'd feel much better if a Black Knight was stationed near each of the girls…uh… *women*. Not to interfere with the SS Agents, but simply to…*augment* security…to watch. *From the shadows* were the words he used. And that means—"

"*Wha! Wha! Wha!*"

Mac glanced across the conference table. Not in a million years would he ever get used to the sight of Ghost, Mr. Spooky himself, with a baby in his arms.

"Sorry," Ghost muttered, pushing up from the table while his big hand patted his daughter's back, shushing her. "Diaper change. Carry on without me."

Inexplicably, in the last three weeks, Black Knights Inc. had gone from a full-time custom motorcycle shop/covert government defense firm to a part-time nursery. And who would've ever thought that one cooing, pooping, slobbering bundle of joy could turn each of Mac's teammates into baby-talking, *Sesame Street*-watching, fighting-over-whose-turn-it-is-to-give-the-kid-a-bottle idiots?

Okay, yeah, if Mac was being completely honest, he'd fallen into the idiot category, too. In fact, just last evening, he and Ozzie had nearly come to blows over who would give little Jenna Beth her five p.m. feeding.

"Hey, Steady," Boss said, dragging Mac back to the present. "You know Abigail Thompson, right? POTUS's youngest? Didn't you two go to school together?"

With Ghost's defection, Ozzie, Steady, and Mac were the only Knights left at the conference table with Boss. Ozzie, as usual, was nose-deep in a laptop. And Steady looked…Mac tilted his chin…weird.

What was that expression exactly?

And then recognition struck. Recognition because that look of panicked discomfort was exactly how he felt every time Delilah walked into the room.

Delilah…

Ten times a day he had to stop himself from mounting up on Siren and roaring over to her bar. Ten times a day he had to toss his phone aside lest he dial her number. And ten times a day he had to remind himself of the danger she posed to his future plans, his future sanity, his…heart.

"*Sí*, we went to school together," Steady acknowledged, trying, and failing, not to fidget in his seat. "But I wouldn't say I *know*—"

The sound of boot heels racing up the metal stairs from the floor below caught everyone's attention, cutting Steady off mid-sentence. The sound of boot heels and…*what the hell is that?*

And then Mac knew. Dog claws. It was dog claws clacking against the treads. His heart lurched, then stopped altogether when Fido burst onto the scene, tongue lolling, goofy grin splitting his furry face, doggy goggles sitting atop his head and…Mac tilted his chin again…a freakin' red bandana tied around his throat like he was the canine version of the Red Baron or something. He'd heard Delilah had attached a sidecar to Big Red for Fido. Now, he could imagine them tooling around the city together. And the picture in his head was…well…adorable.

Then his eyes lifted…

Did the floor drop out from under him? Was he falling through space? Or was that simply the feel of his stomach sinking into the soles of his boots?

Because, there she was. Delilah. The woman he loved. The woman he refused to let himself have. She looked…good. Better than good, *great*. As always. Temptation on two legs.

It took everything he had not to race to her. Not to take her in his arms and damn any future consequences. It took everything he had to simply clear his throat and say, "Hey, Delilah."

"Don't you *hey, Delilah* me, you idiot-minded jerk!" she yelled.

"Uh." Ozzie glanced up from his laptop, allowing his gaze to flit from Delilah to Mac. "Should the…um… should the rest of us leave?"

"Sounds like it," Mac said, never taking is eyes off her, his heart thundering so hard he wondered that his T-shirt wasn't fluttering against his chest.

There was some scuffling as the three Knights pushed away from the table. Some whispered exchanges as they shuffled into Boss's office and quietly shut the door. Mac waited a beat, then two before asking, "Something on your mind, darlin'?"

She stalked forward, the swing of her hips enough to have his hands curling into fists. Fido trailed her like the good dog he was, glancing up at her adoringly—Mac totally understood the sentiment. Reaching into her hip pocket, she came out with what appeared to be a photo and slammed it down on the table in front of him.

"Mommy issues!" she hissed, planting her hands on her hips. "I'm forced to give up the man I love because he has *mommy issues*?"

Mac's hair threatened to leap off his head. His tongue swelled until it was nearly impossible to breath. Two things struck him about that last sentence. The first was that she knew about Jolene. The second was that...she loved him.

Chapter Twenty-four

"ZOELNER NEEDS A LESSON IN KEEPIN' HIS MOUTH shut," Mac grumbled, his jaw sawing back and forth and making his adorable dimple twitch.

Delilah gaped at him. "Seriously? I just dropped the L-bomb, and you're talking about *Zoelner*?"

"I—" He opened his mouth, but she waved him off with an impatient hand. Zoelner said she needed to be tough, to not take *no* for an answer if she had any hope of breaking through all Mac's barriers. Well, Zoelner's definition of tough and *her* definition of tough might be two different things. Because she had a whole lot more than talking and not taking *no* for an answer in mind...

Skirting the conference table, she grabbed Mac's wrist—oh, how she'd missed the heat of him, the crinkly prickle of his hairs against her skin. Hauling him to his feet, she dragged him toward the stairs leading to the third floor. When he saw their destination, he began backpedaling like a kid on his way to the dentist. "Whoa, wha—"

She turned and placed his hand on her boob, trying not to smile when all the blood drained from his face a second before he adjusted his stance like his pants were suddenly too tight. Seemingly of its own accord, his thumb trailed over her nipple, bringing the peak to instantaneous life. She felt a tug in her womb but ignored it. She had to play this smart if she wanted to reach her goal.

"Delilah," he gulped, shaking his head. She went up on her tiptoes, threading her arms around his neck and sealing their lips.

At first, he kept his mouth closed. But one swipe of her tongue and he growled, his arms coming around her waist, his lips parting. She moaned. She couldn't help herself. He was so big, so warm, so...*Mac*.

It took everything she had to pull back, to break the wet, hot suction of their lips, but she managed it. Then she whispered in his ear, "Come upstairs with me. I want to make love to you."

She heard him swallow. Heard his throat *click* dryly. "Delilah, I—"

"I'm not asking you for promises or pledges or vows right now," she assured him. "I'm not asking you for anything more than what you're willing to give me." She pulled back so she could see his face, his electric blue eyes. "Are you willing to give me this?"

Her lungs waited to draw breath, her heart waited to pump blood, every cell inside her body waited for his answer. And when he shook his head, she nearly lost faith. "I can't—"

"Forget I asked for permission," she cut him off. *Don't take* no *for an answer,* Zoelner said. Well, by God, she wasn't. "Let me put it to you this way... you're *taking* me upstairs and you're *going* to make love to me."

"But—"

"No *buts*," she growled, stepping from his embrace, once again yanking him toward the stairs. He trailed her slowly, grudgingly. She could almost hear the thoughts and arguments spinning through his head over the *clink-clink* of Fido's nails on the metal staircase. He followed them happily, panting and smiling and thinking it was all a great adventure. When they reached the landing, Delilah saw a long row of gray doors. "Which is yours?" she demanded.

"The second one, but—"

"What did I just say about no *buts*?"

"Delilah—"

She ignored whatever he was about to say, instead marching over to the second door and pushing it open. The room inside screamed Mac. A queen-sized bed in a big mahogany frame sat center-stage, the fall-colored linens atop it in disarray. Two comfy armchairs in burgundy leather were pushed against the far brick wall, flanking a small occasional table where a stack of files sat. An old-fashioned Tiffany floor lamp sat next to a massive armoire. It cast warm, dappled light around the small space. And above the bed was a framed black and white panoramic picture of a long, lonely fence line and a big, arching iron gate. At the top of the gate, a faded wooden sign read *Lazy M*.

So, that's Mac's home… And, yeah, she could see the allure. The beauty in the vastness of the land. The windswept wonder of it all.

Fido walked around the room, sniffing furniture and shoving his snout into a wastepaper basket. Then he climbed atop one of the leather chairs, curling himself into what she'd come to term the doggy-doughnut—where his nose met his furry butt—and immediately closed his eyes. She turned to Mac. He was hovering on the threshold, looking ready to bolt. "You coming?"

He shook his head. "No, I—"

Rolling her eyes, she grabbed his arm and hauled him inside the room. When she kicked the door closed, the look on Mac's face went from merely startled to flat-out terrified. Her heart clenched for him. But she couldn't give in to the desire to comfort him *or* confront him. He wasn't ready for either. That would come later, when he was softened up, during the warm afterglow of hot, sweaty sex. For now, she needed to focus entirely on seduction.

Lucky for her—and all women, really—seducing a man didn't take much.

Bending to yank off her biker boots and socks, she instructed Mac to do the same. Her shirt and bra went next, followed by her jeans and panties. When she was standing buck naked in front of him, the cool air in the room raising goose bumps over her skin, she looked up to find him still completely clothed. Not that she was surprised. He was going to fight this. She'd known on the ride over that he was going to fight this every step of the way.

Fortunately, she was a stubborn woman. And once she set her mind on task, woe to any man, woman, child, fruit, vegetable, mineral, or *other* that stood in her way…

She strolled over to him, making sure to give her hips an *extra* little swing, delighted that his eyes were super-glued to the bounce of her boobs. When she reached for the hem of his T-shirt, he grabbed her wrist, his Adam's apple bobbing in the tan column of his throat. "W-we had a deal. A one-night stand only. No strings. No hurt—"

"I'm reneging on that deal," she said, feeling not one ounce of regret even when his wonderfully dimpled chin jerked back. "We're going to make a new deal," she said, reveling in the feel of his hot skin along the backs of her fingers where she was still gripping his shirt. "A new deal where we take this thing one day at a time. Every day, I'll wake up and remind you that I'm not your mother and that *you* are not your father."

The muscle in his jaw ticked frantically as his nostrils flared wide. She saw she'd distracted him enough to whip his T-shirt over his head. The sight of him, of all that tanned, toned flesh made her throat constrict and her nipples furl.

"Every day I'm going to wake up and tell you I love you."

His eyes became overly bright. His big chest began to quake. It caused tears to prick behind her nose—seeing big, bad Mac McMillan so scared and vulnerable—but she swallowed them. She had to remain strong, resolute. It was the only way she was going to win this game. Win against years of hurt and confusion. Win against plain ol' wrong-headedness.

"And every day I'm going to wake up and tell you that I'm not leaving you."

She could see him struggling. Struggling against his past. Against the desire to believe her words. Against the tears that filled his eyes. She knew he was hovering on the precipice, and she knew this could go one of two ways. Either he'd admit his love for her and agree to her terms, or he'd fall back on his old patterns and kick her out of his bedroom…

In such a volatile state, she didn't trust him to make the right decision. So, she put it off for a bit longer by reaching for his belt buckle and saying, "So, what'll it be? The dresser again?"

"Huh?" he gulped, shaking his head, blinking rapidly.

"It just seems to me," she whipped off his belt and started in on the buttons of his fly, "that you're a bit partial to dressers."

"I—"

He stopped talking, his eyes rolling back in his head when she reached into his pants, into his boxers, and wrapped her fist around the hard, hot, pulsing length of him.

"Mmm," she murmured, stepping up to him, thrilled by the warmth radiating from him as she pressed a kiss to his delectable Texas tattoo. "I've *missed* this." She grabbed his hand and placed it on her breast, simultaneously licking the flat brown disk of his nipple, delighted when the little nub sprang to life against her tongue. "Have you missed this?"

"God, *yes*," he admitted, his fingers plucking at her, causing a liquid ache to build and throb between her thighs.

When her hand slid to the end of his shaft and she felt a silky drop of moisture waiting there, she couldn't help herself. She dropped to her knees, simultaneously dragging his jeans and boxers down his large thighs.

Mary and Joseph, just look at him…

So unapologetically male. So big and…and *angry* looking, all red, violently veined skin and shiny, plump head. Saliva pooled on her tongue. She leaned forward to kiss the tip of him, to clasp his shaft in a hard fist just as he'd showed her, to cup his tight, warm balls in her free hand.

"Delilah!" Her name was barely discernible his voice was so guttural. And when she opened her mouth and swallowed the head of him, drank in the salty essence of him, he was reduced to nonsensical syllables.

Both his hands were fisted in her hair. His hips moving slightly, the muscles in his thighs twitching as if he were struggling to keep himself from thrusting forward violently. The feel of him against her tongue was amazing. Such soft skin covering such unyielding hardness. His veins were bumpy. They pulsed rhythmically when she pressed her lips against them.

In and out.

In and out.

He tasted good. Like male. Like sex. Like Mac…

"God, Delilah," he gasped, pulling from her mouth, from her hands. "You've gotta stop, darlin', or you're gonna make me lose it."

"So lose it." She smiled up at him, past the impressive jut of his shiny erection, past the corrugated muscles of his flat belly, past his big chest and shoulders to his beautiful, sparkling eyes.

She could see him hesitate, could see that he was tempted. But he shook his head, the muscles in his five-o'clock-shadowed jaw clenching. "No. I want to come inside you," he growled, grabbing her by the shoulders and hauling her to her feet. His callused hands spanned her waist, and the next thing she knew, she was airborne…

———❧———

Delilah landed on the mattress with her silky thighs spread wide, and Mac couldn't strip out of his boots, socks, and pants fast enough. Launching himself atop her…ah, *God*…she instantly wrapped her legs around him, her slick channel welcoming the length of his aching erection as he pressed it against her.

He knew he shouldn't be doing this. Knew it flew in the face of the vow he'd made himself. Knew that it was incredibly dangerous. Was this how it'd been between his parents in the beginning? Would it end for him the same way it'd ended for his father? Would—

Delilah fisted her hands in his hair, hungrily claiming his mouth, and every single thought in his head slid out through his ringing ears.

"Mac," she gasped against his lips, her breath hot. "Make love to me."

And it would be love. Because he *did* love her, and by God, he *believed* her when she said she loved him, too. Reaching down between them, he tested her readiness with two fingers. When he found her hot and wet and pulsing, he grabbed his shaft and teased his head against her opening.

"*Yes*." Her thighs rode high against his sides. "Yes. I want you inside me."

Her hands skimmed down his back. Her fingers digging into the muscles of his ass as she pulled him close.

"Delilah…" he breathed, slowly sinking into her tight, sultry body, ducking his chin to suck the peak of one rosy, hard nipple into his mouth.

"Unnnhhh." She arched into him, trying to seat him to the hilt. He had to pull out slightly and press in again before he could accommodate her, before her body finally yielded to his, before his heated balls slammed against the warm curve of her ass.

Right…

That's how it felt. *Right* in a way that it'd never been

before with any other woman. It thrilled him almost as much as it scared the living shit out of him.

"Please," she begged, squirming beneath him, hips bucking, urging him to move. And move he did, pulling out only to plunge home. He set a rhythm that drove them both to the edge within minutes, a slow, pumping, in-and-out slide that had her writhing and mewling and begging, and him gritting his teeth against coming too soon. Then, suddenly, she detonated. Just like he knew she would. Taking him with her in the process. Her body milking his orgasm from him in pulsing, greedy tugs.

Long seconds later, after they'd both managed to catch their breath, after he rolled onto his back, she threw a leg over his, twirling her fingers in his chest hair. Then, she said the words that simultaneously thrilled him and chilled him. "I love you, Mac. And I know you love me, too, even if you haven't said it."

He wanted to say it. Knew he probably *should* say it. That's what normal folks did when they loved each other. They *said* it, right? But the words stuck in his throat like a damned cocklebur.

"And I'm never going to leave you like your mother left your father," she continued, kissing his shoulder. "I'm never going to break your heart like your mother broke your father's. I'm in this thing until the end," she said, her voice husky as one more poignant, promising kiss landed near his Texas tattoo. "And when you're lying on your deathbed at the ripe old age of one-hundred-and-ten, and you're calling my name in the darkness," damn Zoelner and his big fucking mouth, "I'm going to be right there holding your hand. We're

Notebook-ing it, you and I. A real-life Allie and Noah. Staying together until we *go* together."

Sweet God, he couldn't stand it. He wanted that to be true so badly…

Crying like a fucking baby, that's what he was doing. Unwelcome tears leaked from the corners of his eyes, wetting his hair and the pillow beneath his head. His chest shook. His stomach trembled. He hadn't cried like this since the night his father died. Since the night he sat vigil by the man's bed, holding his hand, trying to lend comfort but knowing he wasn't enough as his father yelled for Jolene. *Jolene, where are you? Jolene, come back!*

"I'm s-scared to death," he admitted on a hiccupping sob, embarrassed to let her see him like this but unable to stop the strangled tears catching at the back of his throat.

She lifted her head from his shoulder, placing the gentlest of kisses on his lips, her breath the sweetest he'd ever tasted. "Shhh. It's okay," she told him, smiling softly, her eyes bright. "I know you're scared. I'm scared, too." She pressed soft kisses to the corners of his lips, his cheeks, his eyes. "Love is a risk for everybody." And that was the understatement of all time. "But, like I said, we're going to take this slow. One day at a time. But we *are* going to take this, we *are* going to give this a chance."

That wall he'd built up around his heart began to crumple beneath her words, beneath her delicate caresses. Could he do it? Was he brave enough to take the chance on her? To take the chance on *them*?

"Because I've lost a few people I've loved during

my life," she continued, "and this is what I know. In the
end, the love we withhold, not the love we give, is what
we wind up regretting. I don't want to die with regrets,
Mac. Do you?"

"No," he told her, pulling her close, kissing the top of
her head when she laid it on his shoulder. "No, I don't want
to die with regrets. And I *do* love you, Delilah." Another
sob shook him, cracking his voice. "I swear to God I do!"

"Shh." She hugged him close. "I know you do, Mac.
I know you do."

He nodded, his heart full to bursting. The wall he'd
built around the organ decimated by the love of one
flame-haired temptress. Then a thought occurred to him
and everything inside him stilled. "Zoelner told you I'm
buyin' back the ranch, right?"

"Yes." He felt her nod.

"It's my legacy," he stressed. "Even if I didn't love
it, which I do, I'd still *have* to go back there. I'd have to
take back what's been in my family for—"

"Mac." She pushed up on one arm to frown down at
him. "I'm *delighted* you're going to buy back the ranch.
It's the right thing to do. And I can't wait to own a pair
of cowgirl boots." She bit her lip, winking. "And maybe
some of those shirts with the fringe and rhinestones."

Yeah, she thought it was romantic now, from afar.
"Ranchin' is hard," he warned her. "And it's lonely.
You're used to all the fun and excitement of Chicago.
You're used to fifty people a day comin' into your bar
to flirt and banter and—"

She placed a finger over his lips, clucking her
tongue and shaking her head. "And there you go again.
Comparing me to your mother."

"I—" He tried to talk around her finger but was forced to stop when she used it along with her thumb to squeeze his lips together.

"I'm only going to say this once, Bryan McMillan," she declared, her eyes impossibly green, "I'm *not* Jolene." And, *damnit*, there went the waterworks again. "She was a shallow, foolish woman who needed constant attention and adoration from the outside because there was nothing to her on the inside. Sorry to speak ill of your mother"—she made a face—"but from what I understand, it's true." He nodded. She was absolutely right. It *was* true. "*I* don't need all that." She firmed her jaw, her expression daring him to naysay her. "I don't need adoration or attention from the masses to feel good about myself. I feel good about myself because I'm smart and loyal, caring and kind. And I can mix up a martini that would make James Bond weep."

It was hard to smile when she was smashing his lips together. Not a shy or a humble bone in Delilah's body. Just one of the reasons he absolutely adored her.

Reaching up, he tugged her fingers away from his mouth. "Speakin' of those martinis. Won't you miss the bar? You love it there."

She shrugged. "To tell you the truth, it's lost its appeal since Buzzard died. I've been thinking for a while now, especially after the fun I had helping the CIA track down some of Agent Winterfield's foreign deposits, that I might want to turn forensic accounting into a full-time gig. I'm sure there are telephones and Internet hookups in Texas, right?"

He nodded, tears standing in his eyes even as a smile

pulled at his lips. Was it possible? Could he really have it all? The ranch? The girl?

"Don't you get it, Mac?" she asked, shaking her head. "I just need you. Wherever we go, whatever we do, I'll be happy because I'm with you. *You* are my home."

And with those words, red-hot Delilah Fairchild stopped being That Woman. Because those words gave him the courage and strength to call her His Woman...

In Rides Trouble

Prologue

"WE'RE DEFINITELY CHANGING THE NAME." FRANK "Boss" Knight pulled the Hummer up in front of the sad little pre-fab building and glanced at the hand-painted wooden sign screwed over the front door: BECKY'S BADASS BIKE BUILDS.

"Too much alliteration for you?" Bill Reichert snickered from the passenger seat while unbuckling his seat belt and throwing open the door. The frigid winter wind whipped into the interior of the vehicle, prompting Frank to grab his black stocking cap from the dashboard and tug it over his head and ears before zipping his parka up to his chin.

If this thing actually worked out, Chicago winters were definitely going to take some getting used to. Of course, freezing temps were a small price to pay for a good, solid cover for his new defense firm. And joining Bill's kid sister in her custom Harley chopper business, posing as mechanics and motorcycle buffs, promised to be a freakin' phenomenal cover for all the guys he'd recruited away from the various branches of the armed services. Especially considering most of them were bulky, tattooed, and—without regulation military haircuts—just scruffy enough to pass for their own chapter of Hell's Angels.

He pushed out of the Hummer and had to lower his chin against the gust of wind that punched him in the face like an icy fist. Shoving his hands deep in his coat someone had shoveled in the thick blanket of snow.

Bill applied a gloved thumb to the buzzer, and five seconds later, a familiar noise sounded from the behind the metal door, making the hair on the back of Frank's neck stand up.

How do you know you've been in the business too long? When you recognize the sound of a .45 caliber being chambered from three feet away, that's how.

"Who is it?" a deep, wary voice inquired from within.

"I thought you said she knew we were coming," Frank hissed over Bill's shoulder.

"She does." Bill grinned. "But she also knows she can never be too careful in this neighborhood."

And that was no lie. The graffiti tagging every vertical surface for six blocks in each direction announced that they were smack dab in the middle of some very serious gang territory. The Vice Lords ruled the roost, and they wanted to make damned sure everyone knew it.

Raising his voice above the shrieking wind, Bill yelled, "Open the damned door, you big ape! We're freezing our dicks off out here!"

And that was no lie either. Frank couldn't even begin to explain to his family jewels why he hadn't jumped into a pair of thermal underwear this morning and instead opted to go commando.

Big mistake. *Huge.*

One he sure as hell wouldn't be making again.

The front door swung open with a resounding clang, and they were met by a giant, red-headed man who looked like he should be wearing a face mask and leotard while smashing a folding chair over some guy's back.

Frank could almost hear Michael Buffer shouting, *Arrrrre you ready to ruuumbllle?*

"Manus," Bill said, stepping over the threshold and motioning Frank through, "this is Boss. Boss, meet Manus. He and his brothers work security for my sister."

Frank waited until Manus tucked the .45 into the waistband of his jeans before cautiously stepping into the small, tiled vestibule. The walls were covered in rusted motorcycle license plates, and as soon as the door closed behind him, the aroma of motor oil and burning metal assaulted his nostrils.

"You the guy who wants to partner with Becky? Invest some money and learn to build bikes?" Manus asked while pumping the hand he offered, a smile splitting the big man's ruddy face and making all his freckles meld together.

Yeah, that was the story they were tossing around until he could get a look at the set-up...

"I haven't decided yet," he answered noncommittally, and Manus's smile only widened.

"That's only because you haven't seen Becky's bikes," he boasted. "Once you do, you're gonna want to give her all your savings and have her teach you everything she knows."

Frank lifted a shoulder as if to say *we'll see* and watched as Bill opened the second set of glass doors.

His ears were instantly assailed by a wall of sound.

The pounding beats of hard-driving rock music competed with the hellacious screech and whine of grinding metal. He resisted the urge to reach up and plug his ears as he followed Bill into the custom motorcycle shop, skirting a few pieces of high-tech machinery.

And then he wasn't thinking about his bleeding eardrums at all.

Because his eyes zeroed in on the most beautiful, outlandish motorcycle he'd ever seen.

It was secured on a bike lift. The paint on the gas tank and fenders was bright, neon blue that sparkled iridescently in the harsh overhead lights. It sported a complex-looking dual exhaust, an outrageous stretch, and intricate, nearly whimsical front forks. It also had so much chrome it almost hurt to look at it.

In a word: *art.*

It made the work he'd done restoring his vintage 1952 Harley-Davidson FL look like amateur hour.

And just when he thought he couldn't be any more blown away, the sound of grinding metal slowly died down and a young woman emerged from behind the bike with a grinder in one hand and a metal clamp in the other.

He nearly swallowed his own tongue.

This couldn't be...

But obviously it was. Because the instant the woman caught sight of them she squealed, clicked off the music pouring out of the speakers of an old-fashioned boom box, and dropped both tools on the bike lift before jumping into Bill's arms, hugging him tight and kissing his cheek with a resounding smack that sounded particularly loud in the sudden silence of the shop.

This was Rebecca "Rebel" Reichert, Wild Bill's little sister.

Little being the operative word. If she stood two inches over five feet Frank would eat his biker boots for dinner.

He didn't quite know what he'd expected of a woman who ran her own custom chopper shop, but it wasn't long, blond hair pulled back in a tight ponytail, intense brown eyes surrounded by lush, dark lashes, and a pretty, girl-next-door face that just happened to be his own personal weakness when it came to women.

Something about that wholesome, all-American thing always managed to bring him to his knees.

Well, hell.

Bill finally lowered her to the ground, and she came to stand in front of Frank, small, grease-covered hands on slim, jean-clad hips. For some inexplicable reason, he felt the need to stand up straighter.

It was probably because she had the same unyielding look in her eye that his hard-ass drill sergeant always had back when he'd been in Basic.

"So." She tilted her head until her ponytail hung down over her shoulder in a smooth, golden rope. "You must be the indomitable Frank Knight. Billy has told me so very *little* about you."

And that voice…

It was soft and husky. The type that belonged solely in the bedroom.

"Everyone calls me Boss," he managed to grumble.

"I think I'll stick to Frank," she said with a wink. And for some reason, his eyelid twitched. "After all, there can be only one boss around here, and I'm it. Now, I hear you want to get into the business of building bikes?"

"I'm considering it." He couldn't help but notice the way her nose tilted up at the end or the way her small breasts pressed against the soft fabric of the paint-stained, long-sleeved T-shirt she wore.

Kee-rist, man, get a grip.

"Well, then." She nodded, pushing past him as she made her way toward the front door, "let's go take a look at that bike you brought with you and see if you have any talent at all."

For a split second, he let his eyes travel down to the gentle sway of her hips before forcing himself to focus on a point over her head as he followed her back through the various machinery. Bill was right behind him, which helped to keep his eyes away from the prize… so to speak. Because the last thing he wanted was to get caught ogling the guy's kid sister.

Talk about a no-no of epic proportions. Especially if he didn't fancy the idea of finding one of Bill's size-eleven biker boots shoved up his ass.

Once they reached the first set of glass doors, she pulled a thick pair of pink coveralls off a hook on the wall. Balancing first on one foot then the other, she stepped into the coveralls and zipped them up before snagging a bright purple stocking cap from a second hook and pulling it over her head.

She looked ridiculous. And feminine. And so damned cute.

He gritted his teeth and reminded himself of three things. One, she was way too young for him. Two, if things worked out, then despite what she thought now, *he* was going to be *her* boss. And three, he'd made a promise not to—

"How much money are you thinking of investing?" she interrupted his thoughts as she pushed through the double doors and into the vestibule.

As much as it takes..."We'll talk more about that later." He held his breath, waiting to see how she'd respond to both his authoritative tone and his answer. It was a test of sorts, to determine if they had any hope of working together.

She regarded him for a long second, her brown eyes seeming to peer into his head. Then she shrugged, "Suit yourself."

When she opened the outer door, he once again had to dip his chin against the icy wind. The three of them slogged through the snow to the small, enclosed cargo trailer hitched to the back of his Hummer, and he fished in his pocket for the keys with fingers already numb from the cold. Once he opened the trailer's back door, she didn't wait for an invitation to jump inside.

He and Bill were left to follow her up and watch as she walked around his restored bike before squatting near the exhaust.

"You do all the work yourself?" she asked.

The bike he'd been so proud of thirty minutes before seemed shoddy and unimaginative by comparison.

"Yes," he admitted, amazed he actually felt nervous. Like maybe *she* wouldn't want to work with *him*.

"Your welding is complete crap," she said, running

a finger along a weld he'd thought was actually pretty damned good. "But it's obvious you're a decent mechanic, and that's really what I need right now, more decent mechanics. Plus," she stood and winked, "it might be nice to have a big, strong dreamboat like you around the place day-in and day-out. Something fun to look at when my muse abandons me."

He opened his mouth...but nothing came out. He could only stare and blink like a bewildered owl.

Holy hell, was she *flirting* with him?

He was saved from having to make any sort of answer—*thank you, sweet Jesus*—when Bill grumbled, "Cut it out, Becky. Now's not the time, and Boss is definitely not the guy."

"No?" She lifted her brows, turning toward Frank questioningly.

And now he was able to find his voice. "*No*." He shook his head emphatically, trying to swallow his lungs that had somehow crawled up into his throat.

"Well," she shrugged, completely unflustered by his overt rejection, "you can't blame a gal for trying." She offered him a hand. "I'm in, partner. That is, once I know exactly how much you're thinking of investing."

"Bill will get back to you with the specifics," he hedged, taking her hand only briefly before releasing it, more eager to get the hell out of there than he'd care to admit.

Again she did that head-tilt thing. The one that caused the end of her ponytail to slide over her shoulder. She regarded him for a long moment during which time he thought his heart might've jumped right out of his mouth had his lungs not been in the way. Then she shrugged and said, "Fine. Go ahead and do that whole mystery-man thing. I don't really give a rat's ass as long as you're good for the green."

And with that, she hopped down from the back of the trailer.

He moved to watch her traipse through the snow to the front door of her shop. Only once she disappeared inside did he turn to Bill. "You sure she's trustworthy enough? She seems a bit impulsive to me."

Impulsive and arrogant and bold and…way too cute for her own good.

Bill smiled, crossing his arms. "Despite all evidence to the contrary, Becky's as steady as they come. We can depend on her to keep our secrets. You have my word."

"And what about the hierarchy? How's she going to react once she realizes I'm the one calling the shots?"

Bill clapped a heavy hand on his shoulder and chuckled. "I have no doubt you can handle her, Boss."

Uh-huh. He wished he shared Bill's certainty. Because there was one thing he could spot from a mile away, and that was trouble.

And Rebecca Reichert?

Well, she had trouble written all over her…

Chapter One

Three and a half years later…

PIRATES…

Wow. Now there's something you don't see every day.

That was Becky's first thought as she ducked under the low cabin door of the thirty-eight-foot catamaran named *Serendipity* and stepped into the blazing equatorial sun. Her second thought, more appropriately, was *oh hell*.

Eve—her longtime friend and owner of the *Serendipity*—was swaying unsteadily and staring in wide-eyed horror at the three dirty, barefoot men holding ancient AK-47s like they knew how to use them. Four more equally skinny, disheveled men were standing in a rickety skiff tethered off the *Serendipity*'s stern.

Okay, so…*obviously* they'd been playing the oldies a little too loudly considering they'd somehow managed to drown out the rough sound of the pirates' rusty outboard engine motoring up behind them.

"Eve," she murmured around the head of a cherry Dum Dum lollipop as her heart hammered against her ribs and the skin on her scalp began crawling with invisible ants. "Just stay calm, okay?"

Yep. Calm was key. Calm kept a girl from finding herself fathoms deep beneath the crushing weight of Davy Jones's Locker or under the more horrifying weight of a sweaty man who didn't know the meaning of the word *no*.

When Eve gave no reply, she glanced over at her friend and noticed the poor woman was turning the color of an eggplant.

"*Eve*," she said with as much urgency as she could afford, given the last thing she wanted was to spook an already skittish pirate who very likely suffered from a classic case of itchy-trigger-finger-syndrome, "you need to breathe."

Eve's throat worked over a dry swallow before her chest quickly expanded on a shaky breath.

Okay, good. Problem one: Eve keeling over in a dead faint—solved. Problem two: being taken hostage by pirates—now *that* was going to take a bit more creativity.

She wracked her brain for some way out of their current predicament as Jimmy Buffett crooning, "Yes I am a pirate. Two hundred years too late," wafted up from inside the cabin.

Really, Jimmy? You're singing that now?

Under normal circumstances, she'd be the first to appreciate the irony. Unfortunately, these were anything but normal circumstances.

The youngest and shortest of the pirates—he wore an eye patch...*seriously?*—flicked a tight look in her direction, and she threw her hands in the air, palms out in the universal *I'm unarmed and cooperating* signal. But a quick glance was all he allotted her before he returned the fierce attention of his one good eye to Eve.

She snuck another peek at her friend and...oh no. Oh *crap*.

"Slowly, very slowly, Eve, I want you to lay the knife

on the deck and kick it away from you." She was careful to keep her tone cool and unthreatening. Pirates made their money from the ransom of ships and captives. If she could keep Eve from doing something stupid—like, oh, say flying at the heavily armed pirates like a blade-wielding banshee—they'd likely make it out of this thing alive.

Unfortunately, it appeared Eve had stopped listening to her.

"Eve!" she hissed. "Lay down the knife. *Slowly*. And kick it away from you."

This time she got through.

Eve glanced down at the long, thin blade clutched in her fist. From the brief flicker of confusion that flashed through her eyes, it was obvious she'd been unaware she still held the knife she'd been using to fillet the bonito they'd caught for lunch. But realization quickly dawned, and her bewildered expression morphed into something frighteningly desperate.

Becky dropped all pretense of remaining cool and collected. "Don't you even think about it," she barked.

Two of the men on deck jerked their shaggy heads in her direction, the wooden butts of their automatic weapons made contact with their scrawny shoulders as the evil black eyes of the Kalashnikovs' barrels focused on her thundering heart.

"You don't bring a knife to a gun fight," she whispered, lifting her hands higher and gulping past a Sahara-dry knot in her throat. "Everyone knows that."

From the corner of her eye, she watched Eve slowly bend at the waist, and the unmistakable *thunk* of the blade hitting the wooden deck was music to her ears.

"Look, guys," she addressed the group, grateful beyond belief when the ominous barrels of those old, but still deadly, rifles once more pointed toward the deck. *That's the thing about AKs*, Billy once told her, *they buck like a damned bronco, are simpler than a kindergarten math test, but they'll fire with a barrel full of sand. Those Russians sure know how to make one hell of a reliable weapon*—which, given her current situation, was just frickin' great. *Not.* "These are Seychelles waters. You don't have any authority here."

"No, no, no," the little pirate wearing the eye patch answered in heavily accented English. "We *only* authority on water. We Somali pirate."

"Oh boy," Eve wheezed, putting a trembling hand to her throat as her eyes rolled back in her head.

"Don't you dare pass out on me, Evelyn Edens!" Becky commanded, her brain threatening to explode at the mere thought of what might happen to a beautiful, unconscious woman in the hands of Somali pirates out in the middle of the Indian Ocean.

Eve swayed but managed to remain standing, her legs firmly planted on the softly rolling deck.

Okay, good.

"We have no money. Our families have no money," she declared. Which was true for the most part as far as she was concerned. Eve, however, was as rich as Croesus. Thankfully, there was no way for the pirates to know that. "You'll get no ransom from us. It'll cost you more to feed and shelter us than you'll ever receive from our families. And this boat is twenty years old. She's not worth the fuel it'll cost you to sail her back to Somalia. Just let us go, and we'll forget this ever happened."

"No, no, no," the young pirate shook his head—it appeared the negatives in his vocabulary only came in threes. His one black eye was bright with excitement, and she noticed his eye patch had a tacky little rhinestone glued to the center, shades of One-Eyed Willie from *The Goonies*.

Geez, this just keeps getting better and better.

"You American." He grinned happily, revealing crooked, yellow teeth. Wowza, she would bet her best TIG welder those chompers had never seen a toothbrush or a tube of Colgate. "America pay big money."

She snorted; she couldn't help it. The little man was delusional. "Maybe you haven't heard, but it's the policy of the U.S. government not to negotiate with terrorists."

One-Eyed Willie threw back his head and laughed, his ribs poking painfully through the dark skin of his torso. "We no terrorists. We Somali pirates."

Whatever.

"Same thing," she murmured, glancing around at the other men who wore the alert, but slightly vacant, look of those who don't comprehend a word of what was being said.

Okay, so Willie was the only one who spoke English. She couldn't decide if that was good or bad.

"Not terrorists!" he yelled, spittle flying out of his mouth. "*Pirates!*"

"Okay, okay," she placated, softening her tone and biting on her sarcastic tongue. "You're pirates, not terrorists. I get it. That doesn't change the simple fact that our government will give you nothing but a severe case of lead poisoning. And our families don't have a cent to pay you."

"Oh, they pay," he smiled, once again exposing those urine-colored teeth. "They always pay."

Which, sadly, was probably true. Someone always came up with the coin—bargaining everything they had and usually a lot more they didn't—when the life of a loved one was on the line.

"So," he said as he came to stand beside her, eyeing her up and down until a shiver of revulsion raced down her spine, "we go Somalia now."

And she swore she'd swallow her own tongue before she ever even thought these next words—because for three and a half very long years the big dill-hole had refused to give her the time of day despite the fact that she was just a little in love with him, okay *a lot* in love with him—but it all came down to this…she needed Frank.

Because, just like he always swore would happen, she'd managed to step in a big, stinking pile of trouble from which there was no hope of escape.

She absolutely hated proving that man right.

———〜〜〜———

Briefing room onboard the navy destroyer, USS Patton
Six days later…

Sometimes Frank hated being proved right.

"Well Bill," he said as he skimmed through the plans detailing Becky and Eve's rescue for what seemed like the umpteenth time. No way was he letting this op go off with even the slightest hiccup, not with Becky's neck on the chopping block. "It appears your little sister has finally landed herself in a big, stinking pile of trouble. I always knew it'd happen."

Bill sat at the conference table with his desert-tan combat boots propped up, placidly reading a dog-eared copy of *The Grapes of Wrath* as if his kid sister wasn't currently in the hands of gun-toting Somali pirates.

Un-fucking-believable.

But that was Bill for you. The sonofabitch was the epitome of serenity, *always*, even when balls-deep in the wiry guts of an IED. Which was why two hours after Frank made the decision to open his own private shop, he'd recruited Bill from Alpha Platoon. The commanding officer of Alpha still hadn't forgiven him for that little maneuver, but Frank didn't much care, considering it was a known fact within the spec-ops community that no one knew his way around things that went *kaboom* like Wild Bill Reichert. And Frank accepted nothing but the absolute best personnel—the elite of the elite—for Black Knights Inc.

"It's not like she *intentionally* put herself in the path of Somali pirates, Boss," Bill murmured as he licked his finger and turned a page.

"I don't care if she *intentionally* put herself in the path of Somali pirates or not." He nearly popped an aneurism when the words evoked a starburst image of Becky in the merciless hands of those ruthless cutthroats. "The fact remains, she should've known better than to travel to this part of the world."

"Seychellois waters are considered secure. Pirates have never attacked a vessel so close to Assumption Island, so it is reasonable to assume the women believed they would be perfectly safe," rasped Jamin Agassi.

Frank glanced over at one of Black Knights Inc.'s newest employees and, not for the first time, felt a shiver of trepidation run down his spine. How could you trust a guy who knew the adjective form of Seychelles was Seychellois?

And it didn't help matters in the least that Agassi had been dubbed "Angel" by Becky because the man's features were so perfect they were almost unearthly. Of course, the plastic surgeries he'd undergone after defecting from the Israeli Mossad and before Uncle Sam decided to conceal him within the ranks of Frank's Black Knights no doubt had something to do with the perfection of the man's mug.

Goddamn pretty boy.

Which only served to remind Frank of all the other goddamned pretty boys who worked for him. The ones who'd been out on assignment when the call for Becky's ransom came in, leaving him to catch the next transport onto the USS *Patton* with only Bill and the FNG—the military's warm and fuzzy acronym for the fucking new guy.

"Yes, Seychellois waters," he unnecessarily emphasized the word, "have never before seen pirate attacks, but military ships from across the globe have increased patrols and secured the shipping lanes around the bottle-necked Gulf of Aden, which anyone with a smidge of gray matter will tell you has only chased the pirates farther south around the Horn of Africa. So it stands to reason that it was only a matter of time before the waters around the Seychelles and Madagascar started seeing pirate activity."

See, just because he didn't know the adjective form of Seychelles didn't necessarily mean he was a slavering idiot. He knew some shit about some shit even though his vocabulary—liberally sprinkled with four-letter words on a good day—tended to indicate otherwise.

"It's not really their fault, you know," Bill said quietly, never taking his eyes off the text as he turned another page.

"Of *course* it is," Frank rumbled, throwing his hands in the air and wincing when his trick shoulder howled in protest of the sudden movement. Damn, getting old sucked...hard. "She didn't have to go on this asinine vacation halfway around the world to potentially pirate-infested waters. If she wanted to get some sand and sun, I know of some very nice beaches in Florida and California, on *U.S.* soil," he emphasized as he rolled his shoulder and reached into a zippered pocket on his cargo shorts to pull out his trusty bottle of ibuprofen.

He was never without the pain pills these days...

Goddamnit.

And that fun little fact was beginning to make him feel like he was just one step away from Metamucil and Viagra, and *that* just pissed him off.

"I wasn't talking about Becky," Bill said, "although you know as well as I do a mere weekend stroll along a beach in Florida or California wasn't going to do it for her. She needed to get away, *far* away, to clear her head."

Ah God. Why did no one agree with his decision to keep Becky from risking her fool neck by becoming an operator? Had everyone suddenly gone completely kill-the-bunny crazy?

Obviously. Because before he'd found out and eighty-sixed their activities, a few of the Knights had been teaching her—upon her repeating wheedling, no doubt—such dubious skills as computer hacking, sniping, explosives, demolitions, FBI investigative techniques...and God only knew what else. He was still mulling over some really inventive ways to kill his men for that.

She was supposed to be their *cover*. Nothing more. End of story.

Author's Note

For those of you who have ever been to Cairo, Illinois, you'll notice I embellished a bit on the decline of its population. Although the lynchings at the turn of the century; the race riots, boycotts, and "white flight" in the 1960s; and the 2011 Mississippi and Ohio River floods all struck major blows to the number of residents in Cairo, there are still many intrepid souls who are proud to call the town home. This book is dedicated, in part, to them and the inspiration their fascinating little burg afforded me.

Acknowledgments

Ever and always, I must thank my husband. Sweetheart, you'll never know how much it means that you graciously and uncomplainingly put up with missed dinner dates, uncombed hair, and my wearing of a seemingly endless—and terribly unsexy—array of grungy sweatpants when I'm on deadline. And I'm *always* on deadline. So, simply put, you're the best.

Next up, I must give a shout-out to my 4D gals—Chicago divas who dine, drink, and dish. Divas, without your advice, encouragement, and willingness to share a bottle of wine, I don't know if I would have kept my sanity in this cutthroat world of publishing. Three words: Writers unite! Huzzah!

Also, hugs and kisses to Amanda Carlson, Amanda Bonilla, Kristen Callihan, Roxanne St. Claire, Louisa Edwards, and Kristen Painter. You guys never fail to make me laugh or get me a little tipsy…usually by way of Cards Against Humanity and peach champagne. Until the next conference…Monkey Toes!

And, as always, *thank you* to our fighting men and women, those in uniform and those out of uniform. You protect our freedom and way of life so we all have the chance to live the American Dream.

About the Author

Julie Ann Walker is the *New York Times* and *USA Today* bestselling author of the Black Knights Inc. romantic suspense series. She is prone to spouting movie quotes and song lyrics. She'll never say no to sharing a glass of wine or going for a long walk. She prefers impromptu travel over the scheduled kind, and she takes her coffee with milk. You can find her on her bicycle along the lake shore in Chicago or blasting away at her keyboard, trying to wrangle her capricious imagination into submission. For more information, please visit www.julieannwalker.com or follow her on Facebook www.facebook.com/jawalkerauthor and/or Twitter @JAWalkerAuthor.